THE THIRD LAW

Lawrence Ricketts

The Third Law
Copyright © 2017 Lawrence Ricketts

No part of this publication may be reproduced, distributed, or transmitted in any form or by any means, including photocopying, recording, or other electronic or mechanical methods, without the prior written permission of the author, except in the case of brief quotations embodied in critical reviews and certain other non-commercial uses permitted by copyright law.

tellwell

Tellwell Talent
www.tellwell.ca

ISBN
978-1-77370-474-6 (Harcover)
978-1-77370-473-9 (Paperback)
978-1-77370-475-3 (eBook)

Table of Contents

PROLOGUE IX

CHAPTER ONE 1

CHAPTER TWO 9

CHAPTER THREE 15

CHAPTER FOUR 19

CHAPTER FIVE 23

CHAPTER SIX 29

CHAPTER SEVEN 35

CHAPTER EIGHT 43

CHAPTER NINE 53

CHAPTER TEN 61

CHAPTER ELEVEN 71

CHAPTER TWELVE 77

CHAPTER THIRTEEN 85

CHAPTER FOURTEEN 91

CHAPTER FIFTEEN 99

CHAPTER SIXTEEN 105

CHAPTER SEVENTEEN 111

CHAPTER EIGHTEEN 119

CHAPTER NINETEEN 129

CHAPTER TWENTY 137

CHAPTER TWENTY-ONE 145

CHAPTER TWENTY-TWO 153

CHAPTER TWENTY-THREE 157

CHAPTER TWENTY-FOUR 163

CHAPTER TWENTY-FIVE 171

CHAPTER TWENTY-SIX	177
CHAPTER TWENTY-SEVEN	187
CHAPTER TWENTY-EIGHT	197
CHAPTER TWENTY-NINE	203
CHAPTER THIRTY	209
CHAPTER THIRTY-ONE	217
CHAPTER THIRTY-TWO	223
CHAPTER THIRTY-THREE	231
CHAPTER THIRTY-FOUR	241
CHAPTER THIRTY-FIVE	247
CHAPTER THIRTY-SIX	251
CHAPTER THIRTY-SEVEN	259
CHAPTER THIRTY-EIGHT	263
CHAPTER THIRTY-NINE	277
CHAPTER FORTY	287
CHAPTER FORTY-ONE	291
CHAPTER FORTY-TWO	297
CHAPTER FORTY-THREE	305
CHAPTER FORTY-FOUR	309
CHAPTER FORTY-FIVE	319
CHAPTER FORTY-SIX	325
CHAPTER FORTY-SEVEN	331
CHAPTER FORTY-EIGHT	339
CHAPTER FORTY-NINE	345
CHAPTER FIFTY	351
CHAPTER FIFTY-ONE	359
CHAPTER FIFTY-TWO	365
CHAPTER FIFTY-THREE	373
CHAPTER FIFTY-FOUR	383
ACKNOWLEDGEMENTS	395

For Stacy

Gone too soon but always in my heart

For every external force that acts on an object there is a force of equal but opposite magnitude on the object that exerted the external force.

— *Newton's third law of reciprocal action*

If he's gonna want to personal, then i'm gonna want to get personal.

— *John Gotti (Mafia Boss)*

I have no knowledge of what kind of weapons will be unleashed against one another in ww iii, but I can guarantee ww iv will be fought with sticks and stones.

— *Albert Einstein*

PROLOGUE

07 APRIL 1998
Miami Florida
0300 hrs

THE BEAT UP, BLACK VAN SCREECHED TO A STOP BESIDE THE JAGUAR convertible, blocking it from pulling away from the curb. The driver of the Jag glared up at the van and, as the passenger window lowered and the side door slid open, yelled: "The fuck you think you're doin' you—" The deafening blast of a twelve-gauge tore into his neck and face. The passenger beside him tried to open the door as more bullets from a Mac-10 sprayed across his chest and head. The lone passenger in the back seat launched himself onto the trunk and rolled off the back as another blast from the twelve-gauge ripped into his right thigh. He landed on his side in the gutter, struggled to his feet and managed one or two steps onto the sidewalk before the leg caved under him. The van's passenger door opened and the man holding a sawed-off twelve-gauge stepped out and casually walked to the back of the Jag. He flicked his long dreadlocks back, ejected the spent shell, and racked another into the chamber. The man squirming on the sidewalk holding his shattered leg seemed to know the sound well, slowly turned his head, possibly wondering if he might know who was about to kill him. He didn't.

The face at the other end of the barrel smiled but said nothing. The injured man murmured something in French that could have been a plea or a prayer. Whatever, it didn't matter. The shotgun blast bounced his body five or six inches off the sidewalk, then lay motionless in a spreading pool of dark red.

The shooter wiped some specks of blood off his face, grinned at the mess on the sidewalk, turned, and walked back to the van. It roared off as soon as he climbed in. From start to finish, the killing had taken less than twenty seconds.

The Miami Herald chronicled the event on page two along with photographs showing a white plastic sheet covering a body on the sidewalk, and an orange tarp draped over the two bodies in a black Jaguar convertible. The arm dangling below the tarp on the driver's side sported a blood-soaked Rolex. Photo journalism 101. If it bleeds it leads, and it read like so many others

> *Three men were shot and killed last night as they left a popular nightclub in the Coconut Grove district. Police describe it as an execution-style hit carried out by members of a rival gang. At this point there are no suspects or witnesses. Investigators say it is part of an ongoing turf war. Two of the victims were well known to authorities. Sources say that one was the nephew of Pablo Costa, the head of one of the biggest cocaine cartels in Columbia. It is not known if the third victim, a Canadian, was involved in the drug trade. Canadian authorities are checking his identity and any criminal association he may have had with the other two victims. Police say that if one of the victims is Costa's nephew, it will likely escalate the violence.*

CHAPTER ONE

10 APRIL 1998
Miami Florida
1430 hrs. local time

PAUL GOLDMAN COCKED HIS HEAD AND SQUINTED DOWN THE neatly-trimmed cedar hedge separating his property from their neighbors, the Wilsons. He walked a few feet forward and clipped back two branches that stuck out slightly. Satisfied, he smiled and nodded. "Not bad, Goldman," he said out loud. At fifty-three he had remained slim and fit due to a rigid routine of exercise and of running the equivalent of a marathon each week. Staying in shape for Paul was a given, something he'd been doing for over thirty years.

"How's that look, hon?" he called over his shoulder to his wife.

Anna Goldman stood up from the flower bed she'd been weeding and stretched.

"Humm ... not bad. I figured the hedge would win for a while the way you were cursing under your breath, but you showed it who's boss," she said smiling.

Paul laughed and eyed it one last time. "Yeah ... well, that's as good as my landscaping prowess gets I'm afraid. God, I can't believe people actually do this every day for a living."

Anna brushed herself off and followed him onto the deck. "And what do you think a landscaper would say about what you did for a living?"

Paul put the clippers on the picnic table. "Hey, my job had its boring times, too."

"What? You mean the times you were in the hospital. Yes, I'm sure they were boring. You're just lucky you married a nurse, Goldman," she said, nudging him with her elbow.

"So how would my personal nurse like a cold drink?"

She put her trowel and hand rake on the table. "Sounds great. There's lemonade or beer in the fridge."

"I like the sound of a cold beer myself," he said, opening the screen door. "Want to split one?"

"I think I'll settle for a tall lemonade with lots of ice, thanks."

Stepping inside, they heard their son Ben running down the hall to the kitchen.

"Mom! Dad!" he hollered. "It's here."

· · · · · · ·

For the past week Ben had been intercepting the mailman at the front door, and today the envelope had finally arrived. The logo on the top left read: University of Miami. He waited until they were both in the kitchen, and then took a deep breath.

"Man," he said, rolling his eyes. "I'm almost afraid to open it." After a few seconds he tore open the end of the envelope. "Here goes," he said and removed the single sheet of paper. At six foot he had a couple of inches on his dad but shared the same wiry build. Ben started reading to himself. Within seconds his worried look disappeared.

Anna glanced at Paul then back at Ben. "You're in?"

He nodded, not raising his eyes from the page. "Oh, man, listen to this," he said, clearing his throat. "Ahem. Dear Mr. Goldman, uh, that'll be me," he said, nodding to both of them. "We are pleased to advise that as a result of your high achievement in the prerequisite courses you have been accepted into the M.D. program at the University of Miami, Leonard M. Miller School of Medicine."

"Well, I'll be," Paul said.

Anna threw her arms around his neck. "Oh, Ben! Congratulations, honey. That is so wonderful."

"Thanks, Mom. Man, I was getting worried cuz I hadn't heard anything. Wow. Can you believe this, Dad, I'm really in."

"And all this time I thought you were just chasing girls around the campus," Paul said, laughing and giving him a hug and pat on the back.

Ben struck a profile pose "Dad, when you look as good as this. You are the chase-e, not the chase-or."

"Oh boy," Paul said rolling his eyes.

"Yes, you're incredibly handsome," Anna said. "Now, please read on. What else does it say?"

Ben scanned down the page, reading half to himself and half out loud. "Hmmm, hmm, hmm … excellent results in neuroscience and molecular biology … hum … high standards displayed. Oh, and get this, they want me to call to make an appointment for an interview at "my" earliest convenience." He looked up and smiled. "Better check my schedule to see if I can fit them in."

"I'll tell you what," Paul said. "If you can fit them in, I'll make a reservation for dinner tonight at some place befitting a future doctor."

"That's a deal," Ben said, picking the desk calendar off the counter. "Hmm ... I appear to have a free day for whenever they want me."

Anna shook her head. "Well, aren't they the lucky ones."

· · · · · · ·

Paul washed up then called and made reservations at one of Miami Beach's more popular seafood restaurants, The Deep Six.

"Can I meet you guys there?" Ben called from his bedroom. "I've got a bunch of calls to make and want to hit the gym for a workout."

"Sure," Paul said. "Reservations aren't until seven. You go ahead and we'll meet you there."

"And drive carefully," Anna said, wagging a finger at him as he came down the hall carrying his gym bag. Stock words she always gave both men in her life.

"Sure, Mom. Not to worry," he called over his shoulder as he headed out the front door.

· · · · · · ·

Ben, who would turn twenty in two weeks had, since being a toddler, thrived on challenges. Throughout school and collage he had accepted nothing less that A's, and now it had all paid off. Shortly after they arrived in America four years ago, Ben told his parents that he'd decided to become a doctor. Paul and Anna were, of course, happy with his choice but realized that at age sixteen plans for the future changed numerous times; Ben, however, had never considered anything else.

They watched him jog down the driveway and climb into his eighteen-year-old, but so far dependable, blue Volkswagen van. As he pulled out, he pumped his fist out the window and let out a loud whoop.

Paul smiled at Anna. "Ever see anybody that excited?"

"Never," she said, then let out a long sigh. "He's going to make a great doctor."

"He sure is, honey. He sure is."

· · · · · · ·

Paul Goldman had spent the majority of his adult life in the Israeli military, and if the never-ending violence hadn't caught up with him, he would probably still be working within its ranks. Five-and-a–half years ago, he, Anna, Ben, and their fifteen-year-old daughter Rebecca were nearing the end of a three-day mini-vacation on a beach near the northern city of Haifa. The weather each day hovered between twenty-five and thirty Celsius under cloudless skies, and made the cool Mediterranean a welcoming relief from the sweltering heat. While Paul and Anna laid out a lunch of sandwiches and fresh fruit on their beach blankets, Ben and Rebecca went to the shops on the promenade above the beach to buy some cold drinks.

On the road that ran along the promenade a beat-up Land Rover inched slowly through the congestion of vehicles and pedestrians. Packed with a hundred pounds of high explosives and bags of nails, it was heading south, destined for what the driver prayed would be a crowded market in Tel-Aviv. Whether it was a short in the detonator or the driver felt something was wrong and panicked, no one would ever know. It detonated as it passed in front of the shops. Rebecca had just walked out the door of the confectionary. She was carrying a paper bag with four cans of ice-cold juice, with Ben a few steps behind her. Then it happened. The massive explosion killed her and eighteen others instantly. Ben, protected by the brick wall of the store, was thrown back by the blast and suffered a bad concussion and numerous cuts from flying glass and debris. He spent two weeks in hospital and underwent a delicate but successful operation to repair a detached retina. After a year or two, his scars were pretty much gone, but his nightmares would last a lot longer.

· · · · · · ·

Paul tried to keep working, but he soon realized his lack of focus brought him too close to the line that separates being an asset to being a liability. He loved Israel, but had given so much. Three years ago his brother Ira, a major in the bomb disposal unit, was killed by a sniper while disarming a truck bomb in one of the disputed settlements in the West Bank. Paul himself had the scars of a half-dozen near misses, and now the violence had taken Rebecca. He was empty. Even Anna, the eternal optimist who prayed every day for peace, became increasingly worried about Ben having to do compulsory service when he turned eighteen, so they made the decision to immigrate to America, a country not torn by war, a country filled with opportunities. Paul's expertise in electronics and the fast-growing computer technology sector formed the foundation for their new life. Now, four years later, life for the most part had become completely normal, especially after Ben's great news today.

· · · · · · · ·

At 6:15 PM, Anna checked herself in the hall mirror, picked up her purse and announced herself ready. Paul opened the front door.

"Umm," he said as she walked past him. "Lookin' good."

She batted her eyelashes at him. "Play your cards right, sailor, and this could be your lucky night."

He laughed and locked the door behind them. "Oh, I'll play them right alright."

Anna leaned on his arm as they walked to the car. "I can't get over the look he had on his face when he opened the letter."

"Yeah. I don't think I've ever seen him so happy," Paul said, opening the passenger door. She got in and watched him walk to the driver's side.

"You know," she said as he climbed in, "he looks so much like you when you were his age."

"Thanks, Babe, but any good looks he's got come from your side of the family

"Doctor Benjamin Goldman," she said. "Yeah ... I like that."

`1820 hrs.`

Not far from Miami International, at the Blue Tide Motel three men sat around the table in unit number six. They spoke in low whispers and stopped when the phone rang. The oldest, in his mid-forties and a good fifteen years older than the other two, reached over and picked up.

"Si ... si ..." he said, then listened, nodding slowly every few seconds. "Bueno ... si."

Hanging up, he checked his watch then reached under the bed, pulled out a large aluminum case and put it on the table. Flipping the lid open he undid the velcro straps that held the contents securely in place. Without a word he handed a Machine pistol and thirty-round clip to one, and a sawed-off five-shot Brushmaster twelve gauge to the other, then took a Gloc 9mm. pistol for himself. No silencers. The more noise the more panic, and panic made people keep their heads down and concentrate on surviving rather than trying to identify who was doing the shooting. They had more than enough firepower but in a crowded area, with so many Americans packing guns these days, the outcome was pretty hard to predict. What tonight accomplished didn't concern them. It was a job, riskier than most, but that just put a bigger price tag on it.

After changing clothes they left the motel and walked two blocks to where the caller said their car was waiting. The oldest got into the driver's seat. The other two got in, one in the back and one in the passenger seat. The driver then twisted the wires dangling below the dash. The engine turned over immediately.

CHAPTER TWO

1850 hrs.

BY THE TIME PAUL AND ANNA ARRIVED AT THE DEEP SIX, THE RUSH hour traffic had eased.

One of the uniformed valets opened the passenger door for Anna, then handed Paul a ticket stub.

"Thanks," he said, slipping it into his jacket pocket and putting his arm around Anna as they walked to the front door.

The restaurant, built on a jut of land surrounded on three sides by the ocean, was one of Miami's high-end eateries and considered by culinary experts as an experience not to miss. No matter where one sat, the wrap-around floor-to-ceiling windows offered every customer a panoramic ocean view. Light-brown tablecloths, white linen napkins, and a crystal candleholder adorned each table, along with a single white rose. The staff—with the exception of the maître d' ,who wore a black tuxedo—were dressed in crisply-tailored white slacks and in shirts with tan-colored vests. It gave the feeling of dining on a luxury cruise ship.

The maitre d' ran his finger down the reservations list.

"Ahh, here we are," he said. "Your table is ready, Mr. Goldman. I can seat you right away."

Picking three menus off the shelf behind him, he bowed politely to Anna then led them through the crowded dining room to a table by the window. The maitre d' removed an ornate brass 'Reserved' sign off the table and pulled a chair out for Anna.

"I hope this is satisfactory."

"Oh, yes," Anna said, looking out the window. "Wow."

"Thank you," Paul said. "This is excellent."

The maitre d' smiled. "You're welcome, sir. Your waiter will be right with you, and I hope you will enjoy your evening."

· · · · · · · ·

As the sun slipped below the horizon, it sent millions of diamond sparkles shimmering across the waves. Anna stared out the window, mesmerized, a peaceful Mona Lisa-like smile on her face. Paul watched her quietly, not saying a word.

· · · · · · · ·

From the first day he'd laid eyes on her over thirty years ago, he knew she was the one he wanted to spend the rest of his life with. She had been working as a nurse at a military hospital in Jerusalem when Paul dropped in to visit one of his men, who was recovering from shrapnel wound. He literally bumped into her as she was leaving the room. After apologizing, he stared at her, speechless. Anna smiled, saying it was she who should have been watching where she was going. Paul watched her walk down the hall. Just as she turned the corner, she looked over her shoulder at him. Later Anna would admit she was hoping that when she turned he would still be watching her. Over the next few weeks, Paul made almost daily visits to the hospital, all on the pretext of checking on the condition of the soldiers in his unit, and some he didn't even know from other units. It soon became apparent to all the staff that his visits always coincided with Anna's shifts. He finally built up the courage to ask her out for a coffee, and

THE THIRD LAW

when she smiled and said, "I'd love to Sergeant Goldman," he was elated. He couldn't believe she'd even found out his name and rank; then he remembered it was stitched on the front of his tunic.

• • • • • • •

Anna looked over and caught him staring at her. "I love you, too, Paul Goldman."

"I should get you a job on one of those psychic T.V. shows," he said, shaking his head.

A waiter appeared at their table and placed glasses of ice water in front of the three place settings. At the table directly behind them, three men were becoming quite loud, all speaking with obvious Jamaican accents.

"May I get the lady something from the bar?" the waiter asked, glancing over at the table behind them.

Anna seldom drank, but this was a special occasion. She thought for a second. "Perhaps a glass of Chardonnay please. The house brand will be fine."

He nodded politely and turned to Paul. "And for you, sir?"

"Johnny Walker Black, please, on the rocks."

• • • • • • •

Johnny Walker Black had become his celebratory drink of choice since the conclusion of a successful mission in 1984—a joint British/Israeli search-and-destroy operation consisting of five Mossad and five S.A.S. members. Their target? A terrorist training camp operating from a remote area in the central Libyan Desert.

• • • • • • •

The night jump landed them to within five kilometres of their objective, and by 0215 hours from atop a windswept ridge they studied the darkened camp less than a hundred yards away. The two guards patrolling the perimeter paid little attention to the cold, black desert, seeming more intent on trying to keep warm. Meanwhile, in international waters off the Libyan coast, the aircraft carrier U.S.S. Ranger received and passed on information from a re-positioned KH-11 reconnaissance satellite. One of the first of its kind, capable of transmitting digital high resolution imagery, it showed individual human heat signatures as blobs of yellowy green and their exact location in the camp. At 0230 hours, two snipers took up positions on either end of the ridge to provide cover-fire if necessary. The remaining eight made their way silently towards the camp, their desert camouflage and blackened faces melting them into the landscape. In less than a minute, the two guards, moving in opposite directions, simultaneously disappeared without a sound.

• • • • • • • •

The camp consisted of six bell-tents in a semi-circle, all under camouflage netting. Information passed on from the USS Ranger indicated no heat signatures coming from the two tents on the far right of the camp. These were likely supply tents. Three of the other tents showed four signatures in each, and in the last one, three. The team broke into pairs. There would be no prisoners.

• • • • • • • •

By 0237 hours, the twelve, would-be terrorists lay in their cots, throats sliced wide, while their souls went off to have a one-on-one with their respective Gods. The three mercenary instructors, one American and two Germans, shared the same fate. The attack would go unreported. Libya, standing by its claim not to train or harbor terrorists had to ignore it, and when no government or group came forward to claim responsibility, it sent a strong message to other training camps. The victims would quietly be hailed as martyrs, having died defending a fanatical religious belief, or in a struggle to overthrow a despised political system.

• • • • • • • •

The operational reporting of the event by the participating countries would be so thoroughly sanitized that for all accounts, it had never happened.

• • • • • • • •

THE THIRD LAW

By first light the team had been choppered into Remada Tunisia, then trucked on to Tunis. Over the next twenty-four hours, some in pairs and others individually, left via commercial airlines to Gibraltar, then home. The last to leave were twenty-nine year old Major Goldman and his counterpart, an S.A.S. Major, William Smythe. Dressed in business suits, the two toasted each other's homeland with a complimentary Johnny Walker Black Label. For what had been done, there was no remorse. The dead were killers of the innocent and combatants in conflicts that seemed to have no end.

· · · · · · · ·

The restaurant was full when Ben arrived. The waiter pulled out his chair and handed him a menu.

"Would the gentleman like a refreshment?"

"Uh, just a Perrier on ice would be great, thanks."

"Right away, sir."

He was still beaming from the news. He looked around then leaned over and gave his mother a kiss on the cheek.

"Hi Mom. Great spot, Dad. Jeez, check out the view."

The clouds were now streaks of crimson and yellow with soft, purple edges against a sky that was changing from pale to dark-blue. At the table behind them the three Jamaicans were still being loud, but for the most part it was just with laughter.

Ben took a breath and said. "Mom, Dad, uh, I've got some more news, and I don't want you to get mad or anything."

Paul and Anna looked at each other, then at Ben. "What do you mean, son?" Paul asked. Anna just looked on, saying nothing.

"I'm going to get a tattoo."

Anna frowned. "A tattoo! Why would you want a tattoo?"

"Ben, what you want today may change in a year or so, and tattoos are there for life," Paul said, glancing at the worried look on Anna's face.

Ben nodded. "I know that, and I want it there for life."

Anna lowered her voice to a whisper. "Why, on earth would you want a tattoo?"

"Well," he said. I remember when I was a kid, I asked Gramma what the mark on her arm was, and she told me she got it from the Nazis when they sent her to Auschwitz. I was only about six, and so I didn't have any idea what she was talking about, and then she died and I never got a chance to talk to her about it again. A few years ago I was looking through a bunch of my old stuff and came across a drawing I'd done from around that time. I'd written down the number A-11963 on the bottom of the paper and remembered it as the number on Gramma's arm. I know now what she must have gone through and how strong she must have been to survive, or, I wouldn't be here ... so I'm going to have her number tattooed on my wrist. That way, I can cover it with my watch band, but I can see it whenever I want."

Paul and Anna stared at him. They were quiet for what seemed like a long time. Finally, Paul cleared his throat and said: "I, uh, I think that's a great idea, son. A great idea."

Anna wiped her eyes with her napkin, and gave Ben's hand a little squeeze. "Honey, your Gramma would be so proud."

1935 hrs.

The brown four-door Monte Carlo moved with the flow of traffic and made its way south along I-95. Stolen an hour earlier from a theatre parking lot in Hialeah, the odds were it wouldn't be reported for another hour, that is, unless the owner decided to leave before the show ended. Plenty of time. The three men in the car said nothing. The success of what they were about to do depended on surprise, confusion, and a lot of luck. Their instructions had been very clear. Do it inside the restaurant.

CHAPTER THREE

1945 hrs.

AS THE WAITER REMOVED SALAD PLATES FROM THE GOLDMAN'S table, the first stars were beginning to appear in the darkening sky. The table behind them was being served by a parade of waiters carrying trays of oysters on the half shell, steaming pots of mussels and clams and three platters, each with a lobster, a twelve-ounce beef tenderloin, garlic mashed potatoes and a medley of colorful vegetables.

"Holy ..." Ben whispered, turning to look at what was being delivered to their table.

"Bet they're musicians with all that jewelry and stuff. "

Anna half-turned so she could see the table then looked back at Ben. "Could be, they certainly do look like it."

Paul kept his thoughts to himself. The one with the shaved head had caught his attention when he and Anna first arrived. He watched everyone who came in. Paul had seen the look many times, both in predator and prey, and it bothered him. The one with long dreadlocks was acting like he'd just won a million dollars and the heavy- set one ignored everyone and started in on the mountain of food as soon as it arrived.

Anna reached over and touched his arm. "Paul," she whispered. "What is it?"

"Hmm. Oh, nothing. It's nothing, honey," he said, smiling and turning his attention back to the view.

Anna nodded over her shoulder towards the Jamaican's table. "You look ... is something wrong?"

"No, really, everything's fine," he said. "Just fine." But he couldn't shake the feeling that something wasn't right.

· · · · · · · ·

The maitre d' looked up from his station near the front door when it opened. "Good evening, sir," he said as the middle-aged man approached the reservations desk. "Do you have a reservation this evening?"

The new customer opened his jacket and put his hand on the butt end of the Gloc 9 mm protruding from his waist band. The maitre d' was more surprised than stunned. Few paid with cash nowadays, and so a robbery seemed rather ill thought out. But this guy definitely looked serious, and what little English he did speak was more than enough to be understood.

"You go *el banos*, amigo. Go now ... or I kill you ... *comprende?*"

Dropping his pen and pressing his back to the wall, the maître d' edged his way around the reservations desk, his eyes riveted on the gun. He scurried to the end of the short hall, opened the door to the men's room and quickly disappeared inside. The driver of the Monte Carlo then removed his jacket and tossed it on the floor behind the maître' d station. Underneath he wore a white shirt, tuxedo vest, and a black bow tie. The restaurant door opened again. He nodded at the two younger men, both wearing three-quarter-length leather jackets, then picked up a couple of menus, held them in front of his right hand, and led them into the dining room.

· · · · · · ·

No one paid any attention as they moved through the room, past a table for two where a young couple oblivious to everything smiled and spoke quietly to each other. Next to them a table of four couples were engrossed in conversations and appetizers, and beside them, at a table for one, a businessman looked up briefly then turned his attention back to his glass of merlot.

· · · · · · ·

Paul noticed the one with the shaved head at the table in front of him watch with growing interest as the two new customers were being escorted through the dining room. Paul could see there weren't any empty tables or chairs, yet they were making their way towards the table occupied by the Jamaicans. He felt the hackles go up on the back of his neck. When they reached the table, it clicked. It wasn't the same maître d'. The one with the shaved head had put it together too. He pushed his chair back and reached inside his jacket as the one dressed as the maître d' dropped the menus and raised his Gloc. Paul lunged across the table, grabbing both Ben and Anna.

"Anna! Ben! DOWN!" he yelled as a staccato of sharp cracks, and the deafening blast of a shotgun filled the air. Terrified customers and staff scrambled to get out of the line of fire as bullets ripped through tables and chairs, shattering three of the floor-to-ceiling plate-glass windows.

· · · · · · ·

It felt like a sledgehammer hit him in the chest, followed by a searing pain that jerked his head to the side. Then, like someone turning the volume down, the sounds of gunfire and screams melted away, as did the pain. Then all became silent, then dark.

CHAPTER FOUR

```
11 APRIL
Miami Fl
Mercy Hospital
0700 hrs. local time
```

AT FIRST THE VOICE MADE NO SENSE. DISJOINTED SOUNDS. THEN, slowly it began to register. It was calling him.

"Paul ... Paul Goldman, can you hear me?"

He struggled to open his eyes. It was a woman's voice. Anna? Yes Anna. Thank God. He could make out a blurry form above and tried to call her name, but his words came out as a low, moaning sound.

"Mr. Goldman. Can you hear me?"

Paul squeezed his eyes shut a few times, and nodded his head.

"You're in Mercy Hospital. Do you understand?"

Things came into focus. Not Anna. A nurse. On either side of the bed, intravenous bags dangled from metal stands, their tubes disappearing under the sheets. He made the mistake of trying to take a deep breath. It sent a searing pain through his chest. He let out a groan and remembered the restaurant.

"My wife ... son," he whispered, his voice cracking. "Where ...?"

• • • • • • •

Nurse Carla Thatcher looked over her shoulder at the doctor standing behind her. He nodded and she stepped back. He took off his sweat-stained surgical Cap and scrunched it into a ball.

"Mr. Goldman, my name is Doctor Phillips." He paused. God he hated this part of his job. "You're in the recovery room at Mercy Hospital, Mr. Goldman. Do you remember what happened?"

Paul nodded ever so slightly. "Shot ... restaurant," he tried to say, although he didn't think it came out right.

"That's right. You were shot in the chest, and received a glancing wound to the right temple. We were able to…"

"Anna ... Ben," Paul cut in. "They're okay? Where are they?"

The look on the doctor's face told him the answer.

"Mr. Goldman, I'm sorry, we did everything possible."

He stopped there. Nothing more needed to be said. Paul felt like he was going to be sick. He shut his eyes and, as the tears ran down his face, the blackness folded back around him again.

• • • • • • •

For the next few days he slipped in and out of consciousness. Neighbors, and a few friends who owned shops near his, dropped in to pay their respects; Rabbi Stern came by a number of times as well but, for the most part, the faces and conversations failed to penetrate the wall of sedation that kept him floating in a silent, foggy world where day and night were one.

• • • • • • •

Slowly, bits and pieces of the one-sided conversations lodged in his memory. Especially the one by Rabbi Stern telling him Anna and Ben had been buried at Woodlawn Cemetery. The nurse who spent many hours changing dressings, recording vital signs, and checking on him throughout her shift would talk to him constantly about the weather, how the Miami Dolphins were doing, even how President Clinton was faring in the midst of the Lewinsky investigation. Nurse Carla Thatcher knew that even unconscious, he would pick up parts of the one-sided conversation that would help to stimulate the brain. And in the mist of all these partial recollections, etched crystal clear in his mind were the faces of the men who'd torn his life apart.

CHAPTER FIVE

15 APRIL
0700 hrs.

HE'D BEEN AWAKE FOR ABOUT AN HOUR, STARING AT THE CEILING and for the first time clear headed, when Nurse Thatcher came in.

"Well, welcome back, Mr. Goldman," she said. "How are you feeling today?" she asked, sliding the drapes open. Paul squinted as the morning sun flooded the room. The warmth of the sun on his face felt good, until he shifted onto his side and a stab of pain ripped through his chest.

"To be honest, I've felt a whole lot better, so I was hoping you or the doctor could tell me how I'm doing," he said, looking at the I.V. tubes hanging above him.

She lifted his wrist and watched the second hand of her watch. "You're coming along just fine." She smiled and re-adjusting his pillows.

"Do you think I might be able to get a cup of tea? I've been laying here craving a cup of tea."

"I think that'd be just fine." She glanced at the monitors. "I'll get you one right away." She stopped at the door and turned. "Oh, and I'll check with the doctor to see if maybe we can free you up from some of those tubes you've become so attached to."

"Yes," he said, looking at the tangle of tubes and wires. "That'd be great, before I roll over and hang myself."

"Okay," she laughed. "I'll be right back."

He figured her for somewhere around mid-forties. Hard to tell. Very attractive, light-brown hair cut short, with blue eyes, and a warm smile. Something about her voice sounded familiar, but he couldn't quite put his finger on it.

0905 hrs.

Half-way through his second cup of tea, she came back into his room, a man and woman behind her.

"Mr. Goldman, these are police officers. They're investigating the, uh, shooting. If you feel up to it, they'd like to ask you a few questions."

"Of course," Paul said, putting his cup on the tray and gesturing towards the two chairs at the side of the bed. "Please, sit down."

Nurse Thatcher waited until they were seated. "I'll have to ask that you keep it short. Mr. Goldman needs his rest."

"Absolutely," the male detective said. "Ten minutes max. Promise."

"That's fine," she said and glanced at her watch. "I'll be back at nine fifteen then."

· · · · · · ·

When the door closed he turned to Paul and held up his badge.

"Sir, my name's Morgan Connors, and this is my partner, Bonnie Story. We're detectives with the Miami police homicide unit."

Paul looked at the badge then at him. He looked out-of-place, wearing blue jeans, a denim shirt, light-brown suede sports jacket, and cowboy boots. Only thing missing was a cowboy hat. The detective noticed the look.

"I know. I know," he said smiling. "It's not the Miami look. Truth is, I was born in Montana. Grew up on a cattle ranch an' still go back every spring to help my folks with round-up."

"So," Paul said, arching an eyebrow. "What they say about not being able to take the country out of the boy is true, then."

"You're absolutely right, sir." He grinned, looking over at his partner who rolled her eyes, then opened her purse and took out a notebook and pen.

"We're very sorry for your loss, Mr. Goldman," she said

"Thank-you detective," Paul said. He shifted his gaze to her. Seemed awful young to be a detective. Dark complexion. A touch of an accent. Italian, he thought. High cheek-bones and hazel eyes. Mid twenties. Maybe a bit older but, again, hard to tell. She wore a navy-blue pantsuit and a crisp white blouse; her raven-black hair was tied back in a simple, neat, ponytail. A very professional look. "Sir, we'd like you to look at some photos to see if you can identify any of the people responsible."

Detective Connors opened his briefcase and removed a thick envelope. He opened it and took out a dozen eight-by-ten pictures and handed them to Paul.

Paul started to go through them. "If you have their pictures, I'll be able to identify them, and will testify to it."

"We appreciate that, sir." Connors said

"There's one stipulation we must be clear on though, and should maybe get to that first."

"And what would that be, Mr. Goldman?" Connors asked. He looked at his partner.

"I have the final say on any security arrangements you feel are necessary which, by the uniformed guard I noticed camped outside my door, you believe I do, or will need."

"I can assure you, sir," Connors cut in. "Our department has the best ..."

"Excuse me," Paul said and wagged his finger. "Now, like I was saying, I'll do everything I can to help, but you must allow me this. If you agree we can continue, if not, we have nothing more to talk about."

• • • • • • •

Bonnie put her pen down and looked over at her partner. After a few seconds, he shrugged and nodded. For now, if it made this Mr. Goldman feel better, why not.

"Sure, Mr. Goldman. I think we can agree to that, for the time being."

"Good. Then for the time being, if it can be kept from the press, or at least be kept vague about what you've got so the papers won't be telling the world, then you've got an eye-witness flat on his back in a hospital bed, and I think we can begin."

"Mr. Goldman," Bonnie asked, cocking her head. "What exactly did you do before you got into the computer business?"

"Well," he said, stopping to take a sip of tea. "Back in Israel I spent some time in the military."

Morgan Connors turned away and looked out the window shaking his head. The guy has no fucking idea what he's in the middle of here.

• • • • • • •

The twelve color photos were head and shoulder shots. Each man had black hair and dark complexion. Paul went through them slowly and without any hesitation put the pictures numbered five, nine, and eleven off to the side.

"These are the shooters," he said, handing them to Connors. "This one was dressed as the Maitre d'," he said tapping his finger on the one marked number nine, "and was definitely in charge. These other two followed his lead."

Connors handed him a pen. "Would you mind putting your initials on the bottom of the three pictures you've identified?"

"Not at all," he said taking the pen.

Connors picked up the photos and put them into his briefcase. "Now, is there anything we can do for you sir?" he asked.

"Yes, there are a couple of things. Since I'm sure we will be seeing a lot of each other, call me Paul, okay?"

"Sure, and the second thing."

He looked at Bonnie, then at Morgan. "Please, tell me why my wife and son are dead?"

Bonnie put her notebook in her purse and looked at her partner. He cleared his throat and pulled his chair closer to the bed. "What happened at the restaurant," he said keeping his voice just above a whisper, "was in retaliation for a hit, uh ... a shooting. About two weeks ago, three members of a Colombian drug gang were killed. One was the nephew of the head guy in South America. Name's Pablo Costa. He runs everything. Supplies cocaine to half of North America. Anyway, a Jamaican gang's been tryin' to cut in on Costa's operations here, an' were responsible for taking them out. The three guys at the table behind yours were members of the Jamaican gang and probably the ones who killed the Columbians. They were all killed. Your table was in the line of fire along with the one beside you. A woman an' waiter at that table were hit. They're both gonna make it." He took a deep breath. "The three you identified were picked up at Miami International. Girl at the ticket counter got suspicious when they showed up, very nervous an' tryin' to get seats on the next flight to Bogota without so much as an overnight bag between 'em. She puts a call into the DEA Duty agent who shows up an' figures they'd been up to no good so, being on the ball, decides to turn 'em over to I.N.S. on suspicion of being in the country illegally, an' using phony passports."

"So they've been charged?" Paul asked.

"No," Bonnie said, shaking her head. "They had help. Vehicle was wiped clean, no prints, no weapons, and no witnesses."

"No witnesses! None? Out of all those people, I can't believe no one else, ahhh …" He tried to raise himself up, then moaned as a jolt of pain shot through his chest. He put his head back on the pillow.

"No one from the restaurant's willing to get involved," she added.

Paul lay still, waiting for the pain to pass, then turned his head towards them.

"Well, now, that's all changed, hasn't it."

The two detectives looked at each other. That was just about enough for today. "Oh, and before you go, would you mind cranking this damn bed up a bit, Morgan?"

"Sure," Connors said getting up. "Not a problem, uh, Paul."

· · · · · · · ·

As soon as they left Paul pressed the call button pinned to the side of the bed. At the nurse's station, Carla Thatcher put down a clipboard, checked the room number and hurried down the hall. The uniformed guard outside the door gave her a quick glance, then continued reading his *Soldier of Fortune* magazine.

"Yes, Mr. Goldman, what can I do for you?" she asked.

"Could you tell me the correct time and what day it is?"

"Of course," she said. "It's, uh, 9:25, Wednesday morning, the 15th of April."

"Thank you. One more thing, if you don't mind. Would it be possible to bring me a phone? I have to call someone."

"Sure, I'll arrange for one right away. Are you sure you feel up to making calls?"

"For now, there's only one I have to make, then I'll rest."

CHAPTER SIX

15 APRIL
San Diego Ca.
0630 hrs. local time

THOMAS CORBET HAD BEEN LAYING IN BED FOR OVER AN HOUR fighting the urge to get up. For most of his adult life he'd been up at five-thirty and at work by six-thirty. No matter what time he went to bed, he couldn't re-set his mental alarm clock, so, two years after leaving the Central Intelligence Agency, everything in his life had changed, except waking up at five-thirty, and he hated it.

• • • • • • •

Like all three of his marriages, retirement seemed like a good thing at the time, especially with the ever-mounting, bureaucratic red tape that most of the operatives felt was slowly strangling the agency's ability to function. Now, with the exception of Allie—his daughter from his first marriage who worked for AT&T in Seattle Washington—he was alone, and bored.

• • • • • • •

To help fill the void he bought an older, thirty-six-foot wooden hulled sailboat. The ad in the *Marine Traders* magazine had stated it needed a little TLC, and that turned out to be the biggest understatement since Noah said, "It looks like rain." What started as a fun project soon became a full-blown, very expensive obsession.

• • • • • • • •

He ignored the phone when it rang. Always did. His gatekeeper, the answering machine, screened all calls, most of which were telemarketers anyway, except for the Sunday night suppertime call from Allie, but a call this early had to be either a wrong number or something important. He sat up as the answering machine started recording.

"Pick up Tom! It's Paul. It's important … if you're there, pick up."

• • • • • • • •

They'd met a little over fifteen years ago when a secret, antiterrorist unit, formed by a number of western nations was created behind closed government doors. Personnel who were skilled in various languages, weapons, communications and explosives were recruited from the member countries intelligence agencies. Teams were picked from the pool according to the nature of the operation and expertise required. Their mandate? Dismantle and destroy terrorist groups that threatened the members' government's stability, economic interests, or safety of their citizens. Based in Brussels, their theatre of operation was global. The group remained nameless as did the operations themselves. Each was referred to only as "the op." After each mission, debriefings to determine the effectiveness and consequences of the actions were held behind closed doors, with no paper trail whatsoever. When the need arose for an intervention, the plans were formulated and carried out in complete secrecy. Formed in the mid-eighties after an escalation in bombings and political assassinations, the group carried out the mandate with complete anonymity. In November of 1992 political pressure became a bit too much when rumors of a government 'hit squad' leaked to the press. The governments involved denied the existence of any such group, and quickly and quietly disbanded it.

Tom swung his legs off the bed and grabbed the receiver.

"Paul? Hey, man, where are you?"

"Where do you think? I'm still where most old Jews end up. Miami, of course."

Tom laughed. "Yeah. Christ, who woulda figured either of us would still be on the green side of the grass. How you guys doin' anyway?"

"Things … aren't good, Tom."

"What're you talkin' about Paul. What's goin' on?"

"I've, uh … I've lost Anna and Ben," he said, his voice cracking.

"What? Good God, what happened?"

"They were killed. Caught in a cross fire between a couple of drug gangs."

"You hang on, man," he said getting up. "I'll be out there as soon as I can."

"Thanks, Tom, but no. I'm going to come out there. Probably in a couple of weeks. As soon as I get out of the hospital."

"You're in hospital? How bad."

"I'll be fine. Listen, I'll fill you in on everything when I come out and, Tom, I'm going to need your help, if you're willing."

"Anything you need, you got it. You know that."

"I appreciate it. Listen, have you heard anything from Jamie Ryan lately?"

"Not for quite a while. I know he's stuck behind a desk and hates it. Why?"

"I'm going to put a little plan together and his background could really help."

"I like the sound of it already," Tom said. "I'll give him a call. I've got his home number in London around here somewhere, an' I know even if he's on his death bed, he'll be here."

"Thanks, my friend. I'll be in touch as soon as I'm mobile and, Tom, we're not going to have a whole lot of time to get things moving on this, and things could get a little bit hairy. We may have a month, maybe two, tops."

"No prob. We'll be good to go as soon as you get here. Need anything, or anyone else?"

"Right now, I think that should do it. I'll call you in a week or so."

· · · · · · ·

After hanging up, Tom pulled the cord to the venetian blinds and raised them to the top. The early morning sun streamed into the room. He walked into the bathroom, rubbing his hands over a three-day growth of beard. A tingling sensation rippled through his body, something he hadn't felt for a long time. Leaning against the bathroom counter, he checked himself out in the mirror.

"Get your shit together, Tommy, boy. Get your shit together."

· · · · · · ·

He turned fifty-one two weeks ago, and if Allie hadn't called, his birthday would have passed like a stranger on a crowded street. At six feet and a hundred and ninety pounds he kept in shape mostly from working on the boat, a daily thirty-minute weight routine in the mini-gym he'd set up in his basement, and a twice-weekly workout at Shikomo dojo in downtown San Diego. He was still what he looked like, a tough guy, with a weathered face and piercing pale blue eyes that over the years had seen much more than they deserved. As tough looking as he was, there was a softness in his eyes that only women could see. A small box somewhere in the attic gathering dust contained a purple heart and numerous other medals and awards, all of which meant nothing to him. Not that he wasn't proud of his service; it's just that he didn't need flashy trinkets to remind him he'd killed people, and was almost killed himself. The only military thing he hung onto was his hairstyle. A super-short buzz cut. Every two weeks Tom would sit in the chair at Mario's Barber Shop and order in his usual way: "Take'er to the wood Mario."

Home was a fourteen-hundred-square-foot rancher not far from the Gas Lamp district. After paying alimony for years he considered himself lucky to have been able to hang onto the house. Socially he had few friends. A couple of old timers from the agency he'd worked with over the years would call, and they'd meet for drinks and a bite to eat now and then to talk a little about the old times, and a lot about baseball or football, depending on the season. Like most who spent their lives working alone in the shadows, cultivating friendships on the outside had always been difficult. Just too much you couldn't talk about. After Paul's call he'd felt the adrenaline rush, like a returning friend who'd been gone too long. He found Jamie Ryan's home number on his desktop rolodex, coded like all his working contacts. He put in the call.

CHAPTER SEVEN

20 APRIL
Cartago Colombia SA
1145 hrs. local time

ROSA ADONAS OPENED THE THICK, ORNATE DOUBLE DOORS THAT stood ten feet tall. Their balance was so precise even someone as tiny as she could open and close them with ease. Now in her seventies, she had been Pablo Costa's personal maid for twenty-one years. Prior to that she had worked for Pablo's father. After his death Pablo talked her into staying on. She was the only family he had, and treated her like the mother he never knew.

The visitor, although expected, was searched carefully before being escorted across the compound to the main house. Rosa waited at the top of the steps to take him inside.

The sprawling hacienda, surrounded by twelve-foot-high walls with manned guard stations on the turrets at each corner kept watch over the three hundred acres of gently sloping meadows that overlooked the small town of Cartago east of Cali. Heavily armed security patrolled the grounds round the clock aided by cameras and motion detectors that monitored virtually every inch of the property. The road to the hacienda wound its way up from the main highway two kilometres to the south. Approach, day or night without being seen was impossible. Costa loved the hacienda more than any of his other properties. Without a doubt it was the center of his kingdom. Here he felt safe. Here he was treated like a king.

• • • • • • •

Rosa bowed politely and ushered the gentleman in, closing the doors behind him. He had been here only once before, three years ago, for a meeting to arrange financing and routing for large shipments of cocaine. The opulence of the main house had the desired effect, both awesome and intimidating. Three massive chandeliers, their crystals shimmering in the light from stained-glass windows, hung from the high ceiling above the reception hall. Across from the entrance a grand staircase swept up to a landing then split and circled to the left and right continuing to the second floor. The rosewood walls held numerous pieces of art that were reflected in the white, Italian marble flooring. Just inside the main entrance, four life-sized sculptures, two on the left and two on the right, stared through chiseled eyes at each other. Alexander the Great and Julius Caesar on one side, and the Greek philosopher Aristotle and mathematician Archimedes on the other. Knowledge and power. The keys to greatness.

• • • • • • •

The rest of the main floor consisted of a dining hall capable of seating up to thirty dinner guests, a library, study, media room and kitchen. Upstairs in the north wing were Costa's office, the security room, a study, and a large conference room. The south wing housed the sleeping quarters, and consisted of four, self-contained suites, and his own lavishly decorated bedroom where, since his wife's disappearance three years ago after she threatened to leave him, he partied with beautiful young women flown in from Bogota whenever the mood hit him.

• • • • • • •

The visitor, a Canadian named Jean Rheume, had arrived on a flight from Montreal via Miami. A distinguished-looking man, a little over six feet medium-build, with dark hair graying at the temples he looked much younger than the fifty-nine years that his passport declared. Wearing a dark-blue, pin-stripe suit, he could easily be taken for the CEO of a major corporation, rather than one of Eastern Canada's biggest cocaine importers. Security cameras followed them up the staircase and along the second floor hallway to a set of closed, double doors at the far end of the north wing. Rosa knocked quietly. Inside the two men stopped talking.

From behind a gleaming mahogany desk, forty-seven-year old Pablo Costa put down his pen and looked toward the door.

"Come in," he said getting up. His shoulder length gray hair was immaculately styled and accented by a closely trimmed salt and pepper colored beard. Outside the hacienda Pablo always wore a tailored suit, but inside he preferred more casual attire. Today it was a pair of white slacks with an orange-and-white flowered silk shirt.

Rosa opened the door then stepped to the side. "Mr. Rheume to see you sir."

"Thank-you, Rosa. Please, come in Jean," he said spreading his arms. "Welcome to my home. How was your flight?"

Rheume nodded a thank-you to Rosa who smiled and closed the door quietly as she left

"Very smooth, all the way. Good to see you again, Pablo," he said crossing the room. They shook hands.

"And good to see you also. Can I get you anything to drink?" Pablo asked. "A wine, or perhaps whiskey?"

"Thank-you, Pablo, no, nothing right now."

"I don't believe you've met my assistant," Pablo said gesturing towards the slim, dark-skinned man wearing a black suit with a black shirt open at the collar. He was sitting expressionless in one of the two chairs in front of the desk. "Mani DaLucca, Jean Rheume."

Manuel DaLucca rose, and the two men shook hands. They nodded but said nothing. Rheume could care less about some assistant. His business was with Costa. Mani DaLucca on the other hand seemed very interested in the Frenchman and watched him closely.

"Please," Pablo said, patting the high-back, brown leather tufted chair beside DaLucca. "Have a seat, gentlemen." He walked behind the desk and sat in a chair that looked more like a throne. "Jean, I know your concern is what happened in Miami."

Rheume shot a glance towards DaLucca that Costa picked up on right away.

"Don't worry," he said shaking his head. "I keep no secrets from Mani. He is my eyes and ears."

Rheume shrugged and sat down.

"As you wish, Pablo. So, have you been able to find out what happened?"

DaLucca reached inside his jacket pocket and took out his mirrored sunglasses. Wearing them made people uneasy, which was why he wore them. The body language he picked up from the Frenchman, along with the lack of respect in his tone, confirmed his first impression: a man like this could quite easily become an enemy.

"I understand your concerns," Costa said, leaning back in his chair. "Your man, I believe his name was LeFave, along with two of my people, one being my nephew were killed by a group of blacks ... Jamaicans. They have stupidly been trying to expand into our area." Pablo stood and faced the window. "Their leader, a man called Taylor Williamson, has been attempting to widen his interests for some time now. We have tried to correct matters in a more ... diplomatic fashion up to now, but things have changed. The ones who did this have already been dealt with, and Williamson for the time being is still alive, but I guarantee you this is only for a short time."

"So," Rhemue said, "There was no fault from my end at all then?"

"None," Costa said, shaking his head. "All from Miami, completely. The product had not yet been turned over to your man, and so it is still awaiting you, and I regret the inconvenience. I will have my people arrange for delivery direct to Montreal at no extra cost. The details we can discuss later over dinner."

Rheume felt relieved. If the problem had stemmed in any way from Montreal and cost the life of his nephew, Costa's revenge could easily have begun with his death. Their business relationship for now remained intact.

"Thank you, Pablo. That's very kind. If there's anything I can do to help?"

Costa looked at DaLucca then back at his customer. "We will handle everything. We have a bit of minor housekeeping to take care of but that's all. Soon these Jamaicans will realize they should have stayed on their beaches smoking marijuana," Pablo said with a laugh and stood up.

He came to the front of his desk and walked Rheume to the door. DaLucca stayed in his chair, watching.

"If there is anything I can do," Rheume said, shaking Costa's hand again, "anything at all, please let me know."

"I appreciate your offer, Jean." Costa smiled pleasantly. "If the need arises, I may take you up on that. As a matter of fact," he said holding a finger up and looking back at DaLucca. "Mani and I were talking just before you arrived about a little annoyance that may have come up. It appears the Miami police may have a witness, one who could identify the people who took care of the three Jamaicans. I don't think anything will come of it but, if so, perhaps you could help."

Rheume, always quick to seize an opportunity, especially if it meant having someone of Costa's stature indebted to him in any way said: "I have some very talented people with a lot of experience handling such annoyances."

"Excellent, we can discuss this further at dinner also, but for now I'll have Rosa show you to your room. I'm sure you must be tired."

With the meeting over, both were silently glad to be finished with the other. Their association was based purely on the customer and supplier needing one another, nothing else.

21 APRIL
Mercy Hospital
Miami

Hospital rules dictated that patients signing themselves out prior to a doctor's authorized release must be delivered to the front door via wheelchair. Paul refused at first but gave in when Carla Thatcher lied that she could lose her job if he so much as stubbed his toe before getting outside.

"Seems ridiculous if you ask me," he muttered putting the last of his personal items in the plastic bag he'd been given. "If everyone leaving your hospital has to be wheeled out, what does that say about the treatment they received while they were here?"

She laughed and released the brake as soon as he lifted his feet onto the footrests.

"First of all, Paul Goldman, I have two months left in this job and I don't plan on losing it before that. And secondly, you shouldn't even be out of bed for at least another week."

Paul held up both hands in surrender. "Okay, okay. I'm in the chair."

He adjusted himself around a little as she wheeled him into the hall.

"There's a good boy," she said smiling. "Finally doing as you're told."

The guard led the way down the busy and crowded corridor. When they reached the elevators, Paul pushed the down button.

"Why are you leaving?" he asked her, looking over his shoulder.

"Oh, it's something I've been thinking about for a while now. I've been offered a job at San Francisco General. My folks live out there, and they're getting on so it'll be nice to be closer, plus I don't have any ties here anymore."

Paul almost asked what the ties were but caught himself, deciding it was none of his business. The elevator arrived.

"I've never been to San Francisco," he said as she wheeled him in and turned the chair around to face the door. "I hear it's quite beautiful."

"You'd love it," she said. "Cities like New York and New Orleans have their own unique qualities, you know, things that make them special, well San Francisco has its own special things. Lots of them, actually." The doors opened at the main floor lobby.

"Well, here we are," she said stopping beside the front doors and setting the brake.

Getting out of the wheelchair sent a sharp jab of pain across his chest. A lot less painful than a week ago but still enough to make him wince. He forced a painful smile when he turned toward her.

"Thank you for everything. I really mean it."

"Don't mention it. I'm just glad I had the chance to push you around a bit before you got out of here." Then her expression changed. She looked straight into his eyes. "Do something for me would you?"

"Of course. What?" he asked.

"You be very careful, Paul Goldman. I mean it," she said, holding his gaze.

Paul arched his eyebrow. "What do you mean?"

"Well," she said, lowering her voice, "let's just say it was probably the drugs but a few times the past week you did some talking in your sleep."

He wasn't too worried about what he may have blurted out because he knew so little about those responsible that it would no doubt have sounded like the ramblings of a drug-induced patient.

"Dreams," he said with a shrug. "Just dreams, but I promise I'll be careful and … ahh, there's my ride now," he said, relieved when the unmarked Crown Vic pulled up to the curb in front of them. He took her hand and patted it gently "Thank you for your care and your concern. I really appreciate it, and good luck in San Francisco."

"And good luck to you too Paul Goldman," she said, watching him make his way to the car.

CHAPTER EIGHT

PAUL FELT GOOD TO BE SOMEWHAT MOBILE AGAIN, AND TO BE outside. Flat on his back in a hospital bed had made him way too vulnerable. Morgan Connors got out and opened the back door as Paul put the doctor's list of things to do and not to do in his pocket.

"Good to see you up and around, Paul. Hope you're not rushin' things though?"

"No, I'm feeling pretty good, actually," he said, letting out a groan as he adjusted himself and reached for the seat belt.

The conversation during the drive across town remained light. From the excellent care he'd received at Mercy, to the tropical storm that just missed the coast last week, but when Connors mentioned they would have to sit down soon to discuss security options Paul ignored it, so Connors decided to leave it be for the time being. A few blocks from his house they stopped talking and Connors left him with his thoughts. When Bonnie turned left onto Parker Avenue, the sight of the Le Baron parked in the driveway made Paul's stomach tighten. Everything looked so normal. Connors looked at him in the rearview mirror.

"Hope you don't mind, Paul. We brought it over this morning. Thought it'd save you going to the vehicle compound an' all."

"Of course, thank-you. It's just, the whole place looks like nothing ... you know what I mean?" He closed his eyes and shook his head. Bonnie pulled over and stopped at the end of the driveway.

"You want us to come in?" she asked.

"No, no. Thanks anyway, Bonnie, I'm fine, and I've got a lot to do. You know, things to clear up here, and I want to go to the cemetery."

"We understand," she said. "We can put the lineup I.D. off for a day or two if you want."

Paul shook his head as he got out. "Actually, I'd just as soon get it over with."

"Can we pick you up in the morning?"

Paul spoke through the open window. "That's okay. I'll drive myself. After all, nobody's going to know about me until after we do the line-up thing."

Bonnie smiled. "Okay, then. See you at the office at 8:15."

"Sure thing. 8:15 it is," he said.

As he started up the driveway, Morgan called to him. "You got my home number, right? You call me okay? I'm serious, Paul, even just to talk. I don't live far from here."

"I will," he called over his shoulder, then waved without turning around. After they pulled away, Paul stood by his car, staring at the front door. The warm feeling he always felt when he pulled into the driveway had gone. He took the keys out of his pocket and unlocked the door.

It was exactly the way they'd left it. He walked slowly through the living room, then down the hall, filling his nostrils with the familiar smells, not touching a thing. Ben's bedroom door was open. Even though he shared a small apartment with two friends near the college, Anna always kept his room ready for when he came home, usually every other week-end or when in need of a good, home-cooked meal. He studied the posters and pictures that covered every inch of wall space, each image an important part of a Ben's life. Above the desk two shelves held trophies, medals, and awards he'd won over the years. Most were from baseball, but by far Ben's favorite was a bronze surfboard he'd won last summer for placing second in his very first surfing competition. Neatly placed at the side of the desk was the recent letter of acceptance from the University of Miami. Paul picked it up, and started to read it to himself. After a few lines, he put it back exactly where it had been, turned, and walked down the hall to the kitchen. He gazed at a scene where time had stood still. The two coffee mugs, one with lipstick on the rim were on the counter beside the sink where Anna had put them on their way out the door. Her silver lipstick holder lay on the small, oak telephone table in the hallway. She'd searched her purse on the way to the restaurant, sure she'd brought it. He leaned against the kitchen wall, and closed his eyes. The only sound came from the mantle clock in the living room. God it seemed loud. He let himself slide down the wall to the floor. Wrapping his arms around his knees, he buried his face and wept.

22 APRIL
0700 **hrs. local time**

He'd slept in their bed, or tried to. Every time he started drifting off he'd wake in a panic, hoping against hope it had all been a terrible dream. The torture repeated itself over and over until the first light of morning began changing the room from black to grey. It was a relief.

After a hot, painful shower, Paul put a clean dressing on his chest, decided on the tan suit with a dark-brown shirt and got dressed. At 7:45 he locked the front door, climbed into the LeBaron, and headed downtown..

He found a parking spot right across from the Miami Police building. Bonnie was waiting for him on the sidewalk near the front doors. Paul waved, waited for two cars to drive by, and then hurried across.

"Morning Bonnie," he said. "Hope I didn't keep you waiting."

"Hi ,Paul, no, just came down a couple of minutes ago."

She led him in and stopped at the public complaints desk to sign him in, then clipped a "Visitor" pass to his lapel. In the elevator when the door closed, she pressed the button for the third floor.

"How're you feeling?" she asked.

"I'm okay. Didn't get a whole lot of sleep though," he said. "To be expected, I guess."

"You sure you're ready for this?" she asked. "Cuz these things can be tough."

Paul stared at the floor numbers above the door. "Oh, yes, believe me Bonnie, I'm ready for this."

The doors opened. On the wall directly in front of them a sign read HOMICIDE with an arrow pointing right and under it, ROBBERY, with an arrow pointing left. He followed her down the hall to the right.

Morgan got up from his desk when they walked into the homicide office. "Mornin' Paul," he said. "How you doin'?"

"Sore, but all in all, pretty good."

"Come on in," Morgan said, leading him into the captain's office. "Paul, this is Captain Jacobs."

Jacobs was a big man, six-two, weighing in at about two forty, balding on top with silver hair on either side of a round, bulldog face. He looked like an aging football player who'd dropped the exercise but not the appetite. Give him a cigar and black derby, and he could be a stand in for Winston Churchill. He came around from his cluttered desk and extended a meaty hand.

"Mr. Goldman, I want to thank-you for coming down." His voice was gruff but compassionate. They shook hands.

"Sorry we have to do this so soon after your release from the hospital," he said. "But it's necessary so we can get things moving. Hope you understand."

"Of course, captain," Paul said, looking over at the young man wearing a rumpled two-piece grey suit. He was sitting in one of six chairs at a small conference table in front of the desk.

"Oh," said Jacobs. "This is Assistant District Attorney Robert Accardo. He's been assigned to prosecute the case."

Accardo stood and shook Paul's hand. You can tell a lot about a person by their handshake. A firm grip usually indicates self-confidence and a genuine interest in the person they're meeting. Accardo's was limp and impersonal.

"Nice to meet you, sir," Accardo said, then looked over at Captain Jacobs. "So, if we're ready I think we should get this part over with."

"Fine," Jacobs said. "Detective Connors will take you all downstairs, and I'll notify the cells that we're ready," he said, picking up his phone.

· · · · · · ·

Line-ups were viewed from a small room no bigger than a walk-in closet on the main floor down the hall from the cells. A large, one-way mirror gave a clear view of the room where the six or eight members of the line-up would stand side by side facing the one-way glassed-in viewing area. The suspect, prior to entering, would get to pick whatever number he wanted then take that spot in the line. All would be similar in size, age, hair color, and complexion. Because of the age and height differences of the three suspects, there would be three separate line-ups.

Paul took his time before pointing them out. Not unlike the hundreds he'd dealt with in the past, except those had been enemies, who, depending on who you asked, were either terrorists or freedom fighters. Whatever the case, they were driven by a commitment to what in their minds was a just cause. But these people, they killed indiscriminately, and for only one thing: money. When the third line-up was paraded in, Paul studied the face of the one who had dressed as the maître d', and used the Gloc.

"Without any doubt, number six," he said clearly.

As the last line-up filed out, the eldest one of the three shooters, holding card number six, was taken aside, handcuffed and read his rights. Charges of first-degree murder would be laid within the day. The press would know about the existence of a witness in time for the six o' clock news, and the rest of the world would know shortly after that.

· · · · · · · ·

Sitting across from Connors at his desk in the homicide office, Paul finished reading his statement, initialed the bottom of each page then signed it. Connors fastened the pages together with a paper clip and put them in the file marked GOLDMAN-ANNA/BENJAMIN-MURDER OF, then swiveled his chair around, opened the filing cabinet, pulled the middle drawer open and replaced the folder. Paul stared at the file as the drawer closed, gritting his teeth.

"You okay, Paul?" Morgan asked.

"Yeah. It's just a jab of pain here," he said, rubbing his chest.

"Paul," he said spinning the dial on the cabinet lock, "We gotta talk about your security arrangements because, as of now, things have changed, a lot, and we …"

"Yes," Paul said, cutting him off. "I've been giving that a lot of thought, too."

Morgan turned his chair back to face him. "I'm serious man. I know you've got your own ideas, but all bullshit aside, protective custody is the only way to go on this. You gotta believe me. This time tomorrow Costa's people are gonna start looking for you in earnest, my friend, an' they'll keep lookin'."

Two detectives walked by Morgan's desk. Paul waited until they were out of earshot.

"No, you listen, Morgan, that's not what we agreed to, is it? I'll be where you want me when I'm needed and say what has to be said but, damn it, if Costa's as big as you say he is, then sure as hell he's got people somewhere in the justice system, or can you guarantee me he hasn't?"

"Yeah, maybe he does, probably, but I'll hand pick ..."

"No. Then it'll be as we decided. I have some friends I've known for a long time and ..."

"Paul, for Christ's sake man," Morgan nearly shouted. "Will you listen to me. I'm tellin' you, very shortly they'll know who you are and be damned close to knowing where you are. I am not kiddin'. And once he does, the prick'll spend whatever it takes to make sure you don't testify. You gotta understand how this guy thinks. You've stood up to him, an' to him that's a slap in the face."

Paul stared across the desk and locked eyes with the detective. "Isn't that amazing," he said shaking his head. "This man kills my family, and I've slapped him in the face?"

Morgan's voice softened. "Yeah ... something like that, yeah. It's just how the guy thinks."

Paul stood up and clapped his hands. "Okay, then, you're going to have to trust me on this, Morgan. I'll be out of here within twenty-four hours. We'll set up a way to stay in contact with each other in case there's an emergency. Other than that, I'll check in with you every two or three days."

"Wait a minute," Morgan said, waving his hands. "There's no way my boss or the DA are gonna go for this ..."

"Then don't tell them, or say I did it on my own, but this is the way it's going to be."

Connors ran his fingers through his hair and let out a whistle. "Man. Why do I get the ugly feelin' I'm gonna be writin' parking tickets for the rest of my miserable career."

Paul patted him on the shoulder. "Don't worry, my friend. When Mr. Accardo wants to interview me, I'll put myself in your care, I promise. Now I should go. I've got many things to do."

Morgan let out a long sigh. "Yeah, okay. Mind if I drop by your place after work? I have some things I'd like to show you and go over with you."

"By all means, I'll be home all night."

Ten minutes later Bonnie walked into the office and looked around.

"Where is he, Morg?"

He glanced up at her and opened his briefcase. She stared at him, waiting, but he said nothing. "Aw, com'on, you didn't. For the love of God tell me you didn't let him walk out of here?"

"Had to, otherwise we got no witness. It's that fuckin' simple."

"Are you nuts? They'll kill him sure as hell, and you know that." She stormed past him to the window and looked down to the street. "Well his car's gone, so at least he didn't get blown away at the door."

Morgan shook his head and gestured to one of the chairs. "Calm down, Bon, and sit down ... please?"

Bonnie stood where she was, arms folded. After a few seconds she gave in and sat down, but her expression didn't change. Morgan leaned across his desk, keeping his voice low

"We're kinda caught between a rock and a hard place here, but I got this ... gnawing feeling about him."

"What do you mean, gnawing feeling?"

"Don't know. Somethin' about him's buggin' me. Can't put my finger on it, but it's almost like, he's so casual about everything. Been that way since he woke up in the hospital." He opened the top drawer of the filing cabinet. "Right now he thinks he knows how to take care of himself,. cuz he's got Costa pegged as a dummy."

"So, how's letting him wander out of here on his own going to help?"

"Christ almighty, Bon. After what he's been through I'm gonna arrest and lock him up for his own protection? I can't do that to him, plus, you heard him yourself, he won't testify."

"Come on." she stood up and shook her head. "There's got to be something in between protective custody and letting him hang out there on his own. How are you—"

"Hell, suggest something to me. You see how he is. It's his way or the highway. As long he figures Costa's all cash and no brains he won't listen to us. So what we gotta do is convince him we're his best, or rather only bet."

She shrugged. "Maybe because of his military background he feels he can take care of himself."

"Shit, Bon, you read the background report we got on him. He was in the supply branch. He handed out uniforms and sent barrels of oil and gasoline to the front lines, probably by phone for Christ's sake. His entire military career was about as exciting and dangerous as watching paint dry."

"Okay, maybe you're right but coming up through the ranks he'd have to have learned enough to get promoted, wouldn't he?"

Morgan put three, thick files in his briefcase. It barely closed.

"There's nothing to indicate he even knew what end of a fuckin' rifle to point."

"So. What are you getting at?"

"So," he said, picking up his briefcase and jacket and walking into the hall. "We gotta change his mind."

She rushed after him. "Like I said ... so what are you going to do?"

"First," he said. "I'm gonna try to talk you into buyin' me lunch."

"Yeah, well, I wouldn't bet the ranch on that one cowboy," she scoffed. "Then what?"

"Then I have to take the bull by the horns, so to speak."

The elevator doors opened.

"I probably don't want to know, but what would that be?" she asked, giving him a suspicious look.

He checked over his shoulder to make sure no one was around, then whispered in her ear.

"I gotta get through to him what this guy's all about, so I'm gonna sit down and go through the file with him."

Her eyes widened. "Are you talking about the Costa…you're not. Are you?"

They stepped in. Morgan waited until the doors closed and the elevator started moving before continuing. "It's the only thing I can think of that may scare some sense into him."

She shook her head. Even though they were alone, she looked over her shoulder before whispering. "What! Are you crazy? You're going to give him a top secret file?" The doors opened. They walked past the complaints' desk, through the front doors. He waited until they were in the parking lot before he answered.

"I'm not giving it to him, Bon, I'm hoping that after he gets a clearer picture of what the guy's capable of." He tapped his briefcase. "He'll let us do our job … and hopefully save his life."

CHAPTER NINE

22 APRIL
1700 hrs. local time

MORGAN CONNORS LAY THE THREE FILES OUT ON PAUL'S KITCHEN table and had just explained what they were and was half way into a "do you have any idea the kind of shit I'd be in if anyone found out about this" speech when his pager went off. A suspect from a two-year-old shooting had just been picked up at Miami International getting off a Chicago flight. He called Bonnie and arranged to pick her up at her place in fifteen minutes. He thought about taking the files with him, but he figured they'd be safer here than in the trunk of his car. Thieves didn't discriminate between cop cars and civilian vehicles at night.

"You got a safe place for these, Paul?"

"Don't worry," he said reassuringly. "I'll lock them in my safe upstairs."

"Okay. That'll be good, cuz this could take some time. I'll be here first thing in the morning an' we can go over things then."

"Sure, I'll have the coffee on for eight?"

"Eight is perfect," Morgan said putting on his jacket and heading for the door. He hesitated before opening it, as if he was having second thoughts.

Paul smiled and said: "Really. Don't worry. I'm locking them up right now."

....

It took an hour and a half to dismantle, photocopy and reassemble the three thick folders, but at least Paul didn't have to rely on his memory, which is what he'd have done if Morgan hadn't been called. The files formed a twenty year time-line chronicling Costa's rise through the ranks of a major drug cartel that was littered with assassinations and brutal murders. When Paul finished, he locked both sets of files in his safe and slipped out the back door. What had to be done next would take a while.

The route to his shop took longer than usual, but it was time to start taking precautions. He parked half a block away and watched the front entrance for any sign that someone may be inside, or on the street watching. After ten minutes he pulled into the rear lane and parked in one of the parking stalls at the back entrance to Spartan Plumbing and Heating, four business's down from his. Paul unlocked the rear door, stepped in, and locked it behind him. He pulled the heavy curtains across the workshop windows then turned on the light over his work bench. It was a little after four in the morning before he got back home.

23 APRIL
0800 hrs.

Paul poured two cups of coffee when he saw Morgan pull into the driveway.

"Morning. Come on in," he called through the screen door.

Morgan went to the kitchen table and sat down, looking around. "Where's the…"

"Oh, right here," Paul said, picking the three file folders off the counter. "And I appreciate the insight into Costa's world. I skimmed though these after you left. He certainly is driven, isn't he? Here you go." He handed him the three files.

Morgan put them in his briefcase and locked it, looking very relieved.

"Oh, he's driven alright. "Driven? That's a nice way to describe an obsessive homicidal psychopath," he said and put the briefcase on the floor beside him. "So, now you've got an idea about the type of mentality we're dealing with here?"

Paul nodded and put the cream and sugar on the table, sat down and passed a cup across the table.

"I hope you don't mind decaf. Anna's idea, and she finally got me hooked on it."

Morgan shook his head. "No, decaf's fine."

"I think, my friend," Paul said, "in a different time, the government would, with what's in these files, remove him once and for all."

Morgan took a sip then added a bit more sugar. "True. Trouble is, we're playing' by the rules of a system that today's got so many loop holes that most of the time it's the bad guys who get portrayed as the victims. Collecting evidence is getting harder, an' every move seems to become an infringement of the poor dirtbag's rights. Getting a conviction, even with the slam-dunk cases, it's like a flip of the coin." He took another sip. "Umm ... that's better. An' believe me, I'm sick of the ongoing bullshit and misery people like Costa cause. Problem is, he sits in Colombia shipping dope and countin' dough, surrounded by the best protection money can buy, an' I don't just mean his goons. I mean lawyers, politicians an' cops. So we're left runnin' around with our heads up our asses."

Paul rolled his mug back and forth in his hands. "Strange isn't it. Everyone knows who he is, what he's doing, and how he's doing it, but we're so tied up in laws and rights that we can't do anything but sit on the sidelines and watch him tear apart the very fabric of our society. If another country tried to poison our young and destroy our system we'd call it an act of war and defend ourselves. But if an individual does it, the safeguards within the very system being attacked automatically jump to his defense."

"No argument there," Morgan said, putting his cup down. "An' add to that the bastard's got enough money to pay off the national fuckin' debt, it gives him the resources to buy almost anyone, anytime, anywhere."

Paul nodded slowly. "Almost everyone, Morgan, but not everyone. By the way, any idea when I'll be needed? To testify, I mean," he asked topping off both cups.

"Not sure. Probably seven or eight weeks at the earliest ... why?"

"Well," he said, looking around the kitchen. "I've decided to go visit an old friend for a while."

"What are you talkin' about? Jesus Christ, man, after what you just read, can't you see you don't have a lot of options, and one of em' sure as hell isn't going to visit an old friend. Listen to me, Paul, I can guarantee your safety if you'll just let me handpick the right people. No matter how well connected these guys are—"

"Exactly," Paul cut in. "So let it be known you've moved me into a, a cabin in, I don't know ... Virginia or wherever you want. Or you're moving me all over the damn country, it doesn't matter, as long as the only information about my whereabouts comes from you. If it does filter down to a leak, they'll spend their time chasing shadows. You agree?"

"Okay, maybe for a while, maybe, but what about the fluke? You know, the, it's- a-small-world shit. Then what happens? How you gonna protect yourself against crap like that?"

· · · · · · ·

Paul leaned across the table and, for the first time, Morgan noticed something different in his face. The sad, vulnerable look of a victim had disappeared.

"Listen to me," he said, his voice quiet, and resolute. "You and I, we have an agreement. Remember?"

Morgan closed his eyes and sighed. "Here we go, yeah, yeah, yeah, I remember."

"Look," Paul said. "I know you're trying to help, and I appreciate it, but you don't know anything about me or my life, so I'll tell you this much. I know what I'm doing and it's the right thing. You're going to have to trust me on this."

Morgan studied him for a few seconds. "In other words, don't believe everything you read, right?"

Paul didn't answer. Morgan pushed his cup off to the side and clasped his hands together in front of him. "Okay, so what's next?"

"I could use a drive to the airport later today, around noon if you're not too busy," Paul said. He picked up the cups, the softness returning to his voice. "I'm booked on a two o'clock flight."

"Sure, the airport, of course, why not," Morgan sighed. "Anything else?"

"No, I don't think so. Oh, maybe bring your personal car so it doesn't attract any attention."

"My personal car, sure. Is that it?"

Paul thought for a few seconds before nodding. "Yes, I think for now that should be it."

1145 hrs.

Morgan Connors pulled into Paul's drive way in his red Miata convertible. He tapped the horn twice and saw Paul wave from the living room window. The first couple of weeks after he'd bought the convertible, Morgan had been the brunt of a stream of mid-life crisis jokes. Bonnie called it his reward for reaching male menopause before anyone else his age.

Paul locked the front door behind him and carried a suitcase, suit bag and briefcase down the steps. He stopped at the bottom and stared at the car.

Morgan climbed out of the driver's door and opened the trunk. "You want me to water your plants or anything?"

"No, thanks, I've given them all to my neighbor," he said, shaking his head and frowning. "Morgan. What is that?" he asked pointing at the tiny sports car.

"Oh, man, not you too."

Paul watched as he put the suit bag and briefcase in the small trunk then secured the large suitcase on the chrome trunk rack with two bungee cords.

"Seriously, Paul, what do you think of her?" he asked.

"Well, the suitcases, okay, they fit but how does a normal-sized human get in?" He asked, looking at the passenger seat.

"Hey, trust me," Morgan laughed. "By the time we get to the airport you'll probably be makin' me an offer on this little gem."

Paul groaned as he wedged himself into the seat. "Why would I want to spend big money on such a little car, especially when I can fall down a flight of stairs and get almost the same feeling."

• • • • • • • •

Pulling out of the driveway, Morgan circled the block once checking his rear-view mirror after each turn. Out of the corner of his eye, he saw that Paul was doing the same thing with the side mirror. It made him feel a little better. Maybe he did know a little about taking care of himself. Still, Morgan had real bad vibes about what he was doing.

• • • • • • • •

It took twenty minutes to get to the airport and find a parking spot. Inside the terminal the line-up at the American Airline counter was short and moved quickly. After the ticket agent attached the luggage tag to his suitcase and stapled the other half to his ticket, she smiled pleasantly. "There you are Mr. Wallberg, open return to San Diego. Your flight departs from Gate C-thirty-four at 1:50. You can go to the boarding gate now, if you wish."

"Thank you, Miss," Paul said taking his ticket and boarding pass.

"You've got I.D. in the name of Wallberg?" Morgan asked as they walked away.

"Yes. I thought it might be a good idea. Don't you agree?"

Morgan smiled and nodded. "Yeah ... a handy thing to have for a guy who sends uniforms and gasoline around Israel."

On their way to the security screening area Morgan watched the people moving around them. The departures level was fairly quiet, which made it easy enough to spot a potential problem, but difficult to melt into the crowd. No doubt Costa would know by now, and so still being in Miami and out in the public was really pushing the envelope. Ahead of them a young man moving quickly through the crowd towards them caught his eye. As he got closer Morgan slipped his hand into his jacket pocket and stepped in front of Paul. The young man passed by looking lost, and late.

· · · · · · ·

Morgan breathed a sigh of relief. "Look, Paul. I'm goin' along with this, but I'm not real excited about it. At least give me a damn contact number."

They stopped by the security entrance. A large sign above it read gates C-16 to C-35.

"I'll call every few days like we agreed. To your home. If you're not there, I'll leave a message with the time I'll call back so you can be there. For anything else," he said, handing Morgan a piece of paper. "It's a pager number in case you need to get a hold of me." Paul unzipped the side compartment of his suit bag and took out a black plastic bag. "Oh, and if you could keep these locked up in your office until all this is over They're albums and pictures of Anna, Ben, and myself. I didn't want to leave them in the house."

Morgan took the bag. Not bad, he thought. Making it difficult for anyone to get their hands on something that could put a face to him. "No problem. Anything else?"

"I don't think so," Paul said as he lifted his briefcase and suit bag onto the conveyer belt that moved them inside the x-ray scanning machine. They shook hands.

"Hey, take that look off your face detective. I'm not a fool, and I don't have a death wish. I'll come back when I'm needed."

Morgan looked around and shook his head. "Christ, I don't know how you got me to go along with this, Paul ... I mean, Mr. Wallberg, cuz if the shit hits the fan, I'm screwed, big time."

"You're a good man," Paul said, smiling and patting him on the shoulder. "Don't you worry, and say good-bye to Bonnie for me." He turned and walked through the metal detector, setting it off. Morgan watched the security guard run the wand over his body. After removing his watch, the second attempt was successful. He winked at Morgan, who smiled back and waved.

He waited outside the departure security area until Paul's flight showed on the wall monitor as DEPARTED, then headed for the parking lot. He'd take his time driving to the office, because he had to come up with some kind of believable story that Captain Jacobs would buy when the time came.

CHAPTER TEN

23 APRIL
Miami, Fl.
2300 hrs. local time

THE ANSWERING MACHINE ON THE KITCHEN COUNTER CLICKED ON after the fourth ring. The recorded message was short. "You've reached the Goldman's. We are away right now but will be checking for messages. Please leave your name, number and the time you ..." click. The caller hung up.

· · · · · · ·

Minutes later, two shadows moved silently along the darkened hedge that ran along the edge of the Goldman's property. They reached the back door, hidden from view by a six-foot privacy fence around the patio. It took only seconds to pick the lock. Inside, the two moved quickly and quietly from room to room. In the master bedroom, the closet door was wide open. Most of the men's clothes were gone. On the kitchen counter next to the answering machine, a pad of paper half-covered by a metal cookie tin caught their attention. One of the intruders took a penlight from his jacket and held it above the pad. The thin beam lit up an address partially hidden by the cookie tin. His partner picked it up and put it off to the side, revealing the complete address: Number 7, White Caps Motel, 7621 Bremner St., Ft. Lauderdale. After a few whispered words, one of the men tore off the top page, and they left through the back door. Seconds later the deadbolt clicked back into the locked position.

```
23 APRIL
San Diego, Calif.
2000 hrs. local time
```

Paul squinted at the display screen on his pager, then waited until their waiter removed some dishes from the table and walked away.

"Appears someone is paying me a visit back home, Thomas," he said, taking the cell phone out of his pocket. He pressed one, the area code, then his home number, and when the answering machine came on he punched in, star-eight-eight-three. The tape rewound and began to play. He covered his other ear to muffle the noise of the restaurant.

He looked at Tom and held up two fingers. "Speaking Spanish."

He listened until he heard the click of the lock then put the phone back in his pocket.

"Not bad," Tom said, pouring the last of the wine into their glasses. "Thought it'd take a little longer than that. Gotta have people in the right places."

"Yes, quite impressive," Paul said and took a piece of paper out of his wallet. "So now we throw a little wrench into the works by letting him think someone else is in the game. Someone he won't be able to find no matter how many people he pays off." He unfolded the paper and began dialing a Ft. Lauderdale number. After a series of beeps he punched in a long combination of numbers. "There. That should stir things up a bit for him," he said, motioning to the waiter for their bill.

· · · · · · ·

When they got back to Tom's place, Paul spread the files out on the dining room table. Just after ten, his pager buzzed again. Three time zones away, residents living near The White Caps Motel were jolted out of their sleep by an explosion from inside unit seven. The two stun grenades, or 'flash bangs', rigged together blew out one of the windows and caused some minor damage to the carpets and bedding. The two men who had opened the window far enough to break the connection lay dazed and temporarily blinded on the sidewalk. Paul pushed the off button, and the buzzing stopped.

"Well, if he's as compulsive as they say, that should keep him busy for a little."

"Night Cap?" Tom asked and took two glasses out of the dining room cabinet.

"Sounds great. Then we'd better get some sleep. Things could start getting pretty hectic around here real soon."

Tom handed him a glass. "Paul. I've known you for years an' we've planned and done, Christ, dozens of missions together, but this is different, man."

"What are you getting at, Tom?"

"Aw, shit. How can I say this. It's just that ... Anna and Ben, they're all you can think about right now, and rightly so, an' you just got outta hospital, an' you're hurtin' that way too. Are you sure you shouldn't give it some time, like a couple of months?"

Paul sipped his drink and stared at his friend. After a few seconds he slowly shook his head. "I understand what you're saying, Tom, and any other time you'd be right. I am hurting, bad not just the chest, I've got pain killers for that, but time isn't on our side here. This will be in court within a couple of months, and we have to have done what has to be done by then. So until it gets done, Anna and Ben will be in my heart twenty-four seven, but I've got to try to keep them in the back of my mind."

Tom clicked his glass against Paul's. "Copy that. Then I say … let's get the son-of-a-bitch. Oh, by the way, Jamie'll be here tomorrow. Said he's got a ton of leave to burn up and couldn't think of a better way to use it."

Tom looked down at a surveillance photo of Costa stapled to the front of one of the files and raised his glass. "Okay, you little shit, let's play hard ball. Your bat an' ball, but our field an' rules."

30 APRIL
Montreal, Canada
0840 hrs. local time

Jean Rheume ate breakfast every morning without fail at Le Café Royale, a small diner across the street from his apartment building. Nothing fancy, but the food was okay, and it saved him from doing what he hated—cooking. The morning customers were pretty much all regulars with the exception of the odd person running in to grab a coffee to go. The owner, Maurice Talbot, used to be one of Montreal's busiest bookies back in the old days. Back then he used Le Café Royale as a front for his bookmaking operation. When the bookie business dried up with the coming of casinos and online gambling, Maurice was surprised to find that the café could actually generate enough business to bring in a half-decent, legitimate living. He and Rheume had known each other for years. The two old-time rounders had no axes to grind, because they'd always worked opposite sides of the street. If Rheume ran into someone who wanted to place a bet he'd send them to Talbot, and if any of Talbot's customers wanted dope, he'd return the favor. In his usual back booth facing the front door, Rheume finished his breakfast by mopping the remaining egg yolk and catsup with the last of his toast. His daily routine. Three eggs over easy, five strips of bacon, toast with loads of butter, and two or three coffee. This routine changed only on Sunday when the Royale was closed and he would make toast and coffee at home. He took the postcard out of his jacket pocket and re-read it. It had arrived by Fed-Ex as he was leaving his apartment half an hour ago, and the message was very clear.

THE THIRD LAW

Jean:

Having a wonderful holiday. The weather has been lovely. I've been on a number of tours and am learning a lot about this beautiful country. Hope things are well with you and everyone is healthy. Things are fine here except I still have that nagging cold I had when we talked. You mentioned a remedy your mother used. Could you let me know about it.

Regards: P.

Jean left a ten on the table, waved at Maurice who smiled and nodded from behind the counter, then crossed over to his apartment. Inside he opened the sliding-glass balcony door and stepped outside. The morning air was crisp and the sky an electric blue. The weatherman had been right on. Another warm, dry spring day. In the distance, freighters from all over the world glided silently back and forth along the St. Lawrence Seaway. Below him the streets were clogged with morning commuters. Montreal is probably the only city in Canada where drivers use their horns more than their turn signals. But the sounds of honking, screeching tires and sirens were all part of the ambience of living downtown. Sitting at the small, wrought-iron table Rhemue lit the corner of the postcard and held it over an ashtray. In the three years they'd been doing business, Costa had never asked him for a favor. This could be an excellent opportunity. When the flames had done their job, he went inside, took the keys out of his pocket and unlocked the middle drawer of his desk.

Whenever he had business to discuss over the phone, no matter how insignificant, he took precautions. He changed his codes every couple of weeks. As simple as they were, so far they had been good enough to stay a step ahead of the cops. He picked up the phone and dialed the pager number of his most trusted man, Marc Tasse. At the sound of the beep he punched in three numbers, 3, 8, and 2. The first two added together indicated the time Tasse should call. In this case eleven o' clock. The third number, a 2 meant he would call the second phone number on his list.

· · · · · · · ·

Both men would then go about their day, which included more than usual checks for surveillance. A few minutes before 11:00 Marc Tasse randomly picked a payphone. Today his choice of payphone was outside an office building on the corner of Sherbrooke and Harvard streets. Some twenty blocks away, Rheume pulled into the underground parking at the Cartier Hotel, took the elevator to the lobby where he bought *a Montreal Gazette* and leaned against the wall by the row of payphones. The phone beside him rang exactly at 11:00.

The conversation was kept short. No details. Those would be discussed in person later. Rheume hadn't done jail time for twenty-five years and even then not much. A few 'bits' as cons call anything under a deuce, or two years. Getting caught or killed depended on how you conducted business. Generally, police got their information from customers who got arrested and were trying to cut a deal, or the competition. Customers, if treated right would give up the dealers who sold shitty dope or were light on the weight, so Rheume always tried not to piss people off, and so far had kept himself off anyone's "get out of jail free" list. Handling problems with the competition was different. That's where people like Marc Tasse came in.

Competitors were a constant danger. Whatever they were planning to do to you, you had to be ready to do to them, only sooner. Then of course, there were the cops. Throwing money around and driving exotic cars attracted cops faster than flies to cow shit.

Lastly, if you became a creature of habit, you were easy to find, follow, and therefore easier to put in jail.

After hanging up, Marc Tasse couldn't have been happier. He loved Miami, and to get the chance to show the people down south how good he was would no doubt do a lot for his future. At five-foot-five he sported an Elvis-style hair-doo to make him look and feel a bit taller. Although he looked more like a standup comic than any kind of threat, in reality, his appetite for violence had grown over the years to become insatiable.

· · · · · · ·

He'd grown up in Northern Quebec, and life had been hard from the get go. The constant beatings by an alcoholic father fuelled Marc's hatred towards him, and any other type of authority. So when his father passed out in his truck one February and froze to death, Marc felt cheated out of fulfilling his reoccurring dream of one day killing him. Throughout his teens he bounced from foster homes to juvy detention centers, escalating his distrust of society in general. Then at eighteen, high on a combination of booze and L.S.D., he committed his first murder. The victim, a drifter making his way to the West Coast, had his fate sealed by bearing a slight resemblance to Marc's father. Lured to an abandoned building with the promise of a half bottle of whiskey, Tasse wound up, and smacked him from behind with a piece of angle iron. When the drifter came to he found himself tied to a chair, gagged, and his execution already underway. With an eight-inch butcher knife Marc Tasse spent the next hour crossing the line from being a problem child, to a cold-blooded killer. The sheer brutality of the murder earned him two things: the nickname 'Le Petite Boucher' meaning The Little Butcher, and ten years in Archambeault Penitentiary.

All maximum security prisons are worlds unto themselves, and surviving until your parole date means doing whatever necessary to get through each day. No matter how violent the crime that put you in, your reputation on the outside counts for very little.

It's the one you earn on the inside that determines the degree of respect or abuse you receive.

At the end of his second week, the inevitable happened. During showers, two lifers, Alain Dupuis and Michel LaRose decided to share the small, young newcomer. Word passed quickly for the dozen or so other inmates to leave. Rinsing the soap out of his hair, Marc noticed the loud talking above the hiss of the showers had stopped. He opened his eyes and saw the two forms walking towards him through the steamy mist. He knew exactly what was about to happen. He backed up against the tile wall, his eyes darting from side to side. No one knew that his father had beaten fear out of him a long time ago; now, everyone who tried to hurt him merely filled him with rage. They, in effect, became his father.

LaRose moved in front of Dupuis. At about ten feet away he saw the grin on Tasse's face. Bending down, Marc let out a high-pitched howl, jumped up, grabbed the copper showerhead and, using all his weight, snapped it off. He landed on his feet, went into a crouch, and sprang forward like a wild animal. LaRose, caught completely off guard, didn't have a chance to react before the jagged end of the showerhead pipe ripped into his right eye. He let out a blood-curdling scream as he grabbed at his eyes and threw himself back in agony. Blood squirted from between his fingers, turning the shower water crimson as it swirled around the drain. Alain Dupuis, a three-hundred-pound biker from Quebec City stopped dead. He stared at LaRose in disbelief, his smile and erection disappearing pretty much at the same time. He stepped forward and took a wild round house swing that Tasse easily ducked. The momentum spun Dupuis around on the slippery tiles; his feet shot out from under him. He went down hard on his back, smacking his head on the floor. Dazed and semi-conscious, he struggled to get up, but Tasse was on his chest. By the time things started to register, the sharp end of the shower head had already torn his face and throat open. Dupuis flailed his arms in a slow-motion death dance, eyes wide, mouth gaping. Just before the last spark of life ebbed out of the tough guy from Quebec City,

Le Petite Boucher calmly dropped the bloody shower head, rinsed himself off and mingled with the stunned audience of inmates. None could believe what they'd just seen. Pierre Trembley, a dope dealer from Montreal doing six for trafficking heroin, yelled at the guards as they pushed their way through the crowd.

"Hurry ... there's two guys killin' each other in there!"

Marc Tasse had earned the reputation he needed to be left alone, and Trembley, on the day of his release would introduce him to Jean Rheume.

Since then he'd killed many people. Some were bad customers who refused or couldn't pay their debts; others were competition that had become a problem for his boss. Tasse was totally loyal, and Rheume soon became the father he never had. So if his friends in South America needed help taking care of someone, he wouldn't let Rheume down.

He waited as instructed until 3:30 then called the number he'd been given. A Miami area code, and picked up on the first ring by some guy with a thick Spanish accent. Tasse identified himself as the friend from up north, and the voice on the other end got right to the point. An invitation to come fishing. He'd be contacted as soon as the fish are running. His written invitation is in the mail, and he should bring it with him. He should not worry about bringing any fishing gear as everything he needs will be provided.

When Tasse hung up he was excited, and pretty clear on the details, at least the most important ones. As soon as they found the target. Marc would be contacted. In the meantime he'd get something in the mail. When he arrived in Miami he'd be asked to show it to whoever met him. Tasse couldn't have been more pumped. He hoped the target was important, but if not, it didn't matter; he'd make sure his work would impress.

CHAPTER ELEVEN

01 MAY
Miami Fl
0800 hrs. local time

MORGAN CONNORS FIGURED CAPTAIN JACOBS WOULD PUT THINGS together sooner rather than later, and he was right. He gave Bonnie a call; she'd just got the same message. 'MY OFFICE ASAP!!! Morgan told her to meet him in the parking lot so they could go in together.

He met her at her car. "Okay, Bon," he said, looking up at the police building. "Just in case we can't convince Cap, let me do the talkin'. No need for both of us to get suspended. If that happens, you're gonna have to be the buffer between Paul, the system, and the bad guys."

"Got it," she said and nodded.

• • • • • • •

When Jacobs saw them get off the elevator, he stopped pacing, and slammed it the door shut behind them.

"What in hell you think you're, doing Connors?" he hollered, "Where is he?"

"Cap, look, everything's all right, really. In a couple of weeks I'll …"

"No," Jacobs said, shaking his head. "No, Detective, everything's not all right. As a matter of fact, everything's fucking terrible. Now you listen real careful. That witness is under our protection by the end of today, or you're done, mister. Do I make myself clear on that?"

"Cap, would you listen to me for a second? You gotta hear me out. I did this for a reason."

"Reason!" Jacobs bellowed, pacing to the door then back to his desk. "Shit, yeah, I'd love to hear why you decided to say to hell with policy and security procedures, that, I might add, everybody else in the department seems to be able to follow. Yeah, please, let me in on your … reason."

Bonnie started to say something but stopped when Morgan shot her a glance.

"Okay," he started. "We know Costa's gonna do everything he can to get our guy, an' we know he's got people somewhere in the system for sure."

Jacobs plopped himself in his chair, buried his head in his hands and laughed. "Oh, well, isn't this wonderful then. I got the DA, the mayor, and oh, yeah, let's not forget Chief Harelson, all of whom are on my ass, so no big thing, you just want me to tell' em, sorry, boys, but we don't trust any of you? Is that all?" He looked around his office. "Well, gee, why don't I just round off this fun-filled day by sliding on over to "Don's Alligator Ranch" for a quick dip."

· · · · · · ·

Bonnie cleared her throat to get Morgan's attention. He knew what she was getting at. One thing for sure, Jacobs would never go outside the law to make the job easier, but he would dance around a bit of the bureaucratic bullshit to put a bad guy away — fair ball. As much as he deserved to be in the loo, Morgan figured that if

Cap knowingly lied to the chief and the shit hit the fan, it would just make the line-up at the unemployment office a little longer. Still, he had a right to know something.

· · · · · · · ·

"Okay, Cap, the fact is Goldman didn't trust us with his security, and he made it clear he'd testify an' make himself available to the DA, but only if he ...."

"For the love of Christ, Morgan," Jacobs said, slamming his fists onto the desk. "It's your job to build a trust so he won't go off half-cocked and do exactly that. If they find him, he's dead. You know that, right?"

"C'mon Cap, lemme finish here," Morgan said, raising his voice. "The poor bastard's lost his entire family just for bein' in the wrong place at the wrong time. First his daughter gets blown away by some fuckin' terrorist, then just when life is getting back to whatever normal could be after that, bang, a bunch of fuckin' dope dealers take out the rest of his family. I know what my damn job is Cap, an' I'm trying to do it."

Jacobs leaned back in his chair, still frowning, but at least now Morgan had him listening.

"So what's he gonna do, Cap? Put his life in the hands of the good ol' American Justice system an' believe everything's gonna work out the way it's supposed to. The guy's no fool. He knows his chances are better where he is because nobody here knows where he is. As far as the DA and the mayor's office, tell' em you've left it in my hands, and I've got control over him. He'll be available for pre-trial interviews when needed. Tell the same to the chief. Let him know that if anyone starts pressing you to give up a location we're gonna look at that somebody real hard as a possible leak."

He stepped back and waited. Jacobs remained silent, thinking. Morgan hooked his thumbs into the pockets of his jeans. "Bonnie an' me aren't real happy about the way things are either, but short of lockin' him up which is out of the question, it's Goldman's call ... an' like it or not, right now this is how it's gotta play out."

Jacobs stared down at the desk, clicking the end of his pen. After a few seconds he looked up, stared at them and nodded. "An' you're sure he'll stay on side?"

"Gave his word, Cap, an' we believe him." Morgan said. "He needs to. He's a proud man an' it's the only way he can start to find some kind of closure in all this."

"What about trying something on his own?" Jacobs frowned.

"You've seen the guy, Cap. What's he gonna do? No, as much as he's hurtin', he's smart enough to know these guys are way out of his league."

Jacobs picked up a yellow-lined notepad and his pen.

"I don't believe I'm fuckin' doin' this," he muttered. "Okay, here's the official version. I'm advising the chief, the DA and the mayor that security of our witness is strictly need-to-know. Costa's gonna pressure his contacts, so." He looked at the ceiling, searching for the right words, then bent his head and continued speaking as he wrote. "Those with knowledge of his whereabouts will be kept to an absolute minimum. I'm pretty sure Harelson will agree. D.A's office is a different story, probably get a shit-load of flack outta them, but it should do ... for now." He tossed his pen down. "I'll add a little more political bullshit to this, and get it typed up official sounding, but don't be surprised if Harelson or the DA call us on it," he said looking up. "If they do…we are fucked."

Morgan nodded. "Thanks, Cap. Bon an' me'll keep workin' on him. Hopefully by the time he meets with the DA he'll see things more our way."

"I hope so, detective," he said, motioning with his head towards the door. "Cuz if things go sideways you're hangin' out there alone. My pension's so close I can almost taste it, an' I ain't about to screw that up. Now, get outta here."

At the door Morgan turned. He was about to say something but decided to leave well enough alone. Why take a chance of snatching defeat out of the jaws of victory?

At the elevator Bonnie pressed the down button then glanced back towards Jacob's office. "Jeez, not a bad job, cowboy." She said just loud enough for him to hear.

"Cap knows he's doin' the right thing, but we're skatin' near the edge an' draggin' him with us so let's do as he said an' get outta here before he changes his mind."

"Good plan," she said as the elevator arrived. The doors closed, and they were alone. "And you're sure Paul won't try to do something on his own?"

"I been thinkin' bout that since droppin' him off at the airport. Showin' him the Costa file sorta backfired, but still, he doesn't seem like the kinda guy to run off and do something stupid. At least I sure as hell hope he's not. He's gotta know it'd be suicidal to take him on, but the truth is, Bon, there's somethin' about the guy I just can't read."

"And maybe you're reading to much into it," she said.

"Yeah, maybe I am," he said looking at her and nodding. "Shit, I hope so."

CHAPTER TWELVE

02 MAY
San Diego
0900 hrs. local time

FOR OVER AN HOUR THEY'D BEEN SORTING THE STACK OF COMPUTER printouts—separating occurrence reports, source and surveillance information, and photographs—when the front door bell rang. Tom peered out the living room window then walked to the door. "Well, as Paul Revere said, the British are here, and there goes the neighborhood."

Paul laughed and got up from the table. "I'm not sure he said it exactly like that but in modern language that's probably close."

• • • • • • • •

Jamie Ryan stood five foot nine. He was somewhat portly with silver hair and a well-trimmed goatee. He wore a tweed sports jacket complete with brown, leather elbow patches and looked more like an English squire or a character out of a Sherlock Holmes novel than one of the most experienced counter-terrorist operatives in MI-6. He spoke five languages fluently and, over the years, had worked operations in Eastern Europe, Africa, the middle East, Central America, and South America.

Tom's face broke into a broad grin. "Hey, man, how the hell are ya, come on in."

"Thomas, good to see you again," he said shaking hands. "I see your command of the English language remains as challenged as the last time we shared a misadventure."

Tom laughed. "Looks like our odds of being successful just took a dive, Paul."

Paul tossed a surveillance report on the table and shook Jamie's hand.

"Jamie, you look great, thanks for coming."

"Paul. I am so sorry, and thank you for letting me help you on this. It is my pleasure to be on board," he said, and then looked at Tom and smiled. "Besides, there's no way I could leave you to deal with these South American lads, plus Thomas here. That wouldn't be fair at all."

"I think what he's really saying, Paul, is he's always eager to come learn from the real pros."

Jamie frowned and shook his head. "Humm ... professionals ... around here? Highly improbable, but I shall persevere."

Tom laughed, picked up the soft-sided leather suitcase, bowed deeply and pointed towards the hallway.

"If you'll follow me, your highness, I'll show you to the royal suite."

Jamie smiled. "Well, perhaps he's finally catching on Paul."

Tom started to lead the way then turned. "Oh, and Paul, remind me to count the silverware when this little operation is over will you?"

• • • • • • •

Once Jamie got settled in, Paul and Tom spent the rest of the day bringing him up to speed. By late that evening the first phase of the plan was looking good. Tomorrow morning, a little fine tuning, and they'd be ready to begin.

03 MAY
Cartago, Colombia
2200 hrs. local time

Pablo sat alone in his study. He shook his head and re-read the fax. What the hell did it mean? It must have been either the cops or someone close to the witness, but why. And go to all that trouble then use stun grenades. Unless it was meant as a warning, but a warning of what, and from who? He pressed it flat on the desk in front of him, rubbed his eyes and leaned back into his chair. With the amount of money he paid out, someone must have heard something. Time for some of his over-paid contacts to earn their fucking keep. The sooner this witness thing was taken care of the better. It irritated him to have little problems that lingered on.

04 MAY
San Diego
1200 hrs. local time

The I-5 north from San Diego hugs the coastline, winding its way past sandy beaches and crowded marinas that bristle with the masts of hundreds of sailboats and multi-million dollar yachts. Paul spotted a pay phone next to a fruit stand at a pull-off overlooking the Pacific. Except for the fruit vendors pick-up truck, there were no other vehicles. It would do nicely.

Miami, Florida
1500 hrs. local time

Morgan heard the phone ringing as he got out of his car. Running up the front steps, he managed to unlock the door, run down the hall to the kitchen and pick up just before the answering machine kicked in.

"Conners here," he said.

"Morgan, you sound like you're out of breath."

"Paul? Where you been? Its' been four days man. Is everything okay?"

"Yes, yes, everything's just fine. How are you making out?"

Morgan let out a long sigh. "Well, for now Bon an' I got everyone convinced we got you in our back pocket. Don't know how long that'll last though. DA's gonna want to have a sit down with you pretty quick."

"Okay," Paul said, pausing for a few seconds. "Tell them next week I'll be available ... and you'll confirm the exact date later. Will they buy that?"

"Shouldn't be a major problem. I'll tell'em it'll take that long to set up security. They'll understand. Oh, by the way, looks like you might've had visitors at your place the other night. One of your neighbors called it in."

"Really. You think it was. ..?"

"Yeah, has to be. The neighbor saw two guys leavin' your back yard dressed head- to-toe in black. For sure it wasn't kids. Uniforms checked it out, and the place looked secure, but you keep a heads up out there my man."

· · · · · · ·

Paul watched two cars pull in and park beside the fruit stand. A caddy with heavily tinted windows and a red Chevy blazer.

"Don't worry. I'll call in a few days to let you know when I'll be there, okay?"

"Okay," Morgan said. "Anything you need?"

"No, I'm fine. Say hi to Bonnie, and you guys be careful, too."

After hanging up, he stood by the phone. A woman with a small child got out of the Blazer. A few seconds later the doors to the caddy opened and an older couple emerged and walked over to the fruit stand.

· · · · · · ·

On the drive back Paul went over in his mind the rules of the game. Tactics of engagement. Things that hadn't changed much since the first two social groups glared at each other from opposing caves or trees and mutually agreed that the world wasn't big enough for both of them. Following the rules didn't guarantee a win, but it put the odds a little more in your favor. Rule one: Learn everything you can about your enemy—habits, likes, dislikes, plus any fears or phobias. Rule two: Know what his resources are and how far he's willing to go to achieve his goal. Finally, find his weak point, because there always is one, and once you have, you pick the battlefield.

• • • • • • •

The Costa file had explained a lot about his psyche. The string of murders stretching over the past three decades underscored how far he would go to maintain unquestioned control. Bodies left to be found were called "confirmations," and were always extremely graphic examples of what would happen to those who dared cross him. Victims who disappeared without a trace were called '"communions," and from the file it was obvious Costa preferred the fear value of confirmations. His ever-increasing drug profits gave him the ability to buy virtually any resource needed, and with the amount he paid to have eyes and ears at all levels of the justice system and the Colombian government he had layer upon layer of protection. And, judging by how quickly he found Paul's house in Miami, likely there as well. Nothing Paul had seen so far indicated a weak spot in his organization.

• • • • • • •

By 8:00 that evening Tom's dining room had been transformed into an operations center. Charts, maps, and photographs covered most of the walls, and on the fully extended dining room table were the surveillance and intelligence reports, along with individual information on Costa's inner circle. Paul took off his glasses and looked around the room. The first phase of the plan was set. He waited until Jamie finished making his travel arrangements and hung up the phone.

• • • • • • •

"Okay, guys. Let's recap. The file says Costa owns the Mesa Grande Leather Company in Mexico City. It's a legit business that manufactures and exports leather goods all over the world. DEA and the federales figure that's where the bulk of the laundering is coordinated from. They've identified a guy by the name of Fernando Salas coming and going. He's a big-time accountant in Mexico City. Surveillance has put him at Costa's place in Cartago a couple of times over the last year. He's way too high-priced to be doing a leather company's books, and he goes there once or twice a week, and so he's got to be doing the good stuff there. Security looks like video cameras and a twenty-four-hour guard, or guards. The drug boys think there's a computer room where all the interesting stuff goes on at the back of the third floor, seeing as that part's off limits to everyone."

"You planning on hacking in?" Jamie asked.

"No time and too risky," Paul said, shaking his head. "With top-of-the-line fire walls and security, the odds of getting in without setting off alarms are virtually impossible. I'll have to physically go in and get it. I've got a couple of more things to put together before I'm ready to go. .. hopefully later tomorrow. With any luck I should be back within a week. How are you making out?"

• • • • • • •

Jamie picked up a pad of paper. "I leave for Bogota tomorrow morning. My cover is I'm a photo journalist under contract by *National Geographic* researching the historic, cultural, and economic aspects of coca from the Incas to the present. That should allow me to poke around and ask questions without raising too much suspicion. I'll document and photograph Costa's movements, hangouts, and associates and, with a bit of luck, determine where he's most vulnerable, or who around him is. As far as a time-line, I'd say a week. Ten days at the outside."

"Perfect," Paul said and looked over at Tom. "How's this going to fit with your schedule?"

"If you're finished in Mexico in a week, I figure three to four days max to have a sit down with the DA in Miami and be back here." Tom flipped open his note pad. "I've picked two possible hotels that have the location and type of room set ups we're gonna need. It's not prime season, so rooms shouldn't be a problem. Soon as I get word you're finished in Mexico I'll make the flight and hotel reservations. I want three rooms. One for you, Paul, that I'll reserve under your assumed name of Ken Westerby—I'm just about finished putting the I.D. together—and two rooms under my name. I'll be in one room on the same floor where I can monitor everyone comin' an' goin'. The third one'll be directly under yours. That'll be your back door if things go bad. We'll book for two nights."

"What about the police security?" Jamie asked.

"By the time Paul lets them know where he is they won't have time for anything major. Tops maybe a couple of rooms on the same floor an' a few of their people in the lobby. What we gotta remember is if there's a try it's gonna be either a cop or someone from the DA's office behind it. One thing's sure, if they figure it'll be their only crack at you before court, sure as hell they'll go for it. Anyone moves on the room, Paul's outta there an' I'll do whatever has to be done."

Paul and Jamie nodded their approval.

"Sounds good," Paul said and got up. "I've got a few hours work left to do down in Tom's workshop before I'm ready."

"You need a hand?" Tom asked.

"Thanks, no. Just a bit of the finicky stuff left."

• • • • • • •

It was a little after midnight when he climbed the stairs from the basement. What he couldn't buy, he'd built, and disguised, hopefully enough to make it through customs and airport security. Exhausted, he turned the lights out and walked through the house to his bedroom. In the dining room tacked to the wall behind the table, an enlarged headshot of Pablo Costa glared eerily in the darkness.

CHAPTER THIRTEEN

05 MAY
Mexico City, Mexico
1300 hrs. local time

THE TAXI RIDE FROM BENITO JUREZ INTERNATIONAL TO PAUL'S hotel was an experience. The driver, obviously put a lot of faith in the oversized crucifix hanging from the rearview mirror as he chalked up countless near-misses, many of which could have been fatal. Paul had the driver pull over at a small market, there he picked up a dozen bottles of water and an assortment of fresh fruit. It was another five-minute drive to the small three-story hotel called Casa Del Santana. After tipping the driver fifty pesos, Paul waved good-bye, glad he hadn't told him he was in a hurry.

· · · · · · ·

The white stucco on the outside walls of the hotel had chipped away in a number of spots exposing weathered, red adobe bricks. The sun-bleached clay roof tiles were also in need of repair. A fountain in the small courtyard near the entrance dribbled water from the mouth of what years ago probably looked like some kind of sea serpent. Not fancy, but the location made the Casa Del Santana perfect, just two blocks from the Mesa Grande Leather

Company, putting it well within range of his equipment. Paul had called ahead and asked for a room on the top floor facing south. When he checked in, the desk clerk gave him a key marked 302. Paul declined his offer to help with his bags and took the stairs beside the "out of order" sign on the elevator.

・・・・・・・・

His room was small but clean. From the tiny balcony he had an unobstructed view of the roof of the Mesa Grande. Beyond it the city faded into the thick orangey-purple haze of pollution, hiding the blue, cloudless sky.

・・・・・・・・

Paul locked the door, put his suitcase on the bed and began unpacking. From inside the shell of a hand-held camcorder he removed a pouch of tools and batteries and two miniature cameras that were wrapped tightly together. Under ideal conditions the signal would transmit for a maximum of four to five days. Paul had improvised a microwave receiver to look like a metal ruler. When fanned open, it formed the receiver dish. Everything had tested out well in Tom's basement, but bouncing around in the belly of an aircraft, and extreme weather change were just a couple of the many things that could screw up electronic equipment. Other than that, as long as the electricity didn't cut out, which happened fairly often, he should be able to make things work. When he finished checking his inventory, he locked the door behind him and headed down the stairs to the lobby.

・・・・・・・・

At 5:00 PM he was sipping coffee at a small sidewalk café across the street from the Mesa Grande. Like his hotel the Mesa Grande was old and weathered. Attempts had recently been made to make it look better by white-washing the building's front. The glass in the barred windows at street level were painted green halfway up to prevent people walking by from distracting the workers inside, while on the second and third floors the windows were wide open to let in as much light and air as possible.

∙ ∙ ∙ ∙ ∙ ∙ ∙

Paul finished his coffee, left fifteen pesos on the table and walked across the road to a narrow alley that ran between the Mesa Grande and an auto repair shop on its right. Looking down the length of the building he noticed the last three windows on the top floor were tinted to protect against the sun, and that an air conditioner was bolted to a metal bracket outside the end window. On the opposite side of the alley, hanging on the back wall of an auto repair shop, he noticed a wooden extension ladder that looked like it would easily reach the second floor, as long as it could hold his weight. He couldn't see any evidence of video cameras monitoring the outside, so dealing with whatever the inside security turned out to be looked like his only real concern. One last look around, then he crossed back over to the small café, ordered a bottle of water, and sat down at the table he'd just left.

∙ ∙ ∙ ∙ ∙ ∙ ∙

At 6:00 PM the front doors to the leather company opened and workers began leaving. All but a handful were women. Fifteen minutes later the only person left seemed to be one elderly security guard, who stood in the open doorway. He checked his clipboard then returned inside. At 6:55 pm a heavy-set Mexican wearing a similar security guard's uniform walked up to the front door carrying a lunch bucket in one hand and a rolled up magazine in the other. He pressed the buzzer. Seconds later the door opened. The two guards stood in the doorway talking for a couple of minutes before the dayshift guard handed a ring of keys and the clipboard to his replacement, waved good-bye and trudged up the street. Only one guard. Paul gave it another half hour then headed back to the hotel. Inside his room he locked the door, tossed the key on the dresser and started assembling his equipment.

```
05 MAY
Bogota, Colombia
1815 hrs. local time
```

Bogota was a mix of ultra-modern glass towers that boasted ostentatious wealth, and hopeless poverty brought on by the hordes of refugees fleeing civil strife in the outlying villages, and those looking for any kind of work, meaningful or otherwise.

· · · · · · ·

The Zona Rosa District, where high rollers and wealthy tourists played amid the neon lights of clubs and bars, is mere blocks away from the seedier part of the city. Visitors who ventured off the beaten path looking for a little local adventure became easy prey to the pick pockets, rouges, and murderers who called this place home.

· · · · · · ·

The Cantina Dias was, like most of the dingy bars hidden along narrow side streets, a place where locals congregated to share stories and curse their seemingly never- ending misfortunes over a cold Pilsner beer. Tonight, Ramon Malante, a long-time regular walked in with his new friend, a gringo. Every head in the place watched as they made their way to a table near the back.

· · · · · · ·

Jamie Ryan had watched Ramon make two unsuccessful pickpocket attempts at a busy corner near the railway station. As Ramon was about to try his luck in a different area, Jamie approached and introduced himself as Martin Shea. The offer of fifty dollars U.S. a day to be his guide and to help gather information for an article he was doing on the history of the coca plant was too good to be true. With any luck Ramon could stretch this out for a few days, and do quite well.

· · · · · · ·

By the time they'd finished their first beer, two of Ramon's friends had joined the table and quickly accepted the friendly gringo who kept the beer coming while listening to their stories of drug lords, cocaine and murder. Although completely fluent, Jamie pretended to speak very little Spanish. This would allow him to listen in to any conversations his new-found friends may have concerning him. Ramon spoke English quite well, with a little Spanish thrown in now and then.

"Is muy simple, Senor Shea," Ramon explained, putting down his beer and wiping his mouth with the sleeve of his shirt. "If you are importante, and they can one day use you ... they give you mucho dinero, but if you are importante and refuse dineros, then they kill you," he said with a shrug of his shoulders. Two hours and many drinks later, the stories were becoming repetitive and more and more incoherent. The photographer ordered one last round for his new-found friends, then made arrangements to contact Ramon the next day. The gentleman's agreement was sealed with a handshake and a fifty-dollar bill for his first days work.

• • • • • • •

What amazed Jamie was that everybody seemed to know so much about the organization run by Costa and his partner Eduardo Rodriguez. How they joined forces after years of feuding and moved quickly to fill the void when the authorities finally eradicated the notorious Medellin Cartel. Also common knowledge was who their enemies and allies were, even their favorite bars and restaurants. They were feared and idolized at the same time, sort of a cross between Robin Hood and Al Capone, Colombian style. Their business's, both legal and illegal, provided jobs, and every now and then, trucks loaded with flour, fruit and vegetables would make the rounds to the surrounding villages and the poorer areas like Cuidad Bolivar. Their movements were anything but clandestine. They travelled in cavalcades of shiny black SUVs surrounded by an entourage of heavily armed bodyguards. They appeared to operate with immunity, which meant they had people in very high places.

• • • • • • •

Another obvious thing Jamie learned, there appeared to be no competition, so the overkill of security meant that a lot of the concern came from a fear of an internal move. Also, as his wealth grew so did his ego. One thing to be treated like a king. Another to start believing you're a god. Tomorrow he would take a look at Costa's hacienda near Cartago and, with any luck, get a look at the man himself.

CHAPTER FOURTEEN

05 MAY
Mexico City, Mexico
2330 hrs. local time

AFTER A QUICK COLD SHOWER, PAUL BROUGHT THE BLACK CLOTHING he'd hung on the balcony a few hours earlier back inside. Once he made it into the Mesa Grande, any foreign scent could easily give him away. He dressed, packed his equipment into a small black knapsack and, lastly, replaced the clear light bulb on his balcony with a yellow one he'd bought at a shop next to the hotel, then turned it on. He hung the "Do Not Disturb" sign on the door handle and made his way down the stairs to the lobby. The hotel clerk had locked up for the night and guests could leave but had to ring to be let back in. The fire-exit door at the back of the hotel could only be opened from the inside. It wasn't alarmed, and so he wedged a piece of wood between the frame and the door to keep it from locking and walked casually across the Plaza Hidalgo to Avenida Casio, then turned left. Half a block ahead, the Mesa Grande Leather Company was partially lit by the only street light on the block.

· · · · · · ·

Paul found a spot between the cafe across the street and the shoe store next to it where he could watch. The only light in the Mesa Grande came from the window to the right of the front door.

· · · · · · · ·

Paul watched as the guard silhouetted in the window got up exactly at midnight and began his rounds. The beam of the guard's flashlight played across the walls and windows as he made his way through the second and third floors. From Paul's vantage point, he had a good view of the side of the building facing the alley, and the only windows on that side that the flashlight beam didn't illuminate at all were the three at the end on the third floor.

"Not allowed in there are you?" He whispered to himself.

At 12:10 the guard returned to the main floor. Using a small monocular Paul confirmed it was the same guard he'd seen earlier. Twelve hour shifts. Excellent.

At one o'clock, the guard began his rounds again. An hourly routine and the same route. Twelve minutes from the time he started until he returned to his desk. Paul crossed the street and disappeared down the alley. Once his eyes to became accustomed to the blackness, he removed the wooden ladder off the wall of the repair shop next door, extended it fully, and leaned it up against the building. The top rung reached the ledge of a second floor window towards the rear of the building.

After pulling a black balaclava over his head and adjusting the night vision goggles, he tested each rung to make sure it would hold his weight, then slowly began climbing. At the top he used a thin screwdriver to pry the soft wood between the frame and window. In less than a minute he lifted the metal latch, pulled the window open and squeezed through the opening. He stood still, listening for a few seconds. Hearing nothing, he closed the window. It looked like a supervisor's office. A small, wooden desk cluttered with files and loose papers faced the work area that could be watched through a large glass window in the wall. Behind the desk in the corner a cardboard box overflowed with papers and food wrappers, and on the wall to the right of the door hanging in an uneven line were eight or nine clipboards holding invoices, work orders, timesheets and other company paper work.

• • • • • • •

Running his fingers up the side and across the top of the door frame he checked for alarm wires. There were none. The door opened with a bit of a squeak. He closed it slowly and stepped into the work area that consisted of eight rows of benches and machinery. No cameras, at least none in sight. He made his way towards the front of the building, stopped a few feet from the stairs, and listened. The sound of music came from the first floor. The guard had a radio playing.

• • • • • • •

Paul kept as close to the outer edges of each step as he could. The bottom last few stairs were lit up by the light from the security office. He pushed night-vision goggles up and peered around the corner. The guard sat at the desk with his back to the stairs facing the front door, reading a newspaper. A small transistor radio on top of one of two video monitors played softly. The images on the monitors had to be of the third floor. One panned back and forth from the stairs to a short hallway at the far end, and the other looked to be stationary and focused on a door numbered 301. To the right of the guard were two phones. A beige one stained with dirt, and the other black one without a dial. A direct line. A red switch on the 'on' position was above the phones. So there were alarms. Luckily, they hadn't been on the second floor.

• • • • • • •

Paul looked around for a safe place to watch and wait. To his left was a door ajar and what looked to be a small cleaning closet. Perfect. Stepping over two tin pails and around an assortment of mops and brooms, he settled in, making sure the door remained ajar. The sliver of light gave him a view of the guard's back. He held his watch up to the slit of light. 1:49.

• • • • • • •

At two o' clock the guard flicked the red switch to the 'off' position, picked up his flashlight, shuffled past the cleaning closet, and clomped up the stairs. When Paul heard the guard's footsteps moving around on the second floor, he opened the closet door and quickly moved to the desk. A shake of the guard's thermos told him it was about three-quarters full. The thermos top had a little coffee left in it. Paul took out a glass vial, removed the cork and poured a few drops of milky liquid into the thermos.

· · · · · · ·

A check around the desk confirmed the red switch on the wall controlled an alarm on the third floor. A sheet attached to a clipboard recorded times the rounds were made. Every hour on the hour. When he heard the guard making his way down the stairs from the third floor, he wedged himself back into the cleaning closet to wait.

· · · · · · ·

At 2:13 the guard passed the cleaning closet, turned off his flashlight and sat at the desk. He reached over, pushed the red switch to the 'on' position and picked up the black phone.

"Si ... es Marteen en la Mesa Grande ... si, bueno." He hung up, opened his thermos, poured another coffee, then picked up his newspaper.

· · · · · · ·

A few sips and a minute or so later, the guard's head was bobbing as he tried to stay awake. Finally, he gave in and, with a long yawn, he folded his arms on the desk and planted his head on them. Within seconds he was snoring.

· · · · · · ·

Paul came up behind him and moved the red switch to the off position, then quickly climbed the stairs to the third floor. As long as no one called or came to the front door he had at least forty minutes. The third floor looked much the same as the second—lined with work benches, sewing machines and leather cutters. Along the back wall, boxes were stacked floor to ceiling, and to the right of the boxes was a short hallway, and at the end a door marked 301. Paul could see the camera in a small vent in the ceiling above it. A large sign on the door read, MUY RESERVADO.

• • • • • • •

He took out a small leather case from his jacket pocket, studied the Yale dead bolt, then chose two picks. It had been a long time since he picked a lock, and it seemed to take forever before he felt the first of the tumblers fall into place.

"C'mon, Goldman, you haven't got all night," he whispered to himself. A minute later, the remaining tumblers slid into place and, with a click, the dead bolt slid open. He turned the handle and stepped inside.

• • • • • • •

The room measured no more than eight-by-ten and had two desks taking pretty much all the space. Each desk had a computer monitor with keyboard and a telephone. Behind the desks he could make out another door with the same type of lock. This time he had it open in a matter of seconds. Sometimes you get lucky. Heavy drapes covered the windows. He felt around the wall and found the light switch. This office was slightly larger than the first one and consisted of a desk, chair, fax machine and a computer. In the corner a shredder sat on top a five-foot safe. Be nice to have a peek in there, but not enough time.

• • • • • • •

The keyboard was encased in a stainless steel cover with a digital code release switch similar to, but much more advanced than home alarm systems. If the wrong code sequence was entered, the person trying to get in had fifteen seconds to get it right before silent and audible intruder alarms sounded and an automatic message was sent to a deactivation control module inside the computer to shut down all power. Paul had seen them before. Some were set up to alert the operator when he or she logged on that there had been an attempt to compromise the system. One thing for sure, with this type of security, it had to be the machine he was looking for.

• • • • • • •

The two tiny cameras, including titanium battery packs, were, all together, no bigger than a cigarette package. He managed to install both in a ceiling vent above the computer, aiming one at the monitor and the other directly above the keyboard. It took twenty-five minutes to set up. He checked his watch and took one last look around before turning out the light and re-locking the two office doors. Less than twenty minutes left and setting up the transmitter would take all of that.

• • • • • • •

The roof could only be accessed from a metal ladder bolted to the wall at the top of the third-floor staircase. The trap door had a slide lock allowing access to, but not from, the outside. It opened with a loud creak. He listened to make sure it hadn't wakened the guard, then smiled when he heard the muffled sounds of snoring.

• • • • • • •

Judging from the thick coating of dust covering the roof, no one had been up here for a long time. He picked a spot directly above where he figured he'd put the cameras to set up his equipment. After attaching the battery wires he aimed the antenna towards the yellow light on his balcony two blocks away, then tightened the bolts to keep it in place. Giving it a final check, he turned the toggle switch to the 'on' position. He was done.

• • • • • • •

He returned to the first floor. The guard was still sleeping peacefully. Paul emptied the half cup of cooled coffee, wiped it clean, and filled it to the same level. Turning the alarm switch to the 'on' position he adjusted his night goggles and moved quickly up the stairs to the second floor supervisor's office and opened the window.

∙ ∙ ∙ ∙ ∙ ∙ ∙

By 2:55 Paul had replaced the ladder on the wall of the repair shop and was crossing the street in front of the Mesa Grande when he let out a loud, sharp whistle. Inside, the guard lurched forward in his chair. It took a few seconds for the guard's head to clear. He checked both monitors, walked to the front door and looked outside. Across the street a man in dark clothing walked slowly down the road. Back at his desk the guard picked up the coffee cup and took a sip. Must have dozed off for a couple of minutes, he thought. Yawning, the guard checked the clock, reached for his flashlight, and flicked the alarm switch to 'off.' Then turned and started his three o'clock rounds. Another quiet night.

∙ ∙ ∙ ∙ ∙ ∙ ∙

Back in his hotel room, Paul set up the rest of the equipment. He secured the homemade dish receiver to the balcony and aimed it towards the Leather Company. After connecting the leads to two small monitors and recorders he plugged them into a wall socket, pressed the power button and waited. Nothing happened. "Come on ... come on," he pleaded. "Don't do this to me."

A few seconds later the shadowy outline of the keyboard cover slowly appeared. At the same time the dark outline of the computer screen appeared on the second monitor.

"That's better," he said looking at his watch. Now he needed a few hours sleep; tomorrow could turn out to be a long, hot day.

06 MAY
Mexico City, Mexico
0700 hrs. local time

Paul shaded his eyes from the bright glare of the morning sun as he opened his balcony door. Below in the plaza, vendors had been arriving for the past two hours and were busy setting up makeshift tents and tables that would soon hold everything from fruit and vegetables to clothing and appliances. He opened a bottle of water, turned on the monitors and settled in. The accountant usually arrived in the early mornings, but the surveillance information was old, and things may easily have changed. One thing for sure, if he missed whoever came to work on the computer, it could take another week or so before they returned, and that would screw up an already tight schedule.

Paul pulled the drapes closed and propped himself up at the end of the bed facing the monitors. The images on both were crystal clear. On the wall behind him the old air conditioner clacked and trembled, managing to shave a few degrees off the quickly rising temperature.

CHAPTER FIFTEEN

06 MAY
Bogota, Colombia
0800 hrs. local time

JAMIE RYAN LEFT BOGOTA AT SUNRISE AND HEADED FOR CARTAGO, a city of nearly 130,000, mid-way between Cali and Medellin. Although not a tourist destination, there were still a number of quaint hotels and restaurants. Nestled between two mountain ranges or Cordilleras that converged to form the rugged Cauca Valley, Cartago seemed quiet and slow paced. Atop a treeless hill five kilometers to the west, Costa's sprawling hacienda had a commanding three-hundred-and-sixty-degree view of the valley and mountains.

·······

Built to resemble a Spanish castle and surrounded by twelve-foot-high ochre- colored walls with guard turrets at each corner, it offered privacy and excellent protection against anything other than a full-blown military attack. The main house—pastel-pink with white trim and surrounded by lush palms, fountains, pools and manicured gardens— took up most of the compound. The driveway circled an ornate fountain with a larger-than-life statue of Simon Bolivar standing on a high pedestal in the middle.

· · · · · · · ·

Jamie found a bushy area on a piece of high ground between the hacienda and town where with his most powerful camera lens he could make out armed guards patrolling in and around the compound. Fifteen minutes and two rolls of film later he decided he'd been there long enough. If he could see them, it was just a matter of time before they spotted him. After taping the film containers under the driver's seat, he eased his rented Jeep down the narrow, rutted wagon path to the main road.

· · · · · · · ·

Ramon had told him about a restaurant called Leonardo's where Costa preferred to eat and discuss business when he stayed at his villa. At a stop sign Jamie asked a taxi driver for directions; it turned out he was only two blocks away. He drove past it and parked a block down the street. Taking his knapsack and cameras, he walked along the uneven, and in some places non-existent sidewalks, towards the restaurant, pausing now and then to take photographs of shops and pedestrians.

· · · · · · · ·

The restaurant stood out from the other business's on the street. All were light-tan or white while Leonardo's was a bright forest-green with light-green trim. An old woman sweeping off the front steps paid no attention as Jamie walked past and opened the door. It took a few seconds for his eyes to adjust to the dim lighting. On the right, a polished mahogany bar ran the full length of the restaurant, and to the left were about ten tables neatly set with crystal wine glasses and heavy silver utensils. He took a bar stool half way down the bar and put his knapsack on the floor at his feet. The mirror behind the shelves made it easy to keep an eye on the tables without turning around. If need be he would check into a hotel for a few days and become a regular at Leonardo's while he waited to get a look at Costa. Hopefully, it wouldn't take too long.

Right now the only customers were two men who sat at the end of the bar talking to the bartender. They stopped talking when he came in and stared at him suspiciously. The bartender looked from Jamie to the two men. One of the men said something to the bartender. The bartender nodded, wiped his hands on his white apron, then walked towards the newcomer.

· · · · · · · ·

"Buenos diaz, senor," he said eyeing him warily.

"Yes ... uh ... si, I would like a cold beer, please," Jamie answered, using his British accent to the max.

"Senor, you ... uhh." He pointed at the two cameras dangling around his neck. "uh, fotografo, senor?"

"Photographer ... that's correct my good man," he said, smiling and handing him a business card. "I work for a magazine called *National Geographic* ... I'm sure you've heard of it?"

The bartender took the card, looked at Jamie then shook his head. He walked to the far end of the bar and put the card in front of the two men. The shorter one picked it up, looked at it for a few seconds, said something to the bartender, who handed him a phone from a shelf under the bar. Holding the business card in one hand, he picked up the receiver and began dialing.

It was a female voice on the answering machine. "Hello, you have reached the office and studio of Martin Shea. Mr. Shea is on assignment at the present time in South America and is expected back on Friday the fifteenth of May. Please leave a message and ..."

Hanging up, he nodded at the bartender, who opened a bottle of beer, picked up a glass and delivered it to the photographer.

`1145 hrs.`

Jamie had just ordered a second beer when the door opened and two burly and, from the bulges under their jackets, well-armed men entered. One stood inside the front door while the other walked to the two men seated at the end of the bar. The one who had made the call stood and whispered something, gesturing towards the photographer. He strode up to Jamie and nudged the bag of camera equipment with his foot.

"No fotografia, amigo," he said, then, without asking, bent down, opened the knapsack, took a good look then stood up.

"Si ... I understand," Jamie said, putting his beer down and answering in a convincing mix of Spanish and English. "Uh, yo no ... uh, photo aqui. Just cervezas. Okay?"

After studying Jamie's face, he nodded to his partner, who opened the door without hesitation.

· · · · · · ·

Jamie recognized Manuel DaLucca from the surveillance photos. He wore a summer-weight light-brown suit with an open-collar black shirt and, of course, the mirrored sunglasses. His head moved slowly from side to side as he walked to a table at the far corner of the restaurant. Behind him came Pablo Costa, followed closely by two more bodyguards. DaLucca and Costa sat with their backs to the wall. The other two took the table in front of them facing the door.

· · · · · · ·

Over the years Jamie had seen and been involved with every type of security. Good security people were for the most part visible, well-trained and in communication with each other. The fact that Ramon and his friends even had a clue where Costa ate his meals and where his hangouts were broke every security rule. What he saw here looked overly flashy, but not very professional, except for DaLucca. This one acted like a true protector, not a door opener or errand boy. He'd be difficult to trick or catch off guard. Every move he made was deliberate and orchestrated for the sole purpose of protecting his boss. To DaLucca, everyone other than Costa himself had to be considered a potential enemy. He spoke quietly into his cell then leaned over and whispered to Costa.

· · · · · · ·

Seconds later the front door opened again. Jamie sipped his new beer and watched the three men walk past him. From the reflection in the mirror he recognized the one in the middle as Eduardo Rodriguez. Mid-sixties, heavy-set, wearing a crisp white golf shirt. He walked to Costa's table and sat down. It had been six years since the once bitter enemies reached a truce and merged, becoming wealthy beyond their dreams. Even still, Jamie sensed an underlying thread of mistrust between them. Rodriguez sat and motioned for his personal bodyguard, Juillo Sanchez, to sit opposite DaLucca. Jamie felt the eyes behind the mirrored sunglasses watching everyone. The bastard's good, he thought, downing the rest of his beer. Trying not to cause attention, he left a hundred pesos on the bar, picked up his knapsack and left. From a safe distance he made ready to get pictures of all the players as they left.

CHAPTER SIXTEEN

06 MAY
Mexico City, Mexico
1305 hrs. local time

THE SQUEAK FROM THE CEILING FAN HAD BECOME AS IRRITATING as the rattle of the air conditioner. Seems it did nothing but move hot air around. Reaching over to get another bottle of water, Paul noticed a movement on both screens. The camera monitoring the keyboard showed a shadow moving across the lower part of the screen. On the other, a man's face reflected off the computer screen. Paul pushed both record buttons. The metal keyboard cover was removed and a pair of hands began quickly and effortlessly playing across the keys with the skill of a concert pianist.

· · · · · · ·

The slender fingers with manicured nails looked almost feminine. After a lengthy code sequence the ENTER key was pressed and CODE ACCEPTED appeared in the center of the screen. The operator punched in a password. The screen went blank for a split second then lit up, showing two columns of names and figures. Starting at the top left, the operator clicked on each name, bringing up their files. Then line by line he began making changes. Customer accounts, shipment amounts, delivery dates, everything including accounts due and overdue.

• • • • • • •

Half an hour later, the operator logged off and the screen went blank. Paul reached over to turn the recorders off but then the hands appeared again. Same person, only this time the codes were longer and more complex and, like before, the screen flickered a few times then lit up. Moving closer, he looked at the screen and smiled.

"Well, well, what have we here you sneaky little bugger. Gottcha."

A quick check to make sure everything was working, then he sat back and for the next hour watched as millions of dollars moved in and out of businesses and numbered accounts around the world. From Singapore and Hong Kong to Switzerland and the Caymans, the agile fingers moved the organization's drug proceeds through companies and corporations that would eventually filter down into legitimate business investments. The whole process became a sophisticated, confusing maze that would have been impossible to follow, if it wasn't being taped.

• • • • • • •

This time, when the operator logged off the metal guard was locked back onto the keyboard. Paul ejected the tapes, zipped them into the bottom section of his shaving kit and grabbed his camera. He locked the door behind him and ran down the three flights of stairs. When he reached the corner of Avenida Casio, he saw a white BMW parked at the curb in front of the Mesa Grande. The front door to the leather shop opened, and a slim man in his fifties, wearing a three-piece white suit and carrying a black briefcase, stepped into the sunlight. Paul managed to get half a dozen full-body shots and then zoomed in for a couple of head-and-shoulder close-ups. He snapped a few more as he bent to get into the car and another as the BMW left in a cloud of yellow dust. When he got back to the hotel, he began packing. His stay in Mexico City was over.

THE THIRD LAW

07 MAY
San Diego International Airport
1030 hrs. local time

Paul cleared customs and made his way to the exit. Tom was waiting outside the Customs hall. "Here ... lemme grab one of those," he said, taking the larger suitcase.

"How'd it go?"

"We're in." Paul said and patted him on the shoulder.

"Well, I'll be, how'd you get done so fast?"

"Got real lucky. I don't know how often Salas goes there, but he showed up less than twelve hours after I set up."

Tom dug the keys out of his pocket as he and Paul crossed over to the parking lot. "You able to tell if our man's as big as he lets on?" he asked, opening the trunk.

"Much bigger," Paul said. "Tells me at this point it's all an ego thing, cuz he sure doesn't need the money."

• • • • • • •

On the drive home Tom ran through the upcoming Miami trip. High risk operations always consisted of three plans: the principal, which was the way you hoped things would go. The secondary or back-up plan, which usually became the case and allowed for minor changes at the last minute. And the disaster plan, which was the most important and was the plan on how to get out safely when everything that could possibly go wrong, does.

07 MAY
Miami, Florida
0930 hrs. local time

Morgan Connors laced up his runners. Unless he got a call, he'd have time for a quick run before heading to the office. He and Bonnie had worked until 1:00 AM assisting two other detectives, Ron Grange and Keith Wilson, who were the leads in two drive-by shootings in Little Havana. Both shootings happened within an hour of each other. The suspect vehicle was identical in both. The victim of the first shooting, a low-level heroin dealer, was dead at the scene. At the other scene four were hit standing on the sidewalk outside an all-night convenience store. Three had wounds that weren't life threatening, but the fourth, a fourteen-year-old girl, had been shot in the head and back. She wasn't expected to make it. By midnight they had the driver in custody and a positive I.D. on the two shooters. Morgan and Bonnie would be taking the next homicide, whenever it came in, which undoubtedly would be soon, and so they were happy to call it a day.

· · · · · · · ·

Every now and then they'd hang out after shift for an hour or two to brainstorm one of their cases, or just unwind. Bonnie suggested they go to her place and sit out by the apartment swimming pool and have a beer. Morgan said he'd stop on the way over and pick up a six of Bud. As usual, the conversation would come back to their personal feeling about the job and life in general. Morgan never felt comfortable showing too much of his personal side with any of his other partners, but with Bonnie it was different. He'd even contemplated asking her on an actual date a few months back but decided to shelve that idea for the time being. Why risk screwing up a good partnership? No, for now he'd leave things be. If and when the right time came, then maybe. It was nearly 3:00 AM when he got home.

· · · · · · · ·

Morgan slept until 9:00 AM, downed a large glass of orange juice and put on his sweats. Halfway through his warm-up stretches, the phone rang.

He picked up. "Hello."

"Good morning, Morgan. Paul here."

"Good to hear you, pal, uh ... please tell me you're okay and will be coming out soon."

"Yes, I'm just fine and, actually, that's why I'm calling. I'm coming out tomorrow."

"What? Tomorrow! Shit, man, you're not leaving me a whole lot of time to get things ready," he said, opening his junk drawer in the kitchen that housed everything from elastic bands to screwdrivers. He found a pen and paper. "Okay, where and when do you get in? I'll pick you up and..."

"Whoa, now. Hold on. I'll call you once I'm in and let you know where to bring the DA He can have me tomorrow night and all the next day. That should be plenty, don't you think?"

Morgan sighed. "When do I get to do my job for Christ's sake."

"Why, tomorrow, of course. You can arrange a small amount of security, nothing big, though. That'll just attract a lot of attention. Anyway, I've got a lot to do, and so I'll talk to you tomorrow and fill you in on the where and when, okay? Bye."

Morgan stared at the receiver after Paul hung up.

"Thank you for letting me take the appropriate steps to ensure your safety Mr. Goldman ... of course you don't have to worry, after all, I am a professional ... FOR FUCK'S SAKE."

He rubbed the receiver across his forehead, sighed, then gently hung it up. He waited a few seconds and then called Captain Jacobs home number.

· · · · · · ·

He took a few deep breaths as he waited for Jacobs to answer. When at home Jacobs' phone voice switched from an authoritative "JACOBS," to a pleasant, "Hello."

"Hi Cap, Morgan here. Sorry to bother you on your day off."

"No bother, Morg. What's up?"

"Listen, I got our witness comin' out tomorrow for an interview with the DA an' need the go ahead to put a security team together."

Jacobs fumbled for a pen. "How many you need?"

"Uh. .. gonna have to be ten counting Bonnie an' me. Two in the security room and two more in the lobby. We'll do twelve-hour shifts." He winced, hoping Jacobs wouldn't ask what hotel, since he didn't have a clue.

"Okay," he said. "Pick and brief who you want. When you get things figured out call me here or leave a message on my machine at the office so I can make the shift changes. I'm sending D'Angelo and Lomax to Tampa in the morning to interview the suspect in the Campo case, so they won't be available."

"Got it, Cap. Thanks. I'll see if Grange and Wilson are okay for it." Morgan liked Jacobs' style. No bullshit. No grey area. Get it done and done right. There weren't a lot like him in management anymore—ready to make the tough calls and stand by them no matter how they played out. Nowadays most of the 'new breed' officers were more concerned with the political outcome of decisions. They downloaded difficult and potentially controversial calls to others, that way they could jump up and take the bows if things worked, or dump a shitload of grief on someone else if they didn't.

"Just one thing, detective."

"Sure, Cap, what's that?"

"Over the next few days, try to remember your old captain sittin' all alone in his office with no idea what the hell's goin' on, an' when you see a phone an' you feel like reachin' out to touch someone, make that someone me, okay?"

"You got it, Cap, no problem." He hung up quickly before Jacobs could ask any questions.

CHAPTER SEVENTEEN

07 MAY
Montreal, Canada
1845 hrs. local time

WHEN HIS PHONE RANG, TASSE TOSSED THE TINFOIL 'HUNGRY MAN' TV dinner tray onto the coffee table, jabbed at the mute button on the remote and grabbed the receiver.

"Oui ... yes ... this is Marc." He listened carefully, found a pen on the side table and jotted a number down on an unused napkin. When he hung up, he grinned and pumped his fist. They would have a location on the witness soon, so they wanted him to come down there right away. He was given a number to call as soon as he landed. A friend of Jimmy's would come and get him, so be sure to have his calling card. He checked his wallet. The half of the five-dollar bill that arrived by Fed Ex two days ago was tucked behind his visa card. Whoever met him would have the matching half. He stuck the piece of paper with the phone number in beside it, picked up the phone again and called Dorval Airport.

08 MAY
San Diego
0725 hrs. local time

Paul and Tom had time for a quick coffee at the departure gate before boarding their non-stop flight to Miami. At 8:00 AM, right on time, the Lockheed 10-11 roared down the runway, pressing the two hundred and eleven passengers against their seat backs then, with a surge of power, lifted off. Less than a minute later the pilot eased back on the throttle, and the huge aircraft seemed to float into the blue California sky. Paul pulled a set of keys and a list out of his jacket pocket and handed both to Tom.

"These are a few things from my shop we'll need. Once we've checked in, I'll give you an hour until I call Morgan. It shouldn't take more than half an hour to get there and back, and I should be able to get most of our equipment set up while you're gone."

Tom nodded and put the paper in his shirt pocket. "No problem, anything else?"

"Don't think so. There's a gym bag beside the work bench that should be big enough to put everything in. And pretty much everything that's on the list is in the security cage under the workbench. The silver key opens it."

· · · · · · ·

A flight attendant came by offering cold and hot drinks. Paul and Tom both declined. After she moved off, Tom leaned over to Paul, keeping his voice low. "The cops aren't gonna have time to put much of a security plan together. Hotel's pretty booked. They'll be lucky to get a room on the same floor."

"Yeah, Morgan's not going to be very happy about that, but he'll figure a way to put something together. If there is a try, I'd say right at the room, tomorrow night, late."

Tom nodded. "I agree. Only other possibilities are in the lobby or underground as we're leaving, but that's when they'll figure security will be the tightest, and with so many exits a sniper try is pretty much out of the question. Couple that with the fact they won't have a lot of time to put much of a plan together, it's gotta be at the room. Gonna be interesting to see what these pricks have got," he said, easing his seatback down.

"It will that, Thomas, it will that," said Paul. "Then, we've got to find out who's setting us up."

Tom closed his eyes and sighed. "Yeah. We can't move ahead until we do, an' whoever it is, I look forward to punchin' his ticket."

• • • • • • • •

Paul watched the desert creep past some thirty-five thousand feet below. Scattered puffs of clouds hung between them and the earth. Everything on the ground smaller than a house had become microscopic, like it didn't exist.

• • • • • • • •

Tom drifted off listening to the hum of the engines. The sound was a lot different than the deafening drone of the C-141 Starlifters that had delivered him and thousands of other young men into Vietnam back in 1968. That flight to Nam had been his first, and he had been scared to death. Not about going to war, he had no idea what that would be like, but less than an hour into the flight the nineteen-year-old had known one thing for sure—flying wasn't his thing. Every time they hit a little turbulence he thought they were going down. After two nerve-racking landings, first in Honolulu, then in Guam for refueling, they finally put down at Da Nang. He could hardly wait for the ramp to be lowered so he could get out and stand on solid ground.

• • • • • • • •

The TET offensive had been over for a month when he arrived; within hours he and twelve other replacements were assigned to fire-base Geronimo located in the An Loa Valley. The survival learning curve was steep and had to be learned quickly. The Viet Cong had shown their ability to strike anywhere in the south, anytime, almost with impunity.

Every morning Hueys delivered supplies and replacement troops to numerous fire bases, and at the end of the day returned to their base with dead and wounded. It was like some evil thing had set up an enormous meat grinder in the jungle, and every day healthy young men were randomly tossed in. The cardinal rule: stay alert and listen to short-timers. They'd made it this far because whatever they were doing, worked. Tom hated patrol. Hunting the VC in their own back yard meant dealing with traps and ambushes. In the middle of raging firefights, Charlie would literally disappear into a labyrinth of tunnel systems that were hard to find and seemed to be everywhere.

· · · · · · ·

He was the best shot in his platoon and he was soon transferred, as he requested, into the dangerous and elite sniper unit. He quickly proved to be an excellent solo operative, and his growing reputation piqued the interest of Military Intelligence, and the C.I.A.. Under their direction, he spent the next year working with a select group of covert operatives well beyond television cameras and political interference. Slipping across the borders into Laos, Cambodia and North Vietnam, his little group carried out intelligence reconnaissance and something referred to as 'disruptive intrusions.' Getting caught or killed meant being labeled a mercenary, unsanctioned by the U.S. military. He had just signed on for a second tour when he was badly wounded and sent home. After a long recovery, he continued his career with the C.I.A., only now, he operated globally.

· · · · · · ·

The tap on the shoulder from the flight attendant brought Tom out of a sound sleep and back to the here and now.

"We'll be landing in ten minutes, sir. Please raise your seat and fasten your seat belt."

"Yeah, sure, thanks," he said, sitting up and rubbing his hands over his head.

"Good you got some sleep," Paul said. "You've got a long night ahead."

```
8 MAY
Ft. Lauderdale International Airport
```

THE THIRD LAW

1350 hrs. local time

After retrieving their bags, Tom rented one of the Florida tourist's favorite vehicles: a Mustang convertible with tinted windows. There were literally thousands of them all over Miami. The convertibles allowed for optimum views and sun exposure, and gave tourists from the Northern States and Canada a fine tan or a blistering burn, it didn't matter, either one was a status symbol that hopefully lasted for a week or two after the tourists returned home.

Twenty minutes after leaving the airport they turned onto 186th Street and pulled into the underground parking of the Holiday Inn. Paul looked at his watch. "I'll give you a couple of minutes lead."

"Okay," Tom said, opening the trunk and removing a large metal case and his suit bag. "I'll meet you in room 505 after you check in."

Closing the trunk, he headed to a door under a sign marked 'Lobby Elevator.'

• • • • • • •

The walls of the lobby and reception area were a pale green with dark forest-green base boards and matching crown moldings. The arched window frames were white, and the floors were an off-white marble. The reception counter was to the right of the elevators. Two of the three uniformed employees were checking in a small group of guests, while the third busied herself on the computer. In the center of the lobby was a rock pond and fountain stocked with brightly colored koi. On either side of it were two doors; one led to the hotel's dining room and the other to the Glades Lounge. At the end of the hall behind the reception counter was another lounge called Delmonaco's.

• • • • • • •

Between each window along the front wall were two high-back white wicker chairs separated by an ornate, round glass coffee table and on each stood a bronze reading lamp with a jade-colored shade.

• • • • • • •

Tom signed for rooms 611 and 505 under the name Cory Thomas and paid for two nights using a credit card in the same name.

"Are there any more rooms available on the sixth floor?" he asked the front desk clerk.

"I'll check that for you, sir," he said turning to his computer. "Uh, no, sir, nothing on the sixth floor at all. I have rooms on the seventh and eighth if you require something for tonight."

"Thanks. I'll have to check. If I do I'll call down."

"No problem," said the clerk, handing him the keys and waving towards the bellhop. Tom shook his head. "That's okay. I can handle these. Thanks anyway."

He stopped by the fountain and watched the koi swim near him, looking for a handout. When Paul stepped out of the elevator and walked to the check-in counter, Tom scanned the lobby. None of the half-dozen people or staff showed any interest. He moved towards the elevators when Paul finished checking in.

• • • • • • •

Once they met inside room 505, Paul went onto the balcony, leaned over and looked up at the railing of the balcony above. The wrought-iron railings were solid enough so, if he had to, he could lower himself down without a problem.

"Think you're still up to stuff like this?" Tom asked.

Paul squinted down at the parking lot that seemed a lot further than five floors, "To be very honest. I'd much rather take the elevator."

He closed the sliding glass balcony door and left it unlocked. Tom opened the metal suitcase and unwrapped a small, flat Beretta 9mil and handed it to Paul.

"You sure you don't want something with a little more punch?"

"This will do fine," Paul said, putting it in his jacket pocket. "Easy to grab and easy to hide."

Tom checked his watch. "Okay. I'll head to your shop. I should be back in about forty-five minutes."

"Excellent," Paul said and picked up the metal suitcase. "I'll get started with the rooms upstairs." As they left he closed the door and hung the 'Do Not Disturb' sign on the handle.

CHAPTER EIGHTEEN

8 MAY
Miami International Airport
1445 hrs. local time

AIR CANADA FLIGHT 1322 FROM MONTREAL LANDED ON SCHEDULE. The flight had been smooth all the way. From the jovial mood of the passengers the majority were no doubt off to Disney World, a cruise, or a week or two at the beach. Marc Tasse was in a good mood, too; actually, he couldn't have been happier. He loved Miami. One day maybe he would live here. So many French Canadians vacationed in Miami that some referred to it as Montreal South. Everywhere he looked, he saw signs of wealth: expensive boats, luxury cars, and beautiful women. Oh, yeah, Marc thought, definitely my kind of place.

• • • • • • •

He picked up his bag and took his time strolling down the arrivals level until he spotted a couple of payphones near the car rental booths. He took the piece of paper with the number on it out of his wallet, inserted a quarter and dialed. The voice on the other end told him to go to the Trade Winds Bar on the departure level and wait there. He found it one level up at the far end of the terminal. He was about to order his usual dark rum and coke, but he changed his mind and decided instead on a martini. He thought it would look a little more classy and professional. He had just under an hour to kill before Jimmy's friend was to pick him up. He slid his half of the five dollar bill on the bar by his glass.

Half an hour and another martini later, he decided enough of the professional bullshit and ordered a tall, dark rum and coke. He was partway through his drink when someone sat on the stool next to him.

"You waitin' for a friend'a Jimmy's?" the stranger asked.

Marc watched as the matching half of the five dollar bill was shoved over beside his. The guy wasn't what he'd expected. Definitely not Colombian, but the serial numbers matched.

"Yeah," he said, nodding.

"Cool. Name's Rocky, let's get the fuck outta here."

Marc downed his drink, picked up his suitcase and followed. No, this wasn't what he expected at all. Rocky was tall and skinny with a shaved head, scraggly goatee, and jailhouse tats on the back of both hands. Rocky could be taken for a lot of things, but a drug cartel hit man sure as hell wasn't one of them. With any luck he'd just be the driver.

Even standing one step below Marc on the escalator he was still a good six inches taller.

"I usually work alone," Rocky said, turning and leaning close enough for Tasse to get a whiff of bad breath and foul body odor. I don't fuckin' doubt that for a second, Marc thought.

"Yeah ... me, too," he said, moving his head back.

· · · · · · ·

Like Marc Tasse, Robert 'Rocky' Bender came from a totally dysfunctional family. He was born in Louisiana on the outskirts of New Orleans. At the age of thirteen, tired of being abused, he figured he could probably eat better and get slapped around less living on the streets. It worked well until the twenty-eight bucks he'd stolen from his father's wallet ran out, and so Rocky and his thirteen-year-old girlfriend decided to play Bonnie and Clyde, for real. The gas station attendant laughed at the snot-nosed, dirty little kid with the toy gun, until a .45 slug tore a nasty hole through his right shoulder.

With their booty of sixty-one dollars in cash, two packs of cigarettes, a six-pack of coke and four candy bars, they climbed into the stolen Cadillac, fishtailed onto the street and headed for the highway. It would have been a classic getaway except Rocky's driving experience up until then totaled about half an hour, give or take ten minutes, and his choice of stealing the biggest car on the planet meant that he could barely see over the dash. Their short-lived crime spree ended when he rammed the caddy into a row of parked cars less than two blocks from the gas station. It would be the first of many ill- planned and badly executed crimes he'd concoct. Now, violent mood swings brought on in part by years of daily drug and alcohol abuse had left him with few friends. His biggest asset was a willingness to take on any job without question, anytime, anywhere, and, depending on his financial situation, at any price. He and Tasse were a perfect match.

· · · · · · ·

Outside the terminal, Rocky led the way across the parking lot to his 1987 black Trans Am. On the way north on I-95 he filled Marc in on the target, the motel they'd be staying at until the job was over, and why the car's air conditioner hadn't worked since he'd bought it from a guy he'd done time with six months ago.

```
1550 Hrs.
```

After Paul had called to fill him in, Morgan called the front desk of the Holiday Inn. There were no rooms left on the sixth floor, so it took a bit of convincing to get the front desk manager to agree to move the guests out of room 606, directly across the hall from Paul's. Miami's finest would be on the hook for whatever the cost of an upgrade for its occupants, plus, a nice dinner thrown in. It would be a couple of hours until the room was ready, so he called Bonnie and had her brief the security teams and have the night shift on sight by 6:15. The next call was to the DA's office where he left a message for Accardo to get his file together for a seven o'clock interview tonight. Accardo would be good and ticked off at the short notice, and so Morgan was happy to leave the message on his answering machine.

· · · · · · ·

Tom hefted the gym bag out of the trunk and took the stairs from the underground to the lobby. From there he timed the elevator to the sixth floor. With no stops, it was fifteen seconds from the time he pressed the number six to the time the doors opened. Paul was just finishing up in room 611 when Tom knocked.

"Come on in, Tom. I'm almost done," he said, attaching the power cord to the VCR.

Tom stepped in, careful not to get caught up in the wires.

"You able to find everything okay?" Paul asked as he re-adjusted the camera angle slightly.

"Yeah. Threw in some extra battery packs an' a few odds and ends I thought we may need. Any problems here?"

"So far, so good," Paul said, looking around. "Everything seems to be working. Picture's about as good as I can get it considering it's shooting through the security viewer. A little distorted around the edges but clear enough so identification shouldn't be a problem. I was able to hide the microphone wires under the baseboards in the hall. The mike's right under my door so it should pick up in the room and in the hall near the door as well."

· · · · · · ·

The elevator announced its arrival with a ping sound. They watched on the monitor as a bellman, pushing an empty luggage cart, emerged and walked down the hall to room 606. Moments later an elderly couple followed him and their suitcases back to the elevator.

"Okay," Tom said smiling. "We know where the good guys are gonna be."

"Yeah, I'd better head to my room," Paul glanced at his watch. "They'll be here soon."

• • • • • • • •

At 6:15 the elevator door opened again. This time two men in their mid-forties stepped out carrying briefcases. They briefly studied the hallway then walked to room 606. Before going in they both looked over at 605. Tom waited until they had gone inside before he spoke into his portable.

"Your security's arrived, Paul."

"Copy that."

• • • • • • • •

Ten minutes later Paul called to let Tom know Morgan and Accardo were on their way up.

"Yeah, I could hear you on the phone," Tom said. "The mike's pickin' up great."

He had no sooner sat down in front of the monitor when Morgan Connors and Assistant DA Accardo stepped off the elevator. Morgan gave the hallway a good look before knocking on the door.

Paul opened his door. "Good evening, gentlemen. Please come in." Paul closed the door behind them and locked it.

Accardo shook his hand and smiled. "Good to see you again Mr. Goldman," he said, taking a tape recorder and yellow legal pad out of his briefcase and setting them on the table. Morgan sat on the couch and Paul took the chair opposite Accardo, who fiddled with a few dials and adjusted the microphone.

"There. I think we're set if you're ready to begin?" he asked, looking at Paul.

"Absolutely," he said.

• • • • • • •

Accardo cleared his throat and turned on the recorder. "The date is May the eighth, at 6:40 PM. Present in the room are Detective Morgan Connors of the Miami Police Homicide Unit, myself, Assistant District Attorney Accardo, and Mr. Paul Goldman. Okay Mr. Goldman, why don't you begin by going over the events starting from the time you entered the Deep Six restaurant on April the tenth of this year."

Paul recounted the moments leading up to the shooting. He'd re-lived them a thousand times. Ben had just finished telling them about the tattoo he would soon be getting, then, their world ended. Throughout the interview Paul's voice remained clear and strong. Accardo nodded as he jotted down notes and questions, obviously impressed with his witness's almost uncanny recall of the smallest details and his complete descriptions of all the players. The shorter of the three Jamaicans, the more cautious one, had been called Farley by the one with long dreadlocks. When the three shooters got to their table nothing had been said. The two behind the one dressed as the maître d' stayed close and followed his lead. He carried a Gloc semi and fired first. The one standing in the middle had a protruding chin and pronounced under bite and held a Mac-10 in his left hand. The third had a short-barreled twelve-gauge pump. The Jamaican who one of the others at the table called Farley, managed to pull what looked like a nickel-plated .45 from inside his jacket. Paul thought he may have gotten at least one shot off.

"And that's it," he said, leaning back in his chair. "Until I woke up in the hospital."

"Thank you Mr. Goldman," Accardo said, checking his watch. "I have a number of preliminary questions I would like to go over with you at this point."

"Of course," Paul said.

• • • • • • •

For the next hour Accardo went through a list of questions ranging from the lighting, the distance from his table to the Jamaican's, their physical appearances and clothing. When he finished, he turned the tape recorder off and rubbed his eyes.

"You have excellent recall Mr. Goldman. I'd say identification of everyone involved is a shoe-in." He turned to Morgan. "So our big concern now is security. I suggest protective custody for the time being. That way I'll have access to him and ..."

"Excuse me," Paul said, holding up his hand.

"Uhh, yes, sir," Accardo said and shifted his gaze back to Paul.

"Thank you for your concern, Mr. Accardo, but Detective Connors has put together a security package with a number of precautions that I'm very comfortable with, and I have the utmost trust in him and his department."

Morgan Connors rolled his eyes towards the ceiling. Accardo started to say something but stopped, deciding that if something did happen, better if the police were responsible rather than the District Attorney's office.

He snapped his briefcase shut. "Fine then. As long as I have access, and," he said, glancing at detective Connors, "a little more notice would be nice. I'll need the better part of tomorrow. I want to concentrate on key areas the defense will zone in on. I've got a meeting at 9:00 for about an hour, after that I'm free all day."

"How's 10:30 sound then?" Morgan asked, glancing at both of them.

"Fine by me," Paul said and nodded.

"That will be excellent," Accardo agreed, putting on his jacket. "I'll see you then."

· · · · · · ·

As soon as Accardo left, Morgan picked up the phone, called the security room across the hall and asked the two detectives to come over.

"I want them to have a look at you, and you them. I've hand picked them all. The day-shift guys I'll introduce you to in the morning. There'll be no replacements unless you hear it from me first ... anyone else comes to the door ... they'll take care of it."

· · · · · · ·

Tom watched the two detectives come out of 606, cross the hall and knock on the door. When it opened, they disappeared inside.

"Paul," he said. "This is Ron Grange and Keith Wilson. They're from my unit."

They shook hands.

"We'll be covering you through the nights Mr. Goldman. We're right across the hall. If you need anything or have any concerns just call to room 606," Detective Wilson said.

"Thank you, gentlemen. I'll try not to be too much of a bother."

"Thanks guys," Morgan said, nodding towards the door.

Detective Grange opened the door. "No problem, Montana, See you later Mr. Goldman."

Morgan locked the door after they left and sat down at the table.

"Montana?" Paul asked.

Morgan smiled and shook his head "Yeah. Kind of a nickname I've been tagged with. Anyway, there's two more guys in the lobby an' their job is to alert next door to anything suspicious."

"Sounds like you've got everything covered quite well," Paul said, opening the closet and reached into the pockets of his jacket. He removed the two miniature bottles of scotch he'd bought on the flight and brought them to the table. He poured them into two glasses and handed one to Morgan.

"Cheers. Thanks," he said, letting out a long sigh.

"So why the forlorn look, detective?"

Morgan sat at one of the chairs by the table, swirled his glass a few times before taking a sip.

"Paul, I know you've probably got more knowledge about these things than we think. Military service or whatever, it doesn't matter. What matters is unless you let ..."

Paul was already shaking his head. Morgan shrugged his shoulders.

"Christ, man, unless we're shit-house lucky, they're gonna take a crack at you, sure as hell."

"Morgan, listen ..."

"No, Goddamn it, you listen. We both know these assholes don't give a shit. It don't matter to them if they have to blow up a plane load of nuns to get to you, believe me, Costa'll do it without blinking an eye."

"Yes, I know," Paul's voice remained calm and quiet. "So the sooner we get this done, the sooner I can disappear. Morgan, we've been through all this. The more people who know where I am the easier it is for them. When I come back to testify you can give me the full blanket, I promise, but for now, thank you, no."

Morgan downed the rest of his glass.

"How'd I know you were gonna say that," he said, standing up. "How'd I just know." He closed his briefcase. "You're not an easy man to deal with Mr. Goldman."

"Why, whatever do you mean Detective Connors?" Paul said and handed him his jacket.

Morgan looked through the security viewer before opening the door. "See you for breakfast at 8:00?"

"Yes, 8:00 is fine. I'll be up and ready."

"And please ... stay in the room. Wilson and Grange will get you anything you need."

"I don't need anything but a good nights sleep and I promise, as always, I'll be a good boy."

Morgan smiled. "As always? Of course, as always."

Paul arched an eye brow as Morgan closed the door.

CHAPTER NINETEEN

09 MAY
Holiday Inn
Ft. Lauderdale, Fl.
0630 hrs local time

PAUL OPENED THE CURTAINS LETTING THE MORNING SUN FLOOD the room, then picked up the phone on the bedside table and dialed 7-611.

"Morning Thomas," he said. "I hope you managed okay?"

"I couldn't have slept if I wanted to. Man, can you snore," Tom said stifling a yawn.

"Well, you must have been listening to the wrong room, because I've never snored in my life."

"Yeah, right," Tom laughed. "Well if that's true, a real bad tuba player snuck into the room I'm listening to and practiced all night. So … what's your take on when?"

"I'd say tonight," Paul said. "Too much activity during the day, and if the leak's where we think, by now they know our schedule, so late tonight's going to be their only good shot, so to speak."

"You think we should consider getting' outta here after you're finished today?" Tom asked.

Paul slid the balcony door open. A gentle breeze ushered the bright morning light into the room.

"No," he said, squinting at the cruise ships docked in the distance. "Better they make their move according to our schedule. We have to figure out who's talking to Costa, plus it'll give us the high ground."

Tom nodded. "Roger that, and it'll let us know what kind of talent we're up against. Oh, by the way, I called home for messages an' Jamie figures he'll be out of Bogota by the day after tomorrow. Says things are goin' real good."

"Great, listen, you get some sleep when Morgan and Bonnie get here. Tonight could be a long one."

Tom yawned, this time not bothering to stifle it. "Trust me, after last night getting' to sleep's not gonna be a problem."

· · · · · · ·

Paul hung up and began what used to be his daily ritual of fifty pushups. After ten, a sharp jab of pain shot through his chest, reminding him of his wound. He stopped, deciding not to overdo it, and hit the shower. In room 611 Tom watched two men come out of the elevator and knock at the security room door. Shortly afterwards, Grange and Wilson left. The dayshift had arrived.

```
Motel 6
Miami Florida
0750 hrs local time
```

In the dream he's in prison. Most of Rocky's dreams take place in a cell or some other confined space. This one had played through his mind many times over the years, but each time seemed like the first time, and it was always terrifyingly real. Strapped into the electric chair, or "Old Sparky" as it's called by the soon-to-die inmates on Florida's death row, Rocky strains every muscle against the leather straps that hold him frozen in place.

THE THIRD LAW

Faceless guards attach the cold metal electrodes to his arms, legs, chest, and shaved head. He hears nothing but his breathing and soon-to-be-stopped racing heart. The thin eye-slits in the black hood allow partial glimpses of the death chamber. On the wall, the second hand of the clock moves into the final minute on its way to midnight. The guards begin moving further away, out of his view, while the Warden stands by the phone that isn't going to ring. Behind thick glass sit rows of witnesses, witnesses who act more like expectant fans waiting for a long overdue performance to finally begin. He can see his mother and father sitting in the second row, craning their necks to get a better view. They look so happy, like a heavy burden is about to be lifted off their backs. He tries to scream, but there's no sound. Then, as the second hand on the clock touches the twelve, the sound of his pager beeping shot through him like two thousand volts of electricity.

· · · · · · ·

Bolting upright he let out a blood curdling scream. "AAAIIIEEE....NOOOOO."

In the bed next to him, Tasse, ripped out of a deep dreamless sleep, screamed and flung himself onto the floor. Rocky gulped air like a drowning man hitting the surface. His eyes darted around the room until his confused mind put together that it was just that rotten fucking dream again.

· · · · · · ·

They stared at each other, not saying anything. Rocky's eyes darted around the room then, wiping the sweat off his face with the bed sheet, swung his feet onto the floor, took a deep breath and picked his still beeping pager off the night stand. He turned on the lamp and held it up to the light. Marc slowly got up off the floor, glaring at the back of Rocky's head.

"THE FUCK WAS THAT ALL ABOUT?" he yelled, shaking with rage.

Rocky ignored him and squinted at the number on the pager.

"ANSWER ME YOU. .. YOU DUMB FUCK." Tasse came around the side of the bed, fists clenched. Rocky put the pager down and slid his hand under the pillow. The Walther PPK appeared out of nowhere, stopping level with the bridge of Tasse's nose. His mouth dropped open.

"You ever, EVER call me a dumb fuck an' I'll blow your fuckin' head off. You got that?" Rocky snarled.

Marc nodded and stepped back. What kind of fucking jerk am I tied up with, he thought, hoping his new partner couldn't read minds. Then, like nothing had happened, Rocky put the gun down and picked up the phone.

0800 Hrs.
Holiday Inn

Morgan passed the breakfast orders onto the dayshift while Bonnie stepped onto the balcony. Paul watched her methodically check every possible way an approach from the outside could be attempted.

"Balconies on either side are far enough away," she said, stepping back inside. "Awful easy to climb down from the one above though. No building tall or close enough for a shot into the room, so as long as Paul keeps the drapes closed and doesn't go out on the balcony, we should be okay on that one."

Morgan opened his notebook and flipped through the pages. "Here we go. Room 705. Mr. Aiato Tagami, his wife and daughter. They're part of a tour from Japan. Eighteen rooms rented to Nippon Tours until the day after tomorrow."

Bonnie keyed the mike and spoke into her portable radio. "Ray, you there?"

"Go ahead, Bonnie."

"Yeah, Ray, would you check and make sure that 705 is still occupied by the Tagami's."

"Copy that. I'll be back to you ASAP."

A few minutes later, Sgt. Polansky from the dayshift delivered their breakfasts.

```
09 MAY
Cartago, Colombia
0730 hrs local time
```

Pablo especially enjoyed the mornings at his hacienda, and this morning was spectacular. Through the openings in the clouds the sun sent sprays of light, creating a hundred shades of green across the rolling hills and onto the jagged cliffs of the Andes. Things were good again. Other than information of some routine police interest in a few grow areas, everything else was again nicely under control, except the witness thing in Miami, which would be taken care of soon. Pablo picked a few grapes out of the bowl of fresh fruit Maria had put on the patio table. A small bird with a fluorescent yellow breast, blood-red neck band and jet-black head landed on the railing. It cocked its head as if contemplating whether or not to come closer, but flew off quickly when Mani DaLucca opened the glass doors and stepped onto the terrace.

He handed the decoded fax to Costa before sitting down. Pablo read it to himself.

"Well, Mani," he said, placing it on the table. "Tomorrow our little Miami problem will be no more."

DaLucca poured himself a coffee, sat down and stared out over the valley.

"What is it Mani? Something is bothering you?" Pablo valued DaLucca's opinions, so always listened.

"I don't know, Pablo," he said, putting his cup down and shaking his head. "I feel maybe we should leave things be as far as Miami goes. The police are surely expecting us to move against their witness. They'll cover every possible angle to protect him, so if things go wrong and our people get caught, it would be linked to you immediately. Shopping for a judge might be the wiser thing to do. Then later we could arrange an accident for their witness, or a disappearance."

· · · · · · ·

Pablo dipped a slice melon in a dish of yogurt and popped it into his mouth.

"As usual, Mani," he said wiping his lips with a white linen napkin. "You are thinking of all the possibilities, and this is good. But you must agree, if this witness catches a cold, they will feel I am responsible, correct?"

"Yes, that's true," DaLucca answered.

"So," he said, walking to the railing and squinting in the morning sunlight. "To do nothing would be a sign of weakness to everyone we deal with. It's the damned if we do and damned if we don't thing, isn't it. But I share your concerns, and so our friend in Montreal sent one of his people, and Jimmy Santos has someone not connected to us. They'll know it was us, but won't be able to link us to the ones who do it, even if they are caught, or killed."

· · · · · · ·

DaLucca got up and joined Pablo at the railing. Growing up in the slums of Bogota he'd survived by his wits. Life was a cat-and-mouse game, and death always won in the end. It's just that making rational decisions meant being able to play the game longer, and it's much more fun if you're the cat.

"It concerns me also that since the shootings in Miami the police haven't put more pressure on our operations."

"And that is a problem?" Costa asked giving him a puzzled look.

"In the past there has always been an increase in raids and arrests after such things but this time, nothing, or maybe they are in the middle of a larger project against us and aren't quite ready to tip their hand."

Pablo thought, then nodded. "I understand what you're saying," he said, picking up the silver coffee urn and topping off their cups. "And you may be correct that we should distance ourselves from this, however, if we were to always err on the side of caution, it's true we would be much safer, but ..." He put the coffee urn down, spread his arms and looked around. "We would not have all of this."

DaLucca nodded and sat down at the table. Time to leave things alone. He had planted the seed, but clearly Pablo had made up his mind and, who knows, maybe he was right. Still, he had a bad feeling about this witness thing.

CHAPTER TWENTY

09 MAY
Holiday Inn, Ft. Lauderdale
1030 hrs local time

IN THE LOBBY THE SECURITY TEAM CALLED UP BONNIE ADVISING that Accardo had arrived and was on his way up. Bonnie met him as he stepped off the elevator.

"Good morning Detective Story," he said, looking around nervously.

"Morning Mr. Accardo. Right on time," she said.

"I make a point of being on time, detective."

Most anal people do, she thought. "Yes, of course," she said with a smile. He followed her down the hall lugging two bulging briefcases. She knocked twice on the door, and Morgan opened it right away.

• • • • • • •

For the next five hours Paul answered a barrage of questions calmly and accurately. Accardo took on the role of the defense counsel, firing questions likely to be asked. Some were personal, attacking his background and trying to bait him into changing any part of his testimony, ever so slightly, but nothing he tried could alter the story.

· · · · · · ·

At 3:30 after going over his notes one last time Accardo began gathering up his notes and putting them back in the file.

"Mr. Goldman. You're as ready as can be. I can't think of anything else. I'm quite confident that if you give your testimony the way you told it yesterday and today, we'll have no problem convicting, so unless you have something to add, or have any concerns or questions of me, I'll be on my way."

"Nothing that I can think of, Mr. Accardo," Paul said, standing and shaking his hand. "You have covered every aspect quite diligently. I look forward to seeing you at the trial."

He noticed Accardo's grip seemed firmer than when they first met.

"You take care, Mr. Goldman. I'll see you at trial."

· · · · · · ·

Morgan locked the door after he left, walked over to the cluttered table and helped Bonnie pick up the wrappers from the deli sandwiches they'd ordered for lunch.

"You want me to book your flight out of here?" he asked, tossing the wrappers into the wastebasket.

"Thanks Morgan but that won't be necessary. My arrangements are already made. I would ask, though if you could let it be known I'll be departing the hotel at about seven-thirty tomorrow morning."

"You plan on being gone before then?" Bonnie asked.

"Yes."

· · · · · · ·

Morgan looked at Bonnie, who shook her head. Before she could speak, Paul held up his hands.

"Okay ... okay," he said sitting back in the chair he'd spent the better part of the day in. "I'll tell you a bit about myself. I only ask that it go no further."

Morgan took his briefcase off the chair and sat down. "Let me guess. You weren't a guy who issued uniforms and ordered gasoline, were you?"

"The military record you have is the official version. The unofficial one will remain a secret until long after I'm gone." He cleared his throat." I was attached to the Mossad for the majority of my service, conducting covert anti-terrorist operations, some of which made it into the press, like Entebe and a few others, but what and where the majority of operations were, won't ever be known, for obvious political reasons."

"And you retired early because of what happened in Haifa?" Morgan asked before realizing he'd probably opened an old wound. "Sorry, Paul, that's none of my business."

"That's okay. You're right," Paul said. "You see I believed with all my heart that what I did was right, and God was on our side. But the day I lost my daughter to the madness I realized God wasn't on my side. He wasn't on any side. Why would he be? With decades of hatred rooted so deeply between Palestinians and Israelis, let alone the rest of the Mid-East, what peace could there ever be? All those years," he said, shaking his head slowly. "For what? Trying to protect Israel? Hell, I couldn't even protect my little girl."

His mind drifted back to that warm, sunny, terrible day at the beach. Rebecca laughing and playing one minute, the next minute lying amid the carnage with eighteen other souls who were no more.

"So," he said, snapping out of it. "I saw no use in being part of something that had no end. We came here to start over. To a ... safer place," he said sarcastically.

"Paul," Morgan said. "You're not thinkin' bout ... doing anything ... gettin' even are you?"

The five seconds of silence before Paul answered seemed a lot longer.

"Believe me, my friends," he said finally, "nothing I could ever do will bring back what I've lost. What I'm doing, with the help of some very capable friends, is trying to get through this on my terms. Now, having said that, if I have to protect myself, I will, but other than that?" He shook his head. "No."

With that, Morgan picked up the phone and dialed. As it rang on the other end, he covered the mouth piece.

"When will you be out of here?"

"Five, or a little after."

"All right, I'll ... yeah, Cap, Morgan here ... yeah all done ... went fine. Can you arrange with the DEA to fly our boy out at, uh ..." He looked over at Paul mouthing nine o'clock. Paul nodded.

"Say ... nine tomorrow morning? Great .. .flight plan ... uh, Boston," he guessed. "Yeah, Bonnie and I will deliver him to their hanger by eight ... okay ... thanks, Cap, an' tell the DEA I'll let them know if there's any changes. Yeah, okay, bye."

Morgan put the receiver down and let out a whistle. "Oh, boy, am I in shit come tomorrow."

"Your captain sounds like a good man," Paul said reassuringly. "I'm sure he'll understand."

"Yeah, he's understanding all right. Just make sure you've got a spare room in case I need it while I'm looking for a new career."

· · · · · · ·

In room 611, Tom confirmed their seats on United flight 2103 departing for St. Paul at 7:00 AM. The connecting American Airlines flight would land them in San Diego just before 3:00, Pacific time.

```
Miami Fa
Motel 6
1745 hrs local time
```

Tasse pulled back the curtains on the motel window and watched Rocky, who in the parking lot putting a stolen plate on the rear of his Trans Am. It'd be nice if there were a way of getting in touch with Jimmy. He'd feel a lot better doing this alone, without that fucking psycho involved, but this one wasn't a big deal, so why cause waves? Next time though, he'd be the one calling the shots.

· · · · · · · ·

When Rocky finished, he threw the screwdriver in the trunk, removed a worn, brown leather tote bag and slammed the lid twice before the latch caught. Marc stopped shaking his head when Rocky came in.

"C'mon Marc. Let's check our shit out, man," he said tossing the bag onto one of the unmade beds. "You're gonna really get off on this."

Rocky loved guns, and he loved to share his knowledge of them. He gave a running commentary as he took out each piece, carefully checking firing mechanisms and clip fittings. "Mini Uzi ... nine mil, Israeli made, thirty-two round mag, semi or full auto. Twelve hundred rounds a minute, fourteen inches long. She's a beauty."

He laid two loaded clips taped back to back, and a silencer neatly beside the weapon. Tasse couldn't help but be a little impressed.

"Next ..." he said, reaching into the bag. "Ingram, model eleven, nine mil short, made right here in the good ol' U.S. of A. Same size mag an' capability as the Uzi. Total length with silencer eighteen inches." Rocky stood back. "Your choice. Man, I love 'em both so it don't matter shit to me."

Marc picked one up in each hand as if weighing them, then winked. "I got one of these back home," he said, settling on the Uzi.

"Great choice, buddy," Rocky said, giving a thumbs up. "Tonight me an' you'll be able to start a fuckin' war if we want."

Tasse found himself totally caught up in the moment. "Fuckin' "A" man. Fuckin' "A.""

Maybe Rocky wasn't so bad after all.

1805 Hrs

Ron Grange and Keith Wilson arrived to relieve the day-shift security a few minutes before six. Once they were gone, Grange crossed the hall and knocked on 605. The picture on Tom's monitor in 611 was crystal clear as he watched Bonnie open the door and let him in. The microphone picked up everything.

Bonnie: Hi Ron, com'on in. How's it going?

Ron: Great, got word today Barry got accepted to Penn State.

Morgan: So both your kids are gonna be smarter than their old man, huh?

Ron: (Laughing). Hey, I'll tell ya one thing, for what it's costin' they'd better end up a hell of a lot smarter. So what's the scoop for tomorrow?

Morgan: Bonnie and I'll relieve you guys early. Maybe just before five. That'll give us time to get Paul ready, have a quick bite and head out to Ft. Lauderdale International to meet the DEA You and Keith'll still rack up four hours overtime.

Ron: Shit. You know we hate makin' double time. Any chance we could do it for free?

(laughter)

Paul: All this dedication. It's just ...

Bonnie: Nauseating, Paul, it's just nauseating.

Ron: You want anything, Mr. Goldman? I'm gonna order in about fifteen minutes.

Paul: Thanks Ron, no, we had a late lunch and I've got a muffin and a tea bag here for a snack before I go to bed.

Ron: Okay. You change your mind, just call. I'll check in on you later.

Paul: Thanks again.

Tom watched Grange check the hallway before crossing over to room 606.

· · · · · · · ·

Morgan cleared the coffee cups off the table while Bonnie put on her jacket.

"Anything we can get for you Paul?" she asked.

"I don't think so, Bonnie. I'm pretty tired. I may just watch television for a bit. It's been a long day, for all of us."

"Wouldn't you feel safer in a different hotel? We could leave right now and pick one at random," she asked.

"She's right, Paul," Morgan cut in. "Then there's no way anybody could know where you are and ..."

When he raised his hands, they both stopped. It had become a programmed response.

"You have two good men next door and more in the lobby. I couldn't feel safer. To leave now would only bring more attention to ourselves."

The two detectives gave each other a "this is a losing battle and he's probably right again" look. Paul clasped Morgan's hand with both of his.

"I'll be in touch Morgan. Same as before. Till then, you take care of yourself."

Before he could answer Paul turned to Bonnie. "On second thought you'd better take care of 'Montana' here, Bonnie. He never listens to me."

"Yeah, right," Morgan laughed out loud. "I've been leading you around by the nose since we met."

Bonnie gave Paul a hug. "Sure, give me the hard job." She smiled and kissed him on the cheek. "Bye Paul ... and you take care."

They waited until hearing the click of the dead bolt and chain lock before heading to the elevator. Tom watched them get in. When the doors slid closed the hall was quiet.

CHAPTER TWENTY-ONE

2200 hrs
Motel Six

ROCKY AND MARC WERE PUMPED. THE PAPER BAG ON THE TABLE between the two beds contained the ingredients for a small, but well deserved celebration when they finished. A fifth of Jack Daniels and a bottle of Captain Morgan's dark rum. They'd gone over the plan, which should be a piece of cake, and both had memorized the phone number to call when they were finished in case one of them forgot, or didn't make it back. That done, they decided a couple of drinks to settle the butterflies wouldn't hurt. Three hours to go.

2230 hrs

Paul packed everything into his leather suit bag except for the small black plastic bag he had put next to the coffee maker. Sliding the balcony door open, he stepped outside, unfastened one end of the suit bag's shoulder strap, looked to be sure no one was sitting outside on one of the adjacent balconies, then hung it over the railing and began swinging it back and forth. On the third swing he let go, and watched it land with a plop on the balcony of room 505. Back inside he brought out the extra pillows and blankets from the closet. Along with the ones on the bed he arranged them to resemble a sleeping figure and covered it all with the bedspread.

From the plastic bag he removed three ziploc bags and three vials of red food coloring. One vial was emptied into each bag, filled with water, then sealed and taped. Two were placed under the blankets near what appeared to be the torso, and the third where the head would be. When he finished, he moved about the room unscrewing all the light bulbs except for one just inside the door. In the dim light it should sell as long as the sheets weren't ripped off. Hopefully whoever came would figure on having mere seconds before the cops arrived, and with what looked like blood squirting all over the place it should be convincing enough to look like they'd been successful. If nothing happened, Morgan and Bonnie would find the room untouched and know everything went without a hitch.

2300 hrs

The phone in room 606 rang. Keith stopped shuffling the cards and Ron reached over and picked up. "Grange here," he said.

"Hi Ron. It's Paul Goldman. I just wanted to tell you I'm going to bed now."

"That's fine, Mr. Goldman. Have a good sleep. If we don't see you in the morning have a safe flight."

"I will, and thanks for your help."

"Our pleasure, sir. Good night." When Ron hung up, Keith Wilson continued dealing.

"He calling it a night?"

"Yeah," Ron said checking his watch. "Poor bastard's had a long couple of days."

Paul then called room 611. Tom picked up the receiver without taking his eyes off the monitor.

"Yeah, I heard. How you makin' out in there?"

Paul looked around the darkened room. "I think we're set. I've got twenty-three-ten. I'll give it another fifteen in case they call from next door for any reason, then I'm out of here"

"Got it," Tom said, checking his watch. "See you in the underground at zero five hundred, or, when the shit hits the fan."

`2325 hrs`

Paul took one of the oversized bath towels off the rack in the bathroom, walked to the balcony door and slid it open. He hooked an elastic band around the metal trigger lock before stepping outside then, using an extended metal coat hanger to hold the other end of the elastic, gently slid the door closed. About a quarter of an inch from closing he pulled on the coat hanger, stretching the elastic band and putting pressure on the metal trigger lock. The door closed with a muffled thud followed by the click of the lock. The balcony door was now locked from the inside.

· · · · · · ·

Climbing over the wrought-iron railing, he looped the towel around the bottom rail, held onto both ends and slowly lowered himself down. As soon as his arms took his full weight a sharp pain shot across his chest. It took a few seconds for his feet to find the top of the railing on the balcony below. It seemed like an hour.

"That," he said, easing himself onto the balcony deck and looking at the street below, "was a hell of a lot easier a few years ago."

Once inside, he closed the drapes, turned on the bedside lamp and opened his shirt. His dressing didn't show any signs of blood. When the pain subsided he unzipped the side compartment of the suit bag and took out a small portable radio. He sat on the bed and keyed the mike. "I'm in 505, Tom … how do you copy?"

A short blast of static, then: "Got you loud and clear, Paul."

`10 MAY`
`0200 hrs`

The two lounges—Delmonaco's, featuring live jazz and The Glades, featuring a loud rock band—were closing their doors for the night. The music in both had stopped at 1:00 AM and last call announced at 1:30 AM. Delmonaco's had emptied completely shortly after the last set but, as usual, the patrons at The Glades hung on right until two o' clock, then began making their way to waiting taxis or to the parking lot. A handful headed through the lobby to the elevators. Detective Jim Medford, sitting in one of the tall-backed wicker chairs, keyed his mike and spoke quietly: "Lobby to base."

"Go ahead, Jim," Grange answered.

"Heads up. We got the last of the lounge lizards at the elevators cuz she's closin' time, babe."

"Copy," Ron acknowledged, getting up and walking to the door. As soon as he looked through the security viewer, one of the elevators opened. A man and woman emerged arm-in-arm talking and laughing as they made their way down the hall past room 605. When they were out of his view, he opened the door enough to watch them disappear into one of the rooms at the far end of the hall.

Tom watched also.

Less than a minute later, Medford called again. "Lobby's clear, boys, we'll check in every thirty."

"Copy that, Jim," Grange answered, then put the portable on the table and sitting down. "Okay, Keith," he said. "Deal 'em up."

"Okay, partner. No more slight of had shit ... Okay?"

Grange held up both hands and smiled. "Hey, man, I was just testing you to see if you were awake."

"Yeah. Right. Well I'm awake, an' watchin'."

0245 hrs

The ping of the elevator caught Tom's attention. Two men stepped out, looked up and down the hall, then slowly edged their way along the wall towards 605. Tom pushed the record button and whispered into his portable. In room 505 Paul sat up as his earpiece crackled.

"Go ahead, Tom."

"Got two. Number one's short, clean-shaven, light-brown hair, early thirties. Number two: biker type, fortyish, shaved head, six-foot, skinny, goatee, heading to the door now. Looks like they're the whole party. I'll meet you at the car as soon as this plays out."

"Copy that. I'm heading out now," he said, grabbing his suit bag. A quick check. No one in the hallway. He slipped out and walked to the stairway exit.

· · · · · · ·

Without looking away from the monitor Tom chambered a shell into his Gloc. In 606 Grange and Wilson had also heard the elevator. Grange looked through the security viewer as the two figures edged their way closer. "Better come over here partner," he said as his hand slid inside his jacket. Keith Wilson tossed his poker hand on the bed and reached for his pistol.

· · · · · · ·

They were less than ten feet from the security room. Tom watched the monitor. Why the elevator when there's stairs at either end? Unless the T.V. was on you couldn't miss hearing it. The cops must be watching. Shit, these guys don't even have their guns out. The door to the security room opened quickly and Ron Grange stepped out holding a gun in his right hand. Marc Tasse and Rocky Bender froze. Tom relaxed a bit. "You got 'em, man," he whispered, then he heard voices. He turned the volume to high. It was Ron Grange. He handed something to the shorter one.

"Here's the key. And make sure and use this, too, and leave it in there," he said, handing Rocky the pistol equipped with a four-inch silencer.

· · · · · · ·

Tom lowered himself back into the chair. "Well I'll be a son-of-a-bitch," he muttered.

Grange's voice was louder this time. "Go ... for fuck sake ... and be quick. Go!"

Tasse pulled the Uzi from under his jacket and put the key in the lock. Bender nodded, and the door opened. Both disappeared inside. Grange looked right at the camera, then turned and looked at the far end of the hall. Muffled pops blurted, barely audible. Within seconds they stepped back into the hall and closed the door. Bender's T-shirt was blotched with red.

Ron Grange stepped forward, turned his head slightly and closed his eyes.

"Just enough to be convincing. Don't do any fucking damage ... you understand?"

"Yeah ... sure," Rocky said, taking piece of rebar about five-inches long out of his back pocket, and clenching it in his fist. "Just enough to look good." Then he swung as hard as he could. The sound of Grange's nose and skull cracking made a sickening THWACK followed by a loud thump as his head bounced against the wall on the way to the floor.

Tasse stepped over the unconscious detective, stifling a laugh. "Definitely fuckin' convincing Rock ... definitely."

"Yeah," Rocky said, putting the re-bar in his pocket and shaking his right hand, "I jes got this thing about fuckin' pigs man."

They used the exit stairway next to the elevator.

• • • • • • • •

When the exit door closed, Tom turned off the recorder and pulled the camera off the door. He'd packed everything except the camera equipment into the gym bag earlier. It took less than a minute. Leaving the room key on the table, he had a quick look around, then headed for the stairs. He checked Grange for a pulse. Still breathing, but just. Inside the security room, Keith Wilson lay spread-eagle on the floor, his dead eyes staring at the ceiling. Tom took the stairs to the second parking level and hurried to the mustang. Opening the driver's door, he threw his bag on the back seat and climbed in. Paul was in the passenger seat. "Well?"

"My friend," Tom said, turning the ignition key. "Have I got a story to tell you."

CHAPTER TWENTY-TWO

THEY LEFT THE SAME WAY THEY'D COME IN, A REAR DELIVERY DOOR. The Trans Am had been left parked on a side street two blocks from the hotel, and the plan initially was to walk so as not to attract attention, but with the adrenalin rush still in full swing they broke into a run seconds after leaving the hotel. By the time they reached the car and tossed the weapons into the trunk, both were winded. Six blocks away they pulled into an all-night gas station and stopped beside a phone booth.

"Is it six-eight-four-one or one-four?" Rocky asked as he opened the driver's door and got out.

Marc loved that Rocky had to check with him. Should be me makin' the fuckin' call anyway, he thought. "Six-eight-one-four," he answered smugly.

Rocky walked to the booth repeating the numbers while digging into his jeans pocket for a quarter. In Miami Beach, Jimmy Santos was laying in bed wide awake when the phone rang.

10 MAY
Minneapolis St. Paul Airport
0910 hrs. local time

Paul called Morgan's place from a pay phone in the departure lounge and got the answering machine. "Morgan, by now you know we were compromised. Before your department starts pinning any medals on Grange wait until you've looked at the tape I'll courier to you later today. You should have it by noon tomorrow. It pretty much lays out what happened and should help I.D. the shooters. I'm sure you've also figured out I had my own people there. Sorry I couldn't tell you more, but I know you understand. Talk to you soon and, Morgan, you and Bonnie be careful. I mean it. If our friend thinks you two are the only ones who know where I am, he may just come after you."

```
10 MAY
Bogota Colombia
0915 hrs local time
```

The view from his Los Rosales district penthouse was nothing compared the view from his hacienda, but, still, the penthouse provided Costa with all the necessary comforts. He smiled as he read the fax. Finally, everything was back to normal. The witness problem had been taken care of. Soon the charges against the three who took out the Jamaicans would be dropped, and a powerful message would be sent to anyone thinking of testifying against him or his people.

· · · · · · ·

DaLucca poured two glasses of orange juice and handed one across the table. "I am always impressed at your calmness, Pablo, no matter what comes up you analyze things in a logical manner."

"Thank you, Mani," Pablo said raising the glass in a toast. "I function this way only because you do your job, and do it well. It allows me to stay focused," he said, pointing to his eyes then tapping the side of his head. "We are like a finely-tuned machine, you and I."

DaLucca turned when he heard the fax machine in the office.

"Excuse me, Pablo. I'll get that""

"Of course, Mani. Thank you," Pablo said, sipping his orange juice.

In the office, Mani took the one sheet of paper from the fax tray. Another one from Miami, but only a few lines long, so it wouldn't take long to decode.

```
10 MAY
El Dorado Airport
Bogota, Colombia
1220 hrs local time
```

Ramon lifted Jamie's two suitcases from the rear of the jeep and followed him across the parking lot into the terminal. The check-in line moved quickly. When the ticket agent handed Jamie his boarding pass, he motioned for Ramon to walk with him towards the gate. Ramon was all smiles as usual. He liked Mr. Shea. A man of his word, plus he'd been paid in nine days what would have taken months to earn, and with no risk. To bad it had to end.

· · · · · · ·

Jamie stopped and looked around. "Ramon," he said taking a crisp one hundred dollar bill out of his wallet and putting it in Ramon's shirt pocket. "This is a little bonus. Now, I think you understand that the better my stories and pictures, the more money I make and, the more you can help, the more you make."

"Si senor, Shea, I can help make you good story."

"Good. So while I'm gone, I'd like you to check into a few things for me."

Ramon broke into a wide grin. The gravy train was still rolling.

```
10 MAY
San Diego Calif.
1615 hrs local time
```

Tom deactivated the alarm while Paul checked the answering machine. Two messages. The first was from Allison in Seattle. Working for A.T.&T. Security, she had no problem setting up the non-published line her dad needed. Paul pressed the play button.

"Hi, Dad, thought I should let you know there was a call from a place in Colombia South America called Cartago. Whoever it was hung up after listening to the message. Call me when you get in so I don't worry okay? Bye Dad ... love ya."

The second was from Jamie, saying he'd be back later tonight.

· · · · · · · ·

After unpacking, Tom brought the video cartridge into the living room and put it in the VCR.

"Showtime whenever you're ready," he said.

"Okay," Paul said, walking in from the kitchen. "Let's have a look at my execution."

Tom pressed play then sat on the arm of the couch. The sixth floor hallway appeared on the screen. Both the picture and sound were excellent.

There was Ron Grange handing a key to the short one with the Elvis hair-do, and a pistol to the tall, skinny one. Seconds later, Grange stared right into the camera then, muffled shots, lots of them. Grange looked back into his room then checked the hall again. Very nervous. The shooters came out, Grange said something to the tall skinny one, then braced himself and turned his head to the side. The tall skinny one smacked him in the face, hard, then both stepped over him, and walked nonchalantly towards the stairwell out of view. Grange lay in the hall by the open door as the screen went black.

Tom pressed stop.

Paul stared at the blank screen. "This Costa," he said, clenching his fists. "He's really starting to piss me off."

"Yeah, I read ya, man," Tom said, ejecting the video and holding it up. "An' the prick's about to start payin'."

The overnight Fed-Ex delivery would get the tape to Miami by noon tomorrow.

CHAPTER TWENTY-THREE

11 MAY
San Diego, Cal.
0600 hrs local time

PAUL DIDN'T SLEEP WELL. HE WOKE UP WHEN JAMIE GOT IN, SOMEwhere around 1:00 AM and spent the rest of the night tossing and turning, thinking about the access codes for the Mesa Grande computer. At four o'clock he decided to get up and get started since he wasn't going to get any sleep anyway. He put the coffee on and set up the video.

· · · · · · ·

At regular speed the lightening quick fingers made it impossible to determine what keys were being touched on, but slowed down to frame-by-frame, the code sequences gave themselves up. He spent another hour reconfirming the numbers. If he didn't get them right, it could blow them out of the water. By 8:00 AM when he heard Tom and Jamie in the kitchen, he had finished.

Paul took his glasses off and leaned back, stretching. "Well, gentlemen," he called. "Unless they've changed the codes since I got these, we're in business."

"Bloody amazing," Jamie said, coming into the dining room and bending down to look at the screen. "What's next."

"Now I have to take a good look around and create some back doors so we can come and go as we please. After that it won't matter if the entry codes change. I'll have my own way in. So, I suggest we open an account. Might as well bring him down with his own money."

"Gotta love that," Tom said. "Nothin' like a little salt in the wound. Hell, I can't believe you got in so fast."

"Without the access codes," Paul said, "it would've been impossible. The concern now is trying to figure what they've got in place to detect intruders. If Salas gets any indication someone's snooping around, he'll move everything to a backup while he cloaks the transfer and deposit files, and if he does that, we're out of luck. So that means we don't have a whole lot of time to do this thing."

"Electronic footprints," Tom smiled. "Shit, what next?"

"Exactly. Some sign or tracks are always left. With simple text files it's easy. A text editor will erase all traces of being there. The encoded binary files are a little more challenging, but nothing major. So with what's in here," he said, patting the top of the monitor, "and Jamie's new friend in Colombia, we can start turning the heat up a little. Let's make life a little less comfortable for the bastard."

```
11 MAY
Miami, Florida
1225 hrs local time
```

"Who would'a fuckin' thought?" Jacobs growled, breaking the stunned silence. Morgan switched the VCR off while Bonnie opened the blinds. Chief Harelson looked over at Commander Minter, the head of Internal Affairs. "Rotten cocksucker," he muttered, shaking his head.

Chief Donald Harelson was a hard-nose, no bullshit cop who kept politics to a minimum. This had earned him the respect of the rank and file, and the respect of public for his zero tolerance on crime. The words political correctness weren't in his vocabulary. The mayor on the other hand couldn't stand him.

"Use your phone, Cap?"

"Sure, Chief."

Harelson dialed, drumming his fingers on Jacobs' desk as he waited. "Yeah … Harelson here, would you put me through to the mayor please ... no, I have to talk to him right away. Tell him it's an emergency ... thanks … Mornin' Bill, Don Harelson here. Listen, I hope you've had a real good morning so far, because the rest of your day is about to get fucked. Set up a VCR an' I'll be over in ten minutes." Not waiting for a reply, he hung up.

· · · · · · ·

In fact, Mayor William Rice had been having a good morning. The meeting with the Parks Department had gone much better than expected, with a rare unanimous agreement on the proposed new budget for a ball diamond. Good for the kids, and not to shabby for the upcoming election either. But now, even after a short conversation with Harelson, the burning sensation that immediately followed any contact with him began in the pit of his stomach. Rice loathed what he called Harelson's "John fucking Wayne" mentality, though he'd never say it to his face. Rice knew how to play the game when it came to politics, but Harelson never flowered anything up. No bullshit or grey area. Rice flopped back in his leather chair and stared at the phone. His right hand rummaged through the center desk drawer, unconsciously feeling for the antacid tablets.

"I'll just bet the rest of the day is," he said out loud. "I'll just bet it fucking is."

```
11 MAY
Montreal, Que.
1200 hrs. local time
```

Marc Tasse noticed the flashing light on the answering machine as soon as he opened his apartment door. He needed some sleep, but the call was from Rheume, and the message said to call as soon as he got in so they could meet. Tasse hadn't slept on the plane because of some screaming kid and a pounding hangover headache but, the boss was the boss, so a quick shower, a change of clothes, then he'd call. The celebration party he and Rocky had in Miami last night had almost caused him to miss his flight, and the hangover was still a miserable nine out of ten.

```
1 MAY
Miami, Florida
1305 hrs. local time
```

Rocky couldn't believe it. He stared at the dried red stains on his t-shirt. Jimmy had to be screwing him around.

"Hey, man. Whoever it was in that fuckin' room is dead. I don't know who the fuck it was, but the pig gave us the key an', aw, come on, Jimmy, you're pullin' my dick, right? I mean, look at the blood."

Santos ignored him and walked to the window. He opened it as far as it would go. The fresh air helped a bit.

"Rocky, I'm tellin' you, you guys shot the shit out of some blankets an' pillows, an' then caved in the side of our cop's head." He turned, wagging his finger. "Now we got an even bigger problem."

"What's that?" Rocky asked, not grasping the situation at all.

"When our cop comes out of the coma you put him in, he's gonna realize they moved the guy without telling him, right?"

"Yeah ... I guess."

"So, it stands to reason he'll think they're on to him ... right? So what's a guy gonna do, Rocky?"

Rocky thought for a few seconds. "Uh. .. try to cut a deal?"

"Bingo," Jimmy said, clapping his hands. "He's gonna cut a fuckin' deal ... so we gotta take care of this problem real quick, don't we?"

"Me? You mean me?" he asked, pressing his finger into his own chest. "There'll be cops all over the fuckin' place. Hey, man I did what I was supposed ta. It ain't my fault if the cops knew we was comin'."

Jimmy smiled and put his foot on the stained and threadbare armrest of the sofa.

"Lemme better explain our little dilemma here. First. Only four people knew when it was gonna happen." He held up his hand, ticking off each finger as he talked. "There was me, the cop, you, and the Frenchman. So, I know it wasn't me, an' the cop sure as hell wouldn't kill his partner for no reason if it was him, now would he?"

Rocky shook his head, looking at the two fingers Jimmy Santos was left holding up.

"No way, man. It had to be that little French fucker man, cuz it wasn't me."

"I think you're right," Jimmy agreed. "So we gotta fix that too, don't we?"

Rocky nodded, still confused but a least he wasn't being blamed … totally. "Fuckin' rat. I'll fly up an' off the prick, Jimmy. I'll do it just for expenses, no fee."

"First things first, Rocky. We do the cop before he wakes up, then we deal with your little partner."

"Deal man, fuckin' deal," Rocky said, holding his hand out. Jimmy looked at it and put his hands in his pockets.

"Yeah, Rocky … it's a deal."

CHAPTER TWENTY-FOUR

11 MAY
San Diego Calif.
1530 hrs. local time

THE VERY HEART OF COSTA'S ORGANIZATION, EVERY DETAIL, FED out of the printer on seven pages. From Dates and amounts of money transfers and investments, to customer information including monies outstanding, to cocaine shipments and delivery dates, it was all there.

"How soon would you like to get started, Paul?" Jamie asked, handing the printouts across the table to Tom.

"I'll need a couple more days to check things out before I start moving things around. That'll give Miami time to look at the tape and hopefully come up with the shooters identities, which may influence our targeting."

11 MAY
Miami, Florida
2300 hrs. local time
Metro Memorial Hospital

Dora Pratt had been head nurse on the Intensive Care Unit of Metro for the past six years. She was meticulous. At the beginning of each shift she scrutinized every patient's chart in detail, checking medicines, dosages, and changes in vitals. On the plump side, she kept her greying hair tied neatly in a tight bun. She had been nursing for thirty-two years and was the unquestioned final authority on the I.C.U. A mother hen to her staff, and as protective of her patients as a female grizzly is to her cubs. Tonight had been busy as usual, but except for the police officer stationed outside of room 317, nothing out of the ordinary.

"Quiet night everyone, no surprises please," she whispered, looking at the doors down either side of the corridor. Every now and then Dora liked to work the graveyard shift. It gave her time to catch up on paperwork, set up shift schedules and keep in touch with the staff who preferred the midnight to seven shift.

· · · · · · · ·

Sitting in a chair outside room 317, was twenty-three-year old Nicholas Scranton. As of yesterday, he had been out of the police academy for three months, and he took his responsibility seriously. After all, it was a fellow officer he was protecting.

"Evenin' ma'am," he mouthed, waving from his chair outside detective Grange's room.

She smiled and nodded. Nice young man. God, they get younger every day.

· · · · · · · ·

Jimmy's plan was simple. Lure the guard away from the room with a diversion downstairs in emergency, get into the cop's room, and finish him. Rocky, disguised as an orderly, would get that job. Jimmy Santos had given Rocky the go ahead to hire two brothers he'd done time with to cause the diversion. They were biker types and that suited Jimmy just fine. It should help deflect any heat away from his people. Although he would have rather been somewhere else, after the fuck up at the hotel he had to make sure this went as planned.

· · · · · · · ·

Perry and Doug Martens were as close to being Rocky Bender clones as humanly possible. When they weren't in jail, the three of them partied together, which usually ended with someone getting hurt, or something getting destroyed. Both were over six feet, heavily tattooed with long dirty-blond hair. Perry had thick sideburns that met up with his droopy moustache, and Doug sported a full beard. They were crude, violent, and totally unpredictable. Home was a dilapidated twenty-eight-foot rusted-out Travelaire trailer parked behind their mother's house in East Dade County.

Their reputations made them prime suspects in virtually every crime committed within a ten mile radius. The Martens made a living doing anything criminal, as long as it didn't entail a whole lot of brain power. Their forte was selling dope, ripping off dope dealers, break and enters, and smash and grabs. Nothing fancy. When Rocky offered them five hundred, with two hundred and fifty up front just to cause a disturbance, something they usually did for free, they jumped at the offer.

12 MAY
0225 hrs.

Rocky slipped in through the delivery loading dock unnoticed, and made his way to the laundry area. Fishing through a couple of laundry carts, he found a set of orderly whites that came close to fitting. Even with his goatee trimmed, it was a stretch, but the few hospital staff he passed were either too busy or too tired to give him a second look. Using the stairs, he reached the third floor and peered through the small window in the fire door. There were two nurses, one at the desk halfway down the corridor by the elevator, and the other coming down the hall towards him carrying a tray. One cop sat in a chair facing the opposite side of the hall and glanced now and then towards the nurse's station. Everything normal. Rocky checked his watch. 2:30 exactly.

· · · · · · ·

Downstairs, the doors to the emergency ward opened with a hiss. Jimmy Santos casually walked in and crossed to the elevators. Four people sat in the admitting area: a tired-looking mother trying to comfort her baby. An elderly man sitting across from the admitting nurse and holding a bloodied hanky to the side of his face. And, off to the side, a very pregnant woman who rested her head on her husband's shoulder. Beyond the admitting desk were a dozen or so curtained-off cubicles. From the legs showing below the curtains all were hospital staff. With no approaching sirens, at least the next minute or so should be pretty safe. Jimmy stood in front of the elevators. No one paid any attention to him.

· · · · · · · ·

The entrance doors hissed opened again. Perry and Doug Martens stepped inside. Jimmy gave them a nod, then stepped into the elevator and pressed the third floor button.

· · · · · · · ·

The shots and screams were muffled until the elevator doors opened on the I.C.U. floor. Nick Scranton was out of his chair when Santos stuck his head out of the elevator and hollered.

"For the love of God hurry ... they're shootin', an' there's women an' kids down there. Hurry!"

"Call 911 an' tell them to hurry," Scranton yelled as he ran past Dora Pratt into the elevator. Dora grabbed the phone and punched in 911.

Santos pushed the button for the first floor and stepped back behind Scranton who was fumbling to release the leather holster clip. His mouth had gone dry, and he tried to swallow.

"How many ..." he started to ask as more shots rang out. "Fuck. How many are there?"

"Two." The reply was calm.

More shots. Loud. Shotgun maybe. Scranton tried to think. The elevator stopped. "Jesus, don't let me screw up," he whispered out loud, sucking in a deep breath. His gun felt heavier than it ever had. He glanced up. They were stopped on the second floor.

"What the …"

He felt his head jerk to the side, but there was no pain, no feeling at all. Then he was on the floor looking up. The man above him looked distorted and moved in slow motion. Sounds came out of the man's mouth but didn't make any sense, then something in the man's hand pointed down towards his face. Nicholas Scranton, three month veteran of the Miami Police Department, heard his own voice from somewhere deep inside say ... "Ya fucked up, Nick,"

· · · · · · · ·

Dora Pratt, still on the phone with the 911 dispatcher, noticed him out of the corner of her eye. An orderly, running down the hall from the stairway. Must be trying to get out of the way, she thought. As she turned her attention back to the 911 operator, she noticed the floor indicator above the elevator doors had stopped on the second floor. She watched, waiting for it to continue. It didn't.

"What the hell? Something's wrong," she said to the other nurse. She looked back down the hall again. It was empty.

"Damn," she yelled, dropping the phone and pressing the red button on the intercom. "Carol, call security and tell them it's an emergency. Tell them we have trouble in the police officer's room."

Dora Pratt shoved a metal serving cart out of the way as she ran by. It clanged loudly against the wall sending trays of empty juice cartons, water jugs, and plastic glasses across the floor.

Inside room 317, Rocky was moving back towards the door. He glanced back to admire his work. The wooden knob of the ice pick protruded grotesquely out of the right ear of the body of Ron Grange.

"It ain't fuckin' make-believe blood this time," he said and turned to open the door just as Dora Pratt, in a dead run, hit it with all her weight. The metal edge caught him full force between the left ear and his eye sending him crashing over one of the visitor chairs. His head hit the linoleum with a sickening thud. Rocky was out for the count.

0255 hrs

Metro Memorial ER looked like a war zone. Chunks of ceiling tiles, plaster, and shards of glass from the blown-out entrance doors covered the entire waiting room. The pungent smell of the smoke grenade the two brothers had let off still hung in the air. Incredibly, other than some cuts and bruises caused by the panic, none of the staff or patients had been seriously hurt. Bonnie was already there when Morgan arrived.

·······

"Jesus Christ," he said, his cowboy boots crunching on broken glass as he stepped through the door frame. "How many down?"

"None here," Bonnie said, looking up from her note book. "Out and out diversion." She motioned with her head towards the elevators. "And it worked. Grange is dead, along with the uniform who was guarding him."

"Aw shit," he said, shaking his head slowly.

She led the way to the stairwell past the cordoned-off middle elevator that was being treated as a separate crime scene. The lifeless body of officer Nicholas Scranton was sprawled on the elevator floor and was being subjected to the probing attention reserved for those who had met with foul play. Morgan followed Bonnie up the stairs to the third floor.

·······

Things in the I.C.U. looked normal. A few plainclothes cops were quietly taking statements from the two nurses at the nurse's station by the elevator.

"The guy got in fast," Bonnie said, opening the door to 317. A police photographer stood on a chair over the blood-soaked bed and took close-ups of the dead officer's head, while others methodically went about collecting evidence and dusting for prints. "Head nurse cold cocked the perp with the door as he was coming out. He's been taken to Jackson Memorial. Other than a skull fracture and questionable future, he should be able to talk by the time we get over there. Oh, and by the way, I had a look at him when they wheeled him out. Pretty sure he's one of the guys on the tape Paul sent us."

"Guess they wanted to make sure Grange didn't wake up with a conscience. We got any witness's on the other guys?" Morgan asked.

"Yeah. Same nurse got a real good look at the guy who lured the guard into the elevator. She's giving her statement now, and there's six or seven down in emerge who saw the two assholes who caused the diversion."

They stepped back into the hall. Morgan looked around then shook his head. "Man, this was some ballsy hit. Is that the nurse who saw the elevator guy?" he asked, nodding towards the nurse's station where Dora Pratt sat talking to one of the detectives."

"Yeah, and she's a feisty one. Wants to do anything she can to quote: 'catch the piece of dirt who killed the young officer.'"

"Gotta like that spunk," Morgan said. "Let's take her back with us and have her look at some pictures, an' if we strike out there we'll see what the sketch artist can come up with. While she's doin' that, we can interview the guy who did Grange."

· · · · · · · ·

Outside, the media had converged and were scrambling to get film footage and interview anyone who heard anything, saw anything, or anyone who just wanted to speculate on what had happened.

Jackson Memorial Hospital
0400 hrs

Waking up with a terrible headache, disorientated, and feeling like crap wasn't anything new for Rocky. Memory blanks were pretty much a daily occurrence. This time though, he remembered everything clearly, up to a point. Holding the ice pick up to the cop's ear with one hand, then smacking it with the open palm of his other. Yeah, that part went real good. Then he started to leave, then nothing. He tried blinking to clear the fuzzy globs of light. When he tried to move, nothing happened. Oh fuck ... I'm paralyzed, he thought.

"Whas a fuuu...hapin'?" he slurred.

All of a sudden, the blurred images of people appeared on either side of him. He blinked and squinted, trying to focus. Guy in a white kinda smock, a doctor, an'... an' a broad in white, nurse ... yeah, a nurse. A guy an' broad dressed like ... aw fuck, cops. It explained the paralysis. Velcro straps wrapped tightly around his arms and legs held him securely to the bed. They felt like the restraints in his dream.

"Robert Bender," one of the blurry images said. "You're under arrest for the murders of detective Ronald Grange, Officer Nicholas Scranton, and Detective Keith Wilson. Do you understand?" Rocky gave an involuntary nod then closed his eyes and listened as one of them read him what he'd heard a hundred times before, his rights. He knew the name Grange, but not the other two, so after a few seconds he gave his stock reply.

"Ya got the fuckin' wrong guy, man." It sounded a lot less convincing than all the other times. No, this time things would be a whole lot different. This time it had been a cop, or cops. Losing guaranteed that one night or early one morning he'd be led from his cell and put down like a mad dog.

CHAPTER TWENTY-FIVE

12 MAY
San Diego Calif.
0800 hrs. local time

CNN REPLAYED THE FOOTAGE OF THE HOSPITAL SHOOTINGS AS JAMIE came into the living room freshly showered and shaved, knotting his tie.

"Good morning, lads," he said.

Paul waved him over. "Not so good back east. Come look at this."

Jamie sat down as the footage showing the damage to the entrance and a sequence of jerky shots of the inside of the emergency ward played again. The camera panned left to an unmarked police car.

"You'll see Morgan and Bonnie come into the picture ... there," Paul said as the camera zoomed in on them helping an older nurse into the back seat. Spotting the camera, Bonnie tried to shield her but wasn't quite fast enough and, for a split second, a perfect close-up of Dora Pratt's face was transmitted around the world.

· · · · · · ·

Paul waited until the news switched to a tenement fire in Chicago before switching it off. "Okay boys," he said, walking into the dining room. "Time to crank things up. I want Costa so confused he won't be able to tell the difference between shit and shiny metal. As of now, we're leading the parade, not following the damn thing."

```
12 MAY
Bogota, Colombia
1500 hrs. local time
```

DaLucca folded the decoded fax, put it in his jacket pocket and swore under his breath. He'd been right. The small problem that, left alone would have worked itself out, had now become much bigger. He hurried down the hall to the office where Pablo was talking on the phone to Eduardo Rodriguez. When he saw the look on Mani's face he ended the conversation as quickly and politely as he could.

"What is it, Mani? You look troubled."

DaLucca sat down and removed the fax. "Pablo, we have a problem."

"What do you mean?" Pablo asked.

Mani unfolded the sheet of paper. "In Miami," he said. "Things didn't go well." He handed the fax across the table.

Costa snatched the fax out of his hand. "What didn't go well?" As he read, his face reddened.

Mani checked over his shoulder to make sure the door was closed. "I made a call to get the whole story," he said. "Looks like everything that could go wrong did. They got the cop before he regained consciousness, but they killed another one who was guarding him. Jimmy says one of his guys got caught, too. The one with the Frenchman who was sent to do the witness. Two others, hired to cause a disturbance, will more than likely be identified by people in the emergency ward."

"For Christ's sake, Mani." Pablo crumpled the fax and threw it onto the desk. "What the fuck's wrong with Jimmy?"

Mani held up his hand. "There's more, Pablo."

Pablo sat forward, stretching both arms out to the sides. "What? What more could there be?"

"There is a nurse, the one taking care of the cop, she can identify Jimmy."

Pablo stared down at his reflection in the shiny mahogany desk. He shook his head, took a deep breath and looked up.

"I don't fucking believe this, Mani. What's going on here?"

"There's no doubt," DaLucca said. "The one caught will cooperate with the police. He's got no choice."

Pablo swung his chair around to face the window. It had started to rain.

"Can he lead them to us?" he asked, trying to control his rage.

"Directly to Jimmy." Mani answered. "And that's more than enough."

Costa slowly walked over to the liquor cabinet. He took out two glasses and raised one in DaLucca's direction. Mani shook his head. Pablo filled one with Crown Royal and carried it back to his desk. He stared out the window before sitting down.

He took a sip. "Okay," he said. "We move immediately. Have Jimmy arrange to take out the one who got caught, the two who caused the diversion, and the nurse who got a look at him. As soon as it's done, we'll send Jimmy away for a while. Christ almighty, I can't believe this bullshit."

DaLucca shook his head slowly.

Pablo went to take a drink then stopped. "What Mani. What's on your mind?"

"I would agree with you, Pablo, if we weren't talking about cops, but this is different, they'll look until they find him, and when they do ... uh, listen, Pablo, Jimmy is weak, and we both know the cops will go for the death penalty."

Costa slammed his glass on the desk, spilling most of it. "Then what the fuck do you suggest?" he asked, getting angrier.

DaLucca gave him a few seconds to calm down. "My advice would be, as you say, silence the one in jail and quickly. It should look like a suicide or accident. The two who helped, they're apparently brothers who have many enemies. Any one of hundreds would want them dead, and so the police won't be able to link them to us."

"Good, go on," Pablo nodded.

"The French Canadian who Jimmy figures fucked them around on the witness thing."

"Yes, I agree," Pablo said, still nodding.

"And uh ... Jimmy," he said, shifting uncomfortably. "Like I say, if it comes to the death penalty ..."

Pablo moved his glass onto a hand-carved silver coaster. "So, like I say, we take out the fucking nurse, right away."

Mani shook his head. "With the amount of security they'll put on her it will take time to penetrate, and time is something we don't have a lot of."

"Are you saying we hit Jimmy? What the fuck are you talking about Mani? He's Eduardo's nephew, for Christ's sake."

"I know," Mani said, keeping his voice low. "That's why you and I are the only ones who'll know about it. Believe me, I wish there were another way, but there isn't. Jimmy's soft, and he'll talk. We both know that."

Pablo stared down at the desk.

"I'll do it myself," DaLucca said. "And make it look like the Jamaicans hit him."

Pablo ran his fingers through his silver hair. Mani was probably right, but if Eduardo ever suspected that he killed his nephew.

"This is crazy," he said, draining his glass and standing again. "Jesus fucking Christ, Mani ... if Eduardo puts this together we'll be back at each others throats so fucking fast."

He spun around and threw the glass. It hit the wall between the door and a tall oak book case, shattering into hundreds of pieces. He sat down and spun his desk chair around. Outside, the wind howled, lashing the rain against the leaded glass window panes. The black clouds seemed to suck the color out of the landscape, turning everything grey.

After a few seconds and without turning around, Pablo nodded and said. "Do it."

CHAPTER TWENTY-SIX

12 MAY
Bogota Colombia
1700 hrs. local time

FOR A SECOND TIME, RAMON THRASHED THROUGH THE GARBAGE he'd dumped on the floor. His home consisted of one room with a single bed against the wall, a short wooden counter that held a wash bowl and a one-burner hot plate and two shelves above it that held a couple of dishes, a few cans, and a few packages of food. A scarred wooden table and two chairs were placed beside the tiny window that provided the only natural light into his humble abode. A fridge was a luxury he couldn't afford, and even if he could, the electricity seldom ran for more than a few hours at a time. An outhouse behind the building serviced the twelve tiny units. Right now, panic was setting in. He'd already checked every pocket of every piece of clothing he owned, and still he couldn't find the number. Unless he did, his money train had left, for good.

"Fuck is it?" he yelled at the garbage. About the time he was ready to give up, he saw the crumpled piece of paper on the wooden counter under an empty beer bottle. He held it up to the light of the window. The numbers were smeared, but still readable.

"Yes," he yelled, then squinted to read the blurred numbers out loud. "One .. two ... zero ... six, five ... five ... two, nine ... one ... six ... four." He smiled, kissed the paper, then folded it carefully and stuffed it in his shirt pocket. What he had for Mr. Shea would be worth maybe hundreds of U.S. dollars. Hurrying down the stairway and into the sunlight, he walked as quickly as he could to the payphone inside the Cantina Diaz.

```
12 MAY
Dade County Jail
2200 hrs. local time
```

Rocky lay on his back with his hands tucked under his head, staring at the shadow of the bars on the far wall. Weird, he thought, that Jimmy hadn't sent a lawyer yet. Must be a reason. Probably things were in the works right now. Sure, that had to be it. Don't matter shit about a lawyer if you're gonna buy the fuckin' judge. The thought gave him a giddy feeling. They had no reason not to take care of him. After all, he'd done everything they asked. He sat up slowly and looked around. He still felt a little dizzy, and his head pounded when he stood or turned too fast. At least so far he had a cell to himself. Tomorrow he'd check out who had the dope action inside and score enough to ease the pain. Might as well relax and enjoy, till I walk outta here. Then his thoughts turned to Tasse.

"Little cocksucker," he said out loud. "Knew somethin' bout ya was wrong first time I seen ya at the airport. Soon as I get out I'm comin' to Canada and kill ya....ya rat. This is all your fuckin' fault."

```
13 MAY
Miami Fl
0700 hrs. local time
```

Jimmy Santos pondered over the note he'd found in his mail box. Good information always equaled money, and anything anonymous usually smacked of a set up. This though would have to be looked into. The Jamaicans planning a hit on him was easy to buy in light of the events of the past few months. More proof that, unless his uncle and Pablo gave the word to take out those bastards once and for all, this war would drag on indefinitely. He'd let Eduardo know right away. Meanwhile, best keep a few of his people close by.

```
13 MAY
Seattle Wash.
1500 hrs. local time
```

Allison Corbet edged her Volkswagen Rabbit north along the I-5. She had spent the entire day at the monthly A.T.&T. security department meeting in Tacoma. The weather forecast had been typical for this time of year: cloudy with sunny periods and a chance of showers. That chance of showers was coming down in torrents.

Renting an apartment near Sea Tac Airport took a bit of getting used to, what with the busy flight path directly above her, but being within walking distance to some great malls and paying half the rent she would if she lived in downtown Seattle, helped her get used to it.

Allison put her umbrella in the white-and-blue checked ceramic holder, one of the much appreciated house warming gifts she received when she moved in. Walking down the hall to the bedroom, the blinking light on the answering machine she had set up for her dad caught her attention. She pressed the playback button. The excitement in Ramon's voice made him difficult to understand. She had to listen twice to make sure she got the gist of the message and the phone number. After jotting down the message, she dialed her dad's number.

```
13 MAY
Montreal, Quebec
1900 hrs. local time
```

Rheume crumpled the one-page letter and shook his head. What kind of bullshit was this? No way Marc would turn against them or anyone else for that matter. He was the one person, the only person, Rheume could count on. No, he'd leave this for the time being. Let Costa calm down and check his own fucking back yard, because that's where the problem would be. Holding the paper over the ashtray, he lit the corner, and within seconds it was gone.

13 MAY
Miami, Florida
1950 hrs. local time

Every payday, every police club in every city is busy, and the Keystone Klub was no exception. A block and a half from the Miami Police building, it's referred to simply as The Club. A place to unwind, and relive the good, bad and ugly parts of the job without having to look over your shoulder. This payday though, things were different. Although still crowded and loud, the usual party mood was subdued. It had been one of the worst weeks in the history of the department. Three officers killed, well, two good ones. God only knew how many lives and operations Grange had compromised since going to the other side. He had put an ugly stain on the entire department.

· · · · · · ·

Morgan and Bonnie sat across from Captain Jacobs at a table farthest away from the booming speakers that were hammering out Willie Nelsons hit, "Pancho an Lefty." Jacobs got the waiter's attention and circled his finger, indicating another round.

"Minter from Internal called this afternoon," he said. "They found two accounts so far. Not a lot in either of them. Total maybe thirty grand. They figure there must be a safety deposit box or two, but his wife either isn't co-operating or doesn't know."

"Pretty stupid not to co-operate," Morgan said, handing the waiter his empty glass as he arrived with three more pints.

Bonnie lifted her glass of Bud, then put it down.

"Come on, Morg. Hell, a week ago she had a husband, then she's told a hero, then a cop killer on the take, then he's murdered.

Christ, right now she probably couldn't tell you which way up is for God's sake."

"Yeah, you're probably right. Anyway, fuck him, and here's to Keith and the young guy Scranton," he said, raising his glass.

Jacobs clicked both their glasses. "To the good ones. So how're you makin' out with Bender?"

"We talked to him this afternoon, Cap," Morgan said, putting his beer down and wiping his mouth. "An' I mean just that. We talked an' he pretended we weren't there. Wouldn't say dick all. No one from the outside's tried to contact him, so we left him with the impression he's been hung out to dry on this one."

"Plus," Bonnie added. "He knows if convicted he'll fry for sure."

"Who's he got for a lawyer?" Jacobs asked, patting his pockets for the cigarettes he'd given up two weeks ago.

"Court appointed, an' Bender won't talk to him either," Morgan said. "Guy's name's Baxter. He's young, new to the bar, and not a lot of smarts."

"Okay," Jacobs said, downing the last of his drink and getting up. "Work him hard. I don't care if you show him a copy of the video. Don't talk deals, at least not at this point. Let him think they've disowned his sorry ass and he's goin' down for everything, alone."

Morgan looked at his watch. "Will do, Cap. Well, tomorrow's supposed to be my day off, but I'll go ring his bell first thing, seein' as I don't have a life anyway."

Bonnie reached in her purse and put a five dollar bill on the table for the tip. "Yeah, well I do have a life, but what could be more fun than watching the bell ringer in action?"

Morgan smiled. "I'll pick you up at seven-thirty?"

"Wow. Sounds like a date. Are you buying coffee, too?"

"If I'm drivin', you're buyin'," he said getting up. "An' I'm talkin' a latte here."

Jacobs laughed. "Date? Christ, you sound more like an old married couple to me."

13 MAY
Bogota Colombia
1800 hrs. local time

Rodriguez found the message disturbing but no big surprise. He would discuss it with Pablo right away. Definitely time to deal with these low-life Jamaicans once and for all. Eduardo, always the level headed one, opted for peaceful solutions if possible, but not now. Not when it came to his nephew. Pablo, on the other hand would be extremely happy. From the beginning of their partnership, Eduardo's diplomacy and fairness always infuriated him, and it had became their biggest bone of contention. Costa believed in getting rid of problems right away, for good. It saved having to revisit them. In Pablo's eyes, any sign of forgiveness or sympathy were signs of weakness. No, this time the Jamaicans had gone too far. This time they would all have to go.

13 MAY
San Diego, Calif
1830 hrs. local time

Paul pushed his chair back from the computer and rubbed his eyes. His coffee had gone cold, and so he went into the kitchen to give it fifteen seconds in the microwave.

Jamie arrived back from calling Ramon and came into the kitchen as Paul took his coffee out of the microwave.

"So, how'd it go with your boy?" Paul asked.

"Exceptional, much better than expected actually." Jamie smiled. "He's quite the little digger when the price is right and unless he's playing games, which I seriously doubt, we have some valuable information here." Jamie poured a half cup of coffee, sat at the kitchen table and added cream to the top of his mug. Paul watched Jamie stir in five heaping teaspoons of sugar.

"Are you really going to drink that?"

Jamie gave him a bewildered look. "Well, if it were Earl Grey, it would be more civilized, and I would only have to add four sugars."

Paul slowly nodded. "I'm sure, that makes some kind of sense."

Jamie reached into the pocket of his tweed jacket and took out a small notepad. He flipped through the pages. "Yes, here we are. There's a freighter called the *Maco Pride*, departed Buenaventura, Colombia last night. She's heading for Vancouver, Canada, with a stop off in San Francisco. There are five hundred kilos of cocaine on board hidden in a container of coffee. Ramon says it's destined for the eastern United States, probably New York."

Tom came around the corner from the dining room. "How can he be sure it's Costa's?" he asked.

"His cousin works at one of Costa's labs and overheard enough to put it together. It's a rush order, and it sounds like it will be trucked to eastern Canada from Vancouver, then cross into America at some point. The container was loaded right at the lab, so we've got the container number too."

Paul shook his head and smiled. "I'll be damned. That's excellent. I've got a friend with the RCMP who I'm pretty sure is still with the Vancouver Drug Section. I'll try to hunt him down. This, my friends, with the other things we're putting together, couldn't be better."

"Actually," Jamie said, closing his notebook, "it does get better. Seeing as its only photographs I want, for a price he's pretty sure his cousin will give the location of the lab. I gave him a figure of one thousand dollars. Ramon said he'll meet with him in the next few days and get back to me."

Tom put down a surveillance report and peered over top of his reading glasses. "A lab? Christ almighty, wouldn't that ruin his day."

"One thing concerns me," Paul said. "I don't want Ramon thinking he's James bloody Bond out there. Better reel him in some. Once we get the location, wire him the money and tell him to take his cousin on a holiday, and to keep his mouth shut."

"Will do," Jamie nodded. "How are things on your end?"

"Good. I've created doorways into most of the files and accounts. Won't be long till we can come and go as we please, even after they change the access codes. As long as we don't get sloppy and muddy the waters too much, they shouldn't detect us. But, if he's as good as I think he is, it's just a matter of time before he'll get suspicious and change the entire setup, putting us out of the loop completely."

```
13 MAY
East Dade County
2110 hrs. local time
```

Three grams of coke and a twenty-four of Bud ate up the last of the money Rocky had fronted them. Tomorrow they'd figure something out, they always did. Doug and Perry never worried about tomorrow. Nor did they give a shit about Rocky getting busted. Served the prick right for not telling them they were part of a cop hit. They'd already decided to break into Rocky's place later tonight and see if they could find his stash. He sure as hell wouldn't be coming back. So fuck him.

· · · · · · ·

Perry grabbed the flat of beer from the box of their black pick-up. It had taken seven aerosol spray cans and a couple of hours to completely cover the rust, and what remained of an equally bad green paint job they'd done the year before. With his free hand, he yanked the trailer door open, nudged an overflowing plastic bag of garbage out of the way with his foot and climbed in. The inside was as cluttered and dirty as the yard, but that didn't bother them. They could care less and no one in the neighborhood had the balls to complain. The Martens were crazy. No one in their right mind, unless they had an assault rifle or a death wish, would dare provoke them. Doug walked across the overgrown lawn to the back door of his mom's house.

Both front and back doors had been kicked in and repaired so many times that she just left them unlocked. It was less of a problem that way. Claire Martens, watching T.V. in the dimly lit living room, heard the back screen door squeak open. "Who is it?" she yelled

"Hey ... Ma," Doug called from the kitchen. "Whata we got ta eat?"

She didn't take her eyes off the television. "There's some chicken in the orange bowl in the fridge," she hollered over her shoulder. "An' some left over Chinese in the two cartons on the bottom shelf."

A few seconds later she heard the fridge door close.

"Got it, Ma. See ya.

"An' bring them dishes back when you're done, Douglas," she said, but her words were cut off by the slamming of the back door. She returned her gaze to the television just in time to see Jerry Springer duck out of the way of a wild swing from a young, overweight housewife, who had just been introduced to her husband's gay lover.

· · · · · · · ·

"Hey, Per," Doug said, opening the trailer door. "You want chink or chicken? It don't ... "

"KABLAMM"

The deafening blast shook the ground for two blocks, shattering windows in the houses on either side of them. The rusted twenty-eight-foot eyesore disappeared in a cloud of dust and flame. Seconds later, chunks of it and its contents began raining down through the billowing mushroom of grey-black smoke.

Inside her house, Claire Martens picked herself up off the floor. Even though her ears were ringing she could hear things hitting the roof. Her boys were gone. She knew that. She'd known for years it would end something like this. Every time the news reported a body being found, she prepared herself that it would be one of them, and when she found out it wasn't she wondered if they'd done it. Claire Martens couldn't bring herself to look in the backyard. Instead, she hefted herself back onto the sofa and rocked quietly back and forth. Her eyes were glassy, but there were no tears. She'd cried herself out years ago. The police would come again, one last time. She would answer their questions then they'd leave with no reason to ever come back. Claire stared at the snowy television picture and couldn't help wonder what a new antenna was going to cost her.

CHAPTER TWENTY-SEVEN

14 MAY
Dade County Jail
0730 hrs. local time

ROCKY STRUGGLED TO LIFT HIS HEAD OFF THE THIN PLASTIC PILLOW. His prison-issue orange jump suit had turned dark with sweat, and his heart raced. Tyre Washington, a black kid awaiting trial for a string of car thefts, fronted him a flap of heroin, and even lent him his homemade works, which consisted of an eye dropper with a syringe needle, well used, taped to the end. The price had been right, too. He'd pay as soon as his lawyer showed up. Yeah, right. Dumb fuck'll never make money doin' business like that. The high had been instantaneous, and took him up like a rocket then, as his mind spiraled out of control, he couldn't feel his body. He managed to partially open one eye, making out the needle still sticking out of his arm. He fought for control of his brain. If he could just focus better. Sometimes talking out loud helped.

He tried to say, "Get up, Rock ... fuckin' ... gotta ... move round, man." But the words were no more than grunts. The clank of his cell door opening and the sound of voices made no sense either. Then, in slow motion, he was spinning down a dark well, looking back up at the light at the top. As he spun around it got smaller and smaller until it was a tiny dot.

"Ya lil' bastard ... did me," he tried to say as the tiny dot of light blinked out.

0800 hrs.

Morgan's cell chirped as they drove into the parking area of the remand center.

"Conners here," he said, listening for a few seconds before punching the end button and tossing his phone onto the dash. "Overdose, my ass."

Bonnie looked over as they pulled into a parking spot by the front door marked 'Police Vehicles Only.' "What?" she asked. "What happened?"

"Bender," he said, shoving his cell into his pocket. "He's dead."

"When?"

"Right now. Ten fuckin' minutes ago. They got to him ... fuck."

"Jeez, Morg. Ease up. He's a junkie, and that's how junkies usually check out."

"Come on, Bon. The stuff that comes in here's been cut so many times, otherwise there'd be another twenty or thirty bodies. Naw, he was fuckin' hot capped."

They got out of the car and walked up the front steps. Bonnie looked at him. "Okay ... you're probably right, so where's that leave us?"

Morgan's cell rang again. He stepped back into the parking lot for better reception. After a brief conversation, he walked back in, shaking his head.

"Now what?" she asked.

"The two shit rats that got blown up last night?"

"Yeah, the Martens, what about them?"

"Nurse in the emergency room picked them out of a photo line-up."

"Holy shit," Bonnie said. "So that means …"

"Yeah, they're cleanin' house. Jacobs wants us sit on Dora Pratt till we can arrange to have her stashed away."

```
14 MAY
Miami Fl.
0815 hrs. local time
```

Terri Walters stepped out of the shower and wrapped herself in an oversized, fluffy pink towel. Using a face cloth she wiped the steam off the mirror and stared at her reflection. At twenty-six she looked closer to forty. What a change in three short years. Back then she'd been an up-and-coming fashion model on the verge of making it big. Life had been a fairytale of travel, money, glamour, and attention. Looking back now, all those good times seemed so long ago it was as though they'd happened to someone else.

She'd been in Barbados doing a shoot for a swimsuit catalogue when she met the handsome, obviously wealthy young man with dark mysterious eyes and romantic Spanish accent. His name was Jimmy Santos. Four days later when the shoot wrapped, she sadly said good-bye and flew back to New York. Within days she began receiving bouquets of flowers and phone calls. He called in the evening to say goodnight, and in the morning as her wake-up call. He told her that his voice would be the last she'd hear at night, and the first she would hear in the morning. A diamond necklace along with Jimmy's never-ending affections over the next two months swept her off her feet and so, Terri made the decision to leave the big apple and move into Jimmy's beach house just outside Miami, telling her envious friends and frustrated agent she was taking a much needed break, just for a few months.

· · · · · · ·

Jimmy showed his new trophy off like a piece of art, introducing her to the life of non-stop parties and drugs. Drugs to pick her up, calm her down, or put her in whatever space she wanted to be in.

As the parties continued, her interest in modeling began to wane, and so the decision to put her career on the back burner for a bit longer seemed like a no brainer. Why hurry back to long hours and hectic schedules when everything she could possibly dream of was right here? Especially when Jimmy treated her like a princess.

It didn't take long until Terri began depending on him for everything. Her typical day started around one in the afternoon with breakfast that consisted of two or three amphetamines washed down with either a coffee or a tall gin and tonic. Over the next six months Jimmy's attitude towards her began changing. He became more and more distant and verbally abusive. Finally, he rented her a fairly upscale, one bedroom apartment across town, continuing to pay for everything, but his visits became less and less frequent.

A couple of months later Jimmy called her to say his uncle Eduardo from Colombia was in town on business, and he wanted her to take care of him and show him around. He would be at her place at 5:30. Other than his brother Ernesto, Terri hadn't met any of Jimmy's family, and so she wanted to make a good impression. Maybe this meant Jimmy would start paying a little more attention to her.

When his uncle arrived half an hour early, Terri was in her bathrobe and sitting at a makeup table in her bedroom finishing up her mascara. A little annoyed at his timing, she opened the door to the overweight, balding man in his mid-sixties. She apologized as best she could in Spanish for not being ready and asked him to come and sit down in the living room. He smiled politely and stepped inside.

"Gracias," he said, smiling and looking around the room.

"Ah. ... Gracias, senor, con permiso para uno momento por favor," she said, pretty sure it was close enough that he'd understand. Returning to the bedroom, she sat down, picked up an eye brow pencil and carefully accented her dark, curved brows. A shadow reflecting in her mirror made her turn around. Jimmy's uncle was standing just inside the bedroom door. She stood up quickly.

"No, no. You have to stay in the living room," she said, pointing. "Uh ... en la sala, por favor."

He stared at her, his eyes shifting from the top of her short bathrobe to her long tanned legs. A wave of fear came over her. She clutched the front of her bathrobe.

He moved towards her.

"No ...You go ... go now ..." she said, stepping back. As she did, her foot caught the leg of the makeup table, and she lost her balance and fell. She landed hard on her back between the dresser and the bed. Dazed, she turned onto her stomach and started to get up. As she did, he grabbed a handful of her long blond hair and hauled her up onto the bed. She kicked out wildly with both feet. He reached under her housecoat, grabbing at her thigh. Terri twisted sideways. The heel of her foot caught him in the groin. He let out a yelp, let go of her leg, and slapped her across the face.

"You like rough? Good. I give you rough."

With a quick jerk, he tore her bathrobe off, leaving her naked. Before she could react, his hand grabbed her small, trimmed patch of pubic hair.

"Please don't....don't hurt me," she begged and managed to twist herself over onto her stomach.

"What? You want fuck like puppies first? Okay."

Straddling the back of her legs, he unzipped his pants, grabbed a handful of her hair and pulled her up on her knees.

"Jimmy will kill you ... you bastard," she yelled. Then, with a powerful thrust, he was in her. He pushed her face into the pillows muffling her screams then reaching around with his free hand, he grabbed one of her breasts and squeezed hard. He rammed himself forward again and again, grunting louder each time he pushed. There was nothing she could do but wait. When she felt him pulling out of her, she thought it was over. He let go of her hair and slapped her playfully on the cheeks of her ass.

"Now," he said panting. "We fuck in front."

Flipping her over onto her back, he let go of her arms for a split second giving her just enough time to lash out, digging her nails deep into the side of his cheek.

"Ahhhhhhhhhh" he hissed, lurching back and grabbing his face.

Terri rolled off the side of the bed, bolted into the bathroom slamming the door behind her. Shaking with fear, she turned the lock and yanked open the drawer of the medicine cabinet. It flew out, dumping everything onto the floor. She picked up a pair of long scissors, held them above her head with both hands, and waited for the door to open.

After about five minutes that seemed more like an hour, she heard his muffled voice, either talking to himself or on the phone. Every time she mustered up the courage to open the door, she heard someone moving around. Finally, Terri heard the sound of her apartment door opening, then closing. She pressed her ear against the bathroom door, straining to listen. Nothing. The son of a bitch must be gone, she thought. Holding the scissors in one hand, she held her breath and opened the door just enough to peek out. She heard a voice whispering. His.

The bedroom door had been left open to the living room, and she could see the old man talking to someone just out of her view. When he moved to the side she saw Jimmy. The old man rubbed the side of his face, shrugged and patted Jimmy on the shoulder. They spoke quietly in Spanish and Jimmy seemed livid. When his uncle left, Jimmy waited a couple of seconds before slamming the door. He turned and walked quickly across the living room into the bedroom. Terri pushed the bathroom door open, threw down the scissors and ran to him.

"Jimmy," she said, bursting into tears. "He ... he raped ..."

His open hand hit the side of her head, sending her backwards over the bed and onto the floor. She tried to get up, but her legs were like rubber.

"Who the FUCK do you think you are?" he hollered, grabbing her hair and yanking her back up. When she was on her knees he started slapping her.

"I said…WHO…the FUCK…do you THINK…you ARE?" he screamed into her face.

When he let go she slumped against the bed. The taste of blood in her mouth made her feel sick to her stomach. She wiped the blood from her nose and mouth and started to say something, but she stopped when she saw the look on his face. His eyes were wild. She had never seen him like this. Jimmy picked up the over-turned dresser chair and straddled it in front of her. His voice trembled with rage.

"Now get this through your thick, fucking skull, Terri, cuz I'm only gonna tell you once, so listen real good. I give you everything, right?"

Terri stared at him, afraid to answer.

"I pay for this apartment, don't I? An' give you all the booze and dope you want, which is becoming a fuck of a lot lately, right?"

She bowed her head.

He grabbed her head, leaned to within an inch of her face and yelled. "I SAID ISN'T THAT FUCKIN' RIGHT?"

"YES … YES," she yelled back, sobbing uncontrollably.

"Right. So if I ever ask you to take care of anyone," he said, putting his finger under her chin and raising her head. "Just fuckin' do it. Call it whatever you want. Payback, a favor, whatever, I don't care. Now have you got that, Terri? I hope so, cuz if you ever embarrass me by pulling a stunt like this again, I swear to God I'll fuckin' kill you."

Up to that moment everything had been a game, how Jimmy made his money, the fancy lifestyle, everything. She wiped her face with the back of her hand, smearing mascara across her cheeks and nodded. Jimmy stood up and smiled; his voice became quiet, like nothing had happened.

"Good. Now get cleaned up and dressed. I have some calls to make then we'll go out for a bite."

She stayed in the hot shower for over half an hour before she realized she'd never feel clean again.

Since that day there'd been others. Usually people Jimmy owed favors to or was trying to impress. Complaining only led to getting smacked around or having her drug supply cut off, so she didn't. Once she took enough drugs that she could barely answer the door when two of Jimmy's out-of-town customers arrived. She passed out almost right away, and when they finished she was left naked, spread-eagle on the bed. Later, when they told him in front of his friends that she'd lain there like a dead fish, he laughed along with them, then excused himself and drove like a maniac to her apartment. The beating put her in hospital for three days.

· · · · · · ·

Terri hated everything about him but feared him even more. She realized that one day, probably sooner rather than later, he would grow tired of her, and because she knew enough about his business, her fate would be sealed. That's when she came up with a plan. Before she could get out, she had to do two things. Back off the drugs, and get some money. If she got caught stealing from him, he'd kill her in a heartbeat, so it would have to be done carefully, and because of the way things were escalating, she didn't have a lot of time left.

· · · · · · ·

Jimmy arrived last night a little past midnight, drunk, but in one of his rare good moods. He rambled on about a big thing happening in the morning. A guy from back home, the most trusted fixer in the organization, wanted his help with an important job. Within minutes of sprawling on the sofa he was snoring; Terri covered him with a blanket and quietly went to bed.

With the towel still wrapped around her, she walked out of the bathroom and into the kitchen.

"Jimmy," she called. "It's after eight. You want a coffee or somethin'?"

Jimmy bolted upright and squinted at his watch.

"Fuck. Yeah, coffee," he said, getting up and looking down at himself. "Christ Terri, look at my clothes. I look like fuckin' shit. Do I got any clean stuff here?"

"Yeah, honey," she said, filling the coffee maker. "Where they always are, right side of the closet."

"I gotta jump in the shower. Shit I only got half an hour," he said, heading for the bathroom.

When she heard the shower, she hurried into the living room. His keys and wallet were on the coffee table. She opened it. Inside was thirty-four hundred dollars. Terri did what she'd been doing for a number of months now every time he showed up drunk. This time, she removed a thousand, then moved to the tan slacks that lay in front of the bathroom door. The gold money clip was fat with hundreds, fifties, and twenties. She peeled off two hundreds and four fifties. The shower stopped.

Terri stuffed the clip back into his pants pocket, went to the sofa and pushed the money down between the cushions. If he checked and found his money gone he'd blame her. She'd deny it. They'd search and find it where he'd slept. So far she'd managed to collect over twenty-one thousand dollars from Jimmy and some of the friends he'd sent over. One, maybe two more months more, and she'd have enough. All she had to do was keep him happy, and not get caught.

CHAPTER TWENTY-EIGHT

14 May
Ft. Lauderdale, Fa
0845 hrs. local time

DALUCCA ALWAYS FELT UNCOMFORTABLE IN AMERICA. LOTS OF EASY money to be sure, but with so many different police departments the odds of getting arrested or killed were very high. Hard to feel safe with City, County, State Police, Highway Patrols, Sheriff's Departments, and of course the FBI, DEA, ATF, and scores of Drug and Gang Task Forces lurking around every corner. The important thing this trip would be to make sure not be seen by any of their own people. Prior to his flight leaving Bogota he'd called Jimmy, saying he needed his help with an important job the next morning. He was to page at 8:30 with the address where Mani could pick him up, and not to tell anyone anything. A couple of things worried him. One, Jimmy loved to brag, but he had to chance it, and two, not having the time to plan things out better. For DaLucca, a man who calculated every detail this, like all rush jobs, was unnerving.

He rented a van with phony identification, waited until just before dawn, then stashed it in an abandoned warehouse near a couple of bars where the Jamaicans hung out. He would have preferred doing everything under the cover of darkness but getting the afternoon flight home was a must.

· · · · · · · ·

Jimmy paged at 8:35 AM., happy for the chance to redeem himself after the total fuck-up at the hospital, and excited to be asked to do a job with Pablo's most trusted man. This all helped to keep his mind off his hangover. If things went well today it could determine his future in the organization. One thing for sure, sending Mani DaLucca to straighten things out meant that the Jamaican's head guy, Taylor Williamson, was as good as dead.

When DaLucca received the page five minutes late it infuriated him. Meticulous to the smallest detail, anyone who wasn't, as far as he was concerned, always became a problem.

Mani saw him standing on the corner from three blocks away. "Fucking idiot," he said, shaking his head.

There he stood, hands shoved deep in his pockets, watching every car that drove by. The picture of a dope dealer. Dressed all in black with two thick gold chains dangling around his neck. He might as well have been waving a fucking flag. Mani looked around as he slowed. Now he really wished it were dark. He signaled and pulled up to the curb. Jimmy waved and opened the passenger door.

He climbed in and DaLucca quickly pulled out. Checking the rearview mirror, he made a left onto Lennox from Sixth, two more lefts then a right on Eleventh. Satisfied they weren't being followed, he held his right hand out and Jimmy shook it firmly.

"You told no one about this?"

"No way, Mani," he said. "No fuckin' way that sonofabitch is gonna see this comin'."

"So," DaLucca smiled. "You figured out what the job is. Good boy."

Jimmy tried to relax. Nearly impossible when you're about to work with the best. The guy who never fucked up and always preferred to work alone, but today wanted Jimmy Santos as a partner.

They turned left on Meridian and headed north across Dade Boulevard towards Little Havana.

"I've stashed a van in an abandoned building not far from here," Mani said. "We'll use it. Williamson is meeting a couple of his people for lunch at noon. A place called the Sweetgrass Restaurant."

"We gonna whack him there?" Jimmy asked.

Mani ignored the question and made another turn, checking the rearview mirror again.

"With Williamson dead," he said, "It'll take time for them to regroup. He doesn't have a solid number two guy. Too paranoid. Picks a different guy from his top three or four to handle things when he's not around. They never know who will get the nod. So, after he's dead they'll waste a lot of time deciding who's in charge. That'll give us time to move on all of them, once and for all."

"Jesus Christ," Jimmy muttered. "You wanna stop at my place. I gotta lot a hardware there."

"Don't worry," Mani said looking over at him. "I have everything we'll need."

"Yeah but what if he's got a bunch of his ..."

"I said don't worry. It's been taken care of. He'll arrive by himself."

Santos nodded apologetically. Fuck, man, this is Mani DaLucca. Of course he's covered all the angles.

· · · · · · ·

They stopped at the entrance to the warehouse. Most of the chain-link fence that once surrounded the building had fallen and now lay hidden by the long grass. Tufts of yellow and green weeds pushed their way through the crumbling asphalt parking lot once used by employees. Not a single window pane in the entire warehouse had been left unbroken and the two huge metal sliding doors at the far end had rusted in the open position. Above the entrance, a weather-beaten sign, barely readable: 'Avante Imports Ltd.' There was no one around.

· · · · · · · ·

Mani drove slowly around an old box spring and other debris that littered the inside of the musty warehouse. Just past the skeletal frame of a seventies Ford pickup, long since plucked clean of anything of value, Mani pulled up, then stopped beside the black van. He looked at his watch. If he got finished soon there was a chance he could make the three o'clock flight.

He turned off the ignition, got out, and opened the driver's side door of the van. Jimmy watched, then whispered to himself. "Shit ... he's wearing gloves. Fuck, I shoulda brought gloves." Mani took his time checking for any papers in the side panels and glove compartment. When he finished he locked the driver's door and walked to the back of the van. "Jimmy," he said and motioned with his head. "Come here, it's time."

· · · · · · · ·

Santos jumped out and hurried over to the back of the van as DaLucca opened the back doors.

"Mani ... I uh, I got no gloves, just so you know," he said, showing his hands.

"That's no problem, my friend. You have my guarantee no one will ever pin this on you." He couldn't resist smiling.

Taking a last look around, DaLucca pointed to a cardboard box behind the driver's seat.

"Jimmy, climb in and get the box would you?"

"Sure Mani," he said and scrambled into the van, trying not to get the knees of his slacks dirty. He grabbed the box and turned. "It feels empty, Mani."

The silencer on the barrel of the 45 caliber Ruger made it look like a cannon. Jimmy froze, a terrified look on his face.

"Why? I never done nothin'."

He felt the piss running down his leg. "Please, Mani, honest to God I never ..."

DaLucca squeezed the trigger twice. TWAP...TWAP. What housed all the hopes and dreams of one day becoming the richest, most powerful and respected man in Colombia sprayed across the dashboard and windshield.

14 MAY
Mexico City, Mexico
1000 hrs. local time.

Fernando Salas couldn't shake the feeling. Probably his imagination, but he re-checked the figures anyway. Everything appeared to be in order, but something didn't seem right. Maybe the Federales were following him. Pushing back his chair, he got up, walked to the window and pulled back the drapes a couple of inches. Everything on the street looked normal. Sitting back down, Salas sighed and stared at the screen. Tomorrow he'd run some scans just to be safe. For now though there were deposits and transfers to deal with.

CHAPTER TWENTY-NINE

14 MAY
Vancouver, British Columbia
1045 hrs. local time

THE RCMP DRUG SECTION IN VANCOUVER WAS COMPRISED OF FOUR different units, each with its own mandate. Unit three, run by Staff Sergeant Len Cranston, targeted major cocaine and heroin importers. With over thirty years in, and the last twenty-seven on various drug sections across Canada, Cranston had a reputation that made him one of the most valued and respected members in drug enforcement.

In years gone by, he and other selected members of the undercover team were seconded during visits by heads of state to assist in security by infiltrating groups suspected of planning to harm or embarrass foreign dignitaries. In the summer of 1973 he met Paul Goldman, at that time part of Israeli Intelligence, in charge of advance and venue security for a two-day visit by Prime Minister Golda Meir to Ottawa. A bond developed immediately, and they became instant friends. When Cranston's phone rang, he picked up on the second ring.

"Paul? Well, I'll be damned. How the hell are you?"

"Lenny, I can't believe you're still there. What ... have the RCMP built an old-age home around your office for the stubborn ones who won't leave?"

Cranston laughed and tossed the file he was reading to the side of his cluttered desk.

"Believe me, Paul, I'm so ready to leave. And you, where the hell are you?"

"In San Diego right now, visiting an old friend. I wanted to touch base with you on a few things."

Len Cranston tucked the receiver between his shoulder and ear and kicked his office door closed. "Paul, I'm so sorry about Anna and Ben. I just found out a week ago and tried calling but I couldn't get anything out of the Miami cops. I'm sorry I couldn't have been there for you, man."

"I know, Lenny, thank-you. The police were worried about their witness, you know how it goes. As for me I'm doing okay, considering. And you, Lenny, how are things with you?"

Cranston looked around his office. Criminal flow charts and pictures were tacked over all available wall space, including the back of his office door. "Well, there's no shortage of work, so I figure my jobs pretty secure. Trouble nowadays is we spend as much time fighting the system as we do chasing the bad guys."

"I hear you. Listen, Len, I'm working with some people, on a group out of Colombia and could use your help."

"If I can, for sure. Fill me in."

For the next few minutes Paul explained about the five hundred kilos of cocaine in the container aboard the *Maco Pride*, and when it was expected to dock in Vancouver. While listening, Cranston entered the ship's name in his computer, confirming in seconds that it wasn't on their latest "Watch-For" list.

"Our info," Paul went on, "is that the container will be trucked across Canada, then into the U.S., probably somewhere between

Toronto and Montreal. Looks like it'll end up somewhere in New York State."

"So you want us to follow it and take it down at a certain point. That's not going to be a problem at all."

"Uh ... sort of, Len. We definitely want you to take the dope but, to make things work for us, when it's taken, it has to be replaced with a lookalike without the driver's knowledge."

"Without their knowledge?" Len said, picking up his pen. "Okay, difficult ... but maybe not impossible."

"Well," Paul said, "there's a bit of a bigger hook than just that."

"How much of a bigger hook?" Cranston asked, leaning back in his chair.

"Once it's been replaced, it has to be let go. No arrests, no report, nothing."

"I ... uh, run that by me again, Paul. I think I've missed something here."

"Sorry, Lenny. It's the only way we can get an internal thing started back in South America. If they figure it's the cops, it's just the price of doing business, so I need each end to think the other ripped them."

Cranston put his pen down. "Hmm, how the hell am I gonna sell this little gem?" he asked himself out loud.

Like every police force, the RCMP has an annual budget. Investigations that are likely to deplete the budget before the end of the fiscal year usually require special funding. Getting approval from headquarters in Ottawa to spend thousands of dollars and hundreds of man-hours meant the case would have to be very big and very important. With no arrests or seizures, Cranston knew this was no doubt destined to fall on deaf ears.

"Paul. I'll do the best I can you know that ... but ... Jesus, is there anything that'll help me generate a little interest in this?

Something down the road that'll at least show the taxpayers where their money went?"

"I'm afraid not, Len. Looks like it's all going to the one customer in New York. Best I can offer is that when we're done we should have a list of the Canadian customers for you."

There was a long pause before Cranston spoke.

"Okay, Paul. I think just maybe that'll help. Give me one day. This is gonna require a bit more thought. I'll call you back at this time tomorrow."

"Appreciate it, Len, thanks." Paul hung up and looked over at Tom. "I think maybe I just asked for the impossible. We may have to figure something else out."

```
14 MAY
San Francisco Bay
1500 hrs. local time.
```

The *Maco Pride* sailed out of San Francisco Bay on schedule, passing under the Golden Gate Bridge and setting a course due west. Thirty nautical miles out, she'd change headings and make her way north. Built in the early fifties at the Kaiser Shipyards in Portland Oregon, she was identical in design to the Liberty ships used during the Second World War. At four hundred and forty feet long, in calm seas she could maintain eleven knots. The winds were light, and the Pacific rolled gently. If the weather held she should arrive in Vancouver on time.

· · · · · · ·

The *Maco Pride's* captain, sixty-seven-year-old Eric Thornsby had spent the past fifty-one years at sea, and this would be his last run before mandatory retirement, and finishing his career as captain of this beat-up coastal freighter hadn't been his plan. Prior to 1991, he'd been master of the *Charlotte Quest*, a two-hundred-thousand-ton super tanker carrying oil between Alaska and California. Captains of these mammoth freighters were held in high esteem by mariners around the world, but the respect came with enormous responsibilities and, one foggy night off the rocky coast of Kodiak Island, a tide miscalculation by the officer on the bridge ran the *Charlotte Quest* aground. The punctured hull and ensuing oil spill cost the company tens of millions just to repair the environmental damage alone. The investigation determined that at the time of the accident Captain Thornsby had been passed-out in his quarters and, when all was said and done, his reputation and job were no more.

Now, here he was nursing this soon-to-be artificial reef up and down the coast. Its engines were in constant need of repair and its crew, a collection of unreliable dregs who, like him, had managed to work their way to the bottom. First officer Jose Cardova on the other hand, had two things on his mind. His upcoming promotion to captain, and the five thousand dollars that awaited him when he turned over the container number to his contact at the dock in Vancouver.

CHAPTER THIRTY

```
14 MAY
Bogota, Colombia
1700 hrs. local time
```

RAMON USED THE PAYPHONE AT THE CANTINA DIAZ. HE LISTENED for the dial tone, dug into his pants pocket, and pulled out the crumpled piece of paper. Steadying himself, he held it to the light, squinted at the faded numbers and dialed. When the connection completed, he deposited a number of coins. He could feel the effects of the three beer on an empty stomach, but the location of the cocaine lab and what it would be worth was very sobering. When the answering machine came on, he left the phone number of the Cantina Diaz and asked for Mr. Shea to call the next day at noon. Hanging up, he headed back to his table and waved at the waiter to bring another beer.

```
14 MAY
Miami, Florida
Avante Imports
2030 hrs. local time
```

The oldest was maybe twenty and the other four ranged between fifteen and eighteen. They were all members of a street gang called El Diablos. They spread out in a line and moved cautiously through the warehouse towards the black van parked at the far end.

· · · · · · ·

The El Diablos over the past few years had escalated from petty thefts and vandalism, to drug trafficking, extortions, robberies and, on occasion, murder. What they'd stumbled upon here looked like an easy score. If they could get it started, it would be at one of the local chop shops in minutes and, presto, an easy couple of grand in their pockets, plus whatever items of value were inside. The windows were heavily tinted and the doors locked.

As soon as the brick went through the driver's side window, the rancid smell of rotten meat and feces filled the air. In a little over ten hours, with the temperatures inside the van over a hundred, the corpse of Jimmy Santos was already bloated, and flies swarmed around the massive head wound and amongst the bodily fluids that covered the inside of the van.

Their next decision took very little time. Someone could have seen them come in the warehouse, so getting charged with a murder they didn't commit was a distinct possibility. No, they quickly decided to call this one in.

· · · · · · ·

When the police arrived, all five stories were identical. They'd noticed what looked to be someone not moving in the rear of the van. The doors were locked, and so they broke the window. The overwhelming smell convinced them that whoever was in there was dead, and so they called the cops right away. At first the police thought the El Diablos must have been involved in some way, until they discovered the body had over twenty-seven hundred dollars on it, a Rolex, a gold necklace, and two diamond rings. This would make the five good citizens curse their decision to call before checking things out.

```
15 May
Montreal, Quebec
1000 hrs. local time
```

The message on the postcard couldn't have been more clear. Costa wanted confirmation that Marc Tasse had been taken care of. Any delays would only compound the problem.

> *Jean:*
>
> *I am very anxious for news about your friend's declining*
>
> *health. It worries me that you, being so close to him,*
>
> *may catch his sickness. Please keep me informed. If I have*
>
> *not heard from you within a week, I will conclude that you*
>
> *too have fallen ill. I hope you stay well.*
>
> *P.*

· · · · · · ·

No need to read this one a second time. He lit the corner of the postcard, held it over the ashtray and watched it disintegrate into ash. Rheume very seldom drank during the day but felt the need for one now. He grabbed a bottle of Canadian Club from the cabinet over the fridge and a glass from the drying rack, poured the glass half full and sat at the table. He stared out the window, hoping some kind of idea would come to him, some way to convince Costa that Marc wasn't the problem. Hell, he'd never met anyone who hated cops more. So now, because one of Costa's people fucked up, Marc had to go. Things were getting way out of control.

"Goddamned crock of shit," he muttered, shaking his head. Then, with a sigh, he downed the rest of his whiskey and picked up the phone.

· · · · · · ·

In Toronto, the phone at the front desk of the Dumont Hotel rang. After leaving a message Rheume hung up and poured another. Having passed on his usual breakfast and settling only for an orange juice and coffee, he already felt a little lightheaded. The glass shook ever so slightly in his hand. He drank it down in two gulps, picked up the phone, hesitated for a few seconds then said out loud, "Fuck it." and dialed Tasse's number.

"Marc? Jean here." He hoped he sounded normal. "Listen, I need you to go to Toronto, probably later today. I was going myself but other things have come up. How about we meet for coffee in an hour, and I'll fill you in?"

Tasse had just got dressed and was contemplating taking a load of dirty clothes to the laundry on the corner. "Sure, Jean. Usual place?"

"That'll be great. See you there."

Ten minutes later, Rheume's phone rang. It was Alexi Petrov in Toronto. He owed Jean a couple of favors and a considerable amount of money.

```
15 MAY
Bogota, Colombia
0830 hrs. local time
```

When DaLucca arrived, Costa was in his office with the door closed, pacing back and forth. His shoulder-length silver hair, always neat and styled, today was scrunched under a ballcap. He hadn't slept well, or bothered to shave. DaLucca took off his raincoat and hung it on the coat rack beside the door. Pablo motioned towards the two chairs on either side of the coffee table. Mani closed the door and sat across from him.

"Well?" Pablo asked. "What happened?"

Mani spoke quietly. "It's been taken care of. As long as he didn't tell anyone about meeting me, and I told him not to, and there's no reason to think he did, it will be blamed on the Jamaicans."

Pablo nodded and stared at the ceiling. He mumbled something to himself, then looked at DaLucca

"This has caused me much pain, my friend. No matter what, Jimmy was family," he said. "Much pain." He picked up his cup and fought the urge to throw it; instead, he slammed it down on the table. Coffee splashed over the rim onto his hand. Clenching his fists, he glared across the table.

"All of this, this shit, Mani. All this fucking shit because of one stinking witness. An old fucking man." He stood up quickly and, with a sweep of his arm, flung the coffee tray across the room. "I don't care what the fuck it takes, I want this cocksucker dead. Do you understand," he hollered, slamming his fist into the palm of his hand. "This guy is ... just look what's been going on here. I don't care if we have to buy half the fuckin' cops in Florida and kill the other half. I want the fucker dead."

• • • • • • • •

DaLucca remained silent, then nodded. Pablo took a few deep breaths, trying to calm down. "Mani, you know me for a long time. We've done many things over the years to keep our house in order, so we can't deal with a little problem like this? Some stupid little shop owner? I got to be honest, Mani, I won't sleep good till I know he's dead."

He walked to his desk, sat down and closed his eyes. DaLucca stepped over the broken sugar container and stood by the patio doors, hands clasped behind his back. Rivulets of rain ran down the lead glass panes, darting from side to side with each gust of wind.

"Then, if I may suggest," he said, turning back to Costa.

"Please, yes," Pablo said without opening his eyes. "A suggestion would be nice."

Mani sat down. "To try to do this when he comes to court, or meets with the District Attorney is what they expect. The amount of security will make any attempt suicidal but, if we can find out where they are hiding him …"

Pablo opened his eyes and straightened up. "Of course. Of course, Mani. The cop running the case, what's his name, Conners. He must be in touch with him, at least by phone. Okay. Have his phone and house done, and his partner, whatever her name is, do hers, too, and if we don't get anywhere this way … pick up the broad. I'm through fucking around."

DaLucca nodded. "I'll take care of it right away, Pablo."

```
15 May
Bogota, Colombia
1145 hrs. local time
```

Ramon walked quickly from his apartment to the Cantina. He couldn't help smiling. What a great day, he thought. The sun is shining. Mr. Shea gets some pictures, Ramon gets rich, and no one gets hurt. To celebrate, Ramon had bought a white panama hat. He liked the look, and it made him feel rich. He'd had one a few years back, but some lousy bastard ripped it off while he'd been passed out. Today Ramon had decided to have a big breakfast, but out of habit he ordered his favorite beer, a Costena. Ten minutes and a beer later the bartender called out that the phone was for him. Ramon picked up his beer and hurried to the end of the bar.

```
15 MAY
San Diego, Calif.
1230 hrs. local time
```

Jamie checked his notes then, looking up at the map of Colombia tacked to the dining room wall, ran his finger along a section south east of Bogota.

"Got to be right about here," he said, marking an area of thick jungle with a red marker. "And, according to Ramon, it's a big one. Refining, packaging, complete with airstrip. He's not sure what the output is, but with the amount of security it must be one of their biggest."

"Excellent," Paul said. "Jamie. Have you ever dealt with a guy in Colombia named Enrico Messina?"

"Yes, as I recall he was a major in the Anti-Narcotics Police a few years back. We set up a training program for his lads with the help of the C.I.A.. They provided the equipment, communications and weapons," he said, smiling at Tom. "And we provided the brains and know how. Taught guerrilla tactics and close combat. I worked mainly with his boss, but I did meet him a number of times."

"Well, he is the boss now. We'll call him as soon as we hear from Len in Vancouver. Hopefully he'll be able to make that end work."

"How's this looking?" Tom asked, nodding at the computer.

"Done," Paul said, lining up the cursor and clicking on print.

A minute later, he gathered the sheets of paper from the printer tray and handed them to Tom.

As he read through the pages, his eyebrows went up. "Christ! He owns all these?"

"Directly or indirectly." Paul nodded. "Either owns or has controlling interest. Everything from freight companies, hotels, restaurants, casinos, even a hunting and fishing lodge on the west coast of Canada. These guys are very busy, and very rich." He ejected a disc from the computer. "It's all on here. It shows the money trail from beginning to end. At least I'm pretty sure that's all there is, but, hell, he could have two or three places like the Mesa Grande we don't know about. The good thing is, I've found a way of moving things around a bit without them knowing, until we want them to that is."

"So we're ready to go?" Tom asked.

"I'd say a couple of days at the outside," Paul said, looking around at the charts and pictures. "Then, as long as nothing comes out of left field at us, we throw everything we've got at the son-of-a-bitch."

CHAPTER THIRTY-ONE

15 MAY
San Diego Calif.
1300 hrs. local time

"SHE'S A GO, MY FRIEND," CRANSTON SAID AS SOON AS PAUL PICKED up the phone.

"Lenny, you're a genius. How the hell did you pull it off?"

"Long story, pal. I'll tell you all about it when we can sit and have a drink. Now, to make this work I'm gonna need as much information on the container as possible. Colours, lettering, numbers, weigh bills, anything."

Paul put on his glasses and picked up Jamie's notes. "Here we are. The container number is ... Golf... Foxtrot ... two, five, eight, Alpha, zero, zero, nine, one, three." He waited a few seconds before continuing. "It's a "SEARAIL," two-tone light-over-dark blue. Can't help you with a weigh bill number, but the coke is in kilo bricks, in brown burlap coffee sacks, and the sacks we're interested in have a darker stitching across the top."

"Got it," Cranston said and finished writing. "Anything else?"

"That's about it, Len. If we get anything else I'll call, but our guy's not in a position to get much more without raising suspicion."

"Okay. We go with this. One of my guys is checking with Ports Canada Police to get the Maco's arrival time. Got a few loose ends and a bit of fancy footwork to do with headquarters and that should be it. Man … I've spun this one better than a politician caught with his pants down."

Paul laughed. "Lenny, I am impressed, and I owe you big time."

"No problem, but listen, I know this is about Anna and Ben, so I also know you're goin' after Costa and Rodriguez, but I gotta tell you, Costa is without a doubt the meanest prick you'll ever come across."

"I believe that without a doubt he is Len."

"Then you know it's gonna be real tough to stay out of his way once he knows you're making a move on him."

"Yes, I know. He's already taken a couple of runs at me. Luckily I'm not alone. I have some friends helping. They are in the same business as you and I and, with any luck, he won't be able to put things together until it's too late, and by then things should take care of themselves."

"Hope so, Paul. Keep your head up, and I'll be in touch."

"Appreciate it, Len. Thanks"

Paul hung up and gave a thumbs up to Tom who'd been listening to Paul's side of the conversation.

Tom smiled and clapped his hands. "Now this is gonna piss some people off big time."

```
15 MAY
Miami Police Headquarters
Miami, Florida
1315 hrs. local time
```

Bonnie called Morgan's local from the wall phone outside the interview room..

"Conners here," he said.

"Yeah, Morg, I'm in interview room 2. You better come and hear this."

Morgan tossed the autopsy report he'd been reading into his 'in' basket. "On my way, Bon." A few seconds later he knocked on the door marked INTERVIEW ROOM 2. Above the door a red light flashed, indicating an interview was in progress. Bonnie opened it and he stepped inside.

Terri Walter's eyes were red and puffy. The long blond hair that had once turned heads and sold magazines was matted and greasy, hanging lifelessly in front of her face. Her wish had come true. Jimmy was out of her life, for good. No more beatings and abuse, but if Jimmy had done something bad enough for his own people to kill him, would they come after her, too?

"Terri," Bonnie said, motioning with her head. "This is my partner Detective Connors."

She stared blankly at Morgan, then looked down at the table.

"Miss Walters, I'm sorry for your loss," he said and sat down.

"Yeah, I just bet you are," she said. She shook a cigarette out of her package, checked to make sure it was empty, then balled it up and threw it on the floor. "Don't hand me shit, okay."

Morgan held his lighter to the tip of the cigarette that quivered in her lips. She took a long drag and brushed the hair away from her face.

"The fucking truth is, you guys hated Jimmy. You're glad someone killed him, aren't you?" she said, her eyes welling with tears again. Morgan leaned back and studied her before he spoke.

"Look Terri, we didn't like what your boyfriend did for a livin', but he picked the life style not us. Maybe he had a good side to him, whatever," he shrugged. "One thing for sure ... he probably figured the odds were things would end somethin' like this."

She sighed but didn't look up.

"Look, Terri," he continued, "Detective Story and I, we solve murders, for a livin'. It's what we do. Old, new, good or bad, it don't matter. So it don't matter what I thought of Jimmy. The thing that matters is who killed him an' we're gonna do everything we can to find out. That's our job, and that's ... the fuckin' truth."

Bonnie gave it a few seconds before patting her on the hand.

"Go ahead, Terri. Tell him what you told me."

```
15 MAY
North of Toronto, Ontario
1620 hrs. local time
```

The Twin Oaks Motel, north of Toronto on Highway 27 had seen better days, most of them back in the fifties and sixties when Highway 27 was one of the main routes in and out of Toronto from the north. The motel had nine, tiny one-room log cabins painted white with black trim in a semi-circle facing a tiny lake that all but dried up in the hot months of summer. The cabins were spaced far enough apart to allow two cars to park between them. All were basically the same inside: A night table with a lamp bolted to the wall between two saggy double beds, an older twenty-inch television sitting on top of a dresser rimmed with years of cigarette burns, and two white plastic chairs that were stacked by the bathroom door at the rear of each cabin.

The motel's owners lived in the two units closest to the highway that had been joined together to also serve as the office. As the city expanded, Highway 400, a more direct and faster route to the bedroom communities north of the city, had put the motel just far enough off the beaten track that now the Twin Oak's lifeline was dependent on the storms and blizzards that forced travelers to stop there.

Ray and Cora Henderson were delighted when the man with the heavy European accent drove in around noon and rented the two cabins nearest the lake for two days. They were even happier when he paid cash in advance. The others would be arriving later this afternoon. A guy's getaway type of thing. There wouldn't be a need for maid service while they were there, which suited the Henderson's just fine. Ray Henderson made sure to offer the two wooden rowboats that lay upside down beside the dock.

"You're welcome to use the boats, free of charge. I still bring in some nice sized cutthroat outta that lake," he lied.

"Maybe we do little fishing before we go," Petrov lied back.

CHAPTER THIRTY-TWO

15 MAY
Miami, Florida
1530 hrs. local time

MORGAN DECIDED TO SLIP HOME AND TREAT HIMSELF TO A RUN while Bonnie finished taking Terri Walter's statement. Paul wouldn't be calling for a few hours, and he found it easier to think when he was running.

If Walters was right, the hit on Santos fit Costa's mentality of resolving problems by removing anyone who caused him stress, no matter who they were. The FBI had taken over security of Dora Pratt due to the high level of risk and moved her out of state. He checked the answering machine for messages while he changed into his running gear. There were none.

After a series of leg stretches, Morgan locked the door behind him and bounded off the porch heading east to NW17th Avenue. He didn't pay any attention to the dark van parked at the corner. When he reached North River Drive he picked up his pace. This particular route was his favorite and at this time of day not too crowded.

By the time he hit the one-mile mark, his stride had become smooth and his breathing steady. Things were moving fast, and Costa was pulling out all the stops to get Goldman. Luckily, Captain Jacobs had been able to deflect the heat coming from the DA's office, so far anyway. They wanted more access to "their" witness, but with all the bodies piling up, no one dared question the degree of secrecy surrounding his whereabouts. For now things were under control, as long as no one found out that the security package lacked any input from the police whatsoever, and if Paul gets himself killed, Morgan would be hard pressed to get a job as a parking lot attendant.

```
Toronto, Ontario
15 MAY
1745 hrs. local time
```

Marc Tasse drove down Dundas towards Parliament Street. He hadn't been here for a few years and, compared to Montreal, he thought Toronto was a dump. Things had changed since he'd been here though. Now there were specialty shops selling designer coffees, health foods, European fashions, and expensive art, all slowly squeezing out the pool halls, pawn shops, and flop houses of the bad old days. Nowadays, only a handful of the old buildings and businesses were still standing. Tasse turned north onto Parliament street past the old Windsor Hotel that still advertised clean beds by the day, week or month but now with a Starbucks on one side and a Gourmet Cheese and Deli Shoppe on the other, the Windsor got more disgusting looks than customers. A block further on the opposite side of the street and still operating was Tasha's Grill.

Tasse got lucky. A parking spot was right in front. He'd be able to keep an eye on his black 1997 Pathfinder. He learned to do tune-ups from working in prison garages. Washing and waxing he'd learned doing the only straight job he ever held on the outside. As much as he hated washing cars, doing his own was different. Tasse had become closer to his Pathfinder than most people are to their kids.

The phone call wouldn't come in for another fifteen minutes or so. Time for a coffee and maybe a burger. After depositing a couple of quarters into the meter, he watched traffic for a few seconds, then walked in the front door. Tasha's had changed names and owners a dozen or more times over the last few decades, but the consistently poor food and generations of flies swarming on garbage and food alike, hadn't. A faded white-and-yellow Formica counter, chipped and bubbled from years of abuse and cigarette burns, ran the length of the back wall facing the kitchen. The ten or so chrome swivel stools, their maroon padding wafer-thin and held together with strips of duct tape were no doubt as uncomfortable as they looked. Along the windows, three wooden booths, each covered with carved initials, dates, and profanities looked out onto Parliament Street through windows yellowed by years of dust and cigarette smoke. To the clientele, it didn't matter. Cleanliness and food were secondary. What they bought to put in their arm or up their nose was primary.

Marta Kovenko stood on a stool behind the counter reaching as high as she could to tack up the crudely written sign advertising the soup and sandwich special. Today's fare was Cabbage Soup with Grilled Cheese for $4.95. Standing just shy of five feet and close to three hundred pounds, Marta literally waddled. Stepping back to have a better look, she cocked her head, and decided with a grunt that it looked straight enough. Then she turned to deal with her new, and only, customer.

Tasse took the end booth nearest the payphone. He sat down and flicked a few crumbs of whatever off the table.

"A'm comink you," Marta called in a raspy voice. Stubbing out her cigarette, she picked a coffee mug off the drying rack along with a stained sheet of paper that served as the menu and made her way to his booth. The pungent smell of rotting garbage, or possibly the soup special, changed Marc's mind about a burger, or any other food for that matter.

Marta wheezed with each breath and looked exhausted as she plopped the menu and coffee mug in front of him. She managed a smile, exposing the few remaining teeth she had left. "A'm brink coffee you?" she managed to say all in one breath.

"Yeah ... just coffee, I'm waiting for a phone call," he gestured, holding his fist between his ear and mouth and saying it loud, as if it would make her understand better. Marta nodded, mumbled something and made her way back to the counter. She picked up a pot of coffee and came back, slower this time. At the booth she heaved a sigh and smiled again.

"Hokay dokay ... mabee you ead soupa? Marta mak-ed good soupa."

When she poured the coffee, it splashed over the rim of his cup and onto the table.

"Jesus ... watch what you're doing," he said, grabbing the last napkin out of the tin holder. "No soup. No time," he said and tapped his watch. "Very busy. You got that?" he said, louder than before.

"Hokay." She shrugged and picked up the menu. "You coffee ... hokay."

Back at the counter, Marta tossed the menu on a shelf beside the cash register and started coughing. It intensified, turning her face a reddish purple. After one final, loud, lung-clearing hack, she straightened up, reached into the pouch of her soiled apron, and fished the last cigarette out of a flattened pack. Checking around for a match and not finding any, she disappeared into the kitchen. Tasse watched her and shook his head.

"Fuckin' dive," he said out loud. This whole fucking thing seemed a waste of time. All Rheume told him was that Alex Petrov wanted a meet to explain a few things and give a partial payment of what he owed. Probably got some lame fuckin' excuse why he's short again. Still, it wasn't like Rheume to send him anywhere without first going over every detail. Marc sipped the hot, stale coffee and stared out the window. Something about this whole thing bugged him.

THE THIRD LAW

15 MAY
Miami, Florida
1800 hrs. local time

Morgan glanced at the kitchen clock when the phone rang. Should be Paul, he thought, as he picked up.

"Connors here," he said.

"Hello, Morgan," Paul sounded upbeat as usual.

"Paul, I'm glad you called. How's it going there?"

"Fine. Everything's fine. And you, you sound stressed?"

"I'm busy pal, very busy," he said, sliding a chair out from the kitchen table and sitting down. "Looks like your friend's makin' some moves around here, all revolving around you."

"What does it have to do with me?" Paul asked.

Morgan opened the fridge, took out a carton of orange juice and poured a large glass.

"Well, you're definitely at the top of his things-to-do list, that's for sure. Seems anyone connected to the attempt at the Holiday Inn, an' the thing at the hospital are being whacked, including one of their own ... a piece of garbage named Jimmy Santos. He's a nephew of Eduardo Rodriguez, Costa's partner."

"Interesting, so what's your read on it?" Paul asked.

"With three dead cops, they know the pressure ain't comin' off this one, so he's tryin' to remove anybody who can link things directly back to him. Santos matches the description we got from the nurse in the I.C.U. the night they got Grange. She couldn't positively identify him, but this seems to confirm it. The description of the guy Santos was last seen with is Colombian, thinning hair, sunglasses and one of those pencil-thin moustaches. We've got a witness, a girlfriend who says Santos knew the guy from back home. He picked Santos up a block from his place, so probably didn't want anyone to see them together. Now here's the kicker, he dumps the body in Williamson's territory to make it look like a Jamaican job."

"What kind of sunglasses, Morgan?"

"You know those irritating, mirrored kind? Those. Costa's main guy wears a pair, an' it wouldn't surprise me if it was him. Why do you ask?"

"Just wondering. I remember seeing a picture in the file you showed me of one of his people wearing a pair like that. Anyway, wouldn't that give them the reason they need to go to war?"

"Sure, if they needed one," Morgan said, wiping his brow with the sleeve of his sweatshirt. "They already got a cemetery full of reasons. Costa's been pushin' Rodriguez to get on side for a long time now, but Eduardo's always tried to work out some kinda arrangement, so this tells me he didn't sanction the hit, but if he figures Williamson's people did it he'll go along in a heart beat. It works out perfectly for Costa."

"Sounds like his kind of plan all right. Pretty drastic measures though, even for him."

"Yeah it would be, but takin' out Jimmy gets rid of the direct link to him, plus it brings Eduardo on side for a full-blown down and dirty with the Jamaicans."

"So why the worry about me? It looks as though they've got enough on their plate."

"No way, my friend. Not him. He don't work that way. Like I said, you're at the top of his most hated list. Remember what I told you, the prick's driven by revenge, so trust me, nothin's gonna change his mind. Fact of the matter is, in his warped way of thinkin', he'll even be blamin' you for bad fuckin' weather. It's just the way the asshole thinks. By the way, I'm getting pressured big time to get you under a security umbrella from the chief, the DA's office, shit even the mayor. They're all talkin' protective custody."

"Yes, I'm not surprised," said Paul. "How are you getting around all that?"

"With the body count on the rise, and you safe within the incredible security arrangements I've put in place, they're leavin' me alone for the time bein', but I'm tellin' you Paul … you keep your head up."

"So you think Costa does have someone else inside?"

Morgan topped off his glass with more orange juice. "Gotta have. An' he'll be bringin' everything an' everyone he's got outta the wood work. Shit," he said almost to himself. "I thought I knew Grange like a brother."

Paul thought for a few seconds. "Okay, try not to get yourself in any trouble over this. The last thing we need is for you to get pulled off the case. Tell them you want to let things calm down before bringing me back."

"Yeah, right now that shouldn't be a problem. It'll buy us a bit more time, but eventually it's gonna be out of my hands … you know that," Morgan said.

"Yes, I suppose you're right, so let's take it one step at a time. Who knows, Costa may find he has more important problems to worry about. Anyway," he said, changing the subject. "Enough of this. How are you and Bonnie doing?"

"Fine, just fine. She's good. I'm good, everybody's good."

"Okay. You've got my pager number if you have to get hold of me. If I don't hear from you I'll call you in a few days."

"Okay, Paul, take care." Morgan hung up, stared at the phone and shook his head. "Christ, you're up to somethin' you bugger, aren't you."

· · · · · · · ·

Before Paul pulled out to head back to Tom's he felt for his berretta under the front seat, racked one into the chamber and clicked on the safety. After a number of surveillance checks, he made his way into San Diego. For sure Costa would have others like Grange. Time to be a lot more careful. The killing of Jimmy Santos was interesting. Maybe they'd be able to work that into their plan.

CHAPTER THIRTY-THREE

```
15 MAY
Off the coast of Washington State
1500 hrs. local time
```

THE WIND EASED OFF AS THE *Maco Pride* TOOK A STARBOARD heading that would bring her around Cape Flattery at the northern tip of the Olympic Peninsula. Heaving and shuttering through rolling six-foot swells, she held steady at ten knots. Soon they'd be in the more sheltered waters of the Strait of Juan De Fuca and by morning at Vancouver harbor awaiting docking space.

```
15 MAY
Toronto, Ontario
1800 hrs. local time
```

The call came in right at 6:00. The sooner he got out of this stinking restaurant the better. After listening to the message, he slammed the receiver down.

"Fucking kind of shit is this?" he said, pulling a handful of coins out of his pocket and dialing. Marta watched from behind the counter.

In Montreal, Rheume answered on the first ring. The sound in Tasse's voice sent a twinge of panic through him.

"What is it? What's the matter Marc?" he asked.

Tasse tried to keep his voice low. "He wants to meet at some fleabag motel north of the city. What's with that? Seems a bit weird, so thought I better call you first, you know, cuz if there's no reason, I'll tell him to meet me in town."

Rheume tried to remain calm. "Don't worry, Marc. Petrov's being careful, that's all. He's had some heat problems lately and doesn't want you dragging any of it back here. I don't want to say any more on the phone, okay, except, don't worry. Meet him wherever he wants. It's no big deal. "

Tasse thought for a second. He'd never had reason to doubt Rhueme as there'd always been an unconditional trust between them. "Okay," he said. "Not a problem. I'll call you when I get back. Sorry to bother you."

"No bother, Marc. Call me tomorrow when you get back and we'll do lunch."

Rheume hung up and walked to the balcony, slid the door open and let the cool breeze wash over him. It made him nervous that Marc was questioning this, because Rhueme knew very well that, although he looked like a stupid man, Marc Tasse was anything but.

· · · · · · ·

Walking back to his booth, Tasse noticed Marta leaning against the counter watching him. "Fat bitch, the fuck you starin' at?" he said, loud enough for her to hear, and understand, no matter what language she spoke. "You call this shit coffee … how much?"

"One," she said, holding up a fat finger. "One dolla."

Tasse dropped a dollar and a quarter on the counter in front of her as he walked out the door. "Fuckin' dive," he called over his shoulder and letting the door slam behind him.

Marta opened the cash register and plunked the dollar coin in. She stood, rubbing the quarter between her thumb and forefinger.

When the Pathfinder pulled away, Marta Kovenko waddled to the pay phone and used her tip to call Alexev Petrov's pager.

• • • • • • •

In traffic, it would take the better part of two hours to get there. Plenty of time to think things out. With no dope involved, why out in the middle of nowhere? Why not in a night club or restaurant? If Petrov was dragging heat, a couple of guys having a beer would attract a lot less attention than being followed to some shit hole of a motel. Christ, for sure the cops would put that together as a deal going down. The more he thought about it, the more it felt wrong. Marc never trusted the Russians. Bunch of tattooed, no- brain, psycho killers. All liars, cheats, and back stabbers. By the time he turned west on Highway 9, he'd decided that, no matter what his boss said, he'd give this a real good look first.

• • • • • • •

Alexev Petrov drove to the payphone at a Petro-Can gas station half a mile from the Twin Oaks to answer his page. Too easy for the cops to trace a call from his cell. The message confirmed Tasse was on his way. Petrov smiled as he got back into his Mercedes. They were ready. Once rid of the body, they'd be back in Toronto by midnight, dump Tasse's wheels on a side street downtown and have time to go for a drink to celebrate half his debt being cancelled.

• • • • • • •

When Petrov got back to the Twin Oaks he parked beside cabin number nine. The sound of the crunching gravel alerted the two men in cabin eight next to his. Nicoli Trechkoff and Eugeni Timinov opened the door and stepped onto the small porch. "He's on his way," Petrov said, smiling.

1930 hrs.

Marc would have to chance getting a speeding ticket, because he had to get there before dark. The sun was almost touching the horizon when his Pathfinder passed the partially obscured sign announcing, TWIN OAKS MOTEL 2 KMS. He set the trip odometer to zero. Marc hoped this time he was wrong, because if he wasn't, it meant Rheume had turned against him. Just past the Petro-Can station the odometer showed one and a half kilometres. He found a spot a little further where he could pull off the road completely. After killing the engine, he got out, walked to the back and opened the rear hatch.

A pick-up truck roared down the highway towards him. As it went by, the driver didn't even look at the Pathfinder. Marc unscrewed the bracket that held the spare tire in place enough to move it forward a few inches. Behind the tire, he pulled down on a metal handle that released a tightly-wrapped black plastic bag. Unwrapping it he could smell the gun oil. He loved that smell.

The Uzi had two thirty-round clips taped to the short barrel. Not even Rheume knew about it. Tasse considered it his life insurance policy. Moving to the passenger door, he reached in and pulled the hood release. To anyone other than a mechanic it looked like part of the cooling system. He'd fashioned the three-inch-wide hose that ran from the block to the bottom of the radiator. It was capable of holding two kilos of cocaine plus the silencer. He unclipped the hose and removed the silencer. If things were okay there would still be time to get back to his wheels, drive to the motel, and go ahead with the meet. No one would be the wiser.

· · · · · · · ·

After locking the doors, Marc jumped over the ditch and moved into the thick stands of birch bordering the highway. Staying far enough inside the tree line to be hidden from the road and still have enough light to move quickly, he covered the half kilometre in less than ten minutes.

· · · · · · · ·

From the thick brush near the entrance he had a good view of the front of the cabins. Parked beside the one nearest the lake was Petrov's silver Mercedes 380SL. The beat-up Ford F150 pickup in front of the office no doubt belonged to the owners. There were no other cars by the other cabins. Five minutes passed. Nothing.

As he got ready to leave, the curtain on the window of the cabin beside Petrov's moved ever so slightly. Maybe the wind, but he'd give it another couple of minutes.

A few seconds later something else caught his eye. The last rays of light as the sun set were reflecting off something at the back of cabin number eight. Backing into the bush he made a wide circle to get a better look.

"Son of a bitch," he whispered when he saw Timinov's black Corvette backed into the trees. Marc carefully circled around to front again. Darkness was setting in when the door to cabin nine opened. Alexev Petrov, silhouetted against the inside lights, stepped onto the porch. He called out in a loud whisper to the cabin next to him. The door to cabin eight opened slightly. Tasse couldn't make out who it was or understand Russian, but he didn't have to. When Petrov finished talking, the door to cabin eight closed. Alexev stared out towards the entrance, took a final drag off his cigarette, and flicked the butt onto the gravel. He checked his watch then turned and went back inside. Tasse waited another minute before making his way back to the rear of the cabins.

· · · · · · ·

Kneeling down beside Timinov's Corvette, he screwed the silencer to the barrel of the Uzi. Knowing it was a trap gave him the element of surprise. A huge advantage. It completely turned the tables. Once again, the little voice in his head had been right. For a second his thoughts turned to Rheume, the only person he'd ever trusted. He shook it off. He'd deal with that later.

Montreal. Quebec
2030 hrs. local time

Rheume went through the menu a second time. Le Petite Harve in Old Montreal was his one of his favorites, but tonight nothing on the menu seemed appealing. Too much to think about. He flipped open his cell. The battery showed fully charged. Petrov had been told to call as soon as it was over. As soon as he got the confirmation he'd contact down south. What a fucking waste, he thought. His waiter appeared and refilled his wine glass. Taking a sip of the Australian Merlot he decided on the roast duck.

```
Twin Oaks Motel
2000 hrs. local time
```

The ground behind the cabins were covered with a thick blanket of moss that completely muffled the sounds of Marc's movements. Other than the crickets and frogs beginning their nightly serenade, the only sound came from the T.V. in Petrov's cabin. The bathroom window of cabin eight had a piece of two-by-four wedged between the ledge and window, keeping it open a few inches for ventilation. He quietly made his way along the back wall below the window, listened for a few seconds then eased himself up. With the bathroom door wide open he could see Eugeni Timinov in a plastic chair to the right of Nicoli Trechkoff, who sat on the edge of the bed watching the parking lot through the corner of the drapes. They had hung one of the bath towels over the bedside lamp allowing just enough light to move around inside and not be noticed from outside.

Both had their backs to him and were talking quietly. He raised the Uzi and gently rested the silencer on the window ledge. His thumb slid the selector switch from full to semi-automatic.

The metallic click sounded out-of-place and caught Eugeni's attention. As he turned towards the sound, Marc tapped the trigger, twice....PHUTT..PHUTT. Timinov's head snapped back. Both shots hit within an inch of each other on the right side of his face splattering flesh, bone, and dark red against the wall and drapes. His body flopped onto the foot of the bed then slid onto the floor. Nicoli spun around making a grab for his pistol. He looked right at the rear window as Tasse tapped the trigger again. The first bullet entered slightly below his chin. His eyes went wide as he clutched at his throat. The second shot tore through the side of his jaw. He grabbed the bedspread and slid down between the wall and the bed.

"Fuck," Tasse growled, blinking to clear the sweat from his eyes. He watched Trechkoff try to pull himself up. When his bloodied head rose up over the edge of the bed Tasse fired three quick rounds. PHUTT PHUTT PHUTT. There was a thump as Nicoli's dead body hit the floor, then silence.

Tasse took a few deep breaths to calm himself then moved to the back window of cabin nine. With the TV turned up, Petrov hadn't heard a thing. Marc peered in and saw him propped up on the bed with both pillows behind his head. He was smoking a cigarette and watching the New York Islanders in a two-two tie with the Montreal Canadians late in the second period. A bottle of rye and two glasses were on the desk by the T.V. Every light had been turned on. Everything normal. Warm and friendly.

Tasse put the Uzi inside his jacket, crept around to the front and casually climbed the three wooden steps to the door. It was a happy, loud knock. "Shave and a haircut ... two bits." Petrov lurched off the bed, surprised he hadn't heard a vehicle drive in. He looked around the room, ran his fingers through his hair and opened the door. Tasse stood there with a cocky smile on his face.

"Alex, sorry I'm late. Had to walk the last half mile. Got a fuckin' flat. You mind drivin' me back when we're done? I could use your head lights to see what I'm doin'."

Petrov laughed and held the door open, gesturing for him to come in. "Absolutely, my friend, is not problem, but for now you look like you could use drink, yes?"

He turned and walked to the desk. Tasse closed the door.

"Sure, Alex, yeah, a little drink would be great," he said, the smile disappearing as soon as Petrov turned his back. Alex took the paper sanitary wrappings off the two clear plastic glasses and poured a generous amount of rye into each. He turned and handed one to Marc.

"I start to get worried you have got lost, my friend," he said, raising his glass. "I pick this place so we can talk, away from prying eyes ... yes?"

"I totally understand, Alex," Marc said, raising his glass. "Great choice ... good place to do our business. Salut."

He drank it down in two gulps. It burned his throat, but tasted good. Alex took his empty glass, walked back to the small desk and picked up the bottle.

"I'm sure you wonder why we meet, yes?" he asked half filling both glasses again.

"Not really, Alex," Tasse said reaching inside his jacket. "Figured it out driving up here."

Petrov turned off the television. "Really," he said, turning back to to face him.

Tasse stood in front of the door holding the Uzi at hip level.

"Marc ...what is the hell goin' on?" Alex laughed, spreading his arms wide.

"Guess I'm just a careful guy, Alex. Wanted to be sure I wasn't being set up."

"Set up. For what reason would it be set-up?" Alex asked, moving a little to the left. Eugeni and Nicoli would be opening the door any second now.

Marc lowered the barrel of the Uzi slightly. "So, we're alone then. Just you and me?"

"Of course, just you and me," Petrov laughed and waved his arms around. "Why, you see anyone else but us?"

"No, you're right, Alex, it's just you an' me," Marc smiled. "An' the two dead guys next door."

He tapped the trigger. PHUTT.

Petrov dropped the glasses, yelped, and grabbed his knee. He fell on the bed, blood oozing through his fingers.

"Motherfucker," he yelled through gritted teeth. "Little cocksucker."

"Why Alex? Why me?" he asked, raising the Uzi again.

Petrov glared up at him. "Fuck you," he hissed, then signaled his next move by glancing at the pillow before shoving his right arm under it. PHUTT....PHUTT. The first missed, but as his fingers touched the pistol, the second smashed through his shoulder blade. Moaning, he tried to stand, his right arm dangling like a piece of rope. He stumbled, lost his balance and crashed into the television, sending it, the bottle of rye, and himself to the floor.

"Bad move, Alex. Why? What do they think I did?"

The Russian stared up at him. "You know why. You rat out the wrong people, so what you expect? Huh?"

Marc frowned. "The fuck you talking about?"

Alexev Petrov looked at the spreading pool of blood around him. Wincing, he pulled himself up onto his elbow and glared at Tasse..

"You're dead no matter what … asshole. You just don't know yet."

Tasse moved the selector to automatic. "Yeah, well, guess what, fuckhead? I'm gonna outlive you."

In two seconds the remaining twenty rounds raked up and down Petrov's vibrating body.

Marc turned off the lights and waited for his eyes to adjust.

"Son-of-a-bitch," he said, looking at the outline of the corpse as he put the Uzi back under his coat. "The fuck's going on here?"

Locking the door behind him, he slipped around to the back, past the Corvette and disappeared into the bush. As he passed the owners cabin he could hear their television. Inside, Cora and Harry Henderson were settling in to watch their favorite program "Cops." It always reminded them how lucky they were to live in the country, where life was quiet and crime free. Warm and friendly.

· · · · · · ·

Tasse made his way back to his Pathfinder as quickly as he could, ducking into the trees every time headlights came his way. He shoved the Uzi under the front seat, cranked the wheel and made a U-turn. As he headed south towards Toronto his thoughts turned to

Rheume. He fought to control his anger. The bastard had turned out to be just like everybody else in his life. Just like his father.

CHAPTER THIRTY-FOUR

15 MAY
Bogota, Colombia
2015 hrs. local time

"It's San Diego," DaLuca said and hung up the phone. "They don't know exactly where yet, but he's definitely in San Diego."

"Good Mani," Pablo said, clapping his hands. "Get a hold of Luis Montez in L.A. and fill him in. Tell him to get his people ready, and give them his description. Christ, I can't believe there's no picture of this guy anywhere. What do we know?"

"The cop, Connors, gets a call from Goldman every couple of days. He's staying with a friend and, it seems, with no security."

"No security," Costa said, raising his eyebrows. "How can that be Mani?" He stood up and paced to the door and back to this desk.

"I don't know," DaLuca said, shaking his head. "Can't be a cop decision, but the information appears to be good. Now we just have to figure out exactly where he is."

"What if …" Pablo stopped and rubbed his chin. "What if his friend the cop was sent out to meet him alone. They wouldn't feel the need for extreme security measures, would they?"

Mani nodded. "If we can make that happen, we'll have him." He got up and picked up his coat. "I'll get on it right away."

"And, Mani, one more thing."

"Yes, Pablo?"

"Would you check to see if our friend in Montreal has been in touch. I hope he isn't going to become another problem to us."

"Right away, Pablo."

```
15 MAY
Vancouver, British Columbia
2055 hrs. local time
```

Vancouver's Ballentine Pier unloads thousands of containers every week. The process is fast and efficient, and even as the *Maco Pride's* engines were being shut down, two huge cranes swung into place over her deck. Within minutes the first containers were on the dock. As usual, Captain Thornsby monitored the unloading from the bridge while First Officer Cardova oversaw the unloading of the containers from the pier. Half an hour later Cardova was approached by two men, obviously not longshoremen by their clothes.

· · · · · · ·

"Fifteen from Seven."

Len Cranston keyed his mike. "Go seven."

"Okay ... we got one of the ship's officers talking to two suits. Looks like he's pointing out one of the containers. The colors right. Won't be able to confirm the numbers till they move away."

"Copy that Seven. You in a position to get a few pictures?"

"Already done. The lighting could be better, but I.D. won't be a problem."

"Copy. Three and ten, see if you can put the suits to a set of wheels when they leave."

"Ten copies."

THE THIRD LAW

"Three copies."

15 MAY
Montreal, Quebec
2355 hrs. local time

Rheume looked up and down the hallway before unlocking his door. He switched on the light, double locked the door behind him and walked quickly to the hall closet. The timer allowed twenty seconds to enter the code to disarm the alarm. It usually took no more than five or six seconds, but tonight his hands were visibly shaking. When he pressed ENTER, the red light stayed on. His second try turned it green. There were no messages on the answering machine. It had to be over by now. Maybe Marc got lost, but Petrov would have called. After a bottle of wine and three vodkas, he didn't need another but poured one anyway. No, there must have been something that delayed things, he thought. Petrov would call in the next few minutes then, in the morning, he'd call Costa and be done with this whole fucking mess.

· · · · · · ·

It would take close to four hours to get back to Montreal. Marc set the cruise control for one hundred and ten kilometres per hour. The last thing he needed was a speeding ticket that would put him in the area where three associates had just been murdered.

16 MAY
Miami, Florida
0030 hrs. local time

Morgan and Bonnie walked down the hall to Jacobs' office and closed the door.

"You wanted to see us, Cap?" Morgan asked

"Yeah, sit guys. Glad I caught you before you left," he said, closing a file and tossing it into the 'out' basket on his desk.

"Kinda burnin' the midnight oil aren't you, Cap?" Bonnie asked.

"Not by choice. Look at all this," he said, waving his hand at the pile of files and reports stacked overflowing his 'in' basket. "An' most of it admin bullshit. I was hopin' to get through it all tonight, but I've spent the last three hours arguing with the DA's office ... to no avail, I might add."

"What about?" Morgan asked.

"About Goldman."

"Aw, shit. Don't tell me they want him out here again."

"No, not quite. I got a request slash order from the DA's office. Seems they've put together a deposition to have sworn and signed by him."

"A deposition," Morgan frowned. "What the hell kinda deposition?"

"Don't know. They wanted Accardo to go with you, but I was able to put the fuckin' kibosh on that. Bottom line is though, you two are gonna have to take it to him. After Goldman reads it, get it signed and sworn in front of a judge. DA wants to be able to run with the case in the event something happens to him, or he changes his mind."

"Seems a little weird to me, Cap," Bonnie said.

"Yeah, I hear you. I'm not happy about it either, but the thing is it's not entirely out of the ordinary, and," he said, shrugging his shoulders. "At this point they're theoretically in charge and, believe me, they don't like us tellin' them how to run their cases."

"Deposition," Morgan scoffed. "What a crock of shit. Why didn't Accardo do that when our guy was out here?"

"I know what you're thinkin', an' I gotta agree," Jacobs said, getting up and closing his office door. He walked back and sat on the corner of his desk. "Look, we're stuck with this thing, an' with what's been happening around here lately it's a damn site better than bringin' him here, or havin' the entire DA's office goin' with you. Best I can do is tell Accardo you'll be taking it out in a few days. So let's arrange to get the paper here first thing in the morning an' you guys outta here by tomorrow afternoon, without anyone knowin'."

Jacobs flopped down in his chair and rubbed the sides of his head. "Man, this job's turning into one never-ending migraine."

"I'll page Paul and talk to him first thing in the morning," Morgan said. "Then we can make arrangements to leave."

"Okay," Jacobs sighed. "An' I don't want you travelling commercial. I'll set it up with the DEA. They been offerin' to help since this all started. I just won't tell'em who they're takin', or why."

"Okay," Morgan said, raising his eyebrows and shaking his head. "Guess there's bugger-all we can do about it. I'll call you as soon as I've given Paul the heads up."

"An' listen up you two," Jacobs said, pointing his finger at both of them. "You guys be real careful, understand. You suspect anything, anything at all, you call. Not sure what I'll be able to do from here, but I'll do what I can."

They both nodded.

"Will do, Cap," Morgan said. "Call you later."

· · · · · · · ·

Bonnie closed the door behind them as they left. She waited until they were outside in the parking lot before she spoke.

"So, you thinking what I'm thinking?"

Morgan looked at her, then back at the building. "Yeah, for sure. An' he's right. We'd better watch our ass on this one."

Three young cops just off duty hurried past them heading to the Keystone before last call. Morgan waited until they were out of earshot.

"Christ, Bon, do you realize if Costa can orchestrate something like this, we've lost control of the whole fuckin' shootin' match?"

She looked him straight in the eye. "No, you listen. Grange was a leak, right in our office. A guy we both trusted. Now there's probably someone in the DA's office, or the mayor's, or both, well, I say to hell with them. We don't lose unless we quit, and you and I are not going to fucking quit. You got that, cowboy?"

"Whoa," he said, putting both hands up as if to fend her off. "Ease up, Bon. Jeez, it scares hell out of me when you start soundin' like me."

"Okay, then," she said and poked him in the chest. "I'll get the paperwork in the morning, and you talk to Paul."

"Okay ... ouch. ... okay already."

When they got to the parking lot, Morgan dug his keys out of his pocket. "I'll call you first thing," he said. "How much time you gonna need to be ready to go?

"I'll pack tonight," she said, walking to her car three spots further down. "So I'll be good to go any time."

Morgan followed her out of the lot. At Sixth Avenue she turned right and he signaled to go left. Three blocks from his place, he pulled into an AM PM convenience store and bought a quart of orange juice. Deciding against using his cell or home phone, he asked for five dollars in quarters. At the pay phone outside he punched in the number Paul had given him and waited. After the beep he spoke, keeping the message short.

"Paul, it's Morgan. Page me with a number as soon as you get up. Don't call my place. Something's happened an' we have to talk."

After hanging up he drove home, circling the block twice checking for a tail or any strange vehicles. Nothing. He unlocked the front door, pulled out his pistol and methodically checked very room and window. When he was done he phoned Bonnie.

"You okay?" he asked when she picked up.

"Yeah. I did a few heat checks on the way home but everything seems okay ... why?"

"Cuz it's time to really start bein' careful. I did the same. See you in the morning."

CHAPTER THIRTY-FIVE

```
16 MAY
Montreal, Quebec
0445 hrs. local time
```

RHEUME SAT ON THE WHITE LEATHER COUCH IN HIS LIVING ROOM, staring at the wall. He had never felt this nervous. Every time his eyes closed the slightest sound jolted him awake. If that bastard Petrov decided to party and forgot to call, he'd kill him. Then, as though on cue, the phone on the coffee table rang. Rheume lurched forward, glancing at his watch, and grabbed the receiver. Finally, he thought, but the voice on the other end sent a shiver down his spine, and his surprise was obvious.

"Marc. .. I, I didn't expect to hear from you until, uh…later today. So, how'd it go?"

Tasse smiled. Rheume's voice confirmed it. This was going to be quite enjoyable.

"It didn't," he said. "The prick didn't show. I waited till midnight, then figured something must've gone wrong, you know, cops or something. I was going to call from there but figured you'd probably want me to get the hell out. Right?"

Rheume tried to focus. No way Petrov would have passed on the deal without calling. No, somehow Tasse must have figured it out, and somehow killed them all, or else one of them would have called.

"Yeah, of course," he said as calmly as he could. "Good thinking Marc. Where are you now?"

From the phone booth Tasse could see Rheume's building. It was less than a block away.

"Just coming into town," he lied. "Bout twenty minutes away. You want me to go home an' meet you later?"

"No, no," Rheume said, wide awake now. With a good hour until first light there was still time. Whatever went wrong didn't matter now, because now it was up to him to finish things. He pulled the curtains to the side and looked at the street. Everything looked quiet.

"Come over right away. We'll find out what happened. Petrov must have run into some kind of problem." His head began throbbing.

Tasse felt like saying, 'you bet they ran into a fuckin' problem,' but just smiled. Maybe he'd say that just before he put one between his eyes.

"Okay. See you in about twenty minutes."

He sauntered across the street, climbed into the driver's seat of the Pathfinder and, casually, without taking his eyes off the building, replaced the empty clip with the full one.

Rheume threw on a pair of black sweat pants and a dark-blue turtle-neck sweater. He seldom carried a gun but always had access to one. He kept a Beretta 9mm disassembled, and the pieces hidden throughout the apartment. If the cops searched his place, they'd have to find all of them to charge him, because if a gun couldn't be fired, then by law it wasn't a firearm.

It took a good five minutes to locate all the parts and put them together. That done, he unscrewed the vent plate in the bathroom and felt around for the nine-shot clip. Still there. Dusty, but that wouldn't matter. Inserting it into the bottom of the pistol grip, he worked the action, feeding a round into the chamber. He put on his black leather jacket, shoved the pistol in one pocket, and the cordless phone in the other. His heart was racing. Killing had always been delegated to others, but not this time. Now, one of three things was about to happen. One, he could screw up and get himself killed. Two, he could pull it off but get caught, which meant spending the rest of his life in prison. And three, he could kill Tasse and get away with it, which right now didn't seem like a slam dunk.

Rheume left the apartment and took the stairs to the main floor. When he opened the door to the rear parking lot he saw only two cars in the visitors' parking area, both near the far end of the building. Tasse always parked under the light right at the rear entrance. To the left of the door was a blue-grey wooden shed that housed the building's six metal trash cans. The slide bolt allowed residents easy access, and the walls had a one-inch space between the slats that allowed for ventilation, but was still small enough to keep rodents out. Rheume lifted one of the garbage cans, and put it in front of the shed as quietly as he could, then stepped inside, crouched down and closed the door.

• • • • • • •

Sitting in his Pathfinder, Tasse watched the windows of Rheume's apartment. Every light was on. Bastard's in there planning how he'll do it, he thought. Be nice to talk to him first, to find out why, but it doesn't really matter now.

"Gonna smile. Let me walk in, an' shoot me in the back. Yeah, that's your fuckin' style," he said, eyes riveted on the sixth floor lights. "Not tonight, cuz I'm gonna shoot you right in the middle of that friendly fuckin' smile as soon as you open the door."

Not the type to save for a rainy day, Tasse's running money totaled whatever he had in his wallet plus the two or three thousand dollars stuffed in the toe of an old pair of boots at the back of his closet. He did, however, have access to the nine kilos of coke left from Rheume's last order stashed in a rented storage locker in the east end. Not a bad severance package. Maybe a fresh start out in Vancouver, or maybe some place down south where it was always warm, yeah, that would be good.

The clock on the dash showed ten past five. It was time. He started the Pathfinder and slowly pulled out. With the Uzi on his lap, Tasse signaled as he approached 1706 Mont Royale and turned into the driveway that led to the rear of the building. Rheume would be watching, so everything had to look normal. Park in the usual spot, get out like nothing's wrong, and press the buzzer to be let in, just like he did every time he came over.

· · · · · · · ·

Rheume's stomach tightened as the Pathfinder came into view and pulled into the parking spot closest to the rear entrance. For the first time since he'd met Tasse, he was very afraid of him. Peering through the slats of the garbage shed he watched as Tasse studied the two cars at the far end of the lot before opening the driver's door. He walked cautiously to the shallow recess by the rear entrance, took a deep breath, then ran his finger down the name panel. He cleared his throat, and pushed the button beside suite 602, listed on the call board only as 'Occupied.' The glass on the panel gave a dim reflection of the parking lot behind him. The garbage can sitting outside the shed didn't register as a problem until he saw a movement of some kind from inside the shed. Something, no, someone.

"Fuck!" he said out loud, spinning around and reaching into his jacket. Three flashes flared out from between the slats in the shed. CRACK. CRACK. CRACK. The first one sent a searing pain ripping through his upper chest. The other two hit the wall to his left. Tasse managed to squeeze the trigger. The Uzi hissed like a rattle snake, splintering wood in an arc above Rheume's head as he got off two more quick shots The first ricocheted off the bricks to Tasse's right, but the second tore into his racing heart. He slumped into the corner of the alcove. What had been his life insurance policy slipped out of his hands clattering onto the cement. His head wobbled for a second or two, then flopped forward. Rheume stepped out of the garbage shed and over the body. He fumbled with the key for the back door as a half a dozen lights came on in the building. Inside he headed for the storage lockers in the basement.

CHAPTER THIRTY-SIX

16 MAY
San Diego
0700 hrs. local time

PAUL'S CHEST WOUND WAS HEALING NICELY, AND THIS MORNING for the first time his shower was pretty much pain free. Getting dressed he noticed his pager vibrating on the dresser. The display screen indicated two messages. Both from late last night. The first, a voice mail from Morgan, and the other from Len Cranston who'd left three numbers: One, two, and three. Number one meant the container had arrived. Two, picked up. And three, on the move. When the number four came in, it would mean the container had crossed into Alberta. Five into Saskatchewan, and so on.

"Well," Paul said when he walked into the kitchen. "Looks like Lenny's in business."

Jamie raised his coffee cup. "Here's hoping he can pull it off."

"Amen to that. So why don't we see if General Messina would like a drug lab," he said, picking up the phone.

• • • • • • •

General Enrico Messina, head of Colombia's Anti-Narcotics police. fought a war on drugs that really was a war. Last year alone, raids on heavily defended drug labs, bombings, and assassinations claimed the lives of over four hundred. Most of them his men, but a growing number of prosecutors, judges, outspoken politicians, and nosey journalists were becoming targeted as well. This war pitted the Anti-Narcotics police and military against not only the cartels, but also the well-trained and heavily armed Colombian Rebel Army. Once backed by the Soviet Union, they now financed their rebellion by kidnapping business executives, extortions, and hiring out to the drug cartels as security. To assist in the fight, the government invoked a law declaring that any drug suspect shot and killed during a drug raid was deemed to have been shot in self-defense. It cut down on court time, and paperwork.

· · · · · · · ·

The information Paul passed on would be verified by air reconnaissance to determine the exact location, and size, and to get an idea of the defenses they would encounter. Thick jungle made helicopters the only way of getting in, so operations such as these required meticulous planning, and General Messina left nothing to chance. The stakes were too high, and if the lab turned out to be the size described, defenses would be heavy, so the odds of casualties were high no matter how well the plan worked.

· · · · · · · ·

When Paul hung up, he listened to Morgan's message on his pager. It had come in around midnight last night.

"Judging from the sound of his voice, I think I'd better answer this from a pay phone," he said, picking up his jacket. "Be back in half an hour."

"You want us to come with you?" Tom asked.

"No, you'd better keep at it here. Depending on what he has to say, we may have to hurry things up."

Half an hour later, Paul arrived back. Jamie and Tom were working in the dining room.

"Okay, guys, it looks like we may have a little problem coming our way," he said, pulling up a chair.

"What's up Paul?" Tom asked, turning his chair around.

"Seems Morgan and Bonnie have been given some kind of deposition I have to sign. Has to be done right away so they're bringing it out here."

Jamie put an assortment of photographs on the table. "And no doubt our little friend is responsible."

"Yes, it makes sense. They haven't been able to find me, so this would give them the opportunity to follow them to us. Morgan's pretty sure it's linked to the DA's office. Anyway, they're bringing it out. They've arranged a military flight into Camp Pendleton rather than use the DEA. That should make it pretty difficult if it is a set-up."

"Think we oughta speed things up a bit?" Tom asked.

"I'd hate to tip our hand. The general should be making his move in a couple of days. How are the pictures coming, Jamie?"

"Very close. I estimate two to three hours should do it," Jamie said

"Good. So, let's figure out a plan on where and how to deal with this deposition thing. This is going to screw up our timeline a bit but shouldn't be a major problem."

Tom smiled. "I think I know the perfect place."

```
16 MAY
Miami. Florida
1020 hrs. local time
```

Bonnie held the phone between her cheek and neck talking to Morgan as she put her pistol in her handbag and closed it. "Cap says the papers were just delivered to the office, so I'll head over and pick them up. What're our travel arrangements?"

"Cap put me in touch with an old Marine Corp buddy of his. Good guy. He's arranged to get us on a Military flight leavin' from Ft. Myers. DEA'll fly us up there from Ft. Lauderdale. I talked to Paul an' he wants me to call him as soon as we're wheels up."

"Sounds confusing enough. When do we leave?" she asked.

"How about I pick you up at your place at one."

"Sounds good. I've got some running around to do on my way to the office, you need anything?"

"No thanks, I'm good."

"Okay, see you at one."

```
16 MAY
San Diego
0830 hrs. local time
```

The shadow angles, height differences, and coloring matched perfectly. Jamie handed the picture to Paul, who held it to the light, looking for any flaws. There were none.

"If they look at it under a magnifying glass, which I'm sure they will," Jamie said, rubbing his eyes. "They'll find something I put in there that should convince them it's authentic."

"Very impressive," Paul said and handed it across the table. "What do you think, Tom?"

"Not bad. Not bad at all. You sure you're not CIA trained?"

"Quite easy to tell I'm not," Jamie smiled, pointing at the picture. "As you can see, everything's in perfect focus."

Paul smiled. "I'm afraid he's got you there, Thomas. You need a hand with anything to get ready for the deposition thing.

"Don't think so Paul. I've got everything we'll need downstairs. Just gotta bag it up."

```
16 May
Provincial border between British
Columbia and Alberta
```

1000 hrs. local time

The longer the surveillance, the greater the chance of getting burned, so Cranston made sure the five vehicles relieving the Vancouver team at the Alberta border were different colors and makes. Keeping visual contact meant you were visible too, so rotating the vehicle with the eye every couple of miles lessened the chances.

Cranston's successes over the years gave him an edge when dealing with headquarters, so his idea of a training exercise to test response times and capabilities of the major drug sections across Canada had been well-received, since the amount of large drug shipments transported across Canada were on the increase. At the end of the exercise, each drug section would be critiqued to determine which needed more training, and, of course, which one was the best. Cranston explained that it would only be beneficial if everyone involved believed it to be a real investigation, and so it should begin sooner than later. Less chance that it would leak out. Once given the go-ahead, he surreptitiously passed it on to the officer in charge of each division that it was, in fact, an exercise, and the results would definitely reflect back on their management skills. He knew every officer in charge would be determined to win—a guarantee that the best men and equipment would be assigned.

The only permanent part of the entire exercise other than himself were three hand-picked Vancouver drug unit members. One rode with him; the other two followed a couple of miles behind the surveillance in a white cube van. The van carried spare radios, batteries, tracking equipment and ten burlap sacks, each containing fifty-one kilo bricks of simulated cocaine. The "K" Division team from Alberta were waiting on the outskirts of Banff, eager to take over.

16 May
Bogota, Colombia
1030 hrs. local time

Eduardo slammed his fist into the palm of his hand. "Rotten goddamned bastards," he roared. Pablo sat quietly, letting Eduardo vent his rage. They'd met in the small apartment above the Cardaro Club that they used as a safe place to discuss important matters. Pablo's father, back in his day, had set it up with the best electronics available to ensure privacy and Pablo had continued adding state-of-the-art frequency- jamming equipment, making it literally a dome of silence. It was accessible only by one door at the top of a metal staircase leading up from the back parking lot, and video surveillance cameras monitored not only the Cardaro club, but also the surrounding buildings. The furnishings were sparse, a square table with four wooden chairs, a faded blue sofa, and a coffee table. Under the window that overlooked the back lot was a sink with a short counter and a fridge. To the right of the counter, a small storage room for the club below that may have years ago been a bedroom. Pablo's father had told him that the sparseness should always be a reminder of where they came from, and where they could return if they started taking things for granted. DaLucca stood off to the side, stone-faced and silent.

· · · · · · · ·

Pablo shook his head. "We no longer have a choice, Eduardo. The longer we wait the more we look weak. Jimmy was family. We have to make an example of these pricks once and for all."

Rodriguez stopped pacing and sat down. After a few seconds, he nodded. "There is no other way."

"Then, we are as one with this decision, Eduardo?" Pablo asked, glancing at DaLucca, whose expression remained unchanged. Eduardo raised his head slowly.

"Yes ... yes we are."

Out of the corner of his eye, Pablo saw DaLucca nod ever so slightly.

Costa stood up. "Then we will begin immediately. Mani will go to Miami and prepare things, if that is satisfactory with you?"

"Yes, yes that's fine, and I want Williamson to be first," he said, then looked at DaLucca. "Mani, if I were younger I would go and do it myself. Tell whoever does this thing, I want him to feel the pain of losing someone he loves first, then I want him to die very slowly, do you understand?"

"I'll handle it personally, Mr. Rodriguez."

"Thank you," Eduardo sighed. "Uh … Mani, it would be a favor to me if Jimmy's brother Ernesto went with you."

Mani hated the idea. Just someone else to worry about and get in the way.

"Of course," he said. "I think as highly of Ernesto as I did of Jimmy."

"Thank you, Mani."

CHAPTER THIRTY-SEVEN

16 MAY
Ft. Lauderdale International Airport
1400 hrs. local time

THE DEA'S TURBO PROP KING AIR GENTLY LIFTED OFF. IT WAS designed to carry nine comfortably plus a two-man crew, but today the two detectives were the only passengers. The pilot and co-pilot were both ex-fighter jocks, having flown numerous combat missions in Iraq. As soon as they leveled off, the pilot turned to them.

"Ya'all help yerselves to a coffee an' enjoy. Weather looks real good. Should be a beautiful flight. We'll be on the tarmac at Fort Myers in jest shy of an hour."

"Appreciate the lift," Morgan said, giving a thumbs up.

They sat in seats facing each other and Morgan pulled a small table up and out from the bulkhead and locked it into place between them. Bonnie filled two cups from a stainless steel thermos and handed one to him.

Bonnie took a sip. "If it's a set-up, you figure traveling this way will shake them off?"

"It should," he said, opening a pack of sugar. "One thing's for sure, if it doesn't, we're gonna be right in the middle of it."

Bonnie held her cup with both hands as the plane bounced through a billowy white cloud. "So that would make the leak somewhere in the DA's office."

"Sure does look like it. Paul's been able to keep himself pretty much invisible so Costa's figured the only way to get to him is through us. He pulls some strings, gets the deposition thing happening, an' hopes to follow us to our guy."

"Paul worried?" she asked.

Morgan shook his head. "It was like he expected it. Sounded about as concerned as if I'd told him his dinner was gonna be five minutes late."

```
16 MAY Bogota, Colombia
1400 hrs. local time
```

As soon as pre-raid briefings began, the base went on full lockdown. No personal calls in or out, and no passes. The platoon leaders took their seats around the large oval table in the conference room. General Messina stood at the podium waiting for everyone to be seated. Behind him on a viewing screen was an enlarged aerial photograph of the lab and surrounding area. The locations they would be dealing with were numbered one through ten. When Major Alvarez closed the door the room fell silent.

The general turned to the screen. "Number one. .. here," he said, tapping with his pointer. "Is the lab itself."

An enlargement of the lab came on the screen. It showed a long, low building with a roof made of corrugated metal covered with camouflage netting.

"These two smaller buildings on either side of the lab here ... and here, appear to be sleeping quarters and probably storage for chemicals and equipment."

The surveillance photo of the overall area came back up again. "Number two is an observation tower, right here behind the lab, almost hidden by the jungle.

It has a good overall view of approaching aircraft. On the fly-over, infra-red indicated two guards, so for our purposes we'll assume there's always two. Numbers three, four, and five are machine gun bunkers. Two protecting each side of the lab and the third ... here on this stretch of high ground about fifty yards in front of the others. You can see their fields of fire overlap, so all ground approaches are covered. Number six is the landing strip, approximately seventy-five yards from the lab and, judging from its length, capable of handling everything up to smaller executive jets. Number seven, this camouflaged area near the end of the runway, are drums of aviation fuel. Looks like there could be a couple of hundred." He looked around the room. "Keep your men well clear of them. Lastly, off to the east, these areas marked eight, nine and ten, will be our designated landing zones: Alpha. Bravo. And Charlie."

· · · · · · · ·

Major Jose Alvarez made his way around the table handing each platoon leader an operation booklet containing maps, co-ordinates, and an outline of each target.

"The final decision on the LZ s ," the General continued, "will be based on wind direction prior to our departure at 0300 hours tomorrow. As of now it looks like the wind will be from the north at ten to fifteen knots. Unless there's a change, A and B platoons will land at LZ Alpha and C and D here at LZ Bravo." He raised his pointer, tapping both spots on the map. "The distance from the target is approximately two kilometres, so the wind should drown out engine noises. Arrival at the LZ s will be 0330 hours. Questions?" The room remained quiet. "Once on the ground all platoons will make their way here and rendezvous at 0445 hours." He pointed to a spot west of the air strip. "C and D Platoons will follow this creek bed east along the tree line ... to this point here. This will put them in a position to take out the observation tower and provide cover fire on the machine gun bunker to the left of the tower. A and B platoons will circle right and engage the other two bunkers." He stopped again, giving the platoon leaders a chance to make whatever notations they needed. "My chopper will assist taking out the machine gun defenses and the fuel drums. Major Alvarez and his crew will take out the supply sheds and deal with any unforeseen problems." He moved his pointer to the dense jungle behind the observation platform. "We have no way of knowing what they have in the bush back here. Recon didn't pick up heat signatures, but we should expect sensors, booby traps, or even more rebels. Now, if there are no questions, we will assemble in Hanger 1 at 0200 hours. Have your men get some sleep. Tomorrow will be a long day."

Major Alvarez called the room to attention, snapped a salute then turned and dismissed his men.

CHAPTER THIRTY-EIGHT

16 MAY
Camp Pendleton, California
1500 hrs. local time

NO MATTER HOW SEASONED THE FLYER MAY BE, IN THAT LAST minute before touching down, everyone feels a little wave of apprehension. This feeling is brought about by a combination of the weather, the way-too-young pilot, and/or the sudden realization that military aircrafts are built by the lowest bidder. Bonnie watched out the window as they descended towards roof tops and afternoon traffic. As the ground came up to meet them, the sensation of speed increased until, in the last seconds, the edge of the tarmac became a blur. With one gentle bounce the wheels of the C-130 hugged the runway. The roar of the reverse thrusters vibrated everything in the cabin that wasn't riveted down. Outside it was another beautiful sunny day in Southern California.

· · · · · · ·

Camp Pendleton, bordered by Riverside County on the north and San Diego County to the south, is busy twenty-four-seven, all year long. Every type of aircraft the U.S. military has comes and goes from Pendleton. Marines and equipment are constantly shuttled back and forth to U.S. bases and trouble spots around the world.

A member of the cargo crew led Morgan and Bonnie down the transport's loading ramp just as a jeep screeched to a stop at the bottom of the ramp. The driver—wearing an impeccably tailored uniform with razor-sharp creases stepped out—snapped to attention, and saluted.

"Detectives Connors and Story?" he asked.

"Yes ..." said Morgan, almost returning the salute.

"I'm Corporal MacDonald, sir ... ma'am," he said, picking up Bonnie's suitcase. "If you'll please climb in, Colonel Lambert's expecting you."

Morgan helped put their bags in the rear of the jeep and climbed in after them. A little taken aback by the reception, he caught Bonnie's attention and raised his eyebrows. She returned the look.

"Who's Colonel Lambert?" Morgan asked as the jeep sped across the tarmac between two of the huge grey-and-white hangers that lined the length of the runway.

The Corporal turned his head without taking his eyes off the road. "He's the Ops officer, sir. Hell of a guy. Keeps this place running, on time, all the time."

From the back seat, Morgan tapped Bonnie on the shoulder. "I've never been to Pendleton before," he yelled over the noise of the jeep and the roar of the aircraft waiting to takeoff

"Nor me," Bonnie called back.

"I was at Coronado Naval Station on my way to Seoul in eighty-two. It sure wasn't like this. A lot more laid-back, and quieter. Probably cuz ships move slower. It must rub off on you."

Corporal MacDonald laughed and hollered over his shoulder. "Heck, sir. Ol' president Clinton's got us goin' all over the globe, mainly Iraq an' Afghanistan. This is what we call normal around here."

Turning right, they slowed to the posted limit of thirty miles per hour. A couple more turns, and they were on a narrow street that was lined with identical two-story red brick office buildings, each with a small patch of manicured lawn in the front.

· · · · · · · ·

The jeep stopped in front of the building at the end of the road. The sign on the patch of lawn said 'Operation Control Center.'

"If you'll follow me," the Corporal said as he got out. "Don't worry about your bags. I'll take care of them."

He led them through the front doors and down a long hallway lined with windows on the right side and office doors on the left. Highly polished beige linoleum glistened in the sunlight that shone through the windows, and smelled of floor wax and Pinesol. At the end of the hall, the sign on the door of the last office read, 'Col. P. Lambert - Operations Officer.' The door was open; the man behind the desk rose as they approached.

"Welcome to Camp Pendleton folks," he said, extending his hand and smiling pleasantly. "I'm Peter Lambert. Please, come in."

Mid-fifties with thinning grey hair cut in a short brush cut, Colonel Lambert was slim, sinewy, and had a rock-hard build. That, along with a weathered face, spoke volumes about the way he approached the life he'd chosen. "Hope you had a good flight," he said, shaking their hands.

"Excellent, thank-you, sir," Morgan said, not realizing he had come to attention.

Bonnie couldn't help smiling. "Nice to meet you, Colonel," she said.

The office was about the same size as Captain Jacobs', but that's where the similarities ended. The colonel's office verged on sterile. The desk blotter looked like it had never been used—no hastily jotted-down names, no numbers or coffee mug ring stains, not even one doodle. Even the green, metal waste basket was empty. As though no garbage had ever been generated in this place. One grey three-drawer filing cabinet stood in the corner, and it, too, looked like it had been spit polished. The back and side walls were covered with certificates, plaques, pictures, and commendations. Together they provided a capsulated military history of the colonel, from basic training, a stint in the Green Berets, Vietnam, Military intelligence, to Desert Storm. Morgan scanned the walls. It was abundantly clear that this man had managed to place himself in harm's way throughout his entire career.

· · · · · · · ·

Corporal MacDonald brought in another chair, saluted, then turned and left after Colonel Lambert returned the salute. "Thanks corporal." He gestured towards the chairs. "Please have a seat, folks. Paul will be calling in about fifteen minutes. Can I offer you a coffee, or a tea? I prefer tea myself."

Morgan was starting to feel more at ease. "A coffee would be nice, thanks, colonel."

"Please, call me Peter... uh, it's Bonnie and Morgan, right?"

They both nodded. "A tea would be lovely," Bonnie said.

He picked up the phone and passed the order on.

Morgan scanned the plaques and pictures "Colonel, how did you come to know Paul?"

"Well," he said, hesitating. "What has he told you about his past?"

"He filled us in on some of his service in Israel, and about some of the operations he was involved in," Morgan said, trying to make it sound like he knew a lot more than he really did.

"Actually," the Colonel began. "I've only met him once, in the Gulf, just before things got going in '91. I air dropped him and his team into western Iraq one night and picked them up three nights later. Intelligence had confirmed a SCUD storage facility tucked away in the middle of a mountain about a hundred miles from the Syrian border. Short of a nuke it would've been impossible to take out. Colonel Goldman and his boys went in, located it, rigged it, and made their way back without a living soul knowing they'd been there. You got to remember, for Saddam's plan to work he had to get Israel involved so he started lobbing Scuds into and around Tel Aviv. If he'd pulled it off Jordan, Syria, and with a bit of luck, all the other Islamic countries would rally behind him. A long shot, but the guy's always been a poker player, albeit not always a good one. Anyway, what Paul's team did went unreported. They were never there. So a couple of minutes after the first cruise missiles were launched into Baghdad, that mountain disappeared off the map. I'm a close friend with one of the guy's he's working with now, Tom Corbet. We go way back. One thing about the military, the longer you're in, the more you're gonna owe somebody, an' I owe him big time. Must be the same for you guys in the police?"

"Yeah," Morgan said, thinking of Ron Grange. "It's sorta like that."

The colonel opened the middle drawer of his desk, took out two business cards and handed one to each of them. "Paul speaks very highly of you two. Don't know what you folks are up to, but whatever it is, if you need anything, anything at all, whether it's a stapler or a Stealth, call me. I mean it."

There was a knock at the door. Morgan and Bonnie looked at each other.

"Ahh. .. tea," Lambert said. "Come in, corporal."

• • • • • • •

The phone rang just in the nick of time. The colonel had just asked Morgan about his military service, which paled in comparison. Having been between conflicts, so to speak, it was hardly worthy of conversation in the presence of this man. Lambert reached answered the phone.

"Colonel Lambert," he said. "Yes, fine, put him through please. Paul, good to hear you… you're more than welcome ... yes they arrived safe and sound. Not a problem, glad I could help. Pass on my regards to Tom will you? ... great ... yes, he's right here."

He handed the phone across the desk.

"Hey, Paul," Morgan said, then listened as Paul explained briefly what was going to happen. The drive south to San Diego would determine if they were being followed. The colonel would fill them in on any details they needed to know. Morgan noticed there was a distinct difference in the sound of his voice. Friendly, but definitely in charge.

"Okay, Paul, talk to you soon," he said, handing the receiver back to the Colonel.

• • • • • • •

Corporal MacDonald was putting their bags in the trunk of the rented Intrepid as the Colonel walked them out into the parking lot. He handed Bonnie a portable radio.

"Tom had the car dropped off earlier," he said. "You'll be working off channel seventeen. Frequency's scrambled so it's secure. One of Paul's guys will contact you once you've cleared the base."

"One of Paul's guys?" Morgan asked, looking over at him..

Peter Lambert shook their hands and smiled. "Better safe than sorry. Oh, and don't forget, you've got my card"

Morgan put his briefcase on the back seat, rolled the window down, and started the engine. Bonnie smiled and waved from the passenger side. "Thanks for everything, Peter."

"No problem," he said, returning the wave. "And you folks be careful."

• • • • • • •

At the main gate the guard snapped to attention and saluted. The gate rose in front of them and Morgan drove through, turned left and followed the signs to Interstate 5 South. Less than a mile from Camp Pendleton, the portable beside Bonnie crackled to life. The thick British accent and formal tone reminded Bonnie of the beginning of the old television show *Mission Impossible*.

"Good-day Detective Connors...Detective Story. My name is Jamie Ryan. I shall be providing counter surveillance during our little trip today. If I feel you are being followed, we will take steps to confirm and then rectify the situation."

Bonnie picked up the portable radio and keyed the mike. "Copy that Jamie. We're just about to go onto the I-5 South now."

"Excellent," he replied. "Hopefully this will be nothing more than a pleasant drive for all of us. Okay, I believe I have you coming onto the freeway now. Would you confirm by tapping your brake two times."

The brake lights flashed twice.

"Got you. I'll radio check every five minutes."

"Copy that, Jamie, thanks," she said then put the radio on her lap.

Morgan signaled, merged into the slow lane and let out a laugh.

"What's so funny?" she asked.

"Don't you see Bon?"

"See what?"

"Not only does he have his own little army ... he's got the entire U.S. Marine Corp for back up."

Bonnie checked the passenger side mirror. "Yeah ... I'm starting to worry a lot less about his security that's for sure."

· · · · · · ·

Jamie radioed, asking that they stay in the slow lane about five miles an hour below the speed limit. The majority of California drivers pushed the envelope by at least ten over, so any tail should be easy to spot. They drove in silence for a long time. Morgan glanced over. She'd untied her hair, letting the wind from the open window jostle it back and forth. He'd only seen her wear it down a couple of times.

She sensed him staring. "What? Oh, I know. My hair. Looks stupid right. Don't worry I'll do something with it."

"No really, I like it like that ... seriously."

"Yeah, right," she said, giving him a friendly slap across the shoulder.

....

They passed the exit for Oceanside. Fifteen seconds later so did Jamie's rented blue Mustang. He picked up the mike. "So far we're clean. Carlsbad's coming up in a few minutes."

Bonnie picked up the radio. "Copy that."

Jamie watched the Intrepid about a quarter of a mile in front of him. Taking his cell phone out of his pocket, he punched in Paul's number.

....

Paul was putting a large canvas bag into the trunk of Tom's car when his cell rang.

He glanced at the number "How goes it Jamie?"

"Nothing I've been able to spot yet. How are you chaps doing?"

"All set at this end. As soon as you call, we're out of here. If it's going to happen they should be on you by now."

"Yes, I agree. I had a good look when we left Pendleton for non-military aircraft but haven't seen a damn thing out of the ordinary. I'll keep you posted."

"Good. Hard to believe Costa would pass up an opportunity like this."

"Right you are, unless the military flight threw him off, but I think not."

After pressing the end button, Jamie picked up the portable.

"There's a rest stop a few miles ahead. Why don't you pull in for five minutes or so. That'll give me a chance to check out our situation a bit more."

Bonnie held the microphone below the dashboard and answered. "Will do, Jamie."

A white Ford pick-up, red Volkswagen, and a rusted-out black Monte Carlo signaled from the merge lane and pulled in behind the Intrepid. A gold Cadillac followed by a green Chevy van merged in behind Jamie.

• • • • • • • •

Within half a mile all had passed the two slower vehicles except the van. It stayed well behind Jamie. He could see it was an older model and looked like it needed body work. He slowed down a bit, and the van began closing the gap.

He keyed his mike. "Got a green Chev van behind me. Possibly one of the few slow drivers in America, but I'll let him pass, and we'll see what he does. Let's cancel on the rest stop."

"Copy that Jamie."

Signaling, he slowed, pulled onto the paved shoulder and stopped. The van passed. There were no side windows, and the driver was alone in the front. A magnetic sign on the passenger door read 'Standard Electrical Contractors.' Jamie waited a few seconds before pulling back out. The van was still well back of the Intrepid.

"The van is the first behind you in the same lane. Can you see him?" he asked.

Morgan checked the rearview and Bonnie the side mirror. "Just now and then. He's quite a ways back," she answered adjusting the mirror with her free hand.

• • • • • • • •

Jamie kept pace with the van, keeping it about a quarter mile ahead. "Okay," he said, picking a map off the passenger seat.

"Let's slow down another five miles an hour and see what he does shall we."

The van started closing on the Intrepid, then slowed.

"Right then," he said running his finger along the map. "The next exit should be Highway 42, about a mile or so ahead. Turn right when you get off the freeway and pull into the first petrol station you come to."

"Copy that. Highway 42, turn right. What if he doesn't see us take the exit?" she asked.

"If he's by himself and doesn't see you exit he should go right on past. If not, he must have company."

Jamie checked the sky as best he could, but driving made it impossible to be sure.

"We're taking the exit now," Bonnie radioed.

Morgan stopped at the stop sign, signaled and turned right. There was an Exxon station up ahead on the right-hand side.

"Grab the briefcase, Bon," he said, watching the rearview mirror. "Better load 'em."

The van approached the cut off to Highway 42. At the last second it veered into the exit lane. Jamie came off the I-5 just as the van made a right turn at the stop sign.

"We're at the Exxon station Jamie, about half a mile down." Bonnie's voice was calm. They were at work now.

"Right you are," Jamie said. "And our little green friend is coming your way. Okay, we've got brake lights … approaching the Exxon station, slowing down … and turning left into the car lot across the road from you."

Bonnie adjusted her side mirror. "Copy that. We've got an eye."

· · · · · · ·

The knock on the driver's side window startled Morgan. The gas station attendant, a gangly kid with red frizzy hair and a wispy beard smiled. "Fill'er up, sir?"

"Uh, yeah, sure, please," Morgan said.

Jamie scanned the sky carefully. "No sign of any aircraft," he said, speaking quietly into the mike. "Must have got to the car somehow. Got to be a tracker. How they did that beats the devil out of me. What's it doing now?"

Bonnie adjusted her side mirror. "Just sitting between the office of the used car lot and the brick building next to it, facing us. No one's got in or out."

The attendant replaced the gas Cap and jogged back to the driver's window.

"She only took eight bucks worth sir."

"Really," Morgan said, handing him a ten. "Gauge must be screwed. Thanks, keep the change."

"Hey, thanks, man."

Bonnie waited until the attendant headed back to the station before talking into the mike. "What's the call, Jamie?"

"Stand by. I'm checking in now."

"I think you're right, Jamie, must be a tracker," Paul said. "When you get to the exit for Solana Beach head east. It's going to take us at least an hour to get set up," Paul said, nodding to Tom, who grabbed his sunglasses and keys. "Have them stop for a bite to eat. That'll kill some time. We'll get back to you with directions, and better have Morgan call me from a pay phone when you stop"

"Will do. I have exactly fifteen forty-five," Jamie said, checking his watch.

"Fifteen forty-five it is," Paul replied. "We're on our way."

Half an hour later Morgan pulled the Intrepid into the parking lot of the Morrison's Steak and Sea Food House at the junction of the I-5 and the Solana Beach cut-off.

"Take your time," Jamie radioed. "An hour should do nicely. Once you get settled give Paul a call, and he'll fill you in."

"You think I should give the highway patrol a heads up?" Morgan asked.

"Perhaps talk to Paul first," Jamie replied, watching the van nestle in to a parking space between two pick-ups across the street from the restaurant. Jamie parked in front of a business called Kingfisher Charters next to the Steak House. From there he could keep an eye on the van and still see Bonnie and Morgan sitting at one of the window booths. With binoculars, he made out the silhouettes of three, possibly four others in the rear of the van crouched down behind the driver.

Morgan walked to the pay phones near the front door while Bonnie listened to the waitress read the daily specials off the back of her order pad. When she finished, Bonnie ordered two coffee, a tossed green salad with oil and vinegar dressing for herself, and what her partner ate at least once a week, a clubhouse with fries.

When Paul picked up, Morgan could tell from the background noise that he was in a moving vehicle.

"Hey, Paul. It's Morgan."

"Hi Morgan," Paul said. "Has Jamie explained what's happening?"

"Yeah, no doubt what they're up to. Your friend Jamie definitely knows what he's doin'."

"You're in good hands. He's one of the best. Listen, I'm sorry you two have turned out to be the bait in this but …"

"Not to worry, just let me know when you want me to call in the …"

"No," Paul cut in. "I don't want you to call anyone."

An elderly woman picked up the phone beside him and began dialing. Morgan lowered his voice to a whisper and turned his back to her.

"Uh, then what are you thinkin' about doing?"

"Listen, remember a while back I said I would defend myself if I had to?"

Morgan shifted uncomfortably. "Yeah, but what's that got to do with this, I mean we're on to them already?"

"Once they follow you to me I want you and Bonnie to keep going. Check into a hotel in San Diego and let us handle things from there. With any luck it'll be the last time we'll have to worry. Page me later tonight, and we'll meet in the morning for breakfast. I'll sign the deposition and you can tell the DA and the mayor everything went just fine."

Morgan knew it was useless to argue. He looked back at Bonnie who was talking to the waitress as she poured the coffee. The woman on the phone beside him hung up and walked into the restaurant.

"Paul, Bon and I've talked it over. Don't know exactly who your friends are, but I'm startin' to get a pretty good idea, and so what I'm sayin' is, we're in no matter how it goes down and that's that."

"That's not a wise move," Paul said, his voice louder. "Morgan, I want you to understand what I'm saying here. What's going to go down in the next little while isn't going to be anything like a police takedown or arrest. Let me be very clear, the people in that van are here to kill me, and both of you if you're around. It's just that simple. I don't want you guys to be any part of it, because there aren't going to be any arrests."

Bonnie was watching him now.

"I'll call you right back," he said, and hung up.

"What the hell's wrong?" She asked as he slid into the booth. "You look like you've seen a ghost."

He leaned over, keeping his voice low. "We got a decision to make Bon, an' one way or the other, we gotta both agree on this."

A couple of minutes later Morgan walked back to the pay phones.

"Paul?"

"Yes, go ahead, Morgan."

"Okay Paul, here's the deal. Who all's in the van, or how they try to pull this off ...well fuck'em. We're in and that's all there is to it. If not, we'll drive this fuckin' car all the way back to Miami with those assholes followin' us."

"Come on, Morgan. Think for a minute. If you and Bonnie get ..."

"No," he said cutting him off. "Now you listen. We're in, period, end of fuckin' story. We didn't travel across the goddamned country to sit on our ass in some crummy hotel room while that prick takes another run at you. We're sick and tired of his shit, so like it or not you're stuck with us, man."

Paul let out a long sigh. "Morgan, you're making a difficult situation more difficult here. You've both got to be willing and able to live with this. Do you understand? Not just for a month or two. Forever."

"Like I said, we're in. We're armed. End of story."

Paul didn't answer right away, then: "Okay, okay. We'll see you in about an hour, and Morgan?"

"Yeah, Paul."

"When things happen, they're going to happen fast. Changing your mind won't be an option."

"Got it. See you in about an hour."

CHAPTER THIRTY-NINE

16 MAY
Anza-Borrego Desert
1740 hrs. local time

THE REMNANTS OF THE SUTTER MINING COMPANY WERE LOCATED approximately six miles off Highway S22 between Borrego Springs and the Salton Sea. Its glory days went back to the first part of the nineteenth century. It consisted of a man-made pit some fifty-feet deep covering an area of about a hundred and fifty square yards. There were three mine shafts, two of them long since caved in. The entrance to the third was sealed with a thick metal grate and padlock.

In the early twenties the gold per ton ratio began declining and by the time the great depression hit the gold, like the economy, had dried up. The miners walked away broke, leaving everything to the insects, lizards, and snakes. The remains of two small wooden shacks, bleached white from decades of scorching sun, and the rusted skeleton of the mine's conveyer belt system were the only structures still standing. A wooden water tower had long ago succumbed to time and the elements and now lay rotting between two overgrown slag piles that resembled worn down pyramids. The turnoff from Highway S22 was marked only by a post that had probably held a sign years ago. With daytime temperatures well over 100 degrees there was little doubt that if you were looking for the middle of nowhere, the Sutter Mine would be a real good bet. Tom had come across it on one of his five-day survival treks a few years ago, and figured it would do nicely.

1800 hrs.

They could pick intermittent voices out of the radio static.

"They're gettin' close," Tom said, closing the trunk.

"Yes," Paul said, then nodded towards the rusted ladder that led to the top of the conveyer system. "You okay with that?"

Tom slung the leather rifle case over his shoulder and squinted up to what was left of a small, control shed perched at the top.

"Long as it'll hold a hundred and seventy," he said, testing the first rung of the metal ladder. It groaned under his weight. "Well," he said, taking a deep breath, "let's give 'er a shot."

Paul steadied the ladder as Tom carefully started the climb. Finally reaching the top, he wedged himself into the tiny control shed. Not a lot of room to maneuver around but it gave him pretty much a 360 degree view of the mine and anything approaching the top of the depression. Except for the far sides of the two slag piles, he would be able to see everything. He re-arranged a few of the rotted boards to better hide himself.

"Looks good from here," he radioed down. "I should be able to call it no matter how they approach. Christ almighty, they must have been small guys back in the day. I hardly got room to change my mind in this damn thing."

"Yeah, well, don't start dancing around up there or the whole thing'll come down."

"Copy that. Sounds like you've seen me dance."

· · · · · · · ·

Paul found an old forty-five gallon drum between the two shacks and rolled it out front. Inside one of the shacks he found a shovel with the stub of its wooden handle still attached. He used it to fill the drum halfway. Ten yards to his left, what remained of a cast iron boiler once used to power the conveyor belt would make for good secondary cover if needed.

"Paul. Can you copy?" Bonnie's voice was clear now. "We've just turned off the highway onto the dirt road."

Paul put down the shovel and keyed the mike. "I copy you, Bonnie. We're ready for you here. Just stay on what's left of the road, and it will bring you right to us. About five miles and a bit."

Tom indicated he'd heard by touching his earpiece and giving a thumbs up.

Jamie spoke into his radio as he watched the van half a mile ahead of him. "Looks like it's pulling over near the turn off. They're either deciding what to do, or their equipment is giving them problems. No, here we go, they're in. Ladies and gentlemen, show time."

One at a time everyone acknowledged.

· · · · · · · ·

Jamie gave the van thirty seconds before turning off the highway. "The van is confirmed as the only player," he radioed, speeding up to close the distance. The dust cloud, spewing up behind the van, would make it impossible for them to see anything behind.

Ten minutes later, Morgan stopped the Intrepid at the top of the depression. Below he could see one vehicle and Paul standing in front of a shack. No one else.

He looked over at Bonnie. "Christ, I hope he knows what he's doin'," he said, easing their vehicle down the narrow, dirt roadway. At the bottom he drove to the shack and stopped. Bonnie rolled the window down.

"They're about a minute behind us, Paul. Where do you want us?"

"Actually, I'd like you in San Diego, but I know that's not going to happen, so, let's leave the car here and stand with me. Once they're convinced it's just the three of us and they commit to coming down, I want one of you on each of those slag piles, about two-thirds the way up. Tom's got the eye from the shed at the top of the conveyor belt. He'll let us know how many are coming and in what direction. We've got one spare radio," he said, handing it to Bonnie as she got out of the car. "Morgan, you can use the one from your car. Here," he said, handing them each an earpiece. "More than likely they'll split up and come on foot. That'll leave Jamie with the high ground."

They listened carefully as Paul calmly explained the situation. "If any of them have any training at all, they'll split up and try to get us in a cross-fire by flanking us. Now, I know I said it before, but these people aren't here to threaten, rob, or make any kind of deal. They're here to kill all of us, pure and simple, so when you sight in on your target take him out. If you've got a problem with that, and I sure as hell don't blame you if you do, you've got to leave ... now."

Morgan looked over at Bonnie as Tom's voice broke the silence.

"Got dust about a quarter mile ... closin' fast."

Bonnie nodded at Paul. "We're in."

"Okay. How many spare clips?" he asked.

"Four," Morgan said, putting two in each of his jacket pockets. After a couple of shootouts during his career he knew that nobody, cop or bad guy is accurate when being fired at, and running out of ammo during a shoot-out can really ruin your day.

"I've got three," Bonnie said. An excellent shot on the range she'd never had to fire her gun on the job.

"Okay, my young friends, let's stand and chat. Oh, by the way, welcome to California."

"Stand by," Tom's voice crackled through their earpieces. "They're here."

From a slit between two of the planks he watched the van stop twenty or thirty yards from the crest of the depression. The driver got out, crouched down and made his way to within ten yards from the edge, then got on his stomach and crawled the rest of the way. Peering over the edge, the driver spied the two detectives standing talking to a man who fit the description he'd been given. Their car was beside an old shack with another one parked nearby. No sign of a trap, and the only way out was the way they'd come in. He studied the rest of the mine area then, satisfied, squirmed backwards until he could stand without being seen, got up, and jogged back to the van.

· · · · · · · ·

"Okay," Tom radioed. "He's back at the van."

"Go," Paul said, patting them both on the shoulder.

They scrambled up the steep slopes of the slag piles. Near the top, Morgan scooped away a layer of rocks still hot from the afternoon sun to get a better foothold and hopefully conceal himself a little. Across from him on the other pile, he saw Bonnie doing the same.

The side door of the van opened and four men climbed out and gathered around the driver.

Tom held a small monocular with one hand and his portable in the other. "Got a total of five bad guys. Looks like the driver is in charge," he said, watching as one of them opened a duffel bag and started handing out weapons. "Okay, we've got a Ruger mini fourteen with oversized clip, an' one, Christ, it looks like a Sanna seventy-seven with back-to-back forties. Got a short-barrel twelve-gauge pump, no, make that two, an' I can't make out what kind of rifle the driver grabbed, but it's scoped."

Morgan looked at his service pistol. "Well ain't this just fuckin' wonderful," he muttered out loud, then wriggled around to work himself a little deeper into the slag heap.

Paul crouched behind the sand filled drum and keyed his mike. "Jamie, how you making out?"

"I'm on foot. The van is about fifty yards ahead," he whispered into his mike. "I'm closing in now."

"Heads up, people," Tom broke in. "We got the Sanna and a shotgun moving to flank our right, an' the mini an' the other twelve gauge moving left. Looks like the driver's stayin' on the ridge. He'll be yours, Jamie. Don't see any radios or earpieces so they gotta be wingin' it from here on. Okay, I've lost the two on the right behind the slag pile. Coming your way, Bonnie."

"Copy, coming my way," she whispered into her mike.

The sun was at her back so until they made it into the shadows, she'd be impossible to see. She wiped the sweat from her eyes on the shoulder of her blouse and took a firmer, two-handed grip on her pistol. "Calm down now, girl," she whispered. "Deep breaths." From the other side of the slag pile she heard the sound of crunching gravel.

· · · · · · · ·

Tom didn't have time to properly site in the scope before they left, but from this distance it wouldn't make a difference. The heavy-barreled Sterling 7.62 mm had the standard four-round magazine and, although an older model, was still considered to be one of the more accurate sniper rifles.

Jamie reached the back of the van and could see the driver had taken a position at the crest of the depression laying on his stomach, legs spread, scanning the mine site through the rifle's scope.

"Heads up, Morgan," Tom called. "The shotgun just split from the mini. They're comin' round either side. You'll have the shotgun in view any second. Paul, the fourteen's comin' your way."

"Copy that," Paul answered. "I'll have the mini."

Tom shifted to get a better look at the other slag pile. "Bonnie... the Sanna and shotgun are probably doing the same. I've got whoever comes to your right." As he spoke the shotgun came into the cross hairs of the Sterling.

The loud crack echoed through the silent desert, startling everyone except the dead man with the pump twelve-gauge who dropped without so much as a gasp. A split second later the long-quiet Sutter Mining Company exploded back to life.

· · · · · · · ·

From his position at the crest of the depression, the van's driver saw the Sterling's muzzle flash. He quickly re-adjusted himself and aimed at the control shed. It was small enough that, even though he couldn't see, a couple of shots in the middle of it should kill anyone inside. Coming up behind him, Jamie didn't have time to aim. He squeezed the trigger of his M16 twice, sending two, three-round bursts at the prone figure who disappeared in a cloud of dust, but not before he got a shot off. When Jamie reached the twitching body, he heard Tom's voice in his earpiece.

"I'm hit, not bad … but my weapon's fucked. All I can do is spot."

The mini-14 dove for cover as Paul fired, sending stones whirring through the air. He keyed his mike. "Copy, Tom. Jamie where are you?"

"At the van. Driver's down," he said, rolling the corpse over and digging the keys out of a bloodied pocket.

"I'm bringing the van down."

Morgan rolled left as a shotgun blast exploded beside him, sending shards of rock zinging over him. The mini 14 tried to get a shot, but Paul kept him pinned down. Bonnie saw the shotgun fire another blast that hit just above Morgan's head. She fired and missed.

"Shit," she said, firing again. Her second shot hit him just above the knee. He let out a yelp and hobbled behind the slag pile.

"Bonnie," Tom yelled into the mike. "Look out! Roll right! Roll right!"

She rolled onto her back and raised her pistol as the Sanna 77 opened up, sending a stream of bullets snaking up from ten feet below her and tearing across her body. She then toppled forward, falling like a rag doll, arms and legs flailing in a surreal slow motion until her body finally came to rest at the bottom in a twisted heap.

Paul darted towards the boiler. The Sanna tried to make it behind the slag pile but the six or seven feet might as well have been a mile. Paul fired four quick shots and, in one last seemingly defiant gesture, the Sanna 77, advertised in South Africa with the slogan "a farm without a Sanna, is like a yacht without a sail," emptied itself into the late afternoon sky.

• • • • • • •

The van swerved across the floor of the mine. The shooter with the mini 14 scrambled from the far side of the slag pile, waving frantically as the van approached. The initial plan was for it to come down when the shooting stopped, but nothing had gone according to any plan. Morgan used both hands to take aim; he fired until his clip was empty dropping the mini 14 as the van roared by. Jamie slammed on the brakes and skidded to a stop beside the shacks. The firing stopped. For a second no one moved. Then, Morgan lunged down the steep slope.

"Bonnie," he screamed. "Christ, please no," Losing his balance, he tripped and tumbled down the last twenty feet. He clambered to his feet, stumbled to where her body lay, and fell to his knees beside her. Paul covered him and keyed his mike.

"Tom. Give me a count."

"Four confirmed. One twelve gauge missing, must be the other side of Morgan's slag pile."

"Got it." Paul tapped his chest and pointed right. Jamie nodded and moved left.

Morgan rolled her over carefully. Her face and hair were matted with dirt and blood.

"How bad?" Tom's voice crackled through the radio.

"Bad! Real bad, we gotta get help … fast."

"I'm on it," he said, already punching the numbers on his cell.

Paul and Jamie circled around either side of the slag heap. A glint of light reflected off the shotguns barrel as it rose from behind a thicket of scrub brush.

"In front of you," Paul yelled, crouching low and squeezing the trigger.

Jamie fired at the same time. They waited until the dust settled before making their way over. Paul lowered his gun.

"Count's confirmed at five," he called into the radio.

· · · · · · · ·

At Camp Pendleton, Colonel Lambert, finished for the day was about to lock up when his phone rang.

CHAPTER FORTY

16 MAY
Camp Pendleton Military Hospital
2115 hrs. local time

PAUL WASHED UP IN THE RESTROOM ACROSS FROM THE WAITING area. He patted his face with paper towels and stared into the mirror. "The fuck were you thinking, Goldman," he said, lowering his head. "God damn it all to hell."

When he walked back into the waiting room. Morgan stopped talking to Colonel Lambert and looked up.

"Nothin' yet, Paul" he said, shaking his head.

Paul nodded and sat in the chair next to him. "Yeah, could be a while. Damn it, this is all my fault, I shouldn't have ..."

"No," Morgan said, shaking his head. "Our decision. You warned us, we made the call an'..." He stopped as the double doors marked, O.R. NO ADMITTANCE swung open.

· · · · · · ·

The doctor's greens were stained dark with sweat and blood and his expression was grim. He hesitated before speaking, the same way, Paul thought, when Doctor Phillips told him about Anna and Ben.

"Folks, I'm Doctor Henry. Miss Story is still in surgery. We've been able to stop the bleeding and are in the process of trying to repair some extensive damage to her internal organs."

"But she's gonna be okay? Morgan asked.

"Detective, we lost your partner twice and managed to bring her back. If she makes it through surgery, it'll be nothing short of a miracle. After that, the next forty-eight hours should determine whether or not her damaged organs will be able to function well enough to keep her alive. I'd like to be more optimistic, but it doesn't look good. I'm sorry." With that he glanced up at the clock. "I've got to get back."

"We'll be right here," Paul said.

The doctor nodded. "I'll keep you updated," he said, and disappeared through the double doors.

• • • • • • •

Ten minutes later, Tom joined them. The bullet fragments had only done minor damage to his shoulder and upper arm, with the breach of the Sterling luckily taking the full impact of the .223 slug. He'd be a little sore and stiff for a week or so, but other than that he'd be fine.

At a little after midnight Doctor Henry returned to the waiting room. They all stopped talking and stood up at the same time. He got right to the point.

"Miss Story made it through surgery. She's in a coma, which can be expected after what's happened. It can, however, be a blessing, or a curse."

"What do you mean, Doc?" Morgan asked.

"Well, it can assist by letting her body concentrate on repairing the traumatized areas or, on the other hand, if one of the damaged organs shuts down, there's a good chance it could cause a domino effect on the others. The next couple of days should tell."

Morgan's voice was a whisper. "I gotta see her doc. Please."

"Of course," he said. "I'll have a nurse take you to her." He picked up the hospital phone, spoke quietly then hung up. "A nurse will be right with you," he said.

The nurse arrived a few seconds later, looked at the doctor, who nodded towards Morgan.

"If you'll follow me, sir," she said.

Paul patted him on the shoulder. "We'll wait here. Take your time."

Morgan followed the nurse through the doors and down a series of quiet hallways.

Col. Lambert shook hands with Tom and Paul. "Gentlemen, I wish I could've done more …"

Paul shook his head. "You've gone above and beyond Colonel, and we really appreciate it."

"Yeah, well it never feels that way when things go bad. Listen, I've got a briefing at 0600, and so I should catch a few hours. I'll update you whenever I get one from the doc."

"Thanks, Colonel, and again, thanks for everything," Paul said.

"Ditto that, Peter," Tom added.

"Not a problem. If you need anything else, you just call."

As the colonel left, Paul's pager vibrated. When he looked at the display screen, it showed a line of fives. The truck was making good progress.

· · · · · · · ·

The intensive care unit was dimly lit and each bed separated by a wrap-around curtain. A cluster of electronic equipment surrounded Bonnie. She looked so tiny and helpless. He could hear and feel his heart beating as he walked slowly to the side of the bed, ever so quiet, as if he might wake her. He leaned over the bed rail, lifted her hand and kissed it. Then he began to cry.

"Don't leave me, Bon," he whispered between sobs. "Never told you how I felt cuz I didn't want it to mess things up for us being partners an' all." He stood there in silence, holding her hand, just watching her. After a few minutes, he gently placed her hand by her side, wiped his eyes, and kissed her on the forehead.

"Always wanted to tell you this, an' I should have. I love you, Bon," he said, his voice cracking. "Always have an' always will, so don't you think about dying on me, okay?"

After years of witnessing what humans were capable of doing to one another, religion had never played much of a role in Morgan's life. Now, everything important lay in the bed in front of him. He looked up. "Please don't take her away from me. Please don't."

As he opened the curtains to leave, he stopped and looked back. The only sound came from the monitors, and the only sign of life were the jagged lines dancing across the screen.

· · · · · · · ·

Paul and Tom were talking quietly when he came into the waiting room.

"You going to be okay?" Paul asked.

"Yeah. It's just," he closed his eyes and hung his head. "I don't want to lose her."

"I know. Look, why don't you stay here for a while. Tom and I'll get going and you can meet up with us later."

"No, it's okay. I want to help out. I can't just sit an', you know?"

"Okay Morgan, you've got a right to see what we're doing, and be part of it. Peter's going to keep us advised of any change. You sure you're up to it?"

"Yeah, I'm good."

Paul picked up his jacket. "Okay, let's go."

Crossing the dark parking lot, Morgan looked around. "Where's Jamie?"

Tom made sure no one was close enough to hear them before answering. "He's uh, sort of on clean-up detail."

"Oh," Morgan said, sorry he'd asked.

CHAPTER FORTY-ONE

17 MAY
Bogota, Colombia
0250 hrs. local time

THE FOUR BELL MODEL 212/UH-INS, BETTER KNOWN AS HUEYS, whirred to life. Outfitted with side-door 30mm machine guns, they had a range of over 200 miles and a cruising speed of 110 knots. The human payload for jungle raids was a fully-equipped eight-man platoon, plus a crew of four. There were no changes at the final briefing with the winds as predicted: from the north at ten knots, so LZ Alpha and Bravo would remain landing zones, with LZ Charlie the alternate.

· · · · · · ·

General Messina watched the platoon leaders lead their men to the waiting helicopters. Most of them were veterans of many such raids. Once all had boarded, the powerful Pratt and Whitney engines roared to lift-off power then, one by one, they raised a few feet off the tarmac, tilted forward and moved off. At a thousand feet they leveled off and began the twenty-five minute flight into the darkness.

· · · · · · ·

At 0335 hours, the general received radio confirmation that all four platoons had landed without incident and were making their way on foot towards the rendezvous point. The second wave of three choppers prepared to depart. General Messina and Major Alvarez were in the first two, and the back-up "E" platoon with two medics in the third. It would remain in the air near LZ Charlie to be brought in where and when needed.

0445 hrs.

As soon as the ground platoons radioed that they had reached the rendezvous co-ordinates located half a kilometre from the target, the second wave took off. In the eastern sky the first signs of a new day began to lighten the horizon.

· · · · · · ·

Roaring less than a hundred feet above the jungle canopy the general listened to the progress of the ground platoons. "C" platoon had encountered trip wire about a hundred metres up a creek bed. They were flagging it and would need a few minutes to get into position. "D" platoon made a wide arc to come in from the jungle side that would put them close to the observation tower. They confirmed no other buildings or defenses behind the lab and, as suspected, there were two guards in the tower, both armed with AK-47s. "A" and "B" platoons located three trip wires leading to anti-personnel mines protecting the flank of the machine gun bunker to the left of the tower, and were able to disarm them.

0510 hrs.

As the second wave passed over LZ Alpha, the first beams of sunlight burst through the billowing clouds on the horizon sending silver spears of light into the dark-green of the jungle. Puffs of thick fog hung to the tops of trees like a white foam. Above, the support platoons chopper began circling over LZ Charlie.

· · · · · · ·

The ground units would commence firing when they heard the choppers, now less than a minute away. A final radio check confirmed all were in position. Other than a light patch of fog clinging to the end of the runway, the target was clear.

· · · · · · ·

An old DC-3 fired up her number two engine and made ready to taxi to the far end of the runway for takeoff. It's destination? An isolated area north of Cabo San Lucas near the small village of Todos Santos on Mexico's Baja Peninsula. As her engines warmed, a battered flat-deck truck carrying empty fuel drums backed away and headed towards the fuel storage.

0511 hrs.

The second wave roared towards the lab at tree top level. They were a couple of hundred yards away when "D" platoon opened up on the observation tower. Bullets pinged and clanked off the thick, corrugated metal walls while others ripped through the wooden floor and palm thatching of the roof. Both guards died in the hail of fire, but not before one of them detonated a string of anti-personnel mines set out along the tree line. "C" platoon concentrated on the machine gun bunker next to the tower while "A" and "B" platoons poured heavy fire on the other two machine gun positions. General Messina's chopper swooped overhead in a tight circle around the fuel storage. The left side gunner fired a short burst of incendiary shells into the drums. When one exploded it started a chain reaction, and the entire stockpile went up. An enormous black cloud mushroomed skyward. The pilot of the DC-3 made his decision. Faced with the likelihood of being killed on the ground he opted to attempt taking off … with the wind. He'd only seen the one helicopter and figured with any luck it would be kept busy by ground fire. Roaring at full throttle, the aircraft shuttered violently, straining to go. When the pilot released the brakes it began its painfully slow take off.

· · · · · · ·

The right side gunner sighted in on it and was about to fire when the general tapped him on the shoulder and shook his head. With the length of the air strip and weight of its cargo, it passed the point of no return with little chance of reaching lift-off speed. Dust and engine exhaust swirled in its wake as it neared the end of the runway, then, in a valiant effort the fifty-year-old work horse from another era managed to raise her nose into the air one last time. Seconds later, she became a giant fireball plowing into the Colombian jungle.

· · · · · · · ·

Major Alvarez's chopper banked sharply through the smoke of the DC-3 as his right side gunner opened up on one of the machine gun positions. A number of lab workers, there to make a living, not die, ran through a deadly gauntlet of cross-fire to reach the safety of the jungle. One of the workers, Juan Malende, who just a week ago got drunk, talked, and laughed with his favorite cousin Ramon, was shot dead as he ran from the lab past one of the machinegun bunkers.

Circling around the end of the airstrip, the general's pilot yelled into his headset. "Between the buildings ... Stinger! Stinger!"

Messina tapped his side gunner on his helmet and pointed. "There! Take him. Take him." The kneeling figure was poised with the grey cylinder resting on his shoulder raised towards the sky. The one-shot surface-to-air missile had the dubious reputation of being extremely accurate against low flying aircraft. The side gunner fired a steady stream between the buildings but, as a cloud of dust engulfed the kneeling target, a thin, white line shot skyward. In less than a second, its course jogged, locking onto the nearest heat source. Alvarez's pilot didn't have a chance. The rocket exploded into the tail rotor, ripping off the entire rear section. The forward section spun in a tight circle then toppled end over end, slamming into the ground upside down. When it hit, the main rotor blade snapped off and cartwheeled across the compound, slicing through one of the supply huts.

Seconds later, the firing eased off to a few sporadic pops, then stopped. General Messina ordered his pilot to land in the compound beside the lab, and then called for a status report.

"A platoon, no casualties … target secure."

"B platoon, three wounded, two bad … target eliminated."

"C platoon, one with severe head injury, three with minor shrapnel wounds, target secure."

"D platoon, no casualties … target eliminated."

Secure meant there were prisoners. Eliminated meant there weren't.

• • • • • • • •

The back-up "E" platoon landed next to the smoldering wreckage of Major Alvarez's chopper. The medics quickly started on the wounded. The remainder of the platoon would search the entire site for documentation, then gather up and photograph the chemicals and finished product. Explosive charges would be set along the length of the airstrip and, under heavy security, the lab and out-buildings, along with the two thousand plus kilo bricks of cocaine and barrels of chemicals, would be put to the torch.

• • • • • • • •

The wounded would be evacuated first, followed by the dead, then the prisoners.

The five bodies from the downed chopper had been laid in a row. General Messina walked slowly by each one. When he came to the body of his longtime friend Major Jose Alvarez, he knelt down, whispered a few words, crossed himself and stood up. Behind him, the bodies of the nineteen rebels and nine workers killed were being searched for identification and any intelligence information they may have been carrying.

CHAPTER FORTY-TWO

17 MAY
San Diego, Calif.
0730 hrs. local time

PAUL PUT THE CAST IRON SKILLET OF SCRAMBLED EGGS ONTO THE granite counter as the phone rang. He gave his hands a quick wipe and picked up. It was Colonel Lambert.

"Hello Paul."

"Good morning, Colonel. How is she doing?"

"From what the doc says, we're not out of the woods yet, but she's hangin' in there. Even the doctors are surprised. Still too early to tell if she'll pull through, and if she does ... well he's not optimistic that there won't be a fair bit of permanent damage. One of the bullets nicked her spinal cord, and they won't know the extent of damage until they bring her out of the coma, but she's definitely a fighter."

"Appreciate the update, and for sticking your neck out for us."

"No problem. I'll keep you posted. An' how are you guys doing?"

"We're good, thanks."

"Well, good luck, Paul. You need anything else you just call, okay?"

"I will, Colonel. Thanks again."

As Paul hung up, Morgan came into the kitchen. "That was Colonel Lambert," he said, spreading the four plates on the counter. "Bonnie made it through the night. She's a tough little nut, Morgan. Every minute she hangs on her chances get better. For the time being they'll be keeping her in the induced coma."

Morgan let out a sigh. "One thing I know about her, Paul, givin' up isn't in the equation."

"Maybe you should go back to Pendleton to be with her."

"If there was something I could do there I would, but I'd rather stay here, where I can do something, as long as it's okay with you."

Paul handed him a plate of scrambled eggs and patted him on the shoulder. "We talked it over and if you want, you're in."

"Yeah," he said. "I want."

Morgan looked into the dining room where Tom was rearranging the photo board. It looked even more impressive in the daylight. "Man, I can't believe this. I figured you were up to something, but all this," he said looking at the array of charts and pictures. "This is serious stuff. I see what you're tryin' to do, but jeez …"

"Come and eat," Paul said, waving both of them over to the table. "We'll fill you in on everything."

After going over how and what they'd accomplished so far, Morgan looked at them in disbelief. "This is unreal … but how are you gonna get to Costa himself? I mean, he runs one of the biggest cartels in Colombia."

"Well, with any luck he'll soon try to rid himself of a number of, uh … internal problems that we hope to help him see. Our biggest asset is he's got an ego the size of Ohio and doesn't trust anyone, so we'll take advantage of that," Paul said putting his coffee on the table.

"Christ," Morgan said, shaking his head. "I love it, but do you really think he'll buy in?"

Tom smiled and patted him on the shoulders. "He's already bought in, he just don't know it yet."

Paul poured Morgan a cup. "Listen, what happened in the desert yesterday wasn't what I wanted, but we had to have a plan in the event they found me. Better a place of our choosing where no one else would get hurt, I just wish you and Bonnie..."

Morgan shook his head. "Hey, man, like I said yesterday, our call. We both agreed and that's that. And now I've got a personal stake in this too, so, how can I help?"

Paul thought for a few seconds. "Our first priority is finding out who in Miami set us up, and fast. If we don't, once we're into the trial, it'll make it pretty much impossible. What's your gut feeling?"

Morgan took a bite of toast and leaned back. "We talked about it on the drive from Pendleton. Shit, we were blown away by Grange. If you'd depended on us and not had your own plan you'd be dead, he'd be a fuckin' hero an' I'd probably be workin' for the prick one day." He held up his fingers one at a time. "DA's office stands out as number one choice. The mayor's office hasn't been totally in the loop, but there's people there in a pretty good position to get information from us or the DA. Then there's our office, and with Bon an' me really the only ones who had a handle on you, it'd be real tough."

Jamie walked in from the bedroom and held out his hand. "Well, we know who's behind this and why, and this gentlemen is the, how," he said, holding a tiny transmitter the size of a pack of matches in the palm of his hand. "With no aircraft, it meant there had to be a tracker. They couldn't have known about the car so that left your luggage. I found it in the lining of Bonnie's suitcase. Whoever did it was rushed for time. Not the best job, but she probably wouldn't have noticed it right away. They must have gotten into her place after she packed."

Morgan shook his head. "You mean they got into her apartment?"

Jamie opened the living room drapes just enough to see the street. The only two cars parked in view belonged to the neighbors. "Yes," he said. "And no doubt yours, too. Street looks clear."

Paul looked out the kitchen window into the backyard. Other than the clattering of two young boys on skateboards using the speed bumps as mini-jumps the lane was deserted.

Picking up the transmitter, Paul tossed it to Jamie. "Okay, you and Morgan hook this onto something heading either north or east. With any luck our friends from yesterday didn't have a chance to let their boss know things weren't going too well, so they may not realize what's happened yet. I'll drop Tom off at the airport. As soon as you're done head back here. We've got to find our Miami problem, so Morgan, I'll need you to head back to Miami too."

Morgan nodded. "Sure thing."

Paul's pager buzzed. On the screen the area code and number was followed by 911. He picked up the phone and dialed. Cranston picked it up on the first ring.

"Paul, old son, how the hell are ya?"

"We've had a few problems but we're dealing with them and you, Lenny, how's your trip going, well I hope?"

"Smooth as silk so far, but I think we should make things happen sooner than later. They've been running full bore day and night. We just crossed into Ontario, an' seein' as we don't know where they'll cut into the states I figure we'd better create an opportunity pretty quick. Wanted to run it by you first in case there's a problem with us doing it maybe tonight."

Paul watched Jamie and Morgan pulling out of the driveway. "Your timing's perfect, Lenny. Any time now would be great."

"Okay, Paul. I'll set things in motion and hopefully start makin' our move after dark. I'll call as soon as it's done."

"Thanks, Len. Good luck, and I'll talk to you soon."

17 MAY
Montreal Quebec
1500 hrs. local time

They'd kept him as long as they could without laying charges. The Organized Crime Task Force, a combination of Montreal, RCMP, and the Quebec Provincial Police, had played cat and mouse with Rheume's lawyer most of the day, bouncing him from station to station. It gave them the opportunity to interrogate one of their more sought- after targets, but they were pushing the envelope if they screwed his lawyer around much longer. The important thing was, with Rheume's past, and Tasse's murder outside his building, they'd have enough to get a part six warrant signed that would allow them to tap his phone, and wire his apartment for sound.

Throughout questioning, Rheume stuck to his story. Tasse had called and said he thought he was being followed. Rheume told him to come over and, if need be, they'd either call his lawyer or the police. Not long after the call, he heard shots and people hollering in the back parking lot. When he looked out there were two men running down the laneway towards the front of the building. Seeing Tasse's Pathfinder, he ran downstairs. That's when he found him. He was putting in a call to the police when he heard the sirens.

Actually, the police response had been so quick he'd barely made it back from the storage lockers when the first patrol car pulled in. For now, his 9mm with three rounds left in the clip would remain under a box of Christmas decorations in locker #214. Odds were the lockers owner wouldn't have reason to move it for a while.

Rheume always assumed the cops were watching him, and with the bullshit that went on today, no doubt now they'd be doubling their efforts. What really bothered him right now was getting word down south, before Costa had him killed. Parking in the loading zone at the front of his building he ran inside. The lit-up number above the elevator door indicated it was on the eighth floor, so rather than wait he took the stairs.

• • • • • • •

His apartment looked the same as he'd left it, which of course meant nothing. The cops would have, for sure, had a good look around. He'd have the whole place swept for transmitters as soon as things settled down. For now he'd talk as though there was a cop sitting in every room. He went into his study, unlocked the middle drawer of his desk, and removed it. The brown envelope taped to the back contained the coded emergency numbers.

• • • • • • •

Moving his finger down the list of letters and numbers he located the correct month, week, and day code. This allowed him to decipher the contact number. He wrote it down, re-sealed the envelope and taped it to the back of the drawer. When he finished, he locked his door and hurried downstairs, using the stairs again.

Fifteen minutes later, after checking for a tail, he pulled into the Greyhound Bus Terminal, parked, and walked through the front door.

• • • • • • •

Unlike airports and train stations, noise levels in bus stations are generally quieter, with most travelers milling about, waiting for a bus to take them to whatever destination life had put in front of them. Most looked bored and tired as they sat on the uncomfortable wooden benches that lined the middle of the station like pews in a church. The musty smell of stale cigarette smoke and discarded food hung in the air, but Rheume didn't notice. He walked over to the three pay phones on the wall opposite the coffee machine, decided on the middle one, took the piece of paper out of his pocket and dialed.

17 MAY
Bogota, Colombia
1315 hrs. local time

DaLucca walked down the hall carrying the message from Montreal. At least that problem had been cleared up. He broke into a run when he heard Costa yelling.

"What is it Pablo?" he called, flinging the office door open.

"I don't believe it," Pablo said, slamming down the receiver. "How can this fucking be?" His dark eyes shifted from the phone to DaLucca. "The lab." He fought to control himself. "They got the whole ... fucking ... thing. The lab, a fucking loaded DC-3, every fucking thing they got. Why didn't those bastards call? The fuck am I paying for?"

· · · · · · · ·

DaLucca punched a sequence of numbers into his cell, then spoke in a low whisper.

Pablo drummed his fingers, waiting for him to finish. "Well? What?" he snapped, as Mani flipped his cell closed and put it in his jacket pocket.

"Anti-Narcotics by-passed everyone. Looks like they notified the President directly just before they hit it, so our people at the Justice Ministry just found out about it minutes ago."

"Just found out!" Pablo bellowed, pushing his chair back and standing. "Can you fucking believe this?" He began pacing from the desk to the door, like a caged animal. "Isn't this just fucking wonderful. We pay all this money, for...for what? So they can tell us after we've been fucked that we've been fucked?" He slammed both fists on his desk then spun around and faced the window. He took a couple of deep breaths, raked his fingers through his hair and turned back to DaLucca.

"Okay, listen," he said. "I want you to go to Miami, right away, today. Deal with the Williamson matter. I'll talk to Eduardo. We have to put everything on hold until we find out what the hell's going on."

"I'll leave right away," DaLucca said, and turned towards the door.

Costa called after him. "And don't take too long. We've got to get to the bottom of this shit, and soon."

"I'll be back as soon as I can," he said without turning around.

· · · · · · · ·

Two hours later, waiting in the boarding lounge for his flight to board, Mani's cell phone vibrated. Pablo's voice told him something else had gone wrong. The thing in San Diego had somehow gone bad. The last time Montez talked with his people they were about to move in on Goldman and the two cops, some place in the desert. Since then nothing, and now word from Miami is, Goldman was still very much alive.

CHAPTER FORTY-THREE

17 MAY
Miami, Florida
1700 hrs. local time

ERNESTO SANTOS FINISHED FILING THE MONTHLY ORDER FORMS. The complete opposite of his brother, he actually worked, or appeared to. He drove a newer model, maroon Ford Explorer and lived in a modest rancher in a middle-class neighborhood with his wife, two-year-old daughter and a six-month-old son. Most days were spent at his small importing business called South American Treasures. Here he sold everything from native clothing and pottery, to questionably authentic Inca artifacts. He kept a low profile and looked like a typical business man. Jimmy, on the other hand, had preferred the gangster persona and the flashy life style and because of this, Ernesto let his brother deal with matters of violence whenever they occurred, and Jimmy loved that part.

* * * * * * *

Ernesto's driver and bodyguard, Rico Gonzales, had, since Jimmy's murder, been staying closer than usual to Ernesto. He locked the front door while Ernesto finished in the back office. Today had been slow at the South American Treasures shop, but

Ernesto didn't mind. There were more important things on his mind. They still hadn't found Williamson, and Mani DaLucca would be here soon.

Rico Gonzales smirked and shook his head as the Crown Vic pull up in front of the shop. Four doors, no frills, plain Jane, and no-doubt with coffee stains and doughnut crumbs on the seats. An older, plain clothes cop climbed out, checked the address and walked to the front door.

"Ernesto," Rico called over his shoulder. "Got a cop comin' to the door."

"Yeah? See what the fuck he wants."

Gonzales opened the door a couple of inches. "Sorry, officer we're closed, an' we don't give police discounts," he said, starting to shut the door.

Tom flashed a badge that he hoped wouldn't be studied to closely and blocked the door with his foot. "Tell your boss I'm here about his brother's murder, and if I want any shit from you, I'll squeeze your fuckin' head."

Rico looked back over his shoulder. Ernesto motioned with his head to open the door. Gonzales held it open, and Tom stepped inside, bumping Gonzales aside.

"I came to talk to you, Ernesto, about your brother, "Tom said, then shot a glance at Gonzales. "So tell your help to take a fuckin' hike."

Ernesto gave another nod and Rico walked to the back of the shop. Out of earshot, but where he could still keep an eye on things.

"Okay, detective..."

"Warner," he replied, "detective Warner."

"Fine, detective Warner, what about Jimmy?"

"I ain't gonna shit you, Ernesto. You know we were all over Jimmy an' it was just a matter of time before we popped him.

What we didn't know, and I'm pretty sure he didn't either, was he'd been under surveillance by the F.B.I."

Ernesto rolled his eyes. "The fuckin' FBI? What's that all about?"

"Don't know. They don't tell us bugger all. After Jimmy got killed I guess their case wasn't gonna go anywhere so they turned over part of their file in case it might help with the murder investigation."

"My ass," Ernesto scoffed. "How'd he get killed if the feds were following him?"

"Bout all I can tell you on that one," Tom said, "is it takes more than an expensive suit an' some university degree to make a real cop."

Ernesto studied him closely. "Okay … so what's all that got to do with me?"

Tom pulled out his notebook. "Well, seems they got a picture of one of the last guys to be with your brother."

Santos watched him remove a photo from between the pages. "Lemme take a wild, fucking guess. Big black guy, right?"

"Close, dark, but not black, and not very big," Tom said, handing it to him.

"We'd figured it to be the Jamaicans. Guess they could have hired an out-of-towner, but that's never been their style."

Santos moved to the window and held the photo in the afternoon light. It was Jimmy, no doubt about that, standing on the street, smiling and talking to another man. He studied the picture carefully.

"Nope. Don't know him," he said, shaking his head. "Tell you what, Detective. Maybe I could show it to some of Jimmy's friends."

"Naw. Better you tell me their names an' I'll talk to 'em."

"Hey, man, they'll never talk to you, ever, you know that. Me they'll talk to. An' I'll let you know. Really. I mean, he was my brother … right?"

Tom started to put the picture back between the pages of his notebook then stopped.

"You'll call for sure?"

"Swear to God, man, " he said, putting his hand on his chest.

"Okay," Tom said and handed him the picture and a business card. "Just make sure and call, one way or another."

"Like I said, man. Swear to God."

· · · · · · · ·

Ernesto watched the cop climb back into his car and pull out before locking the door. In the back office he turned on the desk lamp, took out the picture and sat down. Good chance the cops were fuckin' him around, but if not it meant they had a big problem.

CHAPTER FORTY-FOUR

17 MAY
Ontario Canada
1815 hrs. local time

THE HIGHWAY SIGN READ, '390 KILOMETRES TO TORONTO.' CRANSTON advised the surveillance team they would attempt the switch sometime after dark as long as they could get the drivers away from their truck for a bit. So far though, other than fuel stops, the truck had gone non-stop since the Toronto Drug Section took over at Kenora near the Manitoba border. Just after dusk, the Kenworth geared down and signaled to pull into the parking lot of a popular truck stop called The Country Kitchen Cafe. The driver found a spot between a couple of fifty-three footers and shut down the engine. He and his partner climbed out of the cab, locked the doors, stretched, and made their way towards the lights and the front door.

· · · · · · ·

Once they were inside, Cranston radioed the team to begin. then put in a prearranged call to the local detachment of the Ontario Provincial Police in Sudbury. While he spoke to the duty sergeant one of his surveillance units parked at the service station next to the restaurant. and the two drug members got out and walked through the parking lot and into the restaurant. They looked like the rest of the truckers, so no one gave them a second look. Taking stools at the counter near the entrance they could keep an eye on their two targets, sitting at a table in the back section of the crowded restaurant. The loud voices and clattering dishes all but drowned out whatever western song was blasting out of the speakers. The middle-aged waitress working the counter handed them menus, put down a couple of coffee mugs and smiled. She hid the life of hard work and partying as best she could behind a generous amount of make-up.

"Hi guys. Coffee first?" she asked already pouring.

"Yeah, great. You got a pay phone here?" the bearded one asked.

"Back there, hon, by the washrooms," she said, wiping down the counter and nodding over her right shoulder.

"Thanks," he said, getting up. "Just coffee's gonna be good for me."

His partner nodded and smiled. "I'll have a coffee and try a piece of your apple pie."

The waitress smiled and reached behind her for the coffee pot.

Len Cranston listened to the update, then radioed the two lock-section members to move on the truck. With a fifty-three footer on either side of the Kenworth, they couldn't be seen from the restaurant. The driver and his partner had just ordered the house special: meatloaf, mashed potatoes, carrots, and peas all smothered in dark, rich gravy, so they would have a bit of time.

Forty-five minutes later they were finished and waved to get the bill. Once paid they left and walked back to the Kenworth. A minute later, it began working through the gears towards the highway. Cranston picked up the radio and gave the Ontario Provincial Police marked unit that had positioned itself a few miles up the highway, a heads up. When the Kenworth passed, the unit pulled in behind it and, when the Kenworth neared a rest stop, turned on its red and blue light bar. The driver noticed strobe lights reflecting in the side mirrors and, glancing at the speedometer, shook his head and muttered. "Aw, shit. What the hell does he want?"

The marked cruiser followed the truck into the rest stop's parking area and pulled in behind it. The emergency lights stayed on, and the officer driving got out and approached the driver's side of the cab.

"Evenin' officer...what's the problem?" the driver asked, rolling down the window.

"Can I see your license and registration please?"

"Sure thing," he said and fumbled through his wallet. "Al, get the registration out of the glove box will ya. I didn't think I was speedin'," he said, handing over his license.

"No, sir, your speed was fine...but you don't have a back plate," the officer said, looking at the license.

"Aw, shit, you gotta be kiddin me," the driver groaned. "It musta come off somehow. Sorry about that."

The officer moved his flashlight from the license to the driver. "I'm sure that's what happened. Anyway your registration should help straighten things out."

"Can't see it in here, Rick," his partner said, emptying the glove compartment completely.

"What? It's gotta be there for Christ's sake."

"No, I'm serious, Rick. It ain't here."

They began a frantic check of the door compartments, behind the sun visors and the storage pouches in the sleeper. Nothing.

"Man, I don't believe this. It's gotta be here somewhere."

"Have to ask you boys to step out of the truck, please." Polite, but an order.

Climbing out, the driver tried to explain what must have happened. "Last time I had it out was about three months ago. Got a warning ticket from a Mountie in Alberta. Maybe he didn't give it back to me. Hell, I can't remember."

His partner Al shook his head and shrugged.

"Me neither...nor can I."

"Okay," the officer said. "You can lock'er up. Our office is only a couple a miles up the road. We'll run the serial numbers an' by the time we get to the station we should have most of what we need. Soon as we straighten it out, we'll make you out a temporary till you get home. Otherwise, you'll be going through this every couple of miles. I can have a car standby and watch your load if you want."

"Yeah, sure, that'd be good," Rick said shaking his head. "Where the hell …"

As he squeezed into the back seat of the police car he wasn't sure if it was the thought of possibly getting a three-hundred-dollar fine for no plate and registration or the meat loaf, but his stomach was starting to act up.

2035 hrs.

The rest stop was secured with a second marked unit blocking off the entrance. Anyone trying to pull in would be told that, due to a police incident, the rest stop was closed. Cranston had one of the surveillance vehicles set up on the O.P.P. station in the event of a communication breakdown, while the rest of the team began working on the exchange. The container was packed with burlap sacks of coffee beans. The ones carrying the cocaine were located all together near the front of the trailer. Ramon's information had been dead on. They'd use the bags the real cocaine was in, in case there were identifying marks they couldn't see. Research on cocaine seizures over the past year that were linked to the Costa/Rodreigez group showed the bricks were always one kilo blocks packaged in green plastic wrap with white adhesive tape around the ends. Luckily they hadn't changed the wrapping method and the phony bricks looked very close.

```
2115 hrs.
```

When the exchange was complete and the container re-sealed the white cube van with five hundred kilos of cocaine headed west back towards British Columbia. Its final destination would be an incinerator near the small town of Langley, not far from Vancouver. The lock section guys had the cab door open in seconds and placed the registration papers under the floor mat on the passenger side with the corner left sticking out just enough to be noticed when they climbed back in. When the door was re-locked a call was put in to the O.P.P. station giving the all clear to bring the drivers back.

```
17 MAY
Miami International Airport.
2105 hrs. local time
```

Captain Jacobs spotted Morgan at the baggage carousel and made his way through the crowded arrivals area to meet him. "Hey, Cap," Morgan said then he spotted Bonnie's suitcase and lifted it off the conveyor belt. "Figured maybe Ident might be able to come up with something. Gonna have to do her place, too," he said quietly. "They definitely got in there."

"Good thinkin'," Jacobs said, picking up the blue weekender. "How's she doing?"

"Not good, Cap, alive, but just."

"Bastards," Jacobs muttered. "How you doin'?"

"I'm okay. Tired is all."

"You look like shit. Let's get you home."

```
2120 hrs.
```

Ernesto held the picture to the light with his free hand as he spoke. "Uncle, I have it right here. I'm looking at it now. There's no doubt. It's Mani for sure, standin' on the street with Jimmy. The time and date are at the bottom."

"Ernesto listen, a picture of Jimmy and Mani standing on the street talking is nothing. Any time and date could be put on it, besides, Mani was here the day Jimmy was killed."

"Did you see him yourself Uncle," he said, putting the picture down. "Because I found something else in the photo."

"What do you mean something else?" Eduardo asked.

"In the background, on the other side of the street, there's a *Miami Herald* newspaper delivery van. Each morning they put a blow-up poster of the day's front page on the side. It's hard to make out, but with a magnifying glass you can see the headlines. It says, "Space Shuttle Delayed Again." I checked with *the Herald* and that was the headline the day Jimmy got killed."

Eduardo was silent. When he spoke, his tone had changed.

"Ernesto, fax it to me. Now. I want to see for myself."

"I'll do that right away, Uncle, but what about DaLucca? I'm supposed to meet him in the morning to go over the other thing."

"That's fine," Eduardo said. "Meet him. Tell him Williamson will be back in a day or two. Say you've talked to me, and I want him to stay in Miami until it gets done. I have to see what Pablo says about where he was. If I'm convinced, then you can take care of him there, and if I find Pablo sanctioned it, I will take care of things here."

"Okay, Uncle. I'll wait to hear from you."

```
17 MAY
San Diego, Calif.
1900 hrs. local time
```

"Have a look at these," Jamie said, handing Paul the two pictures. "All we had were a few surveillance photos of Rheume. The colors were a bit off, but I was able to tone them to match the one's you took in Mexico. I think the one on the left will best suit our needs."

Paul studied the coloring, shadows and, in particular, the edges around each of the two subjects. "Yes...I think you're right. Yes... very, very good," he said, unfolding a piece of paper printed crudely in Spanish and handed it to Jamie. "What do you think of this?"

Jamie read it to himself.

Dear Mr. Costa

I have to tell you that Senor Salas and the one in the picture are stealing your money. Senor Salas told the man, who I feel may be from France, by his accent, that you would never be able to find out. They spoke of a sub account somewhere in Gran Cayman. If I am wrong then I am sorry to trouble you. You have alwaysbeen fair to us, so I wanted you to know.

"Excellent, but how will Costa be able to find the changes and not Salas?" Jamie asked, putting the note on the table beside the pictures.

"That part's easy," Paul said. "Salas has no reason to check for sub accounts attached to any Gran Cayman investments, but Costa will. So," he said, clapping his hands. "Been to Mexico City lately Mr. Ryan?"

"Love Mexico City, Mr. Goldman," he said and put the picture and note in his briefcase and snapped it shut. "Ah...the traffic, pollution, noise. What's not to love?"

"Good. Try to get a flight first thing if you can. I'd like our friend to get this early enough in the day to react. It would be great if you could send it from the fax machine at the Mesa Grande, but there's two banks nearby that will do nicely. Once he finds the accounts, he'll be a believer."

Jamie opened the yellow pages to the Airline section and, minutes later, was confirmed on the 7:00 AM United flight to Mexico City.

```
17 MAY
Near the Ontario, U.S. border
2355 hrs. local time
```

Len Cranston pressed one hand over his ear and held the receiver tight to the other as a West-bound Canadian National freight train roared past. "Looks like it's gonna cross at Cornwall," he hollered.

Paul raised his voice. "I hear you, Len, any problems?"

"Zero... couldn't have gone smoother. You want me to give it a loose one for a few miles on the U.S. side? Might be able to pick off who the customers are for the DEA"

Finally, the train passed.

"No, you've done more than enough. I just hope the customers don't sit on it for too long before they open it."

"Yeah, I read you. Well, if that's it Paul, I'll turn my people around and head 'em home. Got a tired bunch of puppies here"

"Thanks again, Len, and sorry there's nothing in it for you guys."

"Forget it. Glad I could help. Tell you what scares me though."

"What's that?"

"If Ottawa's impressed they may want to make this a regular thing, and I know Quebec's gonna be pissed they didn't have a chance to show how good they are, so they're gonna want to do it over again...and, frankly, at my age living in the back seat of a car twenty-four-seven falls way short of a fun time."

Paul laughed. "Yeah, you're going to have to screen your calls a little better in the future."

"Why bother? You'd find a way around that in no time. Seriously, good luck with everything. If you can ruin that bastard's day, it'll sure make mine."

"If he's as paranoid as I think, we're going to ruin more than just his day. Take care, Len. I'll let you know how things work out."

Jamie looked at him as he hung up. "I can tell by the look on your face that Costa's royal lifestyle is about to deteriorate somewhat."

"Yes, I think he's about to learn that what goes around, comes around, and when it does, it can leave you in a very dark, lonely place."

CHAPTER FORTY-FIVE

18 MAY
Massena, New York
0425 hrs. local time

THE METAL GATE AT THE ENTRANCE TO WHAT USED TO BE THE Atlantis Disposal Company clanged shut behind the black Lincoln that slowly wound its way around water-filled pot holes that pockmarked most of the asphalt. It stopped in front of a large, corrugated metal building. The sign above the sliding doors read, 'Repair Shop.' The doors were pushed open just long enough to let the Lincoln drive inside, then closed. Two men remained outside.

· · · · · · · ·

The container had been removed from the Kenworth and sat in the middle of the shop. When the Lincoln stopped beside it, Antonio "Big Tony" Amado hefted his 350-pound frame out the passenger door and lumbered over to the workbench. With a nod of his head, the rear doors of the container were swung open and the unloading began.

It took less than fifteen minutes for the first sack with black drawstrings to be found and put off to the side. Five minutes later, the rest were stacked beside it. Big Tony smiled. The shipment was on time, a good sign the trip hadn't been interrupted.

"Put one on the bench," he said to no one in particular. Two men standing at the back of the trailer hurried over and hoisted one of the sacks onto a long work bench. Two fluorescent lights hung above the bench. Tony flicked his cigarette onto the floor and walked over to the bench. The click of his switch blade echoed off the metal walls.

Amado sliced the top of the bag open, reached inside and removed one of the tightly wrapped bricks. He inserting the blade, twisted it slightly, then carefully pulled it out. A small amount of granular white powder clung to the tip of the blade. Gently, he tapped it into the middle of a small, stainless steel saucer. Next, using an eye dropper he mixed two drops of marquis reagent to the powder. Everyone watched in silence. Cocaine would turn bright blue in seconds. After that it would just be a matter of taking random samples to their chemist to get an accurate percentage of purity, then a day to cut and repackage it for distribution and, by this time tomorrow, it would hit the street.

Nothing happened.

· · · · · · ·

Amado stirred the mixture with the tip of the blade. Still nothing. "The fuck is this?" he growled. He held his hand out behind him and snapped his fingers. "Gimme another brick and a different bottle of the tester." This time he jabbed the knife in a little more forcefully. He ran the same test. Again, nothing. He took out his cell phone and punched in Vito Sorrentino's number.

"Vito? ...Yeah it's me. No everything's not all fuckin' right...I'll tell you what I mean. We got fucked is what I mean. That cocksucker fucked us. Here, you don't believe me, talk to Joey." Amado tossed the phone to a twenty-something-year-old standing on the other side of the bench.

"Pa...its Joe. Yeah, we're here testin' it right now an' like Tony says, it's all shit. Yeah...yeah...okay...yeah, hang on. Tony," he called and tossed the phone back to Amado. "He wants to talk to you some more."

· · · · · · ·

Twenty minutes later, after five or six more negative tests from different sacks, the Lincoln, followed by two cars, sped through the gates towards the highway. Not long after, the flames from the Atlantis Disposal Company could be seen for miles.

```
18 MAY
Miami, Florida
0615 hrs. local time
```

Hearing the two short horn blasts, Morgan downed the last of his orange juice, grabbed his jacket, and headed for the front door. Most of the night he'd lain awake thinking about Bonnie, a few thousand miles away in a coma she may not come out of. At some point during the night he decided that, as soon as they figured out who'd done this, he'd catch the first flight back. Walking out the front door, he twisted the knob to set the dead bolt. Not that it mattered. Little doubt the pricks could get back in if they wanted to.

· · · · · · ·

Tom reached over and unlocked the passenger door. He looked at Morgan and shook his head. "Christ, man. You get any sleep at all?"

"Couple of hours maybe. I'm okay. How's it doin'?" he asked, nodding towards Tom's shoulder.

"It's fine, comin' along fine," he said, backing out of the driveway. "How are we for time?"

Morgan checked his watch. "Cap's gonna meet us around seven-thirty. I picked a park, away from the office."

"Great, gives us an hour. I want to run by the places I've picked out. Wanna be sure they've got everything we need, an', I wouldn't mind a coffee."

"Yeah, coffee'd be good," Morgan said. As he rubbed his face with both hands he realized he hadn't shaved. "Fuck, I knew I forgot somethin'. Man I'm losin' it."

"Don't worry about it," Tom said pulling into traffic. "Least yours don't come in grey."

· · · · · · · ·

At 7:25 AM they pulled over and parked opposite a small park on Ocean Boulevard. Captain Jacobs' unmarked was the other side of the street. Morgan led the way across the freshly-mowed lawn past a set of swings, a spiral metal slide, and a brightly-painted merry-go-round. They spotted Jacobs sitting on one of the park benches on the promenade, squinting into the morning sun.

· · · · · · · ·

"Mornin' Cap," Morgan said as they approached.

"Oh, jeez," he said, sitting up with a start. "I was damn near asleep."

He got up and held out his hand. "Trevor Jacobs. You must be Tom."

Tom smiled and shook his hand. "Glad to meet you, Captain. Heard a lot about you."

They started walking along the seawall. Other than the usual early morning joggers and cyclists, it was relatively quiet.

"Morgan tells me you've got a plan to flush out whoever set them up. Glad I can help."

"Appreciate it," Tom said.

"So how we gonna do this?" Jacobs asked, throwing his empty coffee cup into a trash can.

Tom waited until two joggers coming up behind them passed. "We know Costa's got someone else here in Miami an' probably right at or near the top. So that's where we start. The DA, the mayor, and your own Chief Harelson. If it don't turn out to be one of them, an' let's hope it ain't, we start workin' our way down."

"If it isn't one of them," Morgan cut in, "I think we should ask everyone in homicide to take a polygraph. At least then we can use our own people to help."

Jacobs let out a sigh. "That's all well and good, Morgan, but I can't force anyone to take it. It ain't legal or admissible. The damn union'll scream bloody murder an' call it exactly what it is... a fishin' trip."

"True," Morgan nodded. "But if you and I took it first. Christ after Grange we gotta know who we can count on here."

Jacobs thought for a few seconds. "Okay, if we rule out Harelson, Accardo, and Rice. Then you an' me will sit down an' come up with a half dozen questions that pertain directly to what's happened. So long as we keep it real specific an', like you say, we go first, I think most of the guys'll go for it."

"An' any who don't." Morgan shrugged. "We keep outta the loop an' take a real hard look at em'."

Jacobs nodded. "You got that right, an' my money's on that little weasel Accardo. Son of a bitch threatened more than once to go over my head to get better access to Goldman."

Tom nodded. "He sounds like a good bet. So, here's the deal. I've rented a room at three different motels for tonight. Accardo, Rice, and Harelson will each be given the name of one of them. They'll be told Paul's arriving at 7:30 tonight to clear up some personal stuff, an' you'll have him outta here before midnight. If we're right, whichever one's in bed with Costa will pass the name of the motel he's been told about to his contact…so depending which motel the bad guys show at, will tell us who's been fuckin' us around."

Jacobs smiled. "Damn thing just might work. So, what do you want me to do?"

"There's a place called the Chestnut Motel," Tom said, taking a piece of paper out of his pocket. "Room number 12, under

Morgan's name. He'll pass the name of the motel and unit number on to Harelson. In case he wants to talk to you about it, Captain, you can give him the same story. Morgan has to talk to Accardo about the deposition anyway, and the mayor'll feel he's being brought up to speed on the latest."

"You want me to get Minter from Internal to have his boys standin' by?" Jacobs asked.

Tom shook his head. "Best we don't have anyone else involved at this point. I'll have cameras set up so the three of us can do the monitoring from my room."

"What about arrest teams if someone does show up?"

Tom shook his head. "For now let's just concentrate on identifying the leak. Once that's done you can handle the rest any way you want."

"Okay," Jacobs nodded. "Sounds good. Need any help setting up on your end Tom? I'm not very mechanically inclined, but don't mind doin' the grunt work."

"I don't think so. Probably best if you guys go about your day as usual. I'm staying at room 1115 at the Whyndam, over on 21st Street. If you guys could be there by 6:30 that would be good."

"6:30 it is." Jacobs said.

Tom shook both their hands. "Okay, boys. If I need anything I'll call. Other than that I'll see you later."

After Tom left, Morgan walked with Jacobs over to his unmarked. "Pretty impressive guy," Jacobs said, opening the driver's door.

"Very," Morgan said and slid into the passenger side. "An' I'm sure glad he's on our side."

"So how the hell did a guy like Goldman get tied up with him?" Jacobs asked, watching in the side mirror for an opening in the traffic.

"It's a long story, Cap. And it's not just him It's them."

CHAPTER FORTY-SIX

```
18 MAY
Miami Fl
0730 hrs. local time
```

WHENEVER HE TRAVELLED, DALUCCA NEVER STAYED IN THE SAME place twice. Sometimes a cheap out-of-the-way motel, other times an expensive downtown five-star. It all depended on the job. He did prefer the higher end hotels. Better security, and easier to pick out the cops hanging around the lobby, always dressed in cheap off-the-rack suits and scuffed shoes.

His choice this time was the Holiday Inn Port of Miami Downtown. When he'd checked in last night he'd asked for a room overlooking Biscayne Blvd. That would give him a good view of any vehicles or people watching the front entrance of the hotel.

Ernesto paged at 7:30 and left a number, DaLucca had already been up for an hour. He called the number and told Ernesto to meet him at a restaurant called Pappa Joe's, just off Biscayne in an hour.

"Sure, Mani. I know where that is. Can I pick you up?"

"No," he said, and hung up.

· · · · · · ·

Pappa Joe's was a family style restaurant where breakfast was served all day and kids were given paper place mats to scribble on to keep them quiet. Ernesto arrived right on time and saw DaLucca already sitting at a window table where he could watch everyone coming and going. Ernesto sat down opposite him.

Without the sunglasses, his deep-set eyes were as cold and lifeless as an executioner's. Fuckin' killin' machine, Santos thought. A chill ran up his spine when Mani shifted his gaze and made eye contact, like he'd said it out loud.

"Hey Mani … good to see you again man," he said, trying to sound calm.

DaLucca's expression didn't change. After a few seconds he nodded slowly. "I'm happy we'll do this together Ernesto. Jimmy was a good boy."

Ernesto was about to say something when the waitress, carrying two mugs and menu in one hand, and a coffee pot in the other, arrived at their table.

"Good morning, sir. Can I start you off with a coffee?"

Ernesto thought for a second then said, "Yeah. Just a coffee is all." And waved the menu away.

· · · · · · ·

DaLucca waited until she was out of earshot. "So what news do you have of Williamson?"

Santos leaned forward and lowered his voice. "He's in Jamaica. Been there for two, maybe three days. Supposed to be back either tonight or tomorrow. He's just got engaged. His girlfriend's got a place on 16th near Little Havana. Word is he ends up there every night. I got some guys watching an' they'll call me when he shows up."

"Good," DaLucca said, "And remember, it's very important she's there with him. Page me when you hear and I'll pick you up." He waved at the waitress to bring the bill and stood up.

"Aren't you gonna have breakfast?" Ernesto asked. "I'll buy. Shit, it's the least I can do."

DaLucca put on his sunglasses. "I've eaten," he said, dropping a ten and walking away.

```
18 MAY
Mexico City, Mexico
1140 hrs. local time
```

Jamie cleared Mexican Customs and made his way through the crowded terminal to the overhead walkway that led to the taxi area. It took forty-five minutes to drive the two miles to the Mesa Grande Leather Company. He paid the driver and offered an extra twenty U.S. dollars to wait for him at a small cafe at the end of the block. The driver pocketed the money, smiled, and said it would buy him forty-five minutes.

· · · · · · ·

As soon as he got out of the taxi he could smell the leather. He crossed the street and opened the front doors. The public area was brightly lit, cluttered, but fairly clean. An attractive girl in her early twenties wearing a white blouse with tight, black leather slacks and a matching vest sat at a desk behind the reception counter, talking on the phone. She looked up when he came in.

"Hola, I'll be right with you sir," she said, covering the mouthpiece. Her English was excellent. She had no doubt determined from Jamie's appearance that he wasn't Mexican.

Jamie bowed his head politely. "Thank you. No hurry at all."

He studied the layout of the office while he waited. Behind the receptionist, against the back wall was a long counter. On it were two printers, a photocopier, fax machine and phone. Off to the right, a door marked 'Seguridad.' On the wall to the left hung a display of leathers showing the different stages of tanning, from stiff rawhides to plush patent leathers. The muffled drone of cutting and sewing machines thumped and hummed from the floors above.

When she hung up, Jamie turned to her and smiled. "Good day, young lady. My name is Ian Frobisher. I'm waiting for Mr. Falcone from International Leathers. I'm a few minutes early. I see he hasn't arrived yet."

"I'm sorry Mr. …uh…. Frobisher," she said, running her finger down the appointment sheet. "I don't see anyone by that name coming in this morning. Was it to meet with Mr. Covera?"

"That's right, Mr. Covera," he said, opening his briefcase and taking out a small appointment book. "Let me just verify … ah, here it is. I have today at 12:15." He looked at his watch. "May I use your phone please?"

"Of course, sir. There's one by the photocopier," she said, turning and pointing behind her.

Jamie walked behind the counter, picked up the phone, and dialed. After a few seconds he spoke loud enough so she could hear. "Yes … oh, I see, of course … no problem whatsoever … I understand … no not at all Mr. Falcone. I was in the area anyway … sure, let me ask Mr. Covera's receptionist." He cupped his hand over the mouthpiece. "Mr. Falcone would like to make an appointment with Mr. Covera, in two weeks if possible."

She turned the page and picked up a pen.

"Yes, Mr. Covera is free anytime on the second of June. What time would Mr. Falcone prefer?"

Jamie murmured into the phone then looked over to her. "Ten in the morning on the second would be lovely."

"Fine," she said, writing it down in the appointment book. "Ten o'clock it is. And he is with, did I hear you say, International Leathers?"

"That's correct."

As she finished writing, Jamie continued talking on the phone. "Yes, sir, I'm sure I can fax those to you right now."

The receptionist overheard and nodded from her desk and pointed to the fax machine beside the photocopier. Yes I have the number ... thank-you Mr. Falcone ... Good-bye."

He hung up and took a manila envelope out of his briefcase.

"Would you like some help sending that Mr. Frobisher?"

"Thank-you, no. I'm fine."

He removed the picture along with the note from the envelope and dialed. As soon as they fed through the fax, he returned them to his briefcase. When the fax confirmed the pages had been sent, Jamie walked back around to the front of the counter.

"You've been very kind Miss ..." he said.

"Maria," she said, blushing slightly.

"Thank you for your help Maria."

"Would you like me to see if Mr. Covera is free to meet you before you go Mr. Frobisher?" she asked.

"Thank you, but no. I have a number of things I must see to. I'll be back with Mr. Falcone on the second of June and look forward to meeting him then."

She smiled as the phone on her desk rang. "Then we'll see you in two weeks Mr. Frobisher."

"I look forward to it," he said smiling. "Good-bye."

CHAPTER FORTY-SEVEN

18 MAY
Bogota, Colombia
1300 hrs. local time

PABLO READ THE DECODED NEW YORK MESSAGE A SECOND TIME. Lying bastards, he thought, crumpling the message into a ball and squeezing it until his fist shook. Shipments were always checked and tested before loading. Routine. Only one person on the ship knew about it, and there was no way he could have switched the entire shipment. Why would he? He got paid very well for virtually no risk. The truck drivers had no idea what they were carrying, and if customs or the police had stumbled onto it there would have been arrests. That amount would have made headlines everywhere. No, there could only be one explanation: fucking Sorrentino was trying to rip him off.

"You got some set of balls," Costa muttered, tossing the crumbled message into the garbage pail and picking up the phone. "Always trying to get something for nothing. Slimy, fucking wops," he said, punching in Eduardo's number. He got the answering machine and left the message that a situation had come up that they should deal with right away. Hanging up, he swiveled his chair around to face the window. Closing his eyes, he took a few deep breaths. That always seemed to help a bit.

His concentration was broken by the sound of light tapping on the office door.

"Yes Rosa, come in," he said without turning.

Only Rosa knocked so daintily. She walked to the desk carrying a sealed envelope. "Mr. Torres delivered this and said you should look at it right away."

Pablo took a final deep breath and swiveled his chair around.

"Thank you, Rosa," he said, taking the envelope from her. "Uh … would you bring me an iced tea?"

"Right away, Mr. Costa," she said.

When she closed the door, he picked up the envelope and opened it.

He read the fax, then studied the picture. His face and neck tingled and felt hot. Across the top of the two, faxed pages was the Mesa Grande Leather Company logo along with the address, and fax number. He'd sometimes worried about Salas having total access without any supervision but never had reason to question his honesty. This had to be bullshit. If someone tried screwing with the books, he'd find it on his monthly audit. The picture, well, that could easily be faked, but why. And if it was true? He tossed the pages on his desk and went to the wall safe built into the floor-to-ceiling book shelf. Removing a brown leather case that held the code book, he re-locked the safe and left the office.

• • • • • • •

Rosa appeared at the top of the stairs carrying a crystal pitcher on a silver tray.

"I have your iced— "

"Not now, Rosa. Can't you see I'm busy?" he growled, pushing her out of his way and storming past her. At the end of the hall he disappeared into the computer room, slamming the door behind him. Rosa wiped the floor where some of the iced tea had spilt then hurried back downstairs. She'd seen his bad moods before and knew when it was best to leave him alone.

• • • • • • • •

Pablo locked the door and quickly sat at the computer and typed in his access code followed by his personal password that showed on the monitor as six stars. When he pressed the enter key, ACCEPTED appeared on the screen followed by the cursor blinking in a box marked MONTHLY CODE. He opened the code book, ran his finger down the page, and then typed in another sequence of letters and numbers. An instant later the screen filled with a list of accounts.

• • • • • • • •

Typing in GR-CAY-IS, a list of eleven accounts appeared on the left side of the screen. Each time he clicked onto an account it listed dates, deposits, transfers and withdrawals, and each amount corresponded with the totals. Nothing was missing. The note said Gran Cayman accounts. Methodically he began sifting his way through the maze of figures, but the bottom line was always the same. Everything balanced. Nothing, he thought … but that damn picture. He started again.

• • • • • • • •

Rosa didn't want to interrupt him, but Mr. Rodriguez sounded very concerned and wanted to talk to him right away. The other caller, a man from New York, also wanted to talk to him right away and seemed very angry. She listened by the closed door. He was talking to himself. She held her breath and tapped lightly.

"What? What is it?" his voice boomed from behind the thick door.

"Mr. Rodriguez phoned," she called from outside the door, having not been asked to enter. "He has to talk to you…and a man from New York left a number. He says it's very important that you return his call." She winced waiting for his reply.

"All right Rosa ... I heard you," he answered, not yelling, but close.

She listened for a few seconds, and when he started talking to himself again she returned downstairs. Usually Rosa enjoyed coming with him to Bogota. A nice change of scenery, and a chance to shop and visit friends. Lately, though, his erratic mood swings made him difficult to be around. She decided as she wiped the tray off and placed it on the kitchen counter that she wouldn't bother him again, no matter what.

• • • • • • •

Two hours went by and still nothing. He rubbed his eyes and leaned back. Sub- accounts, he thought. The note said sub-accounts. Going back into GR-CAY-IS he typed in SUB ACCOUNT after each company, pressed the enter key and each time, NO DOCUMENT FOUND appeared. He tried OTHER ACCOUNT and worked his way down the list again. On the eighth company, Geko Industries, he hit the enter key, and the screen lit up. Pablo's eyes widened. The top of the screen read, S&R Holdings. Below it was a list of dates showing deposits and withdrawals. Deposits into the account had been made on the same day each month. The amounts varied from 15, 600 dollars, to the last one just a few days ago of 48, 700 dollars.

"What the fuck is this?" he said, squinting at the monitor.

At the end of every month, the balance of the S&R Holdings account, except for two or three thousand dollars was transferred. The transfers were equal amounts going to two other accounts, one at a branch of the Canadian Imperial Bank of Commerce in Montreal, and the other at a Banco de Mexico in Mexico City. He slammed his fists on the desk.

"Bastards," he roared. "You rotten bastards."

• • • • • • •

Downstairs Rosa looked over at Pedro Aquino, who stood in for DaLucca whenever necessary. Aquino took orders without question, but decisions of any kind were left to others. He leapt out of his chair when he heard Pablo yelling and started for the stairs.

Rosa shook her head. "Pedro," she whispered as loud as she could, motioning with her hand for him to sit down. "Leave him, Pedro. If you disturb him right now ..." she raised her eyebrows and shrugged.

He listened from the bottom of the stairs not sure what to do. The yelling had stopped. He smiled a thank you to her and nervously sat back in the chair by the front door.

• • • • • • • •

A couple of minutes later the intercom in the kitchen buzzed. Rosa took a deep breath before pressing the speak button. "Yes Mr. Costa."

"Rosa, I'm sorry for raising my voice earlier. I received some disturbing news."

"I understand Mr. Costa. Is there anything I can get for you?"

"Yes, a glass of red wine if you don't mind."

"Right away, sir."

She let go of the intercom button and shook her head. Strange, she thought, he only drank red wine when business transactions had been successful. How things were changing.

• • • • • • • •

Pablo took a sip, then held the glass up to the light, studying its clarity. He would call Eduardo to apologize for taking so long in getting back to him, but first he had to send a message to Montreal and Mexico City.

• • • • • • • •

Eduardo tossed the magnifying glass down beside the picture. This left no doubt. *The Miami Herald* delivery truck seemed to put everything to rest. DaLucca had been in Miami with Jimmy the day he was murdered. Why then had Pablo not mentioned it? Unless Mani had gone to Miami without Pablo's knowledge, which seemed doubtful, but not impossible. The light on his phone began flashing.

"Hello," he said, still looking at the picture.

"Eduardo. Excuse my slowness in getting back to you. Something has come up, and I think we should meet as soon as possible."

"Of course. Where and when?"

Pablo thought for a few seconds. "Have you had lunch yet?"

"No."

"Then how about the club in half an hour?"

"The club in half an hour is fine." Eduardo's grip on the phone tightened. "Oh ... uh Pablo?"

"Yes."

"The day Jimmy was killed. Where was Mani?"

"Here, in Bogota. Why do you ask?"

"Just curious. One of my people saw him at the airport that day."

Pablo could hear it in his voice. He knew something.

"Uh, let me think. Mani said he was going to Cali a while back, but I'd have to check exactly when. Why? Is there a problem?"

"No, no. Just curious. It's nothing. Anyway I will see you in thirty minutes."

"Oh, one other thing," Pablo said. "Would you call our friend with the sharp pencils to meet with us. I think he may be able to help."

"I'll call him now. Good-bye Pablo."

Eduardo hung up and stared at the picture. "What reason could they have to kill you?" he asked, then shook his head and put it in his desk drawer.

Pablo replaced the receiver and slowly pushed the wine glass aside. He sat quietly, mulling over how Eduardo had asked about

Mani. He must have been seen either at the airport, which he could easily cover, or in Miami, which would be impossible to smooth over.

"Fuck!" he said out loud and began printing off copies of the last three months of transactions plus the entire S&R Holdings account information. It was risky to carry them around, but for Eduardo's accountant to figure out how they were skimming and from where, he'd have to see them. Locking the door to the computer room he hurried downstairs. This time he did yell. "Pedro, bring the car, now."

On the drive to the Cardero Club, Pablo couldn't relax. The last thing he needed was a problem with Eduardo, and if his suspicions grew, he would eventually put it together. No, Pablo thought, maybe better to put a little distance between Mani and himself during that time.

CHAPTER FORTY-EIGHT

```
18 MAY
Whyndam hotel
Miami Florida
1525 hrs. local time
```

TOM COMPLETED A RE-CHECK OF THE CONNECTIONS ON ALL THREE monitors. A small toggle switch on each receiver could be moved to zoom in and out, or pan left or right. Each of the motels were within a half dozen blocks of the Whyndam, so with a little luck reception shouldn't be a problem. The camera on the Westgate Inn was a little iffy, but the Chestnut Motel and Coastview Suites were crystal clear. He made sure the units he picked couldn't be watched from the road, so anyone showing an interest would have to come into the camera's view. Everything looked okay, so they were good to go.

"Okay, my little beauties," he said, adjusting the focus on the image at the Westgate. "Let's catch us a rat."

```
18 MAY
Montreal Quebec
1530 hrs. local time
```

Rheume stared at the fax. Not like Costa to thank anybody for anything, so it must be payback for getting rid of Tasse. Whatever the reason, it looked good for him.

> J.
>
> *Glad to hear you are well now.*
> *Things are very busy here.*
> *Would like your help.*
> *Please be here tomorrow.*
> *Call upon arrival and I'll have you picked up.*
> *I feel I must repay you*
> *For what you have done.*
>
> P

Easy to read between the lines. Things were expanding and Costa wanted him to be part of the re-structuring. Definitely opportunity knocking. He smiled and picked up the phone to book a flight.

He packed three of his finest suits, four freshly laundered dress shirts and an assortment of ties. The Air Canada flight to Miami left in three hours and, as luck would have it, there had been a cancellation in first class. The Miami to Bogota leg of the flight had no first class seats left. A little disappointing, but after tomorrow everything would be first class. He activated the alarm and paused at the door to look back into the apartment.

"Time for a bigger place," he said, and closed the door.

• • • • • • •

On the other side of the street a block away, two members of the Montreal Drug Section watched their target flag down Mount Royale Cab #7.

```
18 MAY
Cardero Club
Bogota, Colombia
1600 hrs. local time
```

Geraldo Lopez had been Eduardo's personal accountant for years. He handled the legitimate accounting services of Eduardo's businesses and properties in Colombia. He was short and fat, with thin, wispy grey hair styled in a bad comb-over that looked even more ridiculous when the wind blew. After studying the printouts he wiped the sweat off his brow, pushed his glasses up onto his head and sat back.

"There is no doubt about it, gentlemen," he said. "This would never have been found unless you knew where to look. It is deceptively simple."

Costa and Rodriguez looked at each other. "Could you explain?" Eduardo asked.

The accountant lowered his glasses and turned the pages so they both could see. "This has been done very well. You see right here," he said, pointing to a column of figures with his pen. "The initial amounts deposited and invested are known by you, therefore if subjected to an audit, which I'm sure your man knows is done without his knowledge, any discrepancies would be easily detected. So those figures are untouchable. However …"

Costa wasn't listening now. His fists were clenched, and all he could hear was his voice saying: "They fucked me over. They fucked me over."

Geraldo Lopez was still explaining the method whoever had done this used to divert the monies when Costa started listening again.

"….so the rates of monthly accrued interests fluctuate all the time and are handled and spread throughout the accounts by him alone. Is that correct?"

"Yes, yes that's correct." Pablo nodded.

"What he or they are doing," the accountant continued, "is shaving small percentages off the interest each month, recording the slightly lesser rate over here," he said, pointing to the end of one of the columns. "You see here he, or they, have added the interest of 1.7 per cent to this account. On the same day, the equivalent of .1 per cent was transferred into S&R Holdings. The correct amount that should have gone into your account was 1.8 per cent. No doubt they have done this to most, if not all, of the investments under their control, and with investments growing so rapidly, their take would not only grow each month but also go virtually unnoticed. These monies are then transferred to their personal accounts whenever they wish. As long as they didn't get too greedy, the odds of their actions going unnoticed remained in their favor, and you can see the amounts grew in proportion to the growth of your profits."

· · · · · · · ·

Costa was about to speak but Eduardo held up his hand, stopping him. "Thank you for your help, Mr. Lopez," he said. "I will see that you are reimbursed for your time and effort."

The accountant put his glasses in his pocket and got up from the table. "You are more than kind, Mr. Rodriguez. If I can be of any further assistance," he said, bowing his head to each of them, then backing away from the table. When he was gone Eduardo let out a long sigh.

"What do you think, Pablo?"

"I've contacted both. They suspect nothing and will be here tomorrow."

"Good," Eduardo said, picking up the printouts and giving them back to Pablo. "So much has gone bad lately. It's good you found these things. As for the New York people, I agree it looks like they've turned against us, but until we know more let's tell them another shipment is being put together for them. That will give us time to find out who is responsible and take the steps to correct it."

"Excellent. Can I pour you a glass of wine Eduardo?"

"No, I have some things I must attend to. Let me know if you need anything regarding our two guests when they arrive."

"I will."

They shook hands the way they always did whenever their meetings ended, but something was different this time. Pablo felt it right away, and it wasn't a good feeling.

"Good-bye, Pablo."

"Good-bye, Eduardo."

Pablo watched him walk out. Somehow he'd found out that Mani killed his nephew. There was no doubt. And right now, it didn't matter how he found out, what mattered was how to straighten out this fucking mess.

```
18 MAY
The Whyndam Hotel
Miami Fl
1830 hrs. local time
```

Morgan walked down the hall to 1115 and knocked. Tom opened the door. "Come on in," he said.

Morgan put a paper bag on the table and took out three large coffees, handed one to Tom and took one for himself.

"Cap not here yet?"

"Should be here anytime now," Tom said. "He called about half hour ago an' said he was just leavin' the office."

Morgan tossed his jacket on the bed and sat down in front of the monitors. "Not bad," he said.

"Yeah, let's just hope things don't go sideways on us. These little buggers can get pretty finicky sometimes."

There was a knock at the door. Morgan checked the security viewer before opening it.

"C'mon in, Cap."

"Hey, guys. Sorry I'm late. Traffic's a bitch. We ready to roll on this end?" he asked, sitting on the end of the bed in front of the three screens. He took off his jacket, and threw it behind him, loosened his tie, and rolled up his shirt sleeves.

"Yeah, time to go fishin'," Tom said.

"Want a coffee, Cap?" Morgan asked.

"Sure, thanks. So what kind of reaction you get from Accardo an' the mayor?" he asked.

Morgan handed him a coffee. "Accardo was good and pissed that I didn't give him any notice so he and Paul could get together. Had to dance around that one a bit. When I told the mayor he acted like I was bringing the black plague to Miami. Only thing he seemed concerned with was how long till we could get him outta town."

"An' you must have sold Harelson, cuz he didn't call me," Jacobs said.

"He seemed pretty concerned about the security set-up, and why we brought him back. Told him it was some personal things about his business. Papers he had to sign etcetera. I said it'd be me and you taking care of him, and we'd have him gone shortly after midnight. Other than not being too impressed about being kept in the dark, he seemed okay with it."

Tom checked his watch and gestured towards the monitors.

"Well, it shouldn't be long now boys."

CHAPTER FORTY-NINE

18 May
Holiday Inn, Port of Miami
1830 hrs. local time

DALUCCA USED ONE OF THE PAYPHONES IN HIS HOTEL LOBBY rather than his cell.

Ernesto picked up right away. "Hello."

"You paged?" Mani asked abruptly.

"Yeah. Our long lost friend is back."

"Where is he?"

"He's where we talked about. Got there about ten minutes ago."

"Where are you?"

"At my place. Just off Bayshore on Hardy. I can give you direct ...."

"I have a map." DaLucca interrupted. "Be on that corner in fifteen minutes." He hung up before Ernesto could say anything.

• • • • • • •

The call from his uncle five minutes ago had been short, and crystal clear. "Kill him." Ernesto felt good about this, but just

345

hearing Mani's voice unnerved him. The son-of-a-bitch knows exactly where I live, he thought, and if he suspects the slightest thing, he'll blow my fucking head off.

```
18 MAY
San Diego Ca.
1530 hrs. local time
```

Paul checked the call display when the phone rang. It was from Mexico City.

"Hi Jamie, any problems?"

"None at all. I'm at Benito Juarez waiting for my flight, and would venture to say that as we speak, Costa's beginning to think everyone around him is an enemy."

"Great, I'm putting the finishing touches on the package for the general and have a six o'clock to Bogota tomorrow morning. Tom's thing should be happening any time now and the real good news is that Pete Lambert called and they've upgraded Bonnie from critical to serious. If she remains stable, they'll transfer her out to Mercy in a few days."

"Amazing. Is she out of the coma?"

"Close," Paul said. "She's responding to voices, and the doctors are what they call 'guardedly optimistic.' She's still got a long way to go, but I'd say our girl's going to make it."

"Excellent. Anything you want me to do when I get back?"

Paul thought for a few seconds. "As soon as things get moving down there I'll call you and hopefully you can start dismantling our little operation here."

"Will do. Talk to you tomorrow."

```
18 MAY
Miami Fl
1815 hrs. local time
```

Ernesto ran across the street and got in the passenger side. Even though the sun had slipped below the horizon DaLucca still wore his mirrored sunglasses. Santos shifted as he fastened his seatbelt, hoping he looked calm. He just knew the eyes behind the glasses were staring at him. He was right.

"What is it Ernesto? You look worried."

Shit, he thought, calm the fuck down. "Uh … nothing. It's just, you know … I'm excited is all."

DaLucca turned his attention back to the road after a few seconds, signaled, and turned onto Bayshore Drive. "Relax, my young friend. This will all be over very soon. Are you sure the girlfriend is with him? It is most important that she be there, too."

"Yeah," he said, mustering up a little more confidence. He cleared his throat. "Ahem, she's there, an' don't worry bout me man."

"Good. Now where to?"

Ernesto had picked a quiet spot not far from where Jimmy's body had been found. At the time, he'd thought it be a fitting place to take revenge on his brother's killer, but now it seemed dangerously stupid. As a matter of fact, everything he'd done seemed stupid, right down to the 357 revolver tucked in his waistband under his shirt. Way to big and cumbersome? Christ, a guy could blow his fucking balls off trying to get it out fast. To make things worse, every time he glanced over, Mani's head would turn his way ever so slightly, and with those fucking sunglasses he couldn't tell if DaLucca was watching him, but deep down he knew he was.

· · · · · · · ·

Everyone exhibits some kind of involuntary reaction when they're nervous. Whether lying or being afraid, it can be as subtle as a twitch of the eye or a quick rub of the nose, but there's always something. Ernesto's was clearing his throat. The more nervous he got the more often he cleared his throat, and DaLucca was an expert in human behavior under stress. He picked up on it right away.

"Ahem, not far. About ten blocks to Carlyle Street an' then we turn left. It's the last building on the left, just before it dead ends .. ahem."

Mani rattled off some quick questions and carefully listened to Ernesto's responses.

"What's the address?"

"Uh. .. ahem ... I forget, but I know which apartment building it is ... ahem."

"What floor is she on?"

"Uh…the uh, ahem…first, you know, ground floor."

"Face front or back?"

"Uh….ahem...back, the back...ahem."

Mani made a quick left on Maddox Road and slammed on the brakes. As the car hit the curb he rammed the gear shift into park. Santos lurched forward.

"Jesus, Mani! What are you doing?"

"The fuck's going on Ernesto?"

He couldn't think. Why hadn't he just shot the prick when he got in the car. Now the cornered mouse stared at the cat

"Ahem, what?...ahem, nothin's goin' on Mani ... ahem, honest."

Mani smiled at him. "You're a piss-poor liar, Ernesto."

The chances of pulling it off were real slim, but he had to try. He made a sloppy grab for the butt of the .357, but in the sitting position there was no way. He arched his back but the barrel caught up in his belt and shirt. Pathetic, DaLucca thought and shook his head, then drove his fist into Ernesto's throat. He dropped the gun and clutched at this throat. Mani grabbed him by the hair and drove his face into the dashboard four or five times until he went limp. He looked around to see if anyone had been watching before pulling away from the curb.

· · · · · · ·

Ernesto didn't feel the first slap. The second one tingled, and the third one hurt.

"Wake up, Ernesto," Mani said, his voice echoing off the walls of the deserted warehouse, the same warehouse where he'd dispatched Jimmy less than a week ago.

Ernesto's right eye was swollen shut. From the other he could make out DaLucca silhouetted in the headlights, holding something in his right hand.

The dirt floor was cool and damp and the musty air smelled of diesel fuel and motor oil. He raised himself up on one elbow. DaLucca's voice stayed low and calm.

"I want you to tell me why you tried to do this?"

Ernesto's mind cleared enough to know he'd fucked up big time and would pay the ultimate price. He cocked his head to the side and spit a mouthful of blood onto the dirt floor.

"Why?" he said in a raspy whisper. "You fuckin' know why. You killed Jimmy is why."

DaLucca frowned. "What? Who the fuck told you that?"

Ernesto grunted a laugh. "The fuckin' FBI man, that's who." He had to hold his throat to talk. "They been followin' Jimmy an' seen you meetin' him on the street the day he was killed."

"Bullshit."

"Hey, fuck you, man. You know it's not bullshit. You killed my brother."

DaLucca looked around. It had to be a cop set-up, but if Rodriguez started checking and found he was in Miami, all hell would break loose.

"And Eduardo, he believes this too?"

Ernesto paused. He was dead for sure. DaLucca never left anyone alive who turned on him, but if he thought Eduardo didn't know.

Ernesto shook his head. "He don't know yet. I just found out a few hours ago. I was gonna tell him when I got done."

DaLucca bent down, studied his face then nodded. "Say hi to Jimmy."

It was lightening fast. Ernesto Santos looked surprised as the blade entered the fleshy skin under his jaw, angling up through the roof of his mouth and into the brain. His body stiffened, gave a violent jerk, then went slack. DaLucca wiped off the blade on Ernesto's shirt, stepped over the still body and climbed into the car. Turning off the lights he idled slowly to the far end of the building, through the open doors and onto Delta street.

On the way to the airport, he took out his cell and punched in Costa's private number. As soon as he answered, Mani spoke in his usual quiet tone. "Pablo. It's me. I'll be back about eleven tonight. We have another problem."

CHAPTER FIFTY

```
18 May
The Whyndam Hotel
Miami Fl
2015 hrs. local time
```

THEY ENTERED FROM THE BOTTOM LEFT OF THE SCREEN. THE FIRST one wore a black jacket zipped to the neck and a ball Cap. The second appeared a few seconds later wearing a grey hoody with the hood up. Jacobs lurched forward.

"Okay, guys. Looks like we've got two at the Chestnut. Goin' past the office now."

Morgan and Tom shifted their chairs to get a better view. The dim lighting in the motel's courtyard made it difficult to make out anything other than it was two males until Tom moved the toggle switch forward, zooming in. With his left hand he turned on the recorder. "Okay, the taller guy was with Ernesto Santos at his shop when I paid him a visit," he said, squinting at the monitor.

"That'd be Rico Gonzales," Jacobs said. "He's the main muscle for the Santos brothers. You were at his shop?"

"Yeah," Tom said, moving the toggle switch to the right as they made their way across the parking lot. "Dropped in to say hi the other day."

Jacobs smiled and shook his head. "Any idea who the number two is Morgan?"

The camera followed them between a couple of parked cars and along the covered walkway past the units on the lower level.

Morgan studied the screen. "Don't have a name on him, but I seen him hangin' with Jimmy a little while back. One of his gofers tryin' to work his way off the bottom rung."

Near the door to unit twelve, Gonzales stopped to light a cigarette. He seemed to be listening for any sounds from inside. After a few seconds he continued along the walkway, slowing as they passed to the end unit. He spoke to the guy in the hoody who took a cell phone out of his pocket and handed it to Gonzales. Hoody walked towards unit twelve and stood next to the door, his hand inside his jacket, while Gonzales punched in a number and put the phone to his ear. Half a minute later Hoody looked back at him and shook his head. Gonzales looked around, then started to walk across the parking lot, the hoody following. In seconds they were out of view.

Morgan and Captain Jacobs stared in stunned silence. Finally, Tom leaned over and turned off the three monitors. "How you wanna handle it, Captain?"

Jacobs stared at the blank monitor "Jesus Christ," he said quietly. "The Chief?" It took a few seconds for him to snap out of it. "I'll uh ... call him at home an' have him meet me at his office. Tell him it's important. Something's come up about Goldman. He'll come. I'll call Minter at Internal an' have him meet me there." He looked at Morgan. "Then, I'll arrest the Chief of the Miami Police Department."

Morgan put the video tape in an exhibit envelope, sealed it and initialed across the flap. "You want me to come with you?"

"I don't think that's a good idea, Morgan," he said, shaking his head. "Maybe help Tom clear things up here. Besides, with Bonnie and all, you're too emotionally involved. I'll do what has to be done. And Tom," he said. "Thanks for everything. Couldn't have done it without you."

"Sorry it turned out to be one of yours, Trevor," he said, shaking his hand.

Jacobs nodded and picked up his jacket. "Yeah, who would'a fuckin' thought. Listen, I'll call you guys when it's done."

When the door shut, Morgan tossed the tape in his briefcase and let out a long sigh.

"C'mon, Detective," Tom said. "Shake it off an' let's finish up here."

2100 hrs.

Driving to the office, Jacobs called the chief and asked to meet him at his office right away as something had come up regarding their witness. Harelson said he'd leave right away and should be there in no more than half an hour. That was good, Jacobs thought. Being only ten minutes away from the office would give him time to stop for a quick drink to calm down and figure out how he was going to do this.

· · · · · · · ·

When he arrived at the Miami Police Building things were quiet. Jacobs nodded to the duty Sergeant who looked up from his paper work "Workin' a late one, Cap?"

Jacobs walked by to the elevator. "Yeah, you might say that. The chief come in yet?"

"Yeah. Bout five minutes ago. Looked like he had something big on his mind too," he said, raising his eyes towards the ceiling. "He's in his office."

Jacobs checked his watch "Thanks," he said, pressing three as the doors closed.

When the elevator opened on the third floor, the majority of the office lights had been turned off. One of Harelson's budget-saving ideas. Looking down the hallway, he could see a thin line of light coming from under Harelson's office door.

Jacobs walked silently along the thick carpeting past the row of pictures covering the entire length of the hall. Head-and-shoulder shots of every Miami Chief of Police since its inception. The last picture was of Chief Donald Harelson. Unlike the others who looked authoritatively into the camera, he had a pleasant, trusting smile. At the secretary's desk in front of the door he paused, took a deep breath and knocked.

"Come in Trevor, it's open," Harelson called from inside.

Jacobs stepped in. The chief looked out of place sitting behind the huge mahogany desk wearing a pair of grey sweats. Jacobs looked around and closed the door behind him. He'd been here many times for budget and manpower meetings, but he never dreamed that one day it would come to this.

· · · · · · ·

Harelson sat with his hands clasped together on the desk in front of him. To his right were two doors. One, a private bathroom complete with shower, and the other a small sleeping room used during emergencies when he had to stay at headquarters for long periods of time.

"Come, please sit down," he said motioning to the chairs in front of his desk. "You're pale as hell, Trevor. What is it?"

Jacobs remained standing. "We found out who's been passin' information to Costa's people, Chief."

"You did?" Harelson said, leaning forward. "Excellent ...who?"

Jacobs slowly pulled the pistol from his shoulder holster and leveled it across the desk.

"You, Chief. It was you."

Harelson started to get up but stopped when Jacobs waved the barrel of the gun at him "Me?" he said, easing back into his chair. "Where in hell did you get an idea like that?"

"And'" he said, "I'm here to place you under arrest."

"What? I don't believe this. This is ..."

"Problem is," Jacobs interrupted, "when I got here you panicked. Took an unregistered gun out of the drawer ... and shot yourself." Using his left hand, he removed a snub nose .38 revolver from his jacket pocket. "You see, everyone involved in this investigation as of now is convinced it's you, so it'll all end here."

"Why the hell are you doing this?" Harelson asked, shaking his head in disbelief. "It doesn't make sense. Why? What the hell's going on."

"Well, let's just say if it came down to taking a polygraph I'd have to turn it down, and that wouldn't look good now, would it? I really wanted to make it look like Accardo. That would've steered everything away from the department, but I didn't know the name of the motel they told him about. So, seeing as you're the only one who knew about the Chestnut Motel," Jacobs said shrugging. "I had no choice."

"The Chestnut what? The hell are you talking about?"

From where he stood, the door to the sleeping room was to his left and slightly behind him. He noticed Harelson's eyes glance right. As Jacobs turned they were on him. Both guns were wrenched from his hands and, in a split second, he was on the floor with his arms twisted up behind his back. He struggled against the weight of two Miami SWAT members.

"What the fuck are you assholes doing? Get off me," he yelled. "I'm Captain Jacobs, Homicide, you idiots." Feeling the cuffs on his wrists, he stopped.

"We all know who you are, Cap."

He froze at the sound of Morgan's voice. Turning his head he strained to look up. Morgan and Commander Minter from Internal stood over him. When he was hauled to his feet, his whole body began to shake. Behind them at the entrance to the sleeping room Tom Corbet leaned against the door frame, arms folded.

Jacob's eyes darted from one face to another. "How? How'd you?" He tried to swallow but couldn't.

Morgan circled around him slowly. "We were sure nothin' could've come out of the mayor's office. Rice wasn't gettin' enough information to put things together, an' he definitely wasn't prying. Accardo looked real good, till I found out you were the one who sold him on the deposition idea. The chief didn't know about the flight arrangements to Pendleton, or when Bon and I were leavin'." He stopped circling. "But you did, Cap. So when I dropped in to see the chief today it was to fill him in on what we were doing. I didn't mention the name of the Chestnut Motel. Other than Tom and myself, you're the only one who knew about it."

Jacobs' breathing came in short quick gasps. Morgan moved within a few inches of his face. "You set us up you bastard. You may have killed Bonnie." He took a step back. "You should'a seen her, Cap. The girl who looked up to you like a father for Christ's sake, who trusted you. They shot her so bad they almost cut her in half. Why Cap? How the fuck could you do this?"

Jacobs began sobbing. "They promised me. I made them promise you guys wouldn't get hurt. I made them fuckin' promise, Morgan, honest to God. All they wanted was Goldman. I had no choice. They had me by the balls." Tears were streaming down his face now. "Long time ago I ... I did a really stupid thing. I was a rookie, young, broke, an' my wife pregnant. I looked the other way on a couple of dope deals. Didn't seem like a real big thing at the time, an' I thought that would be it. FUCK. I told 'em never again, ever, but they said that's not how it works. They had pictures, an' a tape. Said I'd lose my job and go to jail if I fucked em' around. One thing led to another an' pretty soon it was like a fuckin' train out of control. I couldn't get off, and I couldn't make it stop."

"And what about Grange?" Commander Minter asked. "You know about him?"

Jacobs shook his head. "No, but they always told me they had a lot of cops in their pocket."

"Who's they?" Harelson snarled. "Who'd you talk to?"

"Couple a different guys in the beginning. Bout five or six years ago it was Pepe Santini. Then nothin'. I thought just maybe it was over, then a week or so ago, fuckin' Ernesto Santos shows up at my house, my fuckin' house. I said no way, so he says the other option is I get to watch them kill my wife an' kids before I die." He started sobbing. "I couldn't let 'em do that."

"Commander Minter," Harelson said, still glaring at Jacobs. " Get this piece of shit out of my office."

Minter gestured at the two SWAT members who each grabbed an arm and led the captain in charge of homicide out the door and down the hall to the elevators. In the booking room after being fingerprinted, photographed and strip-searched, Trevor Jacobs was placed in holding cell number eight.

CHAPTER FIFTY-ONE

```
18 MAY
Bogota Colombia
2330 hrs. local time
```

DALUCCA BROKE ONE OF HIS OWN RULES AND TOOK THE FIRST TAXI in line. There was no time for the precautions. He waited until the cab turned onto Calle 6 before putting in the call.

"I'm here," he said when Pablo picked up. "Where do you want to meet?, fine … yes … I'll be about ten minutes."

Putting the phone back in his pocket, he checked out the back window then leaned forward in his seat. "Calle 13 and Legaro," he called to the driver. The driver repeated it, and signaled to turn left at the next intersection.

When the taxi pulled up opposite from the Cardero Club, DaLucca got out, waited until the taxi turned the corner, and crossed over to the alley that led to the back. Pedro Aquino, standing at the bottom of the metal stairs moved aside and nodded. DaLucca ignored him and climbed the stairs two at a time. When he reached the landing, he knocked and opened the door. Pablo stopped pacing. "So what happened, Mani?"

"He knew."

"What do you mean he knew. Knew what?"

DaLucca walked to the table and sat down. "I don't know how, but he knew I hit Jimmy."

"Jesus Christ. How?" Pablo asked.

DaLucca shook his head. "That's what doesn't make sense. He said I was seen on the street with Jimmy the day he was killed, but there's no fuckin' way. We were in a car the whole time. We were never on the street."

Costa looked confused. "The fuck is going on. Did he say who saw you?"

"Yeah. He said the cops followed us."

"Ernesto said this?"

DaLucca nodded. "But it's got to be bullshit, or why wouldn't they have grabbed me. I always check, and I swear there were no cops."

"So ... what happened?"

"It was a set-up. He was taking me to the same area I killed Jimmy. He told me Williamson was holed up in an apartment with his girlfriend. He got real scared the closer we got, and I couldn't remember any apartments around there. When I called him on it, he pulled his gun."

"And?"

"And, he's dead. I had no choice."

Pablo got up and started pacing again, rubbing his hands through his hair. "Christ almighty, both fucking nephews," he muttered. "So Eduardo knows?"

Mani shook his head. "Ernesto said no. Said he'd just found out and was going to tell him after I'd confessed, and he'd killed me."

Pablo leaned on the counter and stared out the window, mumbling to himself. Mani sat quietly watching him. After a few more seconds, the mumbling stopped and he turned from the window.

"Okay, Mani, here's what we do. I'll handle Rodriguez. In the meantime I want you to stay out of town. It shouldn't take more than a couple of days. Eduardo's always trusted you, more than his own family. I'll figure something out."

"Where do you want me to go?" Mani asked.

Costa thought for a second, then smiled. "As a matter of fact, I have the one from Montreal, you know, the one you're not particularly fond of, and our accountant from Mexico coming for a visit. They have fucked us around big time, and I'd like you to help me take care of them?"

"Of course, Pablo, of course."

Pablo nodded. "Good. And I'll let Eduardo know that Ernesto didn't show up where he was supposed to meet with you."

```
19 MAY
El Dorado Airport
Bogota Colombia
0845 hrs. local time
```

Paul's flight landed on time, and General Messina met him in the custom's hall. The general wore civilian clothes and, except for the obvious bodyguards, looked like any other traveler.

"Welcome to Bogota, Paul," he said smiling.

The guards on either side scanned the crowd in front and beside him. Others were no doubt mingling in the crowd. Over the years, there had been four assassination attempts on his life and, as a result, his routes changed constantly. His residence was walled and guarded around the clock. When he, his wife, and two children moved in four years ago, General Messina had a "safe" room constructed on the second floor between the master bedroom and the kid's bedroom. It was virtually bomb proof, equipped with weapons, a satellite radio system, and enough food and water to last forty-eight hours. It was put to the test two months after its completion when members of the Cali Cartel staged an attack, using hand grenades, RPG's, and assault weapons. After a thirty-five minute firefight, four of the General's guards had been killed along with eleven of the attackers. The entire second floor was completely destroyed, except for the safe room and its four occupants who, other than the trauma of the attack, were fine.

· · · · · · · ·

"Enrico," Paul said, shaking his hand. "Good to see you again. It's been a long time."

"Much too long, my friend. I'm glad you're here. Please," he said gesturing towards the exit. "I have a van waiting. It sounds like you've been very busy lately." He said leading the way to the airline crew clearance line. General Messina nodded at the customs officer, who stamped Paul's passport and handed it back.

"Thank you," he said, putting it in his jacket pocket. "Yes, we've had some pretty full days the last while."

They made their way outside to the three black Escalades parked beside a sign that read, ESTACIONAMIENTO PROHIBIDO. The driver opened the rear door of the second in line for the general and Paul. One of the bodyguards got in the front with the driver while the others climbed into the two remaining security vehicles. Standing off to the side, a well-dressed, recently-arrived passenger waited at the curb. He watched with curiosity as the cavalcade of obviously important people whisked away. No sooner had they rounded the corner when a black BMW came to a screeching stop in front of him. The driver rolled down his window. "Senor Salas?" he asked.

"Yes, that's me," he said, picking up his suit bag and briefcase.

"Mr. Costa sends his regards and will meet you at his private aircraft."

Fernando Salas smiled. "Thank you," he said, getting in the back seat.

When the door closed Salas let out a long sigh and smiled. He enjoyed being treated like this. Something big was going to happen, and he would be part of it. Hard work always pays off.

0945 hrs.

Sergeant Lopez, the General's aide, placed a tray of coffee with an assortment of fresh fruit on the rosewood table that extended from the front of his desk. There were three chairs on either side of the table and, rather than sit behind his desk, the General sat at the table across from Paul. "Please help yourself," he said.

The aide poured two cups, placing one in front of Paul, and the other in front of the General, then left the office. General Messina pointed at two four-drawer file cabinets behind his desk.

"Every one of the files in there involves Costa in one way or the other," he said, stirring his coffee. "He is responsible for the death of many people each year, a lot of them my men. Funerals, I am sad to say, have become part of my monthly schedule."

"These," Paul said, opening his briefcase and handing him a brown envelope, "are the complete banking records and access codes to Costa's money flow and drug transactions. The disc also contains his international investments, company names and locations, customer lists, etcetera. Copies will be sent to the DEA and the RCMP in Canada as soon as you finish your end here."

General Messina held the envelope like it was a priceless piece of art. "Since talking to you yesterday the warrants have been completed and with this," he said, tapping the envelope, "they will be signed within hours. Would you care to join us in making his arrest?"

"I would like that very much, General. Thank you."

"Excellent. There is much I have to do, so I will have Sergeant Lopez show you to your quarters. We will have a briefing at 1400. Until then you should try to get some rest, this could extend well into the night. If you require anything at all just call for the sergeant."

"Thanks Enrico. A little rest sounds good right about now."

The general picked up his phone and within seconds Sergeant Lopez entered.

Paul shook the General's hand and followed the Sergeant to the barracks on the first floor at the far end of the building. The room was the size of a small hotel room, consisting of one neatly-made metal-framed military bed, a two-drawer dresser built into a narrow closet, a desk with one chair, and a private washroom. He sat on the side of the bed and looked at himself in the mirror attached to the closet door. He looked like he felt, tired. Costa had taken everything from him, and put him back into the world of his past, a world where chaos, death and suffering seemed to fill every day.

CHAPTER FIFTY-TWO

19 May
Municipal Airport, North East of Bogota
1030hrs. local time

THE LIMO WAS PARKED BETWEEN A PRIVATELY OWNED HANGER AND an aviation electronics building where it could watch the four-seater Cessna 172 that sat idling just off the taxiway near the small terminal building. With a hum, the limo's rear window lowered a few inches and a set of binoculars rested on the top of the glass. Pablo watched Mani greet Salas. As they talked, another black Mercedes arrived carrying Jean Rheume. When he got out, DaLucca introduced the two men to each other.

"That's right, you little bastards," Costa growled. "Pretend you don't know one another."

They both listened as Mani explained where they would be going and why. A believable story. The Anti-Narcotics Police were putting a lot of pressure on lately and stepping up their surveillance, so for the next while meetings such as these would be held in Esmeraldos on the northern coast of Ecuador. The flight would take just over two hours.

DaLucca's instructions were simple. When they were over the Andes, about half way through the flight, kill them both, dump the bodies, then continue on to Esmeraldos and wait for word that things had been smoothed over with Rodriguez.

1055 hrs.

The binoculars followed the Cessna down the runway and watched it gently lift off. At a thousand feet it banked southeast and climbed towards puffs of white clouds that dotted the morning sky. When it was no more than a tiny speck Pablo raised the window and leaned back in his seat.

"Well," he said, leaning back, "That's that." He took two glasses and a bottle of wine from the built in liquor cabinet, poured, and handed one to Eduardo. Rodriguez tilted the glass then raised it. "Salud, Pablo."

Pablo clicked his glass. "Salud, Eduardo."

1205 hrs.

Nearing the border at five thousand feet DaLucca leaned over, cupped his hand around the pilot's ear and told him to stay calm and on course. He then turned and fired two quick shots. Rheume was asleep, and so he barely flinched when the bullet bore into his forehead. Salas's scream was cut short by the second shot. Mani calmly undid the seat belts of the two dead men, opened the door and tossed the bodies out. The pilot, stared straight ahead at the horizon. DaLucca closed the door, settled back into his seat next to the terrified pilot and patted him on the arm. "It's okay, you're fine ... just relax and fly the plane."

The pilot looked straight ahead, swallowed hard and nodded. DaLucca leaned back and closed his eyes.

1216 hrs.

The drone of the Cessna's engine was replaced by what sounded like a distant clap of thunder that echoed through the deep canyons. A few seconds later all that remained of the Cessna and its occupants was a small, wispy grey cloud that slowly dissipated as it moved with the winds south towards Ecuador.

1345 hrs.

Paul couldn't believe it. Anna and Ben knocking at his shop window, smiling and waving. His heart soared. He tried making his way around the cluttered work bench and stacks of boxes. "Anna ... Ben." he called. "I'm coming. Oh, thank God." But it was like trying to run in waist deep water. The more he tried to hurry, the slower he moved, and so many obstacles. Anna and Ben kept knocking, but they were starting to fade away. "No, wait. Oh, God please," he tried to call, but there was no sound. Then, they were gone. He opened his eyes, but the knocking continued.

"Mr. Goldman?" Sergeant Lopez called.

Paul's eyes opened wide. After a few seconds he swung his legs onto the floor and sat up. "Yes ... yes," he answered, trying to catch his breath.

"Briefing in fifteen minutes, sir, just down the hall, second door on the left."

"Thank you, Sergeant," he said, rubbing his face with both hands. "Fifteen minutes ... yes, thank you." He sat on the edge of the bed for a few seconds, then walked to the washroom and washed his face with cold water.

When he arrived at the conference room Sergeant Lopez met him at the door and showed him to a chair just inside and to the right. General Messina was arranging his notes at the podium, waiting for the last of the team leaders to take their seats around the huge oval table. When he looked up, all talking stopped.

"Gentlemen," he began. "All those who stood up to Costa and his people over the years and paid the ultimate price are responsible for us being here today. Many paid with their lives, and those of their loved ones," he said looking at Paul. "But, I can tell you now that Pablo Costa slept in the comfort of his own bed last night, for the last time." He nodded to Sergeant Lopez, who moved around the table handing out folders to the team leaders.

"What Sergeant Lopez is giving you are warrants for searches and arrests." He waited until the Sergeant finished before continuing. "There are four arrest warrants to be executed. More will follow in the days to come, but for now we concentrate on the main players: Costa, Rodriguez, DaLucca, and Sanchez. Search warrants will be executed on Costa's villa in Cartago, his residence in Bogota and two businesses in Bogota, one being the Cardero Club. Rodriguez's two homes, his shipping warehouses in Santa Marta, and Buenaventura, and finally, the homes of DaLucca, and Sanchez." He walked from behind the podium and stood with his hands on his hips. "The President himself has authorized this operation. Nothing will commence until Costa and Rodriguez have been arrested. Surveillance units are trying to locate them now. Once we have them, the searches will be carried out simultaneously. Everything your team requires is in the folder you've been given. Aircraft are standing by to deliver the teams to the targets outside Bogota." He glanced at his watch then around the room. "You are all well trained, as are your men. I tell you from my heart that I would put my life in the hands of any one of you. You have never let me or your country down, and I am proud to be in your company. What we do today will make Colombia and the world a better place tomorrow. Now if there are no questions, let's get into position."

The mood in the room as the team leaders filed out was electric.

· · · · · · ·

By 1730 hours the teams sent to Santa Marta, Buenaventura and Cartago advised that they were in place. Rodriguez and Sanchez had been spotted in downtown Bogota. They had eaten supper at Alexandria's Restaurant in the Zona Rosa and were now driving along Calle 13 towards the Cardero Club. One of Costa's vehicles was parked at the rear of the Club. DaLucca was nowhere to be found, and his vehicle wasn't at his apartment.

1845 hrs.

The surveillance on Rodriguez radioed saying he had just parked his black Lincoln Navigator at the rear of the Cardero beside Costa's white Mercedes and gone into the upper office. Sanchez and Pedro Aquino were standing guard by the vehicles. Surveillance identified Costa inside when Rodriguez entered. It was time.

· · · · · · ·

Inside the office Eduardo pulled one of the wooden chairs out from the table and sat down. Pablo stopped pacing and joined him. With Mani gone he felt uncomfortable, and very vulnerable.

"Well Pablo," he said. "What about our other problem?"

"Sorrentino? The little prick called two more times today," he said, holding up two fingers. "Asshole's demanding. Fuckin' demanding his front money back or another five hundred keys at a better price ... delivered right away."

"The man has little patience," Eduardo said as Pablo got up and started pacing again. "Pablo, please sit."

"Don't fucking tell me to sit. I'll sit if I want to sit. I think better when I'm walking, so don't fucking worry about it, okay?"

Eduardo held up both hands. "Okay, okay. Calm down. I'll talk to Sorrentino. Make him understand that when something like this happens it takes time to make it right. If need be we can come to some kind of agreement on future prices."

Pablo stopped and threw both arms in the air. "What? Why. Because that little wop asshole yells and stamps his feet we do as he tells us? Bullshit. I say we—"

"No! I'll tell you why," Eduardo exploded, slamming both fists on the table. "That little asshole is one of our biggest goddamned customers. Five hundred keys a month, and we've never had a problem with him. Hell, we don't know if in fact this problem is with him. Remember Pablo, we just threw a hundred kilo buyer out a fuckin' airplane. You see, we need people like him or the way things are going, soon you and I will be selling coca leaves to the fucking tourists."

Pablo came to the table, let out a long sigh and shrugged. "You tell me then, if not Sorrentino ... who?"

Eduardo took a cigar tube out of his shirt pocket and opened it. "I don't know, but we check every one of our people first. Everyone. The drivers, the guy on the ship, everyone who came near it and, if it turns out Sorrentino did rip us, then we take care of him." He held the cigar under his nose, sniffed it, then bit the end off and spat it onto the floor beside him.

"All right," Pablo said, sitting down. "I agree. It's just ... so many things happening at once. I'll have Mani ... I mean, I'll see to it the drivers are talked to."

"Good," Eduardo said. "And don't feel bad about DaLucca. When he told you he'd gone to Miami it confirmed the picture wasn't a fake. The bastard was obviously trying to get a war started with the fucking Jamaicans, or put us at each other's throat."

Pablo raised his head slowly and frowned. "Picture? What picture? You said someone saw him."

Eduardo took the faxed picture out of his pocket, unfolded it and slid it across the table. "Apparently it was taken by the FBI the day Jimmy was killed. At first I thought maybe it was a fake, but when you found out he was there, it had to be real."

Pablo stared at the picture. Mani had been adamant he'd stayed in the car the whole time Jimmy was with him, other than when he shot him. No. This had to be a set up. Somebody set the whole fucking thing up. So maybe the picture of Salas and Rheume ... it did seem like they'd never met.

· · · · · · ·

Eduardo took the photo out of Pablo's hand, crumpled it and tossed it in the garbage can under the sink. "Until we get things back on track we must dissolve our present investment areas and relocate them. Who knows what Salas prepared in the event of his early demise."

Pablo stared at the table where the picture had been. "Yes, yes of course ..." he said, his voice trailing off.

Outside, the setting sun sent shadows creeping up the side of the building.

CHAPTER FIFTY-THREE

19 May
Bogota Colombia
1855 hrs. local time

PAUL SAT WITH THE GENERAL AND FOUR HEAVILY ARMED SOLDIERS in the back of a van that was being followed closely by two others. As they wove their way through traffic along Calle 13, the surveillance on the Cardero Club radioed that the targets were still in the office above the club.

General Messina keyed his mike. "Copy? We are a minute away. As soon as we approach, get into the club and arrest everyone inside." He put the mike down and turned to Paul. "Paul, if you would stay with Corporal Ramos in the van to block the entrance to the parking area."

"Of course, General."

"And, if needed, there is a shotgun there on the rack between the seats."

Corporal Ramos looked over with a nervous smile and said. "I speak good English Colonel Goldman."

"That's good, Corporal, because my Spanish is sketchy at best."

General Messina keyed the mike as the vans approached the Cardero. "Command to base."

The replies came in immediately. "Go ahead Command."

"Commence operations ... NOW."

1900 hrs.

The vans roared into the dusty parking lot at the rear of the Cardero Club.

Costa jumped up and ran to the window when he heard the sound of loud voices and car doors slamming. He got there just in time to see Pedro Aquino pull out his gun. A hail of automatic fire flung his body over the hood of the white Mercedes, leaving a wide streak of red as he slid off onto the gravel. Sanchez ducked behind the black Navigator and managed four or five shots before being killed.

"Jesus Christ!" Pablo yelled, turning and running to the small closet in the storage room.

"What the hell. Is it cops?" Eduardo yelled back. "What are you doing?"

Pablo grabbed a cardboard box off the top shelf and ripped it open. "Here," he said tossing him a mac-ten machine pistol with two thirty round magazines. Eduardo looked at the weapon like it was a poisonous snake. "I don't know ... maybe we should just ..."

"It's a hit, for fuck sake," Pablo hollered, grabbing two nickel-plated .45 caliber pistols and a handful of clips. Then they heard yelling, and the sound feet running up the metal stairs.

Pablo glanced quickly out the window beside the door. They were half way up the stairs. "Fuck you," he screamed and fired off three quick shots. The glass in the window shattered as the officer leading the charge took two of the shots in the middle of his bullet-proof vest. The force threw him backwards into his comrades who crouched down and began returning fire. Pablo ducked as pieces of glass and splinters of the window frame sprayed through the office.

"Eduardo," he yelled over the barrage of gun shots and breaking glass. "When they get to the top of the stairs fire through the door. It'll attract their attention and give me a clear shot from the window in the other room. Our people in the club should be here any second."

Eduardo locked the magazine clip into place. "Maybe we—"

His plea was cut short by a loud explosion that blew the remainder of the window and frame apart leaving a gaping hole.

"Because they're here to kill us you fool," Pablo screamed firing two more shots. Then crouching onto his hands and knees he scrambled towards the storage room. There was little time. Opening the door to the small closet he glanced back and saw Eduardo behind the overturned table, gun aimed at the door. He threw a pile of cardboard boxes off to the side and flipped back the small rug that covered the closet floor. More shots.

Eduardo yelled, "Where the fuck are our people," and fired a burst through the door. Pablo hooked his finger through a metal latch and pulled hard. The trap door barely twenty-inches-square creaked open. Any sounds were drown out by the increasing gunfire.

· · · · · · ·

His father had it built as an escape route and kept it a secret even from Pablo until shortly before he died. It descended into the basement of the Cardero club to what used to be the coal and furnace room. Secreted behind one of the wooden coal bins was a tunnel leading to the basement of the building across the alley. His father had told him, "Never tell anyone about it and one day it may save your life."

When Eduardo fired another burst Pablo stepped onto the top rung of the ladder and climbed down three rungs to where he could reach up with one hand and grab a corner of the rug and the top of the trap door. Two more rungs down he let the door close over top of him. With any luck the rug would cover enough of the trap door to delay it being found. All he needed was a couple of minutes.

• • • • • • •

Eduardo crouched behind the overturned table and loaded his last clip. Bullets ripped through the walls creating pin-points of light. As far as he knew, Pablo was still firing from the window in the storage room, so he concentrated on the door.

Paul and Corporal Ramos knelt behind the van blocking the alley to the rear of the Cardero.

General Messina called for tear gas. Seconds later three canisters were fired towards the gaping hole at the top of the stairs. The first hit to the left of the door and dropped onto the landing where it spun around hissing and belching a white cloud of stinging fumes. The other two sailed through the large opening. From inside came another staccato of shots.

• • • • • • •

Near the body of Pedro Aquino, the entry team adjusted gas masks and started up the stairs. On his order a stun grenade was tossed in and the general led the way up the last few stairs. As soon as it exploded, what remained of the splintered door was kicked open and the team rushed inside. More shots.

Corporal Ramos nodded his head. "I think it is coming to an end now, Colonel."

Paul glanced at the buildings on either side of them. Ramos looked over at him. "What is it, Colonel? Is something wrong?"

"Is there only one way into that place? No other exit?"

"Si, Colonel. That's what we were told. Why?"

"I find it strange that Costa would corner himself in without…"

THE THIRD LAW

The general came running from the smoke-filled room onto the landing, pulled off his gas mask and yelled down. "Rodriguez is dead ... Costa's not here."

Paul and Ramos both turned when they heard the sound of an engine starting up. It was coming from the building to their right, an old vehicle repair shop with a pull-up wooden door.

Paul reached inside the van and grabbed the shotgun as Corporal Ramos pulled his pistol and ran towards the garage. Paul was ten steps behind him when Ramos stopped in front of the garage door.

Paul waved his hand and yelled. "Get back. Get back."

Ramos turned and started to move away as the garage door splintered and all but disintegrated as the Land Rover roared over top of him and spun around onto Calle 13.

Paul ran over to the corporal who lay motionless, his neck snapped off to the side.

"You son-of-a-bitch" he yelled. Running to the van he yanked the driver's door open, threw the shotgun onto the seat and climbed in. The keys were still in the ignition. As soon as it started he cranked the wheel and hit the gas. The van spun in a tight circle and swerved onto Calle 13.

He could see the Land Rover threading its way erratically through traffic three blocks ahead. Nothing on the dashboard looked like a siren switch so he kept one hand on the horn and the other on the steering wheel. The odd car pulled over, but most seemed oblivious to the blaring horn. Still, after a few blocks, the gap between them began to close. At Calle 7 the Land Rover made a sharp, right turn, sliding sideways and narrowly missing a parked delivery van. Paul slammed on the brakes and spun the steering wheel, fighting to keep the passenger side wheels on the ground.

Costa spotted the van in the rearview mirror moving through the traffic behind him. He reached inside his jacket and put one of his pistols on the seat beside him, then fastening his seat belt, pushed the accelerator to the floor. As they approached a street market at La Plaza Castilla, Paul saw a puff of white come from the driver's side window of the Land Rover. Before he could react, the bullet ripped through the windshield, tearing a chunk out of the passenger headrest and shattering the rear window. Paul veered to the right, making it difficult for Costa to get an accurate shot away unless he turned and fired through the back window, and at the speed he was going that wasn't likely. The market had just closed, and the few people left ran to get out of the way as the Land Rover roared across the square with the van a couple of seconds behind it.

Costa turned the wheel and slammed on the brakes, trying to make it around a tight corner. He over-corrected, demolishing a fruit and vegetable stand, then fishtailed into a row of parked cars. The momentum sent the Land Rover towards a group of pedestrians standing at the side of the street. All but two managed to jump out of the way. An elderly woman and her husband stood frozen, as though resigned to their fate as the car ploughed into them. Their bodies were flung up and over the hood like two rag dolls. Paul had no choice. He brought the van to a screeching stop less than a foot in front of the still bodies.

· · · · · · · ·

It took a couple of minutes to inch his way through the crowd that quickly gathered. Costa's vehicle was nowhere in sight. Four blocks ahead the road came to a T-intersection. The arrow pointing right indicated two kilometres to the main road to Medillin and to the left eleven kilometres to the Areopuorto Municipal De Bogota.

"You could have cut over to the highway before now, you bugger," he said turning the wheel hard to the left.

· · · · · · · ·

A mile up the road towards the municipal airport the pavement ended, changing to dirt and gravel. Paul drove as fast as he could, but with the tight, narrow hairpin turns he knew the odds of catching up with him were getting slimmer with every second. On a long, straight stretch Paul spotted a cloud of dust ahead. Closing in on it he reached over and put his hand on the shotgun. As he got closer the vehicle in front slowed. The dust began settling, and he could see brake lights.

Paul tightened his grip on the wheel. He'd already decided he would ram it as soon as he could make out it was Costa. Enough people had died. As the dust cloud began to settle he could make out a beat-up flat-bed truck piled high with sacks and crates. Relaxing his grip on the wheel, he managed to pass it just as the road began snaking its way up a steep hill. What guardrails there were on the sharp turns were dented and streaked with paint from a multitude of near disasters. Hundreds of feet below, partially swallowed by the fast-growing jungle, lay a number of rusted frames of those who over the years hadn't been as lucky.

When he finally reached the summit, he stopped. From here he could see the road winding down to the valley floor and, in the distance, the municipal airport. It was far enough away that Costa couldn't have made it there yet. Paul shaded his eyes and watched the road. Other than a truck, and in front of it, an old yellow bus turning into the airport, no other vehicles.

"Damn it," he said, watching the road to make sure he hadn't missed it. "Guessed wrong." He slammed the steering wheel and made a U-turn.

On the way back, as he slowed for one of the hairpin turns he noticed it—tire tracks in the dirt leading from the road and disappearing over the edge. The glare from the setting sun had made it impossible to see coming the other way. Paul pulled over, turned off the ignition, and got out. It was strangely quiet except for a hissing sound. He walked between the tire tracks to the edge of the road and peered over. Fifty feet down the steep slope the Land Rover lay on its roof, propped against a rotted tree stump that had stopped it from going over a sheer drop of two hundred feet.

It had torn off both doors when it flipped over and rolled down the slope. Wedged between the seat and the steering wheel, hanging by his seat belt and barely conscious, was Costa. Paul made his way carefully down the steep embankment. Steam and smoke were beginning to rise from the under carriage. Costa blinked to clear his eyes, then twisted his head around when he heard Paul's voice.

"Looks like you've got a bit of a problem here," Paul said.

Pablo wiped the blood away from his eyes. "American? Good, I speak English very well I... ahh." He winced as a jab of pain shot up his leg when he tried to move. "I need help ... one of my legs ... I'm stuck."

"Hmm," Paul said, bending down. "I can see that. Smells like the fuel's leaking too. Yes, I'd say you've got a real problem here."

"Yes ... yes. You must hurry," Pablo said.

"Yeah. I'm glad it's not me in there that's for sure," Paul said shaking his head.

Costa looked confused, then like the lights came on. "Oh ... yes, of course, amigo. I'll make it worth your while. Say five thousand American dollars?"

Paul looked over the rotted stump that had nearly torn itself free and gave a low whistle. "Jeez. Look at that drop off. If she comes loose from this thing ... it's not going to be pretty."

"You think it's worth more, eh, amigo," Costa grunted a laugh. "Okay, ten ... ten thousand dollars. Now please, you must get me out of here."

Paul stared at him and stepped back.

"What?" Costa raised his voice. "For Christ's sake man. This thing could blow. What do you want?"

"I'm afraid what I want, you can't give me," Paul said, looking up towards the road.

Costa tried pulling his leg free. All it did was cause more pain. "Ahhh. No. Believe me. You don't know who I am. I can give you anything you want." He had to yell now to be heard as the hissing and crackling began getting louder.

Paul took another step back. "I don't think so, Pablo. You see, I want my family back, and I know I can't have that."

"You know my name?" Pablo said, blinking the sting of sweat from his eyes. "What do I have to do with your family?"

"Yeah," Paul said, looking at the puffs of smoke coming off the manifold as each drop of fuel hit. "I'd definitely say she's going to blow. Well … gotta go," he said, and with a friendly wave started back up the embankment.

Costa watched in disbelief. "What the, you can't just…hey, GET THE FUCK BACK HERE," he screamed.

"You never know," Paul said without turning around. "Maybe someone will come along in time. You seem like a lucky kind of guy."

At the top he turned and called back down. "Oh … as for who I am? I'm a guy who's spent his whole life hunting down and killing very bad people. All I wanted was to live quietly with my family and run a small computer business, but you took that away from me. Amazing what you can do with those darn things, isn't it? Why you can take a picture and make something that never happened appear that it did, and put people together who've never met. You see, when you took that from me, you started playing way out of your league, asshole. My name's Paul Goldman."

Costa strained and jerked to no avail. His leg remained wedged between the steering column and the dashboard.

"You rotten son-of-a-bitch," he screamed, feeling around frantically. "I'll kill you myself, you … you." His fingers touched the barrel of one of his pistols that was laying on the head liner behind him. "I was there, you know, at the restaurant that night. I saw them fuckin' die," he yelled, finally getting a grip on the gun with his left hand. His arm wavered back and forth as he tried to aim.

"Wouldn't if I were you," Paul said taking a step back and shaking his head.

The sharp crack of the .45 was followed by an explosion that shook the ground. Paul watched as the Land Rover became a giant fireball and toppled over the edge.

Getting into the van he checked the side mirror before pulling out. A column of black smoke rose from the bottom of the deep gorge, then, all was quiet.

CHAPTER FIFTY-FOUR

15 JUNE
Miami Beach District Courthouse
Miami Fl.
1530 hrs. local time.

THE PLEA AGREEMENT BETWEEN THE DA'S OFFICE AND DEFENSE Counsel would see Dom Tegara and his two accomplices from the shooting at the Deep Six spared the death penalty. In return for life with no chance of parole, they would cooperate fully and testify on a number of DEA cases. The threat of retribution against them seemed unlikely now with Costa and Rodriguez both dead, and the Jamaican and Haitian gangs battling it out to fill the void left by the Santos brothers. A void that would sooner than later be back filled, and then things would return to what they had been. More bad guys and more bodies, same as before. Nothing ever changed.

• • • • • • •

Outside the courthouse Assistant DA Accardo saw Paul and ran down the steps after him. "Mr. Goldman," he called.

Paul stopped at the bottom and turned around. "Yes, Mr. Accardo?"

"I just wanted to thank you for sticking with this, sir. I know it hasn't been easy, and I uh, I hope this'll help you find some closure for your loss, and well ..."

Paul nodded. "I know what you mean, Mr. Accardo," he said, shaking his hand. He noticed his grip was definitely firmer. "And I thank you for your thoughts."

"I hope you're not too angry about the deal we made. It's just the DEA think they can help clean out a couple of things in LA and New York."

"Not at all," Paul said, shaking his head. "Those men are already dead inside. To sit for twenty-three hours a day for the rest of their lives in a tiny cell is quite satisfying to me." He smiled, patted Accardo on the shoulder and started walking towards his Le Baron parked at the curb. As he reached it, he turned and looked back. "Oh, and Mr. Accardo," he called.

"Yes, sir."

"I want you to know you did a damn fine job yourself. You're a good man."

It was the first time Paul had seen him smile.

"Thanks. Thanks a lot. I appreciate that."

· · · · · · ·

"Where to?" Tom asked as Paul climbed in and closed the door.

"Morgan's over at Mercy with Bonnie. They flew her in from California last night, and he's been there the whole time. Let's head over."

It seemed a long time ago since he'd been there, and most of it he didn't remember. As they parked in the visitor's lot near the main entrance, Jamie looked at Tom, then at Paul.

"Paul. Why don't Tom and I hang about for a few days to help you clear things up? It's not like we're pressed for time and—"

"Yeah," Tom cut in. "An' maybe plan a trip back to my place to do some serious fishin' an relax for a while."

Paul thought for a few seconds. "You know... fishing and relaxing sounds real good guys, but right now I've got to figure out what I'm doing with the house, and the business. I think I need a little time here, by myself."

Jamie held up one hand and nodded. "Totally understandable, old man."

"Absolutely," added Tom

· · · · · · ·

Morgan was in the waiting room when they arrived. He looked up from the *Time* magazine he was reading and tossed it onto the coffee table when they came in.

"Hey guys," he said, getting up. "Bon's doin' good. She's out of intensive care. They're changing her dressings now so we'll be able to go back an' see her in a couple of minutes. The office called an' told me about the guilty plea. They also told me Jacob's is tryin' to make some kinda deal to save his sorry ass in exchange for tellin' all."

A nurse came around the corner. "You can come back in now, Detective Connors, she said.

"Thanks, uh ... and these guys are with me, too, kinda family."

"That's fine," she said, looking at them. "If you'll follow me ... why Paul Goldman, is that you?"

Paul looked up in surprise. "Nurse Thatcher?" he said, walking over and giving her a friendly hug.

"Gentlemen," he said. "This is the wonderful Florence Nightingale who nagged me back to health. How could I die when she would never let me get the last word in?"

"Whatever are you talking about, Mr. Goldman?"

"See, what did I tell you?" Paul said shrugging his shoulders.

"As I recall," she said. "The only time I got the last word in was when you were unconscious."

"You were lucky," Morgan said. "Think what we've been through for the past couple of months."

"You have my deepest sympathy, Detective," she said smiling, then nodded towards the hall. "If you'll follow me, gentlemen."

Paul walked beside her, in front of the others. "I thought you were off to San Francisco?" he asked.

"I am," she said. Friday's my last day, and I start out there on Monday. I flew out two weeks ago and bought a condo not far from Fisherman's Wharf. I'll bunk in with my folks till the moving van arrives. And how are you doing?"

"I'm doing fine, thanks. I'm glad I got to see you before you left," he said, taking her hand and giving it a pat. When he realized after a few seconds he was still holding it, his face reddened.

"Oh ... sorry," he said, quickly letting go. When they reached the door to Bonnie's room she stopped and smiled.

"No need to apologize," she said as the others went inside. "And, if you ever decide to come out to San Francisco for a visit I'd love to show you around, I mean it. Hey, I might even throw in a home-cooked meal with the tour."

"A home-cooked meal and a tour, hmm that's a tough one to turn down. I just may take you up on that, one day," he said, still a little embarrassed.

"Here," she said, taking a pen and piece of paper out of her uniform pocket. "This is a number I can be reached at, if you do come out ... one day," she said, jotting down the number and handing it to him.

Paul looked and the paper, folded it, and tucked it into his wallet.

"Thank you, Carla," he said, for the first time calling her by her first name. "I will call. You have a safe trip and take care of yourself,"

"I will and you, too, Paul."

After a few seconds she started to walk away, hesitated, then came back and gave him a kiss on the cheek. He watched her walk back towards the nurse's station.

· · · · · · · ·

The bruising on the side of Bonnie's face and the swelling were pretty much gone. She opened her eyes when they came in. Paul kissed her on the forehead.

"Well," he said. "How's our little girl doing?"

Bonnie smiled through heavily sedated eyes. "Pretty good I think. Morgan told me we won."

"We sure did, Bonnie," Paul said, moving aside. "I'd like to introduce you to my two friends. The sophisticated looking chap here is Jamie Ryan. He was the voice on your radio."

Bonnie looked at him and smiled. "This may sound weird, but you look just like I pictured you would from the sound of your voice."

"I take that as a compliment of the highest order, my lovely lady," Jamie said with a bow of his head.

"And this old reprobate," Paul continued, "is the other voice you heard. Tom Corbet, and Bonnie, please don't say he looks like he sounds. It'll crush him."

"Don't make me laugh," she groaned. "It hurts. Hi, Tom."

Tom returned the smile and gave a two-fingered salute. "Hey, Bonnie, glad you're feelin' better."

"So, when are they going to let you out of here?" Paul asked.

She cleared her throat. "A week, maybe ten days. Got a lot of therapy ahead, but the doctor says I should be able to come back to eighty percent of what I was. Looks like the whole cops and robbers thing is out of the question though, unless I want to do admin stuff for the rest of my career."

Morgan held her hand and gave it a gentle squeeze. Paul watched them.

"Where are you going to find another partner this good Morgan?"

"Don't think I ever could," he said. "I've got a ton of holiday time built up, an' Bon's never been to Montana, so we've decided to take a little vacation when the doc says it's okay." They smiled at each other.

Bonnie spoke without taking her eyes off of him. "Morgan's mom and dad want him to take over the ranch, and we're thinking about maybe starting up a little P.I. business."

"I think that's a terrific idea," Paul said. "But promise you'll let me know if the partnership is going to go any further than that, okay?"

Morgan nodded. "You'll be the first to know, guaranteed."

Bonnie's eyes welled with tears. Turning to the others, she smiled and said. "Thanks guys, for taking care of me."

"Anytime," Tom said. "Anytime, anywhere."

Jamie smiled. "Be careful, young lady. I believe that's how he proposed to his last three wives."

```
15 JUNE
Miami Police Department
1700 hrs. local time
```

Paul waited in a chair beside the secretary's desk until the last of the reporters and camera crew squeezed into the elevators. When the doors closed, Chief Harelson waved him in.

"Come in Mr. Goldman, please," he said, leading the way into his office. "Have a seat." He sighed and sat behind his desk. "Headlines today, page twenty-nine tomorrow, and by day three, ancient history," he said.

"Nature of the beast, Chief. The need for change is supposedly what makes us the most intelligent of the species, although I've come to doubt that over the years."

"No argument on that one," Harelson said, and then he glanced around and lowered his voice. "You are an interesting man, Paul Goldman, to say the least." He paused, as if searching for the right words. "I'm not exactly sure what's gone on over the last little while, and that's probably just as well … I just hope it's over as far as you're concerned."

"Chief," Paul said. "With Costa gone, as far as I'm concerned, it's definitely over. I want nothing more than to try to get back to some kind of normalcy."

Chief Harelson studied him for a few seconds. "Good," he said, getting up and coming around the desk. "Let me walk you out, Paul. So what are your plans now?"

Paul sighed. "To be honest, I'm not really sure. I've got a lot of things to clear up around here, and I need a little downtime. I don't want to make any big decisions right now if you know what I mean."

"Of course," Harelson said as the elevator door opened. It was empty. Paul stepped in, turned and shook the chief's hand.

"Good luck to you, Paul. Been a real pleasure … and," he looked around and lowered his voice again, "uh, our back yard seems a have a lot less weeds in it now thanks to you and your friends. Kind of proved Isaac Newton's third law, didn't it?"

Paul smiled. "Smart man, Sir Isaac. Good luck to you, too, Chief."

The door slid closed

· · · · · · ·

The elevator door opened on the main floor amid the noise and confusion of a typical Friday night. Paul made his way across to the large, double, brass doors and pushed them open. It bumped the arm of a middle-aged woman standing outside, knocking the papers she was holding to the ground.

"I'm sorry, ma'am," he said, bending down to pick them up. "Here, let me get those for you."

When he handed them to her he could see she'd been crying. "Thank you," she said, wiping her eyes with a balled-up tissue. "It's my fault. I should have been watchin'."

"What's the trouble, ma'am?"

She folded the papers, stuffed them in her purse, then motioned with a nod towards the door of the police station.

"It's, it's my little girl," she said, her voice trembling. "She's missing."

"How old is she?" Paul asked.

"She's just sixteen. She's never run away, like they said in there. God, she's never even been late coming home without phoning."

"Did they have you fill out a missing person's report?"

The woman started sobbing. "Yeah. Then they told me they get hundreds of complaints like this and ninety-five percent of the time the kids show up back home ... but, damn it, I'm not "complaining" I just want help getting my baby back."

"Is that her?" Paul asked, pointing to the picture she removed from her purse.

"Yes," she said, turning it so he could see. It showed the woman and her daughter in a happier moment in time, arm in arm, smiling at the camera. The daughter was an attractive young girl with shiny black hair and beautiful brown eyes.

"That's my Rebecca," she said.

Paul looked up from the picture. "Rebecca?"

"Yes" she stared at the photo. "She's never caused me one minute of grief, ever, and she's all I got in the whole world."

Paul looked at the woman, then again at the picture. "Listen, I've got a friend in the department. Why don't I talk to him and see if there's something that can be done, okay? I can't promise anything, but I'll try."

"Oh, thank you," she said, wiping her eyes with another balled-up tissue. "I got nowhere to turn."

He took a pen out of his shirt pocket, opened his wallet and took out the piece of paper with Carla Thatcher's number on it and turned it over. "Give me your name and the number you can be reached at, and I'll have someone call, or I'll call myself."

"It's Angelina," she said, "Angelina Gomez. My number is 555 2661."

Paul wrote it down, folded the piece of paper and put it back in his wallet. "Someone will be in touch," he said, giving her a gentle pat on the arm.

She looked at him curiously. "Thanks Mr… uh, are you a cop?"

"No," he said.

"Then why are you going to help me?"

"Because sometimes we all need help," he said, walking across the sidewalk and opening the car door. "And nobody should ever have to lose everything."

Climbing into the back seat of Tom's rented Camry, Paul looked out the rear window. Angelina Gomez raised her hand in a half wave as they pulled into traffic.

"Who's that?" Tom asked.

"Just one of the people whose problems get lost in the shuffle. I'll give Morgan a call, see if he can help, or find someone who will. But right now, take me home, boys, take me home," he said, letting his head rest on the back of the seat.

Tom watched him in the rearview mirror. "You okay, man?"

"Hmm … yeah. I'm fine."

"Cuz I could cancel my flight and hang out here for a few days'

"Likewise," said Jamie.

"Thanks guys, but I really need some time alone. Got a lot of things to clear up."

"Okay," Tom said. "But remember, it's fishin' as soon as you clear things up, right?"

"Okay. It's fishing as soon as I clear things up."

"Good, how bout you Jamie? Care to learn the fine art of fishery?"

"You must be joking, Thomas. My little vacation up to now has been quite enjoyable with the exception of the odd irritable moment; however, that said, the thought of tossing about in the ocean all day in a small and, I'm sure if it's been under your care, leaky boat, only to be rewarded by being snagged in the ear by your treble hook rather frightens me. No, thank you so much, but I believe I'll pass."

"Just as well." Tom grinned and turned to Paul. "Dressed like that, he'd put my reputation in question with the guys on the dock, plus scare the hell outta the fish anyways."

When they pulled into the driveway, Paul looked out the window and groaned.

"Oh, man. Look at the lawn. It'll take a week to cut it."

"Should go astro turf, my man," Tom said, popping the trunk lid and getting out. "It's the perfect lawn. Never needs cuttin', rakin', or waterin'. Run the vacuum over it now and then, an' it stays green all year round." He lifted Paul's suitcase and garment bag out and handed them to him.

"And this landscaping tip," Jamie said as he joined them at the back of the car, "has been brought to you by every environmentalist's nightmare, Tom "clear cut" Corbet."

Paul grinned. "Or maybe Thomas is selling vacuum cleaners on the side?"

"That wouldn't surprise me in the least," Jamie said. "What would surprise me is if he actually sold one."

"Okay, okay very funny. But just wait a few years till you have to hire some snot-nosed kid once a week to do a crappy job for twenty bucks a shot. Then just remember what ol' Thomas said." He laughed and shook his head. "Man, you guys are tough."

Paul looked up the driveway, then turned back to them. "Listen guys. What you did for me, it went way beyond ..."

"Ah, bullshit man," Tom cut in. "It's nothin' you wouldn't have done for us. Far as I'm concerned, anytime, anywhere, right, Jamie?"

"My sentiments exactly," Jamie added. "Glad you included me."

"Thanks my friends, and have a safe trip home, and Tom, I'll be out for sure, soon."

Paul embraced both of them and, without another word, they climbed back into the car and pulled out. He watched until it turned the corner at the end of the block before walking up to the front door. Inside it felt different. Knowing Costa's people had rummaged through it defiled the memories of the love that had lived there. He walked down the hall to Ben's bedroom. Sitting on the bed he stared at the array of pictures on the wall. He spotted a drawing that looked like it had been done by a five year old. Under the drawing he had printed 'Grama,' and on the bottom of the page were written the numbers A-11963 in black crayon. He removed the tacks holding it and held it in front of him. He wiped the tears from his eyes and lay back against the pillow.

A couple of hours later he came into the kitchen, taped the drawing onto the door of the fridge, then put the coffee on. He spent the next half hour replacing all the pictures he'd given Morgan to hang onto, back to their original spots. The one of Anna, Ben, and Rebecca he'd taken at the beach in Haifa, he put on the kitchen counter by the table and, after pouring a cup of coffee, sat down and took the piece of paper out of his wallet. On one side was Carla Thatcher's name and number in San Francisco and on the other, Angelina Gomez's. He looked at one side, then the other. When his cup was empty, he placed the piece of paper on the table and picked up the phone.

END

Acknowledgements

Thanks to all my family for helping me through this amazing journey and for their unwavering support.

Manufactured by Amazon.ca
Bolton, ON